S0-AKA-038

"Flashman of the Purple Sage. . . . *Fenwick Travers and the Years of Empire* is the first book in a projected series of 'entertainments' chronicling the fictitious adventures, both military and amorous, of a handsome, egotistical and preposterously lucky American rogue. Although the author's most obvious inspiration is George MacDonald Fraser's sparkling *Flashman* novels, Mr. Saunders . . . has gamely looted the vaults of popular culture as well. . . . And if you don't mind a prose style thronged with exclamation points and synonyms for 'said' . . . you just might enjoy yourself I did."
—*The New York Times Book Review*

"The eponymous hero of this entertaining first novel is a lovable rogue who bounces from one sticky situation to another, always landing on his feet. . . . Fenwick's first-person narration displays an honesty that makes his arrogance, cowardice and womanizing oddly endearing."

—*Publishers Weekly*

Fenwick Travers
and the

Years of

Empire

An Entertainment

Raymond M. Saunders

LYFORD
Books

Except for historical personages, all characters herein are fictitious. Episodes of the novel are based on historical events, but dialogue and the actions of fictional characters, as well as many deeds imputed to historical personages, are the invention of the author.

Copyright © 1993 by Raymond M. Saunders
First paperback edition 1995

LYFORD Books
Published by Presidio Press
505 B San Marin Drive, Suite 300
Novato, CA 94945-1340

All rights reserved. No part of this book may be reproduced or utilized in any form or by any means, electronic or mechanical, including photocopying, recording, or by any information storage and retrieval systems, without permission in writing from the Publisher. Inquiries should be addressed to Presidio Press, 505 B San Marin Drive, Suite 300, Novato, CA 94945-1340.

Library of Congress Cataloging-in-Publication Data

Saunders, Raymond M., 1949–
    Fenwick Travers and the years of empire : an entertainment / Raymond M. Saunders.
        p. cm.
    ISBN 0-89141-479-7 (cloth)
    ISBN 0-89141-571-8 (paper)
    I. Title.
PS3569.A7938P46   1993
813' 54—dc20   93-15105
                                                                              CIP

Typography by ProImage
Printed in the United States of America

To my wife Mia, a true friend and partner.

Judge Thatcher hoped to see Tom a great lawyer or a great soldier some day. He said he meant to look to it that Tom should be admitted to the National Military Academy and afterwards trained in the best law school in the country, in order that he might be ready for either career or both.

Twain, *The Adventures of Tom Sawyer*

The grim three miles an hour
That is empire, that is power
Joyce Kilmer

Prologue

The enclosed papers constitute the memoirs of Maj. Gen. Fenwick Travers, United States Army (Retired). His memoirs were first brought to light in 1948 when MSgt. Willie Dutton, a rum-soaked veteran of two world wars, offered to sell them to the curator of the United States Army Museum at West Point, New York. Before this unusual transaction could be consummated, Sergeant Dutton encountered legal difficulties. Specifically he was court-martialed for black marketeering activities in which he had engaged during his recently concluded tour of duty in Trieste, Italy. Sergeant Dutton unwisely elected to act as his own attorney at his trial. He argued unconvincingly that a mule kick to the head, which he suffered during the 1939 Louisiana maneuvers, had left him incapacitated and not responsible for his conduct. Following his conviction and subsequent transfer to Fort Leavenworth, the mists of time once more enshrouded both Sergeant Dutton and the memoirs.

By happenstance the memoirs surfaced once more, in 1955, when an abandoned footlocker stored in a musty government warehouse in Fort Monroe, Virginia, was inadvertently opened. The papers were found under carefully wrapped packages of occupation scrip from both world wars, two antique Japanese swords, numerous pairs of women's nylons, and an armed German hand grenade of 1915 vintage. The army historical section in the Pentagon was contacted, and that office made a concerted attempt to locate General Travers's family to return the documents. Unfortunately, the general's spouse was deceased, and apparently there had been no issue of the marriage. Rumor at the bar at the Army-Navy Club in Washington, D.C., had it, however, that the general had been quite fecund and had sired a dozen or more illegitimate offspring around the world during his colorful, albeit checkered, career. Frustrated in its attempts to locate any Travers heirs, the army consigned the memoirs to a cavernous archive in Arlington, Virginia.

There matters stood for thirty-five years, until the papers came into my hands. Feeling the need to share General Travers's rollicking and often-bawdy story with the world—and also feeling the need to earn a living—I compiled his collective works into a series of volumes, the first of which follows. General Travers, it turns out, is one of the most enigmatic figures in recent American history. Although virtually unknown to the general public, he was notoriously prominent within the small regular army of his day. The army's sensitivity to any prying into General Travers's career became evident when my initial inquiries were met with a stony official silence. It turned out that the latter part of the general's career involved still-classified intelligence work, and the unclassified parts of his life story involved escapades potentially embarrassing to the reputations of some of the leading world figures of his day.

After years of painstakingly corroborating the general's papers with published histories of the United States Army, I gradually became aware that General Travers, although of flexible moral character and seemingly possessed of an insatiable appetite for female companionship, was one of this nation's most influential military figures in the first half of the twentieth century. Rising from the lowly rank of private, Travers eventually became a major general and along the way participated in campaigns from the Spanish-American War to World War II. A born swashbuckler and an adept social manipulator, General Travers also managed to thrust himself into intimate acquaintance with an astonishingly large number of heads of state, captains of industry, and underworld bosses of his day.

The story is long and rich. The best place to start, of course, is at the beginning, on the first yellowed page retrieved from that footlocker in Fort Monroe many years ago.

1

Plattsburgh Barracks, New York
January 1898

The loud pounding on my billet door slowly roused me from the depths of a whiskey-induced sleep.

"Lootenant! Lootenant Travers, suh!" boomed a deep Southern voice. "Th' guard detail's a-formed up for inspection."

Painfully I lifted my pounding head above the covers. "Who the hell's there?" I croaked through an alcohol-scorched throat, my expelled breath turning into a misty haze in the frigid predawn air.

"Sergeant Richmond, suh," came the reply from outside my door. "I'm sergeant of th' guard and you're officer of th' day. It's nigh on dawn and time to be postin' th' men."

In the background the metallic clanking sounds made by a group of men under arms fell upon my ears and told me that this was no dream. I shook my head in despair, desperately needing several more hours' sleep. "I'm on duty?" I whined weakly in protest.

"Yes, suh," came the uncompromising reply.

"Goddamn," I moaned, sinking back beneath the covers. Why me? Why today? Wasn't it evident that I had completely incapacitated myself for duty? Why didn't Richmond take the hint and simply find a sober officer and leave me alone?

Suddenly my befogged mind screamed in alarm—Richmond, did he say? By God, First Sergeant Richmond was standing outside my door! His wife, Ida Richmond—the regimental laundress and an accomplished temptress—was snoring soundly at my side! I had dallied with her last night in one of the unsavory taverns outside the gates of Plattsburgh Barracks; and by virtue of my not inconsiderable charms, and assisted by the better part of a bottle of Kentucky sipping whiskey, I had persuaded her to warm my lonely army cot. Coyly insisting she could stop by only for "a little tipple," Mrs. Richmond had proven to be up to her reputation as a lusty bed partner.

Now I was fully awake and painfully aware of both my raging headache and my potentially lethal predicament. I struggled to focus my mind on the danger before me: Did Richmond know of his wife's infidelity? My mind panicked at the thought. If not, why then was he, the company first sergeant, performing the guard mount? Usually that task fell to a platoon sergeant. Did Richmond hope to catch me in flagrante delicto?

My galloping mind factored all of this in an instant and decided that if Richmond had suspected the truth, he would have simply fired through the door at the sound of my voice. I knew of his awesome reputation; he was one mean cracker when riled. The troops at Plattsburgh still talked of how he'd nearly gutted a licentious Canadian fur trapper when the unfortunate *coureur des bois* had whistled appreciatively at the sight of Ida, skirts hiked up to her shapely thighs, standing in the shallows of Lake Champlain flogging the regiment's unmentionables.

But why then was Richmond mounting the guard? Probably to cover for one of his sergeants, I decided. First Sergeant Richmond was funny that way. He'd go a country mile out of his way to look after the men below him. For my money, it just wasn't seemly for a first sergeant to be so concerned about the rank and file like that, but philosophical differences were not my immediate problem; finding a way out of this mess without getting my hide ventilated by Richmond was. Richmond was a crack shot and had fists like twin cannonballs, and if he so much as suspected I had been plowing his field, his first official act of the day would be to throttle me and run my carcass up the flagpole.

"Uh, right, Sergeant, right," I stalled, struggling not quite successfully to control the fear in my voice as I leapt from the cot onto the cold wooden floor planks. I shivered violently as I hurriedly pulled on my trousers. "I'll be right with you. Just give me a moment." I desperately hoped that Richmond thought the quavering in my voice was from the brutal cold.

Then I drew back the bedclothes to uncover the firm white figure of Ida Richmond. She was naked as the day she was born and was snoring like a lumberjack. Hardly the picture of the fetching jezebel I had cavorted with last night in the Yankee Trader Inn, I thought grimly; and with each snore she emitted I was suffused with the stale stench of the liquor she had quaffed by the cupful. Reviving her on short notice was clearly going to be a considerable chore. But with her adoring spouse at the front door, I had no choice.

I grabbed the water jug off the rough-hewn stand in the corner, broke the thin crust of ice that had formed, and emptied the contents of the jug into Mrs. Richmond's gape-jawed face.

"Wha—?" she sputtered, clawing out groggily for her unseen assailant.

"Get up, Ida!" I hissed urgently, dragging her from the bed by main force.

"Where am I?" she demanded blearily. "Who th' hell are you?"

"Lieutenant Travers, your paramour from last evening, my dear, and both of us are in big trouble. Now kindly shut up and I'll do my damndest to get us out of this fix. Your devoted husband is standing outside that door, and unless you do exactly what I tell you, there's an excellent chance that neither of us will leave here alive."

"Oh, no!" she squealed, suddenly fully awake, only to be silenced by my hand clamped firmly across her mouth.

"Quiet, damn you, or we're done for!" I whispered through clenched teeth.

She meekly nodded her understanding and I released my grip; her saucer-sized eyes told me that she was now fully alert to the danger, and a certain incipient look of lust also told me that she was starting to recall some of the details of our tryst.

"How'd he find out?" she breathed fearfully.

"He hasn't yet, nor will he if we both keep our heads," I whispered. "The main thing now is that you vamoose, and quickly."

I scampered over to the back of my quarters and cautiously eased open the frost-encrusted window. Outside, the dim light of false dawn reflected off the freshly fallen snow and illuminated the narrow alley that ran behind the row of junior officers' quarters. I carefully scanned the night and saw that the alley was empty. I pushed the window fully open.

"Out you go, my dear," I announced softly. "The pleasure was all mine and we really must do this again soon, perhaps under less trying circumstances."

"But . . . but not like this," she protested, indicating her nakedness. "I can't go out there like this; I'll freeze."

"Ida, it's out the window and freeze or stay and get shot," I observed with forced calmness.

"No, I won't go," she protested with a stamp of her foot, which I surmised passed for finality with her.

"Okay, okay," I conceded; there was no time to argue. "Just keep your voice down." I quickly gathered up her things, which she scrambled into as quickly as her befogged mind would allow. All the while I urged her to make haste, not wanting her recalcitrance to turn me into a target for the straight-shooting First Sergeant Richmond. When she was somewhat dressed, I swept her off her feet into my arms, and set her down in the soft snow outside the window. Beneath the snow, unfortunately, was a sheet of ice, and when Ida took her first step her feet flew up, her skirt billowed out, and down she went.

"Yiii!" she shrieked as her saucy rump hit the snow, but she was instantly on her feet, brushing the snow from her buttocks and sniveling pathetically. She began stamping her feet like an Arctic hare beating out a tattoo as she tried to regain her warmth, but all her ridiculous jig did was to set her generous breasts bouncing about under her tight dress. Fortunately, the wind, blasting down from Canada like a freight train, carried away her caterwauling.

"Oh, my God," she yowled, "I'll die out here."

"Now Ida, stay calm," I reassured her. "Just think of you and me and the thought will keep you quite heated." I bundled up her remaining things—I didn't want any evidence when I opened the door to her husband, you see—and tossed them out the window into her arms. "Run home, Ida. I'll call again when the coast is clear."

"See you again?" she gasped incredulously as she drew her cloak tight over her shivering shoulders. "You throw me out of your room in the dead of night and then invite me to see you again? Why, you brute, I wouldn't see you again if my life depended on it!"

"Then this is the end?" I frowned. "As you wish, my dear," I said, my mind already turning to some of the other equally willing ladies who provided the garrison's officers with lively diversion on cold winter nights.

First Sergeant Richmond pounded at the front door again. "Put a fire under it, Lootenant."

"Hold your damn horses!" I snapped, my West Point–bred disdain for the enlisted ranks rising to the fore. "I'm coming." I nodded to Ida. "Duty calls, ma'am."

"Fenwick, wait," she urged, her face blushing now, but whether from her predicament or from the savage cold I was unsure. "Perhaps we can, er, that is, I may have been a little hasty."

I smiled, giving her that radiant blue-eyed gaze that had carried the day on so many other fields. "Ida, I'm so glad. Perhaps tonight. Now run, my dear, and think of me."

She blew an awkward kiss while keeping her flapping garments pressed to her trembling body, and then she was gone. The pounding from the door came again and broke me from my reverie.

"Lootenant!" demanded Richmond.

"Coming, First Sergeant," I said, hastily drawing on my sturdy leather boots, donning a linen shirt, and throwing a buffalo-skin cape across my shoulders. I pulled my beaver-skin cap onto my head, took my saber down from its peg on the wall, and threw open the door with feigned bravado, while at the same time stealing a furtive look at Richmond's Krag-Jorgensen. The rifle was held loosely at his side, rather than cocked and leveled; I breathed a bit easier.

First Sergeant Richmond saluted none too snappily, shouldered his piece, and stepped aside. Beyond him in the dark was a single rank of troopers, so bundled up against the cold that they looked like small bears on their hind feet. I eyed Richmond carefully. He was not a tall man, but he was built as solidly as a hod carrier. His large, flat face was impassive under the bill of his fur cap, his eyes were shadowed, and his heavy jaw worked at a big wad of "chaw." Well, I thought, if he suspected anything he'd be shooting already; I decided to brazen it out and see what happened.

"Report, Sergeant," I ordered.

"Guard's formed and ready for inspection, suh."

"Let's get it over with then," I said and strode over to the waiting men, Richmond at my heels like a sheepdog anxiously trailing a coyote that was getting too close to the flock.

"Inspection, arms!" he barked, and the ten men moved as one. Each raised his breech-loading Krag to his front, drew back the bolt, looked down to ensure that the chamber was empty, and then brought his eyes to the front to await inspection.

I stopped in front of the first trooper. Inspecting his rifle in this light would be a joke; I would have to be satisfied with the fact that he had one. With practiced speed I snatched the piece from his hands and peered into the breech. I saw nothing but darkness. I crisply brought the rifle down to the port-arms position and thrust it at the silent trooper, who adroitly snatched it back, slammed the bolt closed, and snapped to order arms.

"Harrumph," I growled, and moved on to the next man to repeat my cursory inspection. I made my way down the rank in this manner until I was done with the last man.

"They all seem to pass muster," I yelled over my shoulder to Richmond so as to be heard above the gale.

"Well, they's all good sol'jers, suh," he assured me, despite my direct knowledge to the contrary. Just then the fellow in front of me let out a great belch, and the odor of whiskey wafted past me in the frigid air.

"Sergeant, this man smells like a goddamn still!" I snorted indignantly, hopeful that my own breath was not too pungent.

First Sergeant Richmond leaned past me and sniffed perfunctorily at the impassive figure. "I don't smell nothin', suh. 'Sides, I never knew Olson heah to pull on a jug afore guard mount."

No, I thought to myself, he probably reserved his tippling for during his guard duty. I sniffed at Olson myself. "Well, maybe he hasn't in the past, but he sure as hell has been doing some nipping today."

"Beggin' the lootenant's pardon," countered Richmond, squinting at me wryly, "but mebbe it's someone else's breath you're a-sniffin'."

"I hardly think so, Sergeant," I rejoined stiffly. You bastard, I thought, and made a mental note to roll his wife in the hay at the soonest possible opportunity. I turned, walked back to the center of the rank, and faced the men. First Sergeant Richmond, with practiced tread, took a post directly in front of and facing me.

"Post your men, First Sergeant. I'll be around to inspect them in a few hours."

"Yes, suh," replied First Sergeant Richmond, giving me a salute and holding it until I replied with a nonchalant touch of my glove to the brim of my hat. At that, Richmond about-faced and barked out, "Riii-ght shoulder, arms."

With a dull, metallic thud the troops obeyed.

"Riii-ght face," bellowed Richmond into the wind. Obediently the silent soldiers shuffled about to face to their right, becoming in the process a file facing to my left—all, that is, except Olson. He was lying flat on his face in the snow.

"Jesus Christ!" I sputtered. "He's blind drunk!"

"Not at all, suh, not at all," clucked Richmond. "Olson's jest a mite tuckered. After all, it's pretty early in th' day, don't you reckon?"

Here was a surprise; in my time in the army I had come to understand that being drunk on duty was no crime as long as you could still function, but woe unto him who became so besotted that his condition could not be hidden. Once uncovered, the malefactor almost invariably was consigned to the stockade for a period of enforced sobriety. Richmond's solicitous behavior was uncharacteristic of the noncommissioned officers I'd come to know. But in a small regular army like ours bonds tended to be enduring. Who knows? I thought with a shrug. Perhaps Olson was himself a sergeant in the past, or he and Richmond had served on the frontier together. Or maybe Richmond planned on pounding Olson into a pulp as soon as this pesky lieutenant was gone. It didn't matter; this was a sergeant's problem, and I intended to let Richmond handle it in any way he wanted.

"I reckon," I said at length.

"Kelly! Moran! Give Olson a hand," directed Richmond. Two dark figures fell out of the file and hauled Olson to his feet.

"Will there be anything further, suh?" asked Richmond evenly.

"No. Just stow Olson someplace where he won't freeze before sunrise."

"Yes, suh," replied Richmond. He turned and, with an arm signal, started the troops across the snow-covered parade ground. I watched them go until they faded into the white mist of blowing flakes, and then I trudged back to my bleak billet, closed the door securely, and kindled a small fire in the Franklin stove. I settled into a battered camp chair before the crackling flames and relived yet again the calamitous events that had caused me to be sent off to West Point and to ultimately have the extreme misfortune of being posted to Plattsburgh Barracks as a lowly lieutenant in the 9th United States Infantry Regiment.

2

Elm Grove, Illinois
April 1892

I can still recall the fateful day it all began. I was in my sixteenth year and living in the large clapboard house of my uncle, Enoch Sheffield. We lived in Elm Grove, Illinois, a modest hamlet of whitewashed homes situated on a bluff on the east bank of the Mississippi about fifty miles north of St. Louis. Stretching inland from the village was the verdant agricultural expanse of Black Hawk County, a cornucopia that produced cattle and grain in endless profusion. Elm Grove was the county seat, admirably sited to serve as such since it boasted a sturdy stone quay jutting out into the muddy flow of the Father of Waters. The wealth of the county therefore flowed down Main Street, onto barges, and thence to the commodity auctions of "Sent Looey."

Elm Grove prospered from this trade, which fostered in due course a Farmers' and Merchants' Mercantile Bank, a wholesale feed store, a smithy, a carriage shop, a barrel factory, a slaughterhouse, and a sprawling complex of stables and cattle pens. Being the county center, Elm Grove also had a modest red brick courthouse. This was the bailiwick of Uncle Enoch—"the Judge," as I was taught to address him—for my uncle was the county judge.

At the moment, the Judge was in the study with me and Mr. Overstreet, my instructor from the Elm Grove Academy, the local high school. Mr. Overstreet was relating to the Judge the results of my academic efforts for the past several months.

"The boy simply isn't making any progress, sir. I've seen geese with more native wit than he," piped Overstreet in his ridiculously high voice. "Oh, he's sly enough to feign that he's paying attention like the other pupils, but these examination results are the proof of the pudding. The boy's resisted every effort I've made to teach him anything. I've taken a strap to his hide, sir, but to no avail. He's simply stubborn as a mule, and there's no hope for him."

"Harrumph," rumbled the Judge at this news, a sound I now recognize as his universal response to any unpleasant yet expected intelligence. He turned his dark, grave gaze upon me, and as I stood in a corner trying to melt into the wallpaper, I studied his ominous visage with fear. The Judge was about fifty years of age, of medium height, and had evidently been powerfully built in his prime, for he was still barrel-chested and exhibited only the suggestion of a paunch. He was hard-faced, with high, craggy cheekbones. A few gray strands of hair crossed an otherwise bald pate, and dazzlingly white sideburns wreathed his face, giving him an almost cheery appearance—until you looked into the depths of his calculating black eyes.

Those were the eyes of a man used to wielding authority, and indeed the Judge just about ran Black Hawk County. Despite his title, his main vocation was that of a merchant, selling feed and dry goods to the rustics on the surrounding farms. You see, he owned a large share of the stock in the feed store. He was a sharp trader who charged a pretty penny for his wares, cash on the barrel, thank-you. In addition, he served as a factor for cattle to be sold downriver in St. Louis and also had a stake in the slaughterhouse. Any activity that made a buck interested Uncle Enoch, and he prospered over the years. His labors as a magistrate were in fact only a secondary activity; he rarely held court twice a month, unless there was a rash of hog-rustling afoot. It was beyond dispute that Enoch Sheffield was an established power in Elm Grove, and the townsmen knew that whatever they needed, be it a sack of oats or judgment on a bad debt, the person to see was the Judge.

And indeed, even before the Judge's rise, the Sheffields were well ensconced in local lore. Black Hawk County had been founded by the Judge's father—my grandfather—Mordecai Sheffield. Old Mordecai was a veteran of the Black Hawk War, and had even served in Abe Lincoln's company, or at least so he claimed. Since the same claim was made by most of the county's other veterans of that war, however, I came to believe that the Great Emancipator's militia company numbered some two to three thousand effectives at peak strength.

Whatever the truth of the matter, Mordecai settled down on the virgin banks of the Mississippi after the red man had been run off, and he set his frugal hand to the business of making a living. He prospered and left a few local farms and a respectable amount of hard cash to the Judge and the Judge's younger sister—my mother—Emma. As a wealthy planter, Mordecai had been able to educate his children, and Enoch had elected to read the law in Springfield. After being admitted to the bar, Enoch returned to Elm Grove to become the county's foremost jurist. It was a good choice of careers, because Enoch had a natural inclination for the judiciary, seeing as he just naturally enjoyed telling other people what to do.

As for my mother, Emma, alas, I had not seen her since my birth. There was an old photograph of her on the sideboard in the dining room of the Judge's home. It showed a fair-haired beauty with clear, trusting eyes. Too trusting, as things turned out. One fine day in 1874 a tall, blond stranger strode into the feed store. He was a discharged soldier, he said, an officer. He had tendered his resignation up in Fort Sheridan, near Chicago, and was casting about for a civilian vocation. He had stopped in St. Louis on his way out west, and on a whim had decided to see what lay upriver. What he found was Elm Grove and Emma behind the counter of the feed store.

The soldier was in town only two weeks and then he was gone, never to be seen again. Some said he had gone to the Montana Territory to

campaign against the Sioux. Others said he had gone to the silver mines
of western Colorado. The only thing for certain was that about four
months after his departure, Emma began to show. By five months it
was unmistakable: Emma was in a family way with no husband. In
the ninth month the little bastard, yours truly, arrived—as welcome
as an unemployed houseguest.

All of this, as you can well imagine, set the upstanding village of
Elm Grove on its ear. The Judge's sister despoiled, and by a soldier
at that! What was the world coming to? The Judge was wondering the
same thing as Emma recovered, and he contemplated the blue-eyed
newcomer whose arrival had upset the town's somnolent rhythm of
life. Oh, the humiliation! How could Emma ever hold up her head in
town after this disgrace?

The simple answer was that she couldn't, and one morning shortly
after the lamented birthing the household roused itself to find that Emma
was gone. She left only this short note:

Enoch,
    Raise this boy up. Call him Fenwick Travers after his father.
Don't try to follow me. I'll write when I can.

                                                    Emma

Only she never did, and that note was the last contact I was to have
with my mother. Over the years I caught snatches of whispered conversation between the Judge and his diminutive wife, Aunt Hannah.
From these hushed exchanges I gathered that the prevailing consen-
sus of opinion was that Emma had gone out west to find her soldier
boy. A less-favored theory was that she had taken a steamer from
New Orleans to the Argentine and was now married to some Spanish
cattle rancher.

I grew up in the Judge's household under the dark cloud of my origins.
I was an abomination and an embarrassment, and the Judge did little
to hide this fact from me. As you can imagine, I was the butt of cat-
calls and cruel baiting, both from my playmates in the lanes of Elm
Grove and from the Judge's own numerous brood.

I used to suffer such slings and arrows until I reached early ado-
lescence and began to develop a strength and height that put me somewhat
beyond the ordinary range in such matters. I had a natural disposition

to use my physical prowess to settle scores around town as the need arose. Soon all my peers recognized me as a cunning adversary and a fearsome wildcat in a brawl. With my skill at fisticuffs came a confident belief that I was entitled to lead my peers. If there was devilry afoot, I was usually in the forefront, egging on my social betters. It was exactly my proclivity for such high jinks that had led to my present predicament with the Judge.

"Well, what do you have to say for yourself, boy?" demanded Uncle Enoch ominously.

"Well, er," I began miserably, uncomfortably conscious of the fact that lies would do me no good and that the truth would be disastrous, "it's not so much that I haven't tried, Judge. It's just there's so much to learn." This was true enough, but it wouldn't justify my appalling mathematics test results. But the tactic here was subtle: I was pleading intellectual impairment. Since I was not the fruit of his loins, Uncle Enoch had no cause to be personally offended at my innate intellectual limitations. My plan was to plead ignorance; I would convince the Judge that I was naturally stupid and thereby get him to stop trying to "better me" through the offices of the irksome Mr. Overstreet.

"He's a full year behind the others," snapped Overstreet acidly, gratuitously hammering another nail into my coffin. But I expected as much; the little twit had it in for me because he correctly suspected that I spent most of my time in his classes stirring up my schoolmates against him whenever his back was turned and generally running down his authority at every opportunity. In short, I was a hell-raiser and he knew it, and now it was his turn to exact a pound of flesh. "I'm afraid, Judge," continued Overstreet unctuously, "that there's no academic future for your nephew. Perhaps, er . . . he could be taught a trade?"

The Judge considered this solemnly for a moment and then intoned, "Fenwick, this is most distressing news. Very disappointing indeed. You're a lazy whelp." His voice was taking on a tone of moral outrage that years of experience had taught me to dread. You see, besides being a magistrate, Uncle Enoch was also a lay preacher in the local congregation. His self-righteous and intolerant temperament ideally suited him to judge others in both temporal and ecclesiastical matters. This inherently judgmental nature, when combined with his heart of flint and a tongue that could shoot avenging flames when the mood seized him, rendered Uncle Enoch a true fire-and-brimstone preacher.

To him life in general, and education in particular, were deadly serious matters, and if I didn't realize that fact, he would be more than willing to drive the point home.

"But, Judge," I quailed, trying hard to deflect his mounting anger, "I did the best I could—"

"Silence!" he thundered, and my mouth closed as tight as a bank window in a run; I knew better than to argue when his anger was peaking.

"Fenwick, I can't abide sloth. You've known that as long as you've been under my roof."

True enough; Uncle Enoch drove himself hard around the clock six days a week in pursuit of the almighty dollar. Only the Sabbath enforced a respite in his relentless quest for lucre. It was a dreary, exhausting existence, and it explained Uncle Enoch's dour outlook on life.

"Everything I own, every last thing, mind you, the Almighty Lord gave me because I was willing to work hard. Do you understand what I'm telling you?"

I nodded my head warily, for this was a familiar litany—although inaccurate, since Uncle Enoch had gotten a great boost in life by dint of old Mordecai Sheffield's industry. But I said nothing of that, judging it wiser to weather this storm in silence. Every time I committed some transgression, Uncle Enoch would lecture to me by holding forth as a paradigm his own personal habits of thrift and industry. God liked the Judge and so he prospered, and to show his gratitude he worked all the harder, thereby prospering even more. It was a great celestial circle, you see, which basically involved God and the Judge liking each other very much, and if I mimicked his ways I too would prosper. And maybe God would even like me to boot. Maybe, but not very likely.

"I've labored mightily, boy," the Judge continued forcefully, "and you know I expect nothing less from you. But from what Mr. Overstreet says, your grades are a disgrace and so are you."

I gulped. The boom was inexorably coming down.

"Get down on your knees, sinner!" he roared, his face contorted in a paroxysm of religious fervor. "Get down and pray to the Almighty for forgiveness!"

For a second all I could do was blink at him. "Right here? Right now?"

"Get down on your knees!" he roared, and I dropped as if felled by a poleax. The last thing I wanted to do was to cross Uncle Enoch when he was seized by one of his evangelical fits. Oh, he was a hypocrite all right: In business he was a money-grubbing shylock who would steal the lashes from a blind man's eyes; but on the Sabbath and occasions such as the present, he became a pillar of God-fearing righteousness.

"O God of our fathers," he prayed with awesome ferocity, "shed your light on this pup's benighted soul. Show him the path to everlasting salvation. Show him, O Lord, thy divine Truth."

"Amen!" seconded Overstreet, who had sunk to his knees and joined our revival.

"Hallelujah," I added with all the conviction I could muster. Out of the corner of my eye I caught sight of the slight figure of Aunt Hannah on her knees as well. A bible beater in her own right, she could not pass up the chance to witness to one of her husband's divine petitions.

"O God," Uncle Enoch rumbled on, clearly warming to his task, "you know I've fought the devil many times, and praise be, I'm still thy faithful soldier. I'll be doing thy work until I draw my last breath on this earth. But you already know that, of course."

The Judge presumed that he was on such intimate terms with the Almighty that the latter naturally kept abreast of all Uncle Enoch's efforts on his behalf. Uncle Enoch's arrogance in this regard never ceased to amaze me: He actually thought he could summon the Almighty to the Sheffield residence on demand. But although I thought that Uncle Enoch was a religious fraud, with the ethics of a Barbary pirate, I naturally did not care to share that opinion with my present company.

With the preamble out of the way, Uncle Enoch got to the point. "Almighty God," he bawled, "cast your light on this lost sinner's soul! Give him your divine guidance and show him the path to wisdom. Harken him unto his teachers. Open his pathetically closed mind to thy word and thine inspiration. Lord, lead this stubborn boy to understand life's higher disciplines before it's too late!"

The act was warming up now, and Overstreet was rocking to and fro on his knees, perhaps staggered at the immensity of the job the Judge was attempting to assign to the Almighty. Aunt Hannah rolled her eyes heavenward, either to silently invoke divine intercession or to covertly inspect the accumulation of cobwebs on the ceiling. She, like Uncle Enoch, was an interesting blend of outward religious zealotry and inward grasping materialism. Although I never knew which one of these broad fields of interest occupied her thoughts at any particular moment, she was always careful to invite no censure from Uncle Enoch for lacking a properly humble and beseeching demeanor. Thirty years of marriage to him had taught her to take his fits of moral outrage very seriously indeed. I could vouch for the many times that a slight show of irreverence had provoked marathon prayer sessions on bended knees on the hard oaken floor of the Sheffield parlor. It took only a few of those gatherings to convince everyone in the clan, from Aunt Hannah right down to the youngest Sheffield cub, to humor the Judge in matters of religion and discipline.

"Dear God," Uncle Enoch thundered on, "this lad is beyond mere human help! A hard case, he is. Send down thy light upon him before he is lost to Thee forever." The Judge turned to me with the menacing grimace that for him passed as a look of paternal concern and leveled an accusing finger at me. "Fenwick, do you repent your sinful ways?"

Quivering under his baleful glare, I felt my face redden in distress and fear. "Well, er, I guess so," I heard myself squeak, squirming in torment under the unforgiving gaze of three true believers.

A gasp of disbelief escaped Aunt Hannah, who raised her hand to make the sign of the cross in my general direction.

"What?" roared Uncle Enoch with such force that I involuntarily reared backward in fright, fighting to keep from jumping to my feet and fleeing the room.

"That is, I—yes—I repent!" I quailed miserably. "I do, I do, oh yes, dear God, I do!"

Uncle Enoch was still doubtful. "I don't believe you, Fenwick. It's not true repentance you feel, and nothing I've said here has made the slightest impression on you."

"N—no, that's not so, Judge. I swear, I repent," I stammered, unnerved by Uncle Enoch's ability to hit the nail right on the head at times. "I really repent. I'm sorry as hel—er, that is, I'm really sorry."

"You can't hide your corrupted soul from the Lord, Fenwick, so don't try!" he thundered.

Things were taking a nasty turn here and I knew it; contrition was alien to my nature and I was only capable of faking that emotion. If Uncle Enoch didn't go for my feints, I would be caught in a hopeless dilemma. "I'm not trying to hide anything," I protested wildly. "I'm really sorry. I'll try harder! Honest, I will." I looked desperately at the grim faces around me, searching for a sign of melting to indicate that my abject prevarication was getting through. Their faces remained masks of repugnance.

Then a miracle! Uncle Enoch rose and spoke, and his voice sounded almost mellow. "On your feet, lad," he ordered gruffly.

Warily, I rose. Was this convocation over? Was I to be released? For a second or two the Judge eyed me in icy silence, as though trying to fathom the thoughts behind my darting blue eyes.

And then with the speed of a cobra he struck! He unleashed a thunderous right hand that caught me a staggering blow to the side of my head. I dropped like a stone.

"Umphh," I grunted, stunned.

"Get up, sinner!" hissed Uncle Enoch above me.

And get thumped again? I thought. No, thank you, I'll just stay down and whimper from here. "I'm sorry, Judge!" I wailed pathetically. "I'll be better, you'll see!"

I tried to pitch my whine to a level of wretchedness that would stir the latent maternal instincts of Aunt Hannah. I succeeded; the look of disgust on her face changed to one of concern. She knew that the Judge was capable of dealing out considerable punishment when provoked, and she didn't want a dead sinner on her hands.

"Get on your feet," Uncle Enoch demanded. Deciding that it was probably better to take another blow than to provoke him further through disobedience, I rose like a shot and scurried behind Aunt Hannah, using her as a shield to ward off another assault.

She rose quickly, not wanting to be unceremoniously bowled over should Uncle Enoch charge. "Now, Judge," she clucked nervously, "don't let the boy upset you so."

Uncle Enoch glared at me with his head lowered in a bull-like attitude. I held my breath and tensed for flight, but then he took a deep breath and pulled himself erect. "Go to your room," he ordered sternly. "Stay there until I call you."

"Yes, sir," I chirped with alacrity and was instantly gone. Up the stairs I bounded in a flash, threw open my door, and collapsed gratefully on the bed.

I gingerly felt the rising lump on the side of my head. No doubt there would be a bruise there tomorrow, but nothing was broken and, all in all, I had come through in good shape. Just give me a few days, I thought hopefully, and I'd straighten out this latest tempest. The Judge would calm down, Overstreet would cease his caterwauling, and it would be business as usual. That was the way it had always been, and I was certain that this time would be no exception.

3

I was wrong. The next day the Judge called me to his office in the courthouse. I found him in consultation with Sheriff Weyrick and Mr. Dalton, the prosecuting attorney. The Judge excused himself, ushered me into his chambers, and laid down the law.

"Fenwick, I've had a long talk with your Aunt Hannah. We've decided that further education for you is pointless. It's time you entered the business world."

"I'm not sure I follow you," I said warily. "What do you mean by the business world?"

"The river, boy. You're going to earn your keep from here on out and hopefully learn a skill that will serve you well in life. I've decided that you can best be employed on the river."

"But how?" I asked faintly. "I don't know anything about being a river man."

"Never you fear, Fenwick. What I've got in mind for you is simple enough. All you really need to know is your way to Sent Looey. I aim to make you the mate on a barge that me and Mayor Hobart intend to run on a regular basis to the Sent Looey markets."

"You and the mayor?" I echoed. Mayor Hobart owned the Farmers' and Merchants' Bank and was the county's richest citizen. He and the Judge had formed joint business ventures in the past, the feed store being but one example. I slowly digested what I was hearing and concluded that Mayor Hobart and the Judge had decided to cut out the barge owners from St. Louis who served as middlemen between the farmers of Elm Grove and the downriver markets. It was a natural extension of their business interests, and one that the Judge was apparently ready to make now that he just happened to have a healthy young buck looking for gainful employment.

"Yep, that's the plan," he beamed benignly, so kindly in fact that it set me to wondering why he had not implemented such a simple and logical plan to increase his wealth years ago. A hint of an answer to that question came when he went to a closet behind his desk and produced a venerable Winchester repeating rifle and a box of cartridges. "Here you go, Fenwick. You take this beauty out into the hills behind town and get the rust off your aim. I'll set to finishing the arrangements for a suitable barge, and then you'll be on your way."

I examined the Winchester; it was a Model 1873, .44-caliber, seventeen-shot beauty. I tried the pump action; it was smooth and well oiled. To say the least, all of this was highly perplexing, since the Judge had never before given me anything of value, and here he was lightly handing over a gem of a rifle.

"But I still don't understand. If you want me to be a mate on a barge, why do I need target practice?"

The Judge merely went on as though he hadn't heard me. "Don't stay up in those hills all day. There's still lots of arrangements to be made after you shoot off all that ammunition."

Dubious, I did what I was told. Soon the sound of my firing at empty tin cans had attracted a crowd of other boys. Like me, all were barefoot and clad in overalls and straw hats. Among them was Charlie Hobart, the mayor's boy. Charlie was a pimply-faced little prig, always with his nose in the air because his father was the town's leading citizen. Oh, I could have held my own against his superior airs had I been one of the Judge's progeny, but as a bastard I had no standing in Charlie's eyes, and he let me know it. My only other defense, my fists, was useless against Charlie Hobart because the Judge—well aware of my proclivity for pounding the holy bejeebers out of the other town boys as the mood swayed me—warned me sternly to steer clear of the scion of his business partner.

Hobart pushed to the fore of the gathering of boys as befit his station and demanded querulously, "What'cha doin', Fenny?"

I ignored him, and instead fired three quick rounds, which blew three empty tins into the air seventy-five yards away. The other boys oohed and aahed; it was acknowledged that I was one of the best shots with a squirrel gun in these parts, and now with my evident skill with the Winchester it was clear that I was destined to become one of the county's best riflemen.

With that feat of sharpshooting done and my prowess firmly established, I turned to face Hobart's sneering mug. "I'm off to the river
as a mate, Charlie. The Judge wants me well armed when I'm away."

"A mate is it? Then you've been dismissed from school for good?"
he demanded with a snicker.

I reddened at the barb and muttered, "Who needs school anyhow?
Not me."

"That's because you're a bastard and will never amount to anything,
Fenny." Charlie's remark drew a gasp from the assembled boys, who
knew and feared my quick temper. They dropped back a pace expecting
an immediate assault on Hobart, but Charlie remained before me
undestroyed. Both he and I knew of his immune status, and he enjoyed
it to the hilt. "I for one intend to stay in Mr. Overstreet's school until
I graduate next year"—he was a year behind me, you see—"and then
I'm off to college. Pa says Harvard or Yale, but I don't know about
that. I think maybe West Point or Annapolis. I'm sure I'd make a fine
soldier, like my Uncle Robert. You boys know about him, don't you?"

The other boys nodded dutifully. Hobart's Uncle Robert had been
seen around Elm Grove from time to time when he visited from
Chicago, where he was now a successful barrister. He hobbled about
on a crutch, his right leg having been separated from him by a can-
nonball in Tennessee back in 1863.

"So you think you're off to be a soldier, Charlie?" I smiled with
a narrow grin that my peers had come to know spelled trouble.

"I might," countered Hobart guardedly. "I didn't say for sure, but
I might. Why? You think there's something wrong with that?" As
superior as he thought himself, Hobart was leery of me, for he knew
what a rabble-rouser I was and how I could turn the other boys against
him if I set my mind to it. So although he treated me with outward
contempt, inwardly he knew that he couldn't dismiss me.

"No, I think that's just fine," I said lightly. "That way you can get
your left leg blown off someday, and the Hobart clan will have given
a matched set to the nation. I'd say that would about even the score
for the fact that your Pa bought a substitute when he was drafted back
in '64."

The other boys roared at this, for it was true: Mayor Hobart, to his
everlasting disgrace, had purchased a substitute rather than go to the
front when his number came up in the draft. The substitute, a drifter
from Chicago, was said to have expired of typhus in the trenches before

Petersburg. As you can imagine, this bit of shabbiness did not accord well with Charlie Hobart's exalted view of his family's military prowess, and so he lashed back savagely.

"So what? You damned bastard!" Hobart spat venomously. "The Judge didn't go to the war, neither. He claimed he was a conscientious objector and couldn't bear arms! What a damned lie that was. Everyone hereabouts knows he's not above raising his hands to others if there's a profit to be made from it!"

The boys nodded at this, for this tale too was well known in town, but I only laughed at this riposte. "What do I care if the Judge is two-faced, Charlie? I'm not *his* boy. I'm a bastard, remember? And the only thing I know for sure about my pa is that he was a real soldier, not a draft evader like your pa."

"'Tain't true!" screamed Hobart, almost sobbing.

"'Tis true," I taunted right back. "Your pa had his chance at glory, but he stayed at home with the women and children instead."

This was too much for Hobart, and he lunged forward. But he was a poor fighter, and I easily tripped him up as he bore in and gave him a savage kick in the ribs for good measure. Although the Judge had warned me not to raise my hands to Charlie, he'd never mentioned a word about my feet.

"Owww!" squealed Hobart as the air left him. But he recovered quickly and rolled himself beyond my reach.

I bent and grabbed a handful of empty brass cartridges and threw them in his sniveling face. "Here, Charlie, bring these to your pa. Tell him they're rifle cartridges, since otherwise he wouldn't have the slightest idea what they might be."

Needless to say, this latest breach of the peace did not sit well with the Judge, who cuffed my ear and told me that I was a damned ingrate of a cur. But he was energized by his new enterprise and soon got on to more important things. In a few days he took me down to the quay where his river barge lay at anchor. It was a rugged craft, fully a hundred feet long with a rough crew shack near the bow. Its deck was large enough to hold a small herd of cattle or the better part of a warehouse full of grain sacks. The craft was steered by means of a large sweep secured to her stern, and the principal means of locomotion were the twenty-foot hardwood poles gathered in a neat pile on the deck. Rope coils, called hawsers by bargemen, lay among great barrels of pitch, stored aboard for patching leaks as required. Standing among the coiled

ropes was a feeble terrier that yapped at everything around it. The dog
was a venerable old ratter, I surmised, and was probably included in
the bargain just so that it had a place to live out its days. I returned
my gaze to the barge and gave an appreciative nod; the craft had a
sturdy and thoroughly businesslike air.

"Like her?" the Judge asked with a sharp grunt, which I took to
be a little laugh. When I nodded my assent, he continued, "Got her
for a song upriver near Rock Island. I split the cost fifty-fifty with
Mayor Hobart, so we're equal partners, you see." He neglected to
mention the fact that the price he quoted to Mayor Hobart was inflated,
thereby returning to the Judge his first profit on the deal.

He put an arm around my shoulder and led me aboard. "Here's the
way it's going to work, Fenwick," he explained. "You're to load
whatever cargo I direct you with the help of my niggers"—here he
pointed to a group of darkies lounging about the quay—"and then
you're to pole downstream to Sent Looey. The niggers will be your
crew, so be firm with 'em. When I send you off, it will be with a bill
of sale already drawn up. The only terms to be filled in at Sent Looey
are the price and your signature as my agent when you sell the cargo.
You're to travel straight to market and then lay up off the bank where
you see the warehouse of Julius MacFee. It's unmistakable, boy, there's
a sign announcing the place that's fully twenty feet high, and it's visible
a mile away on a clear day. When you get there, you close the deal.
Understand?"

I shook my head. "Not entirely. How am I going to know what the
selling price is so I don't get cheated?"

That was a good question, so the Judge explained. "Don't you fret
none on that account. The going price for commodities—oats, bacon,
whatever—is always posted on the chalk slates of the wholesalers along
the dock. It isn't any secret, you see, since no wholesale dealer wants
to be out of line with his competitors' prices. The only reason I can't
simply pen in the selling price on the bill of sale before you leave
is that the prices always change a shade up or down. So you read the
slates when you arrive and figure out the going price."

I nodded; that seemed easy enough.

"There's just one thing you've got to remember about MacFee,
Fenwick," the Judge added gravely. "He's a low thief, like all them
grain dealers. You've got to watch him every step of the way. Whatever
you do, don't ever sign the bill of sale and then give it to him to fill

in the price. He'll pen in a discounted price so quick it'll make your head spin. The other thing is to get the cash from him before you hand over the bill of sale. Otherwise he'll pay with a damned promissory note that will be the dickens to collect on. Believe me, I've seen him do it. So you fill in the bill of sale and hold it in your hand until he crosses your palm with hard cash. Understand?" he demanded sharply.

I nodded. "Yep."

"Good boy. When you get the cash, you give over the bill of sale. After that, MacFee has full title to the cargo and it's his to do with as he pleases. Then you arrange to hitch the barge onto one of those river tugs that plies the river between Sent Looey and Rock Island, and pay the fare from the money you get from MacFee. When you get back to Elm Grove, you secure the barge to the quay and deliver the money to me. Don't worry about the niggers; I'll pay them off myself. Whatever you do, boy, don't deal with anyone but MacFee. Sent Looey is filled with vipers, Fenwick, and if you tarry there too long you'll be separated from your money quicker than you can blink your eyes. Now, do you have any more questions?"

I did, and nodded warily.

"Well, speak up then, boy. Don't make me have to drag them out of you."

"First," I asked carefully, "how will I recognize MacFee?"

The Judge laughed outright at this. "He's unmistakable, boy. MacFee is the ugliest man alive, and you'll spot him right off. He sports a derby hat—his lucky charm, he says. And he's only got one ear—lost the other in a barroom fight years ago. Finally, he's fat as a sow. So you just look for a creature that fits that general description and you'll find MacFee. Any other questions?"

I nodded again. "Why did you give me the Winchester?" I knew enough about Uncle Enoch to realize that he never gave anything to anyone out of the goodness of his heart. There was a message in the Winchester that I was not yet able to fathom.

But the Judge was in no mood to clear up my confusion on that point. "Oh, that? Why, it's to shoot wharf rats, boy. They'll scamper right up the hawsers and devour a sack of oats in no time. You need to plug 'em on sight. Keep it stowed in the crew shack at all times, and take it out only if you need to use it. Now set to and get those niggers to work. I want this barge loaded by sunset. You sail in the morning."

4

"Trim her to starboard," I called as the bow of the barge edged toward the tree-veiled shore. In response to my command, the black man on the sweep heaved the rudder to just the right angle, and the ungainly barge headed once more for the open channel. I perched atop the crew shack, taking in the vista that spread before me. The river in these upper reaches of the Mississippi had well-defined banks, and the deep channel was clearly visible in midstream. On either bank, ripples betrayed shoals and snags, but as long as I kept to the middle of the flow, there was no danger of going aground.

On this my maiden voyage, the Judge had loaded the vessel only to a quarter of its capacity. Clearly this was an exploratory journey, designed for me to get the feel of the river and to establish a working relationship with MacFee. I touched the inside pocket of my jacket to feel the bill of sale that Uncle Enoch had thrust at me just as the barge shoved off from the quay. "Just remember my instructions, Fenwick, and you'll be all right."

I hoped he was right. This was my first time away from home and my first time on the river on anything bigger than a skiff. To top it all off, I was entrusted with a cargo worth hundreds of dollars. I prayed that nothing would go wrong, or I'd hear about it for the rest of my days.

The darkies seemed competent enough. The two older ones had worked as barge hands before, and they went about their duties with little instruction. The man on the sweep, a young buck named Henry, I knew well. He was about my age and had been with the Judge all his life. Henry's pa was a freedman sharecropper on one of the Judge's farms, and we had crossed paths all our lives on the streets of Elm Grove. So although Henry was black, I felt as though I had at least one friend aboard.

The barge traveled no faster than the speed of the river's current, which meant that the journey to St. Louis was a leisurely two-day trip. We fished to while away the hours and at night stoked a stove on the deck with cottonwood branches that we pulled from the muddy flow. When the flames were high we broiled the catfish and perch we caught during the day and then sat back to drink coffee and tell stories into the wee hours. The blacks told me the tales of the Old South upon which they had been weaned, the saga of B'rer Rabbit and B'rer Fox. And I told them in return the fanciful tale of Ivanhoe, which I had learned from a novel by Sir Walter Scott that Mr. Overstreet had insisted upon reading to us, although it had taken most of a term to complete. While I readily understood the simple maxims taught by the blacks' folktales, they had a devil of a time figuring out what in blazes chivalry was all about.

I explained chivalry as best I understood it, which wasn't all that good. From their questions, however, I realized that I was speaking Greek to my fellow bargemen. I got basically nowhere until Henry at last summed it all up by saying, "I 'spect white folks is always a mite p'culiar 'bout their lady folks," which prompted all the black heads to nod in unanimous agreement. With that, I gave up my role as dispenser of English literature and rolled over in my blankets to sleep.

The blacks kept a rotating watch day and night. At the end of the second day, a voice sang out: "Sent Looey off de stabboard bow!" I stood on the crew shack and shaded my eyes against the setting sun. There on the bank was the rambling labyrinth of docks, levees, and warehouses that marked the legendary riverbank of St. Louis. It certainly had a functional look to it; many of the wooden buildings were unpainted and had aged to a dull gray over the years. The boats lashed to the levee were mostly working river craft like mine, elegant riverboats having long since been eclipsed by the rise of the railroads. They were nothing fancy to be sure, but they were sturdy enough to survive on a river known for bouts of uncontrolled violence.

And there, as the Judge had promised, was a huge sign proclaiming "MacFee's Wholesaler." We poled toward the sign, sidled our barge between two others in a row containing at least a score of barges, and tied the vessel to both the levee and the neighboring barges. I told the deckhands to stand ready to unload; then I went ashore to find MacFee.

I found him in the street in front of a cavernous warehouse. "Watch that barrel, you one-eyed son of a mongoose!" MacFee bellowed to a stevedore, who grunted as he maneuvered a wheelbarrow bearing a hogshead the size of a small heifer through the open door of the warehouse. "Gently, gently, you blackamoor!" demanded MacFee. "Treat it like it was a giant diamond and you were its new owner, damn your hide."

"Mister MacFee?" I interrupted. The bulky figure turned toward me, and I found myself gazing at the most repulsive face I had ever beheld. One of MacFee's dark eyes bulged out like that of a rat squeezed between two millstones, and his lips were thick and pulpy. His skin was sallow, and bluish scars ran across the beard-blackened jowls and down his wattled neck. One of his ears was sliced clean off, leaving a gaping black hole in the side of his head the size of a rifle barrel. Atop the great head perched a battered derby. I gave an involuntary start and took a step back.

The creature gave a yellow-toothed grin and licked those repulsive lips. "And just who the hell might you be, young'un?"

I cleared my throat carefully, but still shrilled uncontrollably when I spoke. "Fenwick Travers," I piped. "I'm, er, I'm Judge Enoch Sheffield's nephew from up in Black Hawk County."

"Sheffield, eh? And what might the good Judge have sent a whelp to MacFee fer, eh?"

I ignored the pointed insult. MacFee was every bit as boorish as I had feared, but I had come to do business with him and so plunged on undeterred. "He sent me to sell you some goods. I've got one hundred and fifty sacks of oats, fifty of wheat, and two dozen barrels of bacon." I took the bill of sale from my pocket and waved it at him. "The Judge says you'll buy his goods at the established price." I eyed the slates posted before the warehouses that lined MacFee's street and was relieved to see the going price for all commodities plainly displayed.

"Oh, he does, eh?" rumbled MacFee in response to my pronouncement. Catching the direction of my glance, he shook his massive head. "Those figures ain't right, sonny. They're off by ten cents on the dollar. Oh, yes 'deed, too high by 10 percent. They ain't the regular prices I give the Judge."

Uncle Enoch had prepared me for this eventuality on the quay as I departed. He had explained tersely, "Now MacFee usually discounts the price he's willing to pay on Black Hawk County goods by a dime on the dollar. That's his cost for hauling the goods to market, and damned highway robbery it is. But this time we're bringing the goods to him, so there's no need to pay him haulage. You tell him that, Fenwick, you tell him that good and clear."

So I did as I was told, and the news did not sit well with MacFee. "What? Are you telling me that the Judge is in the barge business, you little pipsqueak?"

I affirmed exactly that, which set MacFee to roaring anew. "Goddamn that man! We had an arrangement that worked well for nearly twenty years and now he's gone and broke it all to pieces! Who the hell does he think he is?"

By now a crowd of stevedores and roughnecks had gathered behind MacFee, each one of whom appeared as tough and savage as his chief. I was feeling distinctly uncomfortable now and edged imperceptibly toward the levee and the relative safety of the barge. This trip was turning into a disaster; it was clear that there would be no sale on the Judge's terms. I had best cut my losses and run while I still could. But MacFee spied my design and called out in an almost friendly way. "Hold there, child, this ain't none o' your doing. There's no point in my railing against you, eh?"

I stayed my withdrawal, nodding my head in hopeful agreement. "That's the way I see it, too, Mister MacFee. Seems your fight is with the Judge, not with me."

"There's a bright boy," beamed MacFee with a lopsided leer that seemed to pass as a manifestation of joviality. "Oh, a bright boy 'deed." Even the cutthroats at his back were grinning now, although it seemed that their hard faces might crack wide open at the effort.

"I'll tell you what I'll do, young Fenwick," offered MacFee patronizingly. "I'll settle up with you here and now, and then I'll take up my beef with the Judge direct. Don't that sound fair?"

I readily voiced my agreement. "That sounds square to me, Mister MacFee."

MacFee smiled broadly all around at this. "Then just sign the bill of sale, boy, and hand it over. I'll go and fetch your money."

My eyes narrowed; this was the very trap that Uncle Enoch had warned me against. "No, first I fill in the price, then I sign the bill of sale, then you hand over my money, and then I give you the bill of sale. That's the way it's done," I insisted bravely, although my knees were shaking like saplings in a hurricane.

MacFee scowled at my defiance, but I sensed that he, like any bully, would not take me on directly as long as I faced up to him squarely. If I knuckled under, however, I was a goner.

My instincts proved correct, for my defiance brought forth howls of merriment from MacFee's gang and eventually a forced smile to MacFee's repulsive lips, although his bulging eye glared forth pure malice.

"A spunky young'un. I like that, oh, 'deed I do. And if that's the way you say it must be, that's the way we'll do it, young Fenwick."

He ordered a quill and inkwell to be brought forth, and when they were presented I hastily penned in the price for my cargo, signed my name to the bill of sale with a shaky hand, then held the document before MacFee—but safely beyond his reach should he make a sudden grab for it. He inspected it from afar, grinned sourly, and fished out a great wad of greenback dollars from a pocket in his greasy and tattered vest. He peeled off the sum stipulated on the bill of sale and shoved the greenbacks at me, whereupon I snatched them from his grasp, hurriedly recounted them, shoved them deep in the pocket of my coat, and handed over the bill of sale in return. MacFee inspected the bill, grunted, and shoved it deep in the same pocket whence the greenbacks had appeared.

"I'll be off now, Mister MacFee," I said, fighting to keep the nervousness I felt from my voice. "I'll talk to the Judge about everything you said, I promise," I assured him, even as my feet were carrying me back to the levee.

"You do that, whelp, you do that," called MacFee ominously as I fled.

As soon as I was around the corner I broke into a lope. I wanted to put as much river between me and St. Louis as possible before the night got much older. MacFee had given me the shakes, and I wouldn't feel safe until there was more distance between us.

I sprinted to the levee and called to the deckhands who lounged about on the cargo. "Get those goods ashore fast, boys! We're not staying the night!"

The blacks were disappointed at this; they'd looked forward to visiting the darky saloons and dance halls along the river, and they weren't shy about telling me so. But after I explained to them the unpleasant nature of my confrontation with MacFee, they all saw the wisdom of an early departure. As they put their backs into unloading the cargo, I went up the levee to where a river tug was raising steam. The captain told me she was heading upriver to Davenport, Iowa, and, yes, he would hitch my empty barge to the line of barges he was hauling. Since we'd be last in line, and since I agreed to pay in advance, we could slip the hawsers when he drew even with Elm Grove and thereby return home with the dawn.

I related this to the crew, and we made ready to depart. The deckhands poled to the end of the barge line, where we made fast to the last barge and lashed our vessel securely in place. An hour after sunset we heard a great "Whoot!" in the night, felt a shudder through the line of barges, and felt ourselves being drawn into the current.

We were homeward bound, and not a moment too soon as far as I was concerned. Since we were under the control of the tug, which kept its own watch, I ordered the blacks to stand down, and we all curled up in our blanket rolls to await the dawn and homecoming.

The first hint I had that there was trouble afoot was when a great creaking groan roused me from my sleep. For a second I lay still, getting my bearings. Then I remembered everything: the trip to St. Louis, the encounter with MacFee, and the trip back upriver under the power of the tugboat. Only now I didn't feel the telltale motion beneath me of a barge being towed! We were stopped, by God! Something was terribly wrong.

Alarmed, I leapt to my feet. Perhaps sensing my mounting fear, the crew too was rousing. I quickly glanced about; we were aground on the Missouri bank, and one look at the hawsers lying on the deck near the bow told me that they'd been snapped by the blow of an ax.

"On your feet, boys. There's treachery afoot!" I cried out just as a wooden bumping sound astern drew my attention. A skiff had grappled alongside the barge, and now a dark knot of intruders was clambering up to the deck.

"Boarders!" I roared, and now every man was in motion. I realized instantly that the bushwhackers had secreted themselves in one of the barges ahead of us, and when the time was right they'd slipped down the line to our barge, uncoupled it from the tug by severing the hawsers, and now were in the process of boarding. The two older blacks rushed astern with staves to hurl the intruders overboard, but then a pistol blast split the dark, and one of the blacks staggered backward, his face a mass of blood. He collapsed at my feet, a thick dark puddle of blood spreading across the weathered deck planks. His comrade, seeing the fate of his companion, dropped his stave, dove headlong into the Mississippi, and struck out into the current.

That left only Henry and me. Advancing toward us up the deck were four dark shadows. I had to assume that they were all armed, and the thought rooted me to the spot in fear. But then Henry spoke, breaking the trance. "Fenny! Quick, de hogshead!"

At first I didn't understand, but then I saw his plan. On grounding, the bow of the barge had become elevated slightly in relation to the stern, which jutted out into the Mississippi. Henry was suggesting that we lay some of the huge hogsheads of pitch on their sides and use them like giant bowling balls to topple our assailants.

"Yes, Henry, quickly!" I agreed with alacrity, and straining every fiber in our bodies we muscled a two-hundred-pound hogshead into the path of our advancing foes, keeled it over on its side, and aimed it carefully. Seeing our plan, our attackers fired again. We crouched low and the bullets slammed harmlessly into the great barrel, which served as a breastwork to protect us.

"Let 'er rip!" called Henry, and away the hogshead rolled, rumbling ominously as it picked up momentum on the incline. Now it was our attackers' turn to freeze, then scatter as the hogshead roared into their midst. There was a yelp of pain as the barrel rolled over a foot, crushing it flat. Before the enemy could regroup, Henry and I had a second hogshead down and rolling, and then a third. The second one caught the broken-footed figure flush as he thrashed about on the deck, killing him instantly with a sickening thud. Then the third barrel slammed home, bowling over two of the three remaining assailants. For one of them, this was enough; he dove over the side to follow our fleeing crewman into the current.

The two remaining foemen hunkered down at the far end of the barge, and the gun roared again.

"Duck!" I called to Henry as the bullet ricocheted off the crew house. Then I remembered the Winchester; I ran inside, pulled the rifle from its storage space, fished about in the dark for cartridges, and finally found them. I chambered five rounds and then stepped into the night to settle the score. There was no chance of running, you see, for as long as the enemy was armed, they could pick off Henry and me as we swam downstream. If we fled inland they could track us down and shoot us at their leisure when the sun rose. No, there was no way around it: The place to make our fight was right here.

I put my back against the crew house, aimed the big Winchester where I'd last seen the gunman in the splintered wreckage of the barrels below me, and waited. The false light of dawn was now faintly illuminating the eastern sky behind our assailants, promising a good silhouette for me to fire upon should they show themselves again.

The gunman promptly did just that. I saw his head rise and peer about, and then I saw him raise the pistol to where Henry crouched on the far side of the crew house some ten feet away. I squeezed the trigger, and the Winchester roared.

"Yiiii!" came a scream, and a figure arose, clasping his hands to his face. I'd shot an eye right out of the fellow, and in his agony he hurled himself overboard and sank like a stone in the turgid river. There remained only one enemy.

I signaled to Henry to advance down the left side of the barge, and I set out down the right side. Moving in the open like this was a bold act, and I found my tread involuntarily slowing as I hung slightly back on my flank to let Henry take the lead. What if that fellow down there was armed? Wouldn't he shoot at the person closest to him? That would be Henry now, which would give me the split second I'd need to draw a bead and finish this fight. It's not that I wished Henry ill, you see, but I had the rifle and he didn't, and so my logic was unassailable to me. Accordingly, I let Henry take a full five yards' lead on his flank. Just as he neared the wreckage of the smashed hogsheads, the last dark figure rose up in the growing light.

"I give up! Oh, 'deed I do," he whined piteously. "Don't shoot, please!"

I recognized that voice immediately. "MacFee, you son of a bitch! You were layin' for us, weren't you?"

"Now hold on there, young Fenwick," he protested pleadingly. "It 'twarn't me that started this ruckus. It was the dad-blamed Judge. He broke our deal, damnit! The fault's on his head and not mine!"

"Oh, and all this murder and mayhem's got nothing to do with you, you fat toad? Well, just you step out of that mess and get your hands up, MacFee. We'll see what a jury of your peers has to say about all of this."

MacFee edged into the open, but his hands weren't up. An alarm sounded deep in my brain. "MacFee, you scoundrel, I said get your hands u—!"

Then MacFee had the pistol raised, the one he'd grasped when it fell from the grip of his late henchman. As I had foreseen, he leveled it at Henry, who froze, gasped out a great, "Oh, Lordy!" and sprang a full five feet straight in the air just as MacFee pulled the trigger.

The leap saved Henry's life, for the bullet, aimed where Henry's midsection had been a moment before, missed by a wide margin. When Henry alit, MacFee aimed again, ready now for any last-moment dodges. Henry was clearly a dead man, or so I thought until a furry form scampered past me to lunge at MacFee's pant leg.

It was the old terrier! The gunfire had roused its fighting spirit, and now it was being heard from in earnest. "Aahhh! Get it off me!"

howled MacFee, shaking his leg to loose the aged canine. Finding its grip too strong to break, MacFee lowered the barrel of the pistol and fired. The terrier yelped once and fell to the deck, twitching uncontrollably. Enraged at the gouge taken out of his beefy leg, MacFee squeezed the trigger to finish the job—but the revolver only clicked harmlessly.

I smiled and reversed the Winchester to use it as a club. MacFee was big, all right, but he was a bully who knew he'd been beaten. Now he turned craven, but to no avail, because my blood was up, and I laid into him. I belabored the screaming riverman with the maple stock until there wasn't a square inch of him that wasn't swollen and purple. Although I wouldn't have thought it possible, when the sun was full in the sky and I had a chance to view my handiwork, I saw that I'd rendered MacFee even more hideous than before.

"Let's take this son of a bitch to see the Judge," I told a now-grinning Henry.

5

"Well, what have we here?" demanded the Judge when I hauled MacFee into the feed store at rifle point. I could tell by the looks of mutual disdain that passed between the two men that they were well acquainted with each other.

I related the story of the nighttime ambush and how the crew and I had fought off MacFee's murderous assault. A crowd of townsmen had gathered around and were rumbling ominously at the allegations I was leveling. "That's a hangin' offense fer sho'," opined one worthy, who was vigorously seconded by his fellows. Another chorused, "That MacFee has been rubbin' us the wrong way for years, and now he's due to be whittled down a bit, I sez."

MacFee became agitated at this and began blubbering that he hadn't done anything wrong. He demanded the protection of the law. To my surprise, the Judge took his part; he raised a hand and the crowd fell silent. "There'll be no lynching here, by God. We'll have a trial, all legal and proper."

MacFee was remanded to the custody of Sheriff Weyrick and the crowd obediently dispersed. Indeed there was a trial, not a week later. The prosecutor, Mr. Dalton, with my help drew up a bill of particulars against MacFee. I suggested that murder be charged, since there had been carnage aplenty on the barge that night, but Dalton demurred.

"Nope, I don't see how we can do that," he explained. "Sure there were folks killed, but from what you say, MacFee didn't do the shooting. The fellow to be properly charged with murder was the one you killed. And besides, the only person MacFee's gang killed was a nigger, so I don't think a jury would be very incensed about that anyway."

That was a fine legal point that would have sailed right by me. Chastened but unbowed, I ventured, "But he shot at Henry and me. Ain't that attempted murder, or at least disturbing the peace?"

"Well, to tell you the truth, if it was only Henry that got fired at, it wouldn't even be a breach of the peace. Prosecuting a white for trying to murder a black is just a waste of time, I'm afraid. Since you're white, this charge is a little more serious, but I can't charge him with attempted murder, since his shots never came anywhere near you. They were aimed at the colored boy, you see."

Perhaps something in my look reflected my unease with the state of the law in Black Hawk County, for Dalton patted my back in a consoling way and added, "But I can charge MacFee with assaulting you, and by jiminey, I will."

Mollified at this, I nodded as Dalton drew up the charge, completely omitting any reference to Henry's brush with death in the process. "Well, I guess that's about it, then," I said.

But Dalton shook his head firmly in the negative. "Not by a long shot, Fenny. What about the dog?"

"The dog?" I asked incredulously. "What about it? Sure MacFee killed it, but so what? I mean, if the jury won't give two hoots about Henry nearly getting ventilated, why should they care about a crippled old mutt?"

"Because that terrier was a good old fellow," explained Dalton, "and besides, a barge dog is a public animal just like a horse that pulls a city tram. And it just so happens that we have an ordinance against abusing public animals. No, MacFee must pay for shooting that dog." So Dalton set to and drew up a charge of abusing a public animal— a misdemeanor—and left me scratching my head over how it could be that a jury that couldn't care less about Henry's close brush with death could feel outraged by the death of an old mongrel. Perhaps reading my mind, Dalton paused in his scrivening to announce, "Folks like their hounds here, Fenny. You know that."

I just nodded and Dalton went on. "And don't forget the hawsers on the barge. They were private property that MacFee ordered to be destroyed. That's destruction of private property, and we—"

"Have you got an ordinance against it?" I suggested helpfully. Dalton paused and eyed me; he wasn't an insensitive man, and he knew what I was feeling. "Now, Fenny, stop fretting about that boy Henry. There's no point in going through the motion of bringing charges against a white man for trying to kill a darky when I know that any jury in this county just couldn't be bothered about such a matter. I'm not telling you it's right; I'm just telling you that's the way it is. And besides, Henry came out of this just fine, so all's well that ends well."

I supposed that was so. In any event the trial opened with the charges as Dalton had drafted them. I sat behind the bar just to the rear of Dalton's table so that he could turn and whisper to me as needed. The small gallery was packed to overflowing, which meant that there were about thirty farmers and townsmen in the courtroom. Uncle Enoch was on the bench, magnificent in his black robe, lacking only a white periwig to match the awesome splendor of his cousins in the British judiciary. Into this charged atmosphere MacFee, manacled, was marched by Sheriff Weyrick, who sat him down at the defense table and then took a seat behind the bar, where he could collar the defendant quickly should that prove necessary.

Mayor Hobart strode in with a dapper fellow at his side who stumped down the aisle on a crutch. This would be Robert Hobart, the mayor's brother, I surmised, the Uncle Robert who was the Civil War veteran Charlie always bragged about. What was he doing here? I wondered.

I got my answer when Uncle Robert Hobart made his way to MacFee's table and sat down. Only then did I recall that he was a lawyer in Chicago. He was MacFee's defense attorney, by God! A stir went up at this, for wasn't the mayor a partner in the barge that MacFee attacked? It seemed a bit irregular that the attorney for the accused was the brother of one of the accused's victims. Which then set me to wondering whether it wasn't a bit improper for Uncle Enoch to preside over this tribunal, since he too was an investor in the barge venture. I was no expert in matters of jurisprudence, but there seemed to be conflicts of interest in these proceedings. But if any of this bothered MacFee, you wouldn't know it, what with his horrid face set in his characteristic lopsided grin that made him look like a battle-scarred tomcat that had just eaten a particularly delectable canary.

"Order in the court!" bellowed the Judge, gaveling the assemblage into a respectful silence. He fixed a gimlet eye on the gallery. "I'll brook no more outbreaks during these proceedings."

Lawyer Hobart then rose to inform the court that he would be representing the defendant, and MacFee sweetly assured the Judge that the arrangement was "Just fine with me, Y'onor, oh, 'deed it is."

The stage now set, Mr. Dalton rose to present the state's case. He drew himself up to his full height, fixed the jury with a stern eye, and drew a deep breath to commence his bombardment. But before he could fire the first shot, Lawyer Hobart was on his feet interrupting.

"Your Honor, if I may," he said in the well-oiled tones of a practiced trial lawyer, "would the court be so kind as to allow me to approach the bench a moment?"

"You may," acceded the Judge.

This knocked the wind right out of Mr. Dalton's sails and, a bit perplexed at this opening gambit, he too moved forward, for it was common practice for lawyers from each side to approach the bench whenever a sidebar was granted. But this was no ordinary sidebar, as Dalton quickly found out. "Back away, Mister Dalton, back away," ordered the Judge. "When I require your counsel, I'll tell you."

"But Your Honor," protested Dalton, flummoxed by this rebuff. "An ex parte conversation with counsel for the defendant is improper—"

"Back away," repeated the Judge firmly. Highly indignant and muttering under his breath, Dalton obeyed.

Humiliated in front of the jury, Dalton retreated to his chair. "What in tarnation is going on here?" I could hear him saying to himself, which alerted me that this was not going to be any ordinary proceeding. I smelled a large rat as Lawyer Hobart spoke in hushed, urgent tones to the Judge. The barrister nodded and from time to time glared down at MacFee, who, having been well drilled by his lawyer, kept his rubbery lips fixed in a pursed smile, all the while beaming beatifically with his one bulging eye at the jury foreman. The foreman for his part snorted in disgust; it was obvious that he was itching to find MacFee guilty of something.

Then Lawyer Hobart took his place back at the defense table. "Your Honor," he announced, "my client wishes to enter a plea of guilty as charged."

Dalton rose, dumbfounded. Prior to this very moment, there had not been the slightest hint that MacFee would plead guilty to any of the charges. "Well, Your Honor, this is all news to the state. I'll have to mull it over a bit."

"There's nothing to mull over, Counselor," overruled the Judge. "This sounds like a pretty straightforward proposition to me. Spell out your terms, Mister Hobart."

"A plea to all charges in exchange for an agreement that any confinement you may adjudge will be suspended and Mister MacFee can walk out of here a free man."

"No jail?" sputtered Dalton. "That's not a deal, Judge, that's a giveaway! No, absolutely not!"

But Dalton obviously had lost sight of whose courthouse he was in. "Done!" boomed the Judge and brought down his gavel with a crack. "Mister MacFee, I hereby sentence you to two years in the Illinois State Penitentiary. Further, I hereby suspend that sentence and release you on your own recognizance. The suspension will be lifted if you violate any law of the state of Illinois or any ordinance of Black Hawk County within two years from this date."

Dalton, stunned, sank slowly to his chair, his mouth trying but failing to voice a protest. The biggest villain he had ever prosecuted in his ten years as the town attorney was free, without a legal shot having even been fired by the state. But whereas Dalton was totally confused, the light was beginning to come on for me. Now I clearly saw the elaborate trap that Uncle Enoch had laid for MacFee. I had been sent to St. Louis not so much to trade grain as to confront MacFee. The Judge and Mayor Hobart knew that MacFee had a monopoly on the barge trade north of St. Louis, and that MacFee would not willingly loosen that lucrative stranglehold. So they decided to set me upon him, knowing that I was wild enough to perhaps scare MacFee to terms, and that if bluff and bluster weren't enough and words gave way to fighting, I just might be the fellow to whip MacFee. And if I had failed and died in the trying, well, there was no great loss, since I was generally viewed as a hell-raising inconvenience by the good burghers of Elm Grove. In other words, I was expendable.

That hurt more than I cared to admit. The Judge evidently was prepared to risk my life and limb to secure a business advantage. Had I been more sophisticated, of course, I would have understood the true reasons for Uncle Enoch's antipathy toward me. First of all, I was a bastard and hence anathema. I understood that part, all right, but what I failed to grasp was that, as Emma's son, I was also heir to half of the property the family had inherited from Grandfather Mordecai Sheffield. To the Judge then, not only was I a walking moral outrage, I was also a cloud on the title to what he increasingly regarded as his sole patrimony. The sooner I was gone from Elm Grove, the better. If I had fallen in the murderous confrontation with MacFee, that meant simply that the Judge would have been shed of two vexing problems in one fell swoop. But I had survived, the disappointment of that development being mitigated only by the fact that MacFee had been brought to heel for at least two years, and after that time it was doubtful that he would ever again be able to impose his monopoly on Elm Grove.

The gavel pounded again and roused me from my reveries. "There's just one more matter on the court's docket," announced the Judge. "That's the matter of the death of Mister MacFee's men. The investigation in this case clearly shows that my nephew Fenwick shot and killed one fellow and assisted in the death of the other."

Here Sheriff Weyrick spoke up. "That's right, Your Honor. I fished the one fellow's body out of the Mississippi myself. He was nailed clean, too, right in the eye. Could'na done it no better myself. As for the other varmint, he was squashed flatter'n a flapjack."

At this there was a murmur of approval at my prowess with a Winchester and a barrel, but the gavel pounded the courtroom into silence. The Judge thanked Sheriff Weyrick for this report and announced, "Under the circumstances, this court finds these killings to be legally justified. No further inquiry into the matter is required." The gavel slammed down a final time, the Judge rose and retired to his chambers, and the bailiff announced that the court was adjourned. MacFee gave me a sly wink as Sheriff Weyrick unlocked his manacles, and then the fat rogue was gone.

My first brush with the legal system had left me dazed, shaken, and highly anxious about my future. That anxiety was only heightened when the Judge took me aside a few days later and told me that I was to make another barge trip to St. Louis. Only there was a major catch: I was no longer the mate.

"But I don't see why that should be, Judge," I protested. "Everything went fine on the first trip, and I fought a gun battle to boot. I deserve better than this."

"Perhaps," said the Judge, his tone telling me he didn't think so, "but this barge business is going to be big, and frankly your, er, status won't answer. The mate needs to be on good terms with all the business interests in town, boy. No, you just aren't suited, and that's the end of the matter."

"Then if I'm not to be the mate, who is?"

The answer stunned me: "Charlie Hobart. You're to follow his orders."

"Charlie Hobart?" I echoed incredulously. "Why, that pipsqueak couldn't lead a pack of horseflies into a stable! He couldn't find his way out of a tub of water, never mind down the river to Sent Looey!"

The Judge didn't argue the point, for even he knew that Charlie Hobart could be unusually helpless at times. "That's why you're going along. I want you to teach him the river, Fenwick. Show him the ropes, and teach him everything I taught you on the first trip."

I nodded glumly, fighting back the tears that were welling up in my eyes. Not only was I being cashiered, but I was being told to teach my replacement the very skills that would ensure my own irrelevance! I had always suspected that the Judge considered me a little slow on the uptake—largely because of my dismal performance in Mr. Overstreet's academy—but for him to lay this plan out in front of me made it crystal clear that the Judge considered me to be an absolute moron who could not see his own ruination when it was clearly spelled out for him. It was almost beyond bearing, but I realized that further argument was useless, so I held my tongue.

"Can I rely on you, boy?" he asked gravely.

I fought down my tears and eyed him levelly. "Absolutely, Judge."

6

A week later the barge was outfitted for its next trip. Whereas before the deck had been only a quarter full, now there was not a single square foot that did not hold cargo. The last fruits of Black Hawk County were being lashed aboard as Charlie Hobart and I stepped on deck. From the amount of cargo, I realized that the commission the Judge and Mayor Hobart expected to realize from this trip was considerable indeed. I hazarded a guess that their return from this trip alone would equal a half year's profits from their feed-store business, which was itself an exceedingly profitable venture.

The Judge had detailed two new darkies to serve as deckhands and had also sent along Henry to give Charlie at least one experienced hand. Charlie instantly assumed the role of Admiral of the Ocean Seas and set about belaboring the sweating blacks with a barrage of superfluous and redundant orders. When he was satisfied with arrangements on deck, he ordered the hands to cast off and soon we were in midchannel, drifting slowly south.

Charlie tried to engage me in conversation, for this was a high adventure for him, and he was bubbling over with enthusiasm. But I was in a deep melancholy and could not be drawn out. Abandoning me as a source of entertainment, Charlie turned his attentions back on the hapless deckhands, rounded on them for not poling fast enough, and then for poling too fast, and generally made an ass of himself.

The fourteen hours of the journey went mercifully quickly, and at midmorning on the second day Henry sang out, "Sent Looey, ho!"

"Fenny, lend a hand," ordered Charlie with an imperious air that made me think about tossing him into the river. "Lay us along the riverbank."

Holding my temper despite Charlie's provocations, I took my place at the sweep and helped the blacks to wedge the barge between others of its kind along the levee directly in front of MacFee's warehouse. The blacks threw the hawsers to roustabouts on the levee, and soon we were securely docked. Down went the gangplank, and soon bales and hogsheads were trundling ashore.

"Take me to MacFee," ordered Charlie. "I want to close this deal right now."

I shrugged and did as I was told, leading Charlie up the levee into the mud street that ran past MacFee's office. MacFee was in the street when we approached, and at the sight of me he started violently and stepped back.

"Relax, MacFee," I said. "I'm only here on business. I nodded at Charlie, who screwed himself up to the fullest of his inconsiderable height and tried to look older by putting a ridiculous grimace on his face. "This here's Charlie Hobart, Mayor Hobart's boy. He's come to sell the cargo we got setting on the levee."

This confused MacFee. "Ain't you the skipper, Travers?"

"Not anymore," was all I said, and the wicked grin on MacFee's face told me he understood; I'd been fired and he was pleased as punch at my comeuppance. I also could tell from the appraising way he studied poor Charlie that MacFee was feverishly racking his brain to come up with some way to profit from this unforeseen circumstance.

To MacFee's utter astonishment, I showed him the way. "The Judge told me that I was to teach Charlie here the ropes," I announced, "and that's what I aim to do." Turning to Charlie I instructed, "Here's how the game works. First you and MacFee work out the price."

This Charlie did and the two agreed that the cargo, were it to be bought at Elm Grove, would be worth just over $630. Since we had transported it to St. Louis, however, the price should be increased by the 10 percent transport fee that MacFee usually deducted from the price he paid. The price therefore was set by Charlie at $700, to which MacFee warily nodded his assent.

"Now, Charlie," I continued smoothly, "you sign the bill of sale, then hand it over to MacFee. Then wait right here and he'll get your money." I failed to remind Charlie to fill in the dollar amount of the sale before he signed the bill of sale.

"Shouldn't I get the money first and then sign?" asked Charlie, uneasy at my proposed procedure.

Brutish and repulsive MacFee was, but stupidity wasn't one of his faults. He sensed that I wanted to fleece Charlie—for what reason he couldn't guess—but he was more than willing to play his part. He picked up his cue flawlessly, guffawing loudly at Charlie's question as though the custom of these matters was so well established as to be beyond such second-guessing. "Boy, this here's Sent Looey. I'm known up and down these levees as a man of his word." Lightning didn't instantly strike him down at this mendacity, so he continued saucily along. "You just sign that bill of sale, give it to me, and I'll guarantee that you get your agreed-upon price." MacFee looked at me for confirmation and I duly nodded.

"That's the way I did it last time, Charlie," I lied with a smile.

Charlie was still hesitant, but faced with our combined assurances, he capitulated. "All right, MacFee, but no tricks," which was just a little like telling a flea-riddled hound not to scratch, but MacFee didn't miss a beat.

"No tricks, young sir, no tricks 'deed," MacFee said with the fawning smile that a python would give its prey if it could curl its lips enough to do so.

An inkwell was produced and a quill, whereupon Charlie signed his name. MacFee snatched the document from his hand, then the quill,

and quickly scribbled in a price in the space left blank for that purpose. "Now you young gentlemen wait right here and I'll fetch your
money." He disappeared into his warehouse and reappeared with a roll
of greenback dollars. He thrust them into Charlie's outstretched hand
and tipped his sweat-stained derby in farewell. "A pleasure doin' business
with you, young sirs," he smiled hugely.

"Hold on, MacFee," demanded Charlie. "I want to count out the
money before you leave."

"Oh, it's all there, young'un, 'deed it is," MacFee blithely assured
Charlie as he receded down the street with no slackening of his pace.

Charlie counted the bills as rapidly as he could, blinked as the import
of his calculations became clear, and then bellowed at the top of his
lungs, "Five hundred dollars! By God, MacFee, you shorted me $200!
Stop, thief, stop!"

This cry would have instantly raised a posse of stalwart citizens on
the lanes of Elm Grove, but on the mud streets of St. Louis, Charlie's
clamor drew nary a glance from passersby, other than a yellow cur
that stopped, eyed Charlie idly, then raised a leg to spray a nearby
horse trough. To my surprise, however, MacFee turned at Charlie's
trumpeting and sauntered back to us.

"How can you say such things, young'un?" he asked with feigned
indignation. "Why, I gave you the agreed price."

"That's a lie, damn you!" fumed Charlie. "Look at the bill of sale,
MacFee. The price is on the . . ." His voice trailed off as he realized
the enormity of his error.

MacFee gave Charlie an immense yellow grin and withdrew the
bill of sale from his pocket. "It says right here—$500. And that's what
I gave you. So you see, I'm in the right. Ask your pa, boy, or," here
he chortled gleefully, "the Judge. They'll tell you the law is on my
side this time." Then he threw back his ugly head and gave a great
roar of triumph. "This little deal will more than pay the bill for legal
fees that your Uncle Robert sent me, boy!"

Hobart was beat and he knew it. "Goddamn you, MacFee!" he stormed
impotently. Rounding on me he added furiously, "And damn you too,
Fenny! I'm going to the Judge and tell him the whole story. I've been
robbed, by God!"

"When you see the Judge," I countered dryly, "make sure you tell
him you were stupid enough to hand over your bill of sale before you
got the cash from MacFee. He'll be very interested in that fact, Charlie."

Charlie shook with fury but didn't say another word. He turned and stormed off to the levee. I could hear him muttering dire imprecations about me as he went: "That bastard will pay for this when he gets home, I swear he will!"

Unknown to Charlie, this bastard wasn't going home again. MacFee noticed that I wasn't following Hobart, and he sidled over to me like a scavenging crab. "Fixin' on stayin' around town, eh, son?" he pried.

I didn't reply, for I truly didn't know the answer. If I wasn't going back to Elm Grove, where would I go and what would I do? The whistle of a train rumbling across the Eads Bridge from Illinois drew my gaze; MacFee followed it.

"Thinkin' about travelin' on, are ya?" he asked with a raised eyebrow. "Do what ya want, son, but a smart buck like you might do just fine here in Sent Looey. There might even be a place for ya in the grain business. 'Deed, a place in the business." His stubbly jowls split into a grin at this, for the thought of me working as an enforcer for him gave him a vision of regaining the river monopoly that the Black Hawk County Court had recently pried from his grip.

I eyed MacFee coolly. No doubt he'd pay a good wage for a straight-shooting minion who could mix it up on land or on the river. But he was a repulsive toad, and St. Louis held no charm for me. It was the Gateway to the West, a town that lived by selling things to people who were on their way to somewhere else. It certainly wasn't a place to put down roots. Besides, putting down roots was the last thing on my mind; I had a lot of living to do first.

I was pondering this dilemma and trying to put MacFee's pestering out of my mind when I heard the roll of a drum in the distance. I raised my head at the sound.

MacFee heard it too. "Recruiters," he grunted. "Soldier boys from Jefferson Barracks south of town. They always sweep the docks lookin' for recruits, 'specially when the winter wind starts blowin'." He spat in the street with disdain. "Now there's a fool's game if you ask me. Imagine askin' someone to sign away his life to do another man's fightin'. A fellow would have to be dumber than a headless chicken to agree to a deal like that," he cackled.

But he was talking to himself by now. I was already walking in the direction of the drum.

7

"Come on, boys!" boomed a deep baritone voice. "Which of you are for adventure on the frontier against the Indians and the bandits? Surely there are men among you who crave adventure."

I rounded a corner and came upon a completely outlandish scene. There on a wooden sidewalk outside a tavern stood a recruiting sergeant haranguing a crowd of idlers and habitués of the tavern who had wandered outside to enjoy the show. The sergeant was the picture of military finery; he wore a dark blue coat with sky blue trousers. On his head was a helmet rather like the pith helmet one always saw famous explorers pictured in when they went about discovering the Congo or other such exotic places. The helmet, like the coat, was dark blue, and from its crown a long yellow plume of horsehair flowed gracefully down the back of the sergeant's neck. The plume matched the yellow cords that decorated his breast. The uniform was set off by a leather belt edged with gold from which dangled a cavalry saber. The drumming I heard came from a stripling of a drummer who wore a similar uniform but with yellow herringbone piping across his breast, which denoted him as a bandsman. I knew from reading tales of the Civil War that the yellow details on the uniforms of these fellows meant they were "yellow legs"—cavalrymen.

Curious, I pushed forward into the beer-guzzling crowd. "Who'll be the first to enlist?" cajoled the sergeant. "Ten dollars bounty money, boys! Cash on the barrel. Who'll be the first?"

"Does that include the cost of your casket, or does that come out of a man's pay?" heckled a grizzled riverman, his fellows guffawing at the barb.

But the sergeant was seasoned by having played out this charade in front of a hundred crowds outside a hundred taverns. "The casket's on us, men," he promised unflappably, "and we'll even throw in a brand-new flag to wrap it in. Thank you, sir, for pointing out that very important entitlement. It almost slipped my mind. Now then, who'll be the first? I need some likely bucks who aren't afraid of danger. Men who crave a taste of the wilderness." His practiced eye scanned the crowd and came to rest on me, no doubt because I was almost a head taller than the fellows around me.

"What about you, son? You've got the look of a soldier, by God."

The crowd turned as one to eye me. The grizzled riverman heckled, "Step right up, boy. Get your free room and board. Just make sure t'say your good-byes first."

Another round of laughter greeted this, but to the amazement of all, especially me, I didn't scuttle off. Instead I considered this new possibility. I had by now completely dismissed the thought of returning to Elm Grove, and I had no prospects in this world. I needed to move on, and the recruiting sergeant was offering me the chance of doing precisely that. I pushed through the crowd to face the sergeant.

"What exactly are you offering?"

"What I said, son," he answered with the ready smile of a snake oil peddler. "Good pay—thirteen dollars a month." Here the crowd erupted in laughter and even I snorted, for this was a pittance, but he quickly continued. "And free room and board. Why, we'll even put clothes on your back, son," he added with a glance at my well-worn togs.

"Where will you send me?" I demanded.

"Arizona Territory," he answered in a tone that suggested he was offering a passport to paradise to a specially chosen few. "God's country, boy."

The mention of Arizona drew an involuntary "ohhh!" from the crowd, for that faraway land was like the other side of the moon to most Americans, what with its savage Indians and rugged deserts. Although most of the Indians had been forced onto reservations, Arizona was still infested with outlaws and renegade Apaches. But rather than being deterred by the prospect of going to such an untamed land, I was compelled by my circumstances to press on.

"Where in Arizona?" I asked.

The sergeant smiled broadly now, sensing he had a taker. "Fort Grant. Uh, I didn't catch your name, boy."

"Fenwick Travers," I answered boldly.

"Fenwick Travers, eh?" he echoed, rolling the name off his lips. "There's a fine martial name. Call me Sergeant O'Brien, Fenwick. Yes, son, I'm proposing to send you off to Fort Grant, down by the border with Old Mexico. You'll be a member of the historic 7th Cavalry of Custer and Sitting Bull fame. The regiment was reconstituted after the Battle of the Little Bighorn and sent south to Arizona, a land of unparalleled beauty and wonder. Sign up, Fenwick, and you'll be thanking me for the rest of your life for this magnificent opportunity."

There was more laughter from the crowd at this, but it was good-natured now, as though the idlers were coming to admire the sergeant for the superb salesman he was. Yet I still was not put off.

"You'll pay my way to Arizona?" I pressed.

"That's right, Fenwick," promised Sergeant O'Brien. "We'll send you by train most of the way, too—the ticket's on your good old Uncle Sam."

I considered this a moment; any train would have to pass through large cities on its way to Arizona, and if I wanted to I could desert along the way. Or I could stay for the full ride, see whether or not I liked army life in Arizona, and if not I could desert there. I chewed this over as the crowd drifted away, then I made up my mind.

"I'll sign," I announced.

Sergeant O'Brien beamed and the little drummer smirked. "Fenwick, I knew you had gumption the instant I laid eyes on you. But what about your nigger?"

"My nigger?" I asked, perplexed. "I ain't got a nig—" I started to say, but then turned to see Henry grinning from ear to ear.

"Henry? What in the blazes are you up to? Why aren't you with Charlie Hobart back on the barge?"

Henry fidgeted under my gaze but held his place. "Massa Hobart done stormed back aboard an' tol' us dat you had hightailed it becuz you had cheated him. He swore he wuz gonna tell de Judge, an' dat you would never be able t'set yo' foot in Elm Grove agin'. So I figgered you might jus' need dis." He held up the Winchester.

I took the rifle appreciatively. That was damned thoughtful of Henry and I told him so. He always did seem to do more thinking than any darky I'd ever known.

"But what about you, Henry?" I queried. "As far as Charlie Hobart is concerned, you're just a thieving nigger who's run off with a rifle. The Judge would horsewhip you out of Elm Grove, and that's the truth."

Henry evidently agreed, for he studied the mud and shifted uneasily from foot to foot. He recognized that he'd crossed a line and that returning home was out of the question. "Wal, I figgered I'd jus' tag 'long wid you, Fenny."

"With me?" I exclaimed. "But I don't see how that's possible. I'm off to join the army and then I'm bound for Arizona."

Here Sergeant O'Brien intervened. "Why, it's no problem at all, Fenwick. It was like I was trying to tell you. We'll just enlist the colored boy. It's Henry, isn't it?" asked Sergeant O'Brien with the sweetest smile Henry had ever gotten from a white man in his life.

"Yas, suh," answered Henry nervously.

O'Brien's face clouded over at this, and his voice turned flinty. "Don't call me 'sir,' boy. I ain't no damned officer. I work for a living—I'm a sergeant, a noncommissioned officer. Follow me?"

"Yas, sar'gint," quailed Henry.

But I was still confused. "Sergeant, I don't see how Henry can join the army with me. He's a fine fellow and all, but he's blacker than the inside of a bat at midnight."

O'Brien laughed gently, the picture of genial bonhomie once again. "Why, he won't be in your regiment, son. He'll be in a Negro regiment. Fort Grant has seven troops of the 7th Cavalry, but it's also home to two companies of the 25th Infantry, a colored regiment. What do you say to that, Henry? How does a nice new set of soldier clothes and thirteen dollars a month to boot sound to you?"

Henry's eyes bulged at the prospect of such largesse. First, he had never possessed more than a nickel at a time in his entire life. And second, he had never in his wildest imaginings conceived of such a thing as a colored regiment.

"Ya-yah, suh, uh, sar'gint. Dat sounds jus' fine wid me. I'd like t'join yo' army sump'in powerful!"

"Then you shall, Henry. Come along, men," he ordered. Sergeant O'Brien and the drummer closed up shop on the street corner and the four of us clambered aboard a horse-drawn tram, which carried us to the south edge of town to Jefferson Barracks. Unknown to me at the time, Jefferson Barracks had a long and illustrious history as a jumping-off point for the conquest of the West. At various times both Robert E. Lee and Ulysses S. Grant had commanded the post. Currently Jefferson Barracks served as a depot for the Ordnance Department, but for Sergeant O'Brien it was first and foremost a place where he could find an officer to swear Henry and me into the army.

Sergeant O'Brien ushered us into the presence of the post adjutant, an enormously fat Ordnance Corps captain festooned in the gold aiguillette, cords, and tassels of his office. This officer directed O'Brien to march us over to the post surgeon for a physical examination.

When we arrived at the surgeon's office, Sergeant O'Brien found the fellow dead drunk on his own examining table. Undeterred, O'Brien marched us down the street to the post veterinarian. This officer was glad to examine us and, finding no anthrax or hoof disease, certified us as fit to serve in the regular army of the United States. Sergeant O'Brien then quick-marched us back to the portly adjutant, who perused our freshly signed medical certificates and nodded in satisfaction.

He asked our full names, and Henry said, "Henry Jefferson, suh." Up to that point, although I had known him most of my life, I'd had no idea that Henry had a surname.

The adjutant then produced enlistment contracts, which we promptly signed, and then he administered the oath of enlistment. No sooner did we each say "I do" than the adjutant chortled and said, "Boys, that means if you leave us without permission, we can track you down and shoot you." Then to Sergeant O'Brien he added, "Sergeant, your bounty papers. Congratulations, and have a pleasant trip back to Fort Grant."

Bounty papers? thinks I. Why, O'Brien was getting a bounty for signing us up! But whatever alarm I felt was stilled when Sergeant O'Brien marched us to the mess hall for a hot meal and gave us each two dollars of our ten-dollar enlistment bounties, explaining, "I'll just hold the rest until we get to Fort Grant, men." Then he took us to the St. Louis train station, where he booked passage for the three of us to Wilcox, Arizona, via Memphis and Dallas.

The reason I was still relaxed was that I figured if I got cold feet anywhere along the line, I could simply hop off the train and that would be the last I'd ever see of Sergeant O'Brien. Perhaps O'Brien was reading my thoughts—or maybe he simply had more experience with new recruits than I realized—for just as we were to board he drew us aside and announced in a conspiratorial manner, "Men, there's something the adjutant didn't tell you back there at Jefferson Barracks."

We nodded silently, not having the faintest idea what he was talking about.

"Well, first, you both know that you've got eight dollars apiece waiting for you as soon as we arrive at Fort Grant, right?"

We nodded again. Eight dollars, I told myself, was no princely sum and wouldn't deter me in the slightest from desertion if I set my mind in that direction.

"But what the adjutant was shy about telling you was that you fellows are in line for a national bounty if the three of us get all the way to Fort Grant together."

"A national bounty?" I echoed. "What's that?"

"It's a hundred dollars per man, that's what it is," whispered Sergeant O'Brien.

"A hunner' dollars!" blurted Henry involuntarily, staggered at the thought of so much money.

"Shhh, dammit!" Sergeant O'Brien whispered, glancing furtively about as if trying to determine whether Henry's outburst had been overheard. "It's a secret, you see," he continued in hushed tones. "If the army told everyone about it, we'd be flooded with recruits. We don't want that, you see. We just want the pick of the litter—like you two."

Incredibly, the notion of a national bounty seemed plausible to us, so we nodded our understanding.

"Well, now it's out. I thought you both deserved to know, in case you made some sort of—well, mistake—on our trip out West and cheated yourselves out of a right tidy little grubstake. But I want your word that this will be our little secret."

He got our word immediately.

"Fine, men, fine," smiled Sergeant O'Brien. "Now, not another peep of this to anyone, and when we get to Fort Grant, the first order of business will be to get you both your national bounties."

8

Fort Grant, Arizona Territory
June 1892

"You want a what? A national bounty? By God, of all the gall! What makes you little horse turds think you can march right into a fort belonging to the army of these here United States of America and demand a bounty?"

I gulped and grimaced tightly. My inquisitor was the mustachioed Corporal McCabe, a lean-faced, pockmarked cavalryman with an obviously violent temperament. When the Studebaker supply wagon that had hauled us—Henry, Sergeant O'Brien, and me—from Wilcox to Fort Grant rolled to a stop in front of the post headquarters, Sergeant O'Brien had smiled broadly and announced, "Well, boys, your long wait is over. Just head right in there and claim those bounties."

Which I had done, with Henry and Sergeant O'Brien right on my heels, only to find Corporal McCabe lounging behind the orderly desk before the colonel's office. Had I been more experienced in such matters, I would have realized that he was the orderly of the commander of the guard. That meant he had been the sharpest-looking trooper at guard mount that morning, and as a reward got to stay in the headquarters office rather than walk a guard post. It also meant that he was acting in the place of the officer of the day, and as such he was very much full of himself.

He heard me out only a few seconds before he got the gist of my message and promptly silenced me with a blistering tirade. "You left-handed, sidewinding varmints think you can jes' march up to the colonel's office and demand the better part of the pay that an officer—an officer, by God, not a mewling private—earns in a month! Why, by Christ, I'll see you both shoveling shit from the stable for this!"

This harangue quickly drew the attention of others; a solidly built first sergeant appeared, his august rank denoted by the diamond inside the white chevrons emblazoned on his sleeves. Behind the first sergeant trailed a slim young officer, a lieutenant. He was a little bantam of a fellow, paler in color than the windburned field soldiers around him. The lieutenant looked almost bookish next to these gruff warriors, and I took him for something of a dandy at first, until I realized he merely sported the somewhat individualistic field uniform affected by cavalrymen in these remote wilds: a short blue jacket with epaulets on the shoulders, a gaudy yellow bandanna around his neck, tight trousers with wide yellow stripes down the sides, and knee-high boots set off with glittering Spanish spurs. The lieutenant looked more like a swashbuckling buccaneer than a staid army officer. As for the first sergeant, I could tell from his uniform that he was not a cavalryman, and I quickly concluded that this fellow was a first sergeant of one of the colored companies.

Sergeant O'Brien stiffened at the officer's appearance; he had wanted to enjoy his little joke on these greenhorns, but he had not intended to have his prank come to the attention of his superiors. From the grin on the lieutenant's face, however, I could tell that he was rather enjoying Sergeant O'Brien's discomfiture.

"Now tell me, Sergeant," demanded the young lieutenant with forced sternness, "have you been spinning that same old yarn of yours about the pot of gold at the end of the rainbow?"

O'Brien drew himself up to his fullest height and, with the open countenance of a choirboy on Easter Sunday, affirmed, "By God, no, sir. Where this fellow got such a notion is beyond me."

The stocky first sergeant spoke up. "O'Brien, jes' tell Lieutenant Greer the damned truth for once," he rumbled. The deep Southern accent jarred my midwestern ears. Alabama? Maybe, or perhaps Georgia, I thought.

"First Sergeant Richmond, that was the truth, may God be my judge," Sergeant O'Brien avowed with the unflappable demeanor of a born perjurer.

Lieutenant Greer decided to get to the truth of the matter. "You there, what's your name?" he demanded of me.

"Fenwick Travers," I replied, only to be set on by every noncommissioned officer present. "Lieutenant Greer is an officer, damn you, and you'll address him as 'sir'!"

Which, of course, I instantly did. "Sir, what Sergeant O'Brien is saying is the truth. I heard this tale about a national bounty at the depot in Wilcox when we were waiting for the wagon to take us here. It was none of his doing."

Sergeant O'Brien's eyes went wide with pleasure at this, and then he gave the lieutenant the honeyed smile of a magnanimous man wrongly suspected. "There you have it, sir, straight from the boy's own mouth," he practically purred.

I had quickly decided that fingering O'Brien would not help my situation any, and could only make matters worse, since I was obviously destined to be subservient to him and his fellow sergeants for the rest of my stay at Fort Grant. So I decided to help him in his hour of need and trust that he was the grateful sort.

Lieutenant Greer still seemed dubious, but he could proceed no further in view of my protestation of Sergeant O'Brien's innocence. "Very well, Travers. I'll take your word for it this time. But out here you'll soon find you have to speak your own mind and stand on your own feet if you want to survive. Only hard men make it, isn't that right First Sergeant Richmond?"

First Sergeant Richmond nodded his agreement. "Tha's right, Travers. It's a hard land, and if'n you don't measure up, well, we'll jes' find that out right soon."

"Even the officers are mean out here, Private," Lieutenant Greer continued. "Why, except for Colonel Sumner and me, every cavalry officer and most of the infantry officers on post have been court-martialed at one time or another."

"He's telling it to you straight, Private Travers," O'Brien chimed in. "There's few angels out here."

Then a sudden cloud passed over First Sergeant Richmond's face. Gravely, he asked, "Say, Travers, have you ever been tried fer anything?"

O'Brien went silent at this, for in his eagerness to earn his enlistment bonus, he'd never thought to pry into that part of my background. He held his breath at my answer, fearful that my response would jeopardize his bonus. Before I answered, I thought of the Judge's inquiry at the end of MacFee's trial and then said slowly, "Well, yes, I guess you could say so."

The mirth faded from Lieutenant Greer's features. Enlistment practices were loose in the regular army, but not loose enough to allow known felons into the ranks. "Out with it, Travers," he ordered. "What were you tried for?"

"Murder," I said simply.

"Dat's d'truth," seconded Henry. "Fenny heah was tried for killin' de rascal what tried to shoot me, den he hep'ed squash de other fella."

"God almighty, a killer!" groaned O'Brien, envisioning his bounty flying away.

Greer ignored him and pressed on. "And? Were you convicted?"

I shook my head. "No, sir. The county judge ruled them justifiable homicides. Those rascals needed killing." Henry nodded his head in confirmation, and Lieutenant Greer eyed First Sergeant Richmond, who only murmured, "Seems like a tale we might could check on."

Greer agreed. "First Sergeant, get the particulars and confirm his story by telegram. If it checks out, assign him to my troop. I can always use a man who can shoot straight." Apparently a history of legally excused homicide was a positive character reference in the Arizona Territory. Greer continued, "Put the darky anywhere in the 25th Infantry where there's a vacancy. I'll leave that to you, First Sergeant."

With that the interview was over. I wrote down all the facts First Sergeant Richmond needed to confirm the MacFee incident—all the sergeants being duly impressed that I could write like an officer—and Henry and I were marched out to begin our new lives as soldiers.

Fort Grant was the most desolate place I had ever laid eyes upon. It was located in the Sulphur Springs Valley, a sandy trough about thirty miles long and twenty miles wide, bounded on the east by the Penaleno Mountains and on the west by the Galiuro Range. The valley was at an altitude of about five thousand feet above sea level, which ensured scorching heat until sunset, after which the temperature promptly plummeted. The land around Fort Grant was a desert of gravel and loose stone lightly covered with yucca, mesquite, and cactus. Through this barren scrub crawled lizards, horned toads, rattlers, scorpions, and tarantulas; in the skies above buzzards circled relentlessly. The total impression of such vast emptiness was that God had somehow been interrupted in the act of making Arizona and had never quite gotten around to finishing the job.

Although I thought initially that Fort Grant had been randomly sited, I soon learned that such was not the case. The post had been located so as to sit astride the most direct route between the San Carlos Indian Reservation to the north and the Mexican border to the south. San Carlos served as a warehouse for the most notorious Apache tribes— the Chiricahua, the Mescaleros, and the Tontos—who had been brought to bay in recent years. But an occasional buck still took flight to Mexico to rustle cattle or to kill a miner or two, and when that happened troops from Fort Grant were sent in pursuit. The troops at Fort Grant also curbed the depredations of white outlaws and raiding bandidos from the deserts of Sonora just across the border with Mexico.

As Sergeant O'Brien explained, there was a mounted company of Apache scouts assigned to Fort Grant to assist with this mission. The short, wiry scouts had proven to be the best weapon to use against their fellow Apaches, since whites couldn't match the skill these hellions possessed in ambush and stealth.

As for my training, it was immediate and unrelenting. As directed by Lieutenant Greer, I was assigned to E Troop. Sergeant O'Brien, kindly disposed to me after the bounty confrontation, was my sergeant, and Corporal McCabe was my corporal. It was to McCabe that the responsibility for my training fell. Unfortunately, he had taken an instant dislike to me, and he drilled me mercilessly in what beleaguered recruits called the school of the soldier. The days melted into weeks as McCabe tormented me with endless mounted drill, carbine practice, care of my mount, and innumerable hours spent rubbing saddle soap into my leather equipment until it glowed with a high mahogany sheen.

Although McCabe denigrated me as a "damned greenhorn" at every turn, I progressed so quickly in riflery with my single-shot .45-

caliber Springfield carbine—called a trapdoor Springfield by the troopers because of its wide-swinging breech mechanism—that even the veteran sharpshooters in E Troop were soon talking about the newcomer. Then it was on to advanced horsemanship, which meant introducing me to the Rarey system of horse breaking, a method that taught a cavalry mount to lie placidly on its side while a trooper fired his carbine over its flank at imaginary foes, thus using his horse as a portable breastwork. In the period of a few months McCabe had molded me into a passable yellow leg, not highly skilled yet, but competent enough to hold my own should the troop be called upon to sally forth.

My steady progress did nothing to diminish McCabe's dislike for me, which grew only deeper and more implacable with each passing day. Perhaps it was the way that Lieutenant Greer had taken a shine to me, or maybe it was the fact that I could write, whereas he was denser than a stone; whatever the reason, McCabe made it a point to make my life as miserable as possible. He saw to it that I was always on stable guard, walking between the tethered horses at night to calm them in stormy weather or to free the occasional hoof from an inadvertent entanglement with a tether rope. When I successfully fired enough bull's-eyes on the rifle range to qualify as a sharpshooter—a feat some regulars never attained—my only reward was to spend the rest of the day as a "sand rat" in the pits behind the targets changing targets for other firers.

My peers sympathized with me, for McCabe was widely known in the regiment as a tyrant. The common wisdom was that he had become a soldier only within the past five years. Before that he had run a small spread up in southern Colorado, or at least he did until his cows started "having twins"; that is, they started increasing in numbers at a prodigious rate, while his neighbors' herds mysteriously dwindled at exactly the same rate. To his fellow cattlemen that was a signal that McCabe had gone into the rustling business, and so he had been forcefully urged to move on.

He came to rest at length in the 7th Cavalry, where he had earned a stripe after a few sharp actions against Mexican raiders. A merciless taskmaster he was, but nobody said that McCabe couldn't fight, you see. Knowing his reputation for an aggressive demeanor, I shook off McCabe's attempts to rile me into a confrontation, partly because I wanted to get along in the troop, but also because I knew that conditions in the scorpion-infested guardhouse—or the mill, as it was known to the troopers—were deplorable beyond enduring. I had largely succeeded in avoiding a showdown with McCabe until the day I returned to the barracks from stable call to find him sitting on my bunk.

Now that may seem innocuous to you, but in the regular army no man—not even a corporal—sat on another man's bunk without his permission. To do so was the grossest insult, one that had to be met, or the victim was forever regarded as a craven cur in the eyes of his peers.

"That stable floor clean enough to eat off'a, greenhorn?" McCabe greeted me brazenly. I stopped dead in my tracks, recognizing his calculated effrontery. The other troopers hastily moved their footlockers away from my bunk and snatched their gear off the wooden pegs set in the squad room walls; either a battle royal or an ignominious retreat was about to take place, and they didn't want their few precious possessions damaged should the former be the case.

I eyed McCabe narrowly a moment, and then said quietly: "That's my bunk, Corporal McCabe. I don't recall telling you that you could set on it."

McCabe gave me a sinister smile in return. "I don't generally consult tenderfeet about such matters. I just do as I please, see? Now, do you have a problem with that?"

I edged closer, carefully measuring the distance between us. McCabe was shorter than I was, and probably twenty pounds lighter, but he was older and had a sinewy strength that told me he could be a wildcat when riled.

"Get up!" I almost hissed.

"What's that?" demanded McCabe ominously. "You telling a corporal what to do? Well, looks like it's time I learned you some manners, sonny."

"Why don't you stand up and take off those stripes and just try?" I invited him coldly.

He started to rise to do exactly that when my right fist slammed hard against his temple, sending him sliding across the waxed wooden floor, upsetting the empty ration tins used as cuspidors, until he slammed hard against a locked rack of carbines.

It was a blow that would have stretched a lesser man out cold, but McCabe was on his feet in an instant. "Damn your hide, Travers, I'll whip the holy hell out of you for this!" he vowed as he closed, hands reaching for my throat.

I braced for the shock of his charge and threw an uppercut just as McCabe's fingers touched my throat.

"Urgh!" he grunted as my blow snapped his head back, dropping him to the floor like a rag doll. Blood flowed freely from McCabe's nose when he staggered to his feet again, and murder was in his eyes. He steeled himself for one more rush, when suddenly the excited shouting of the spectators was stilled by the entry of Sergeant O'Brien.

"What the hell's going on here?" demanded the sergeant. When no one replied, O'Brien took it all in at a moment's glance: McCabe's face bloody and swollen, the upset cuspidors, and the depression on my bunk where McCabe had planted his skinny backside. O'Brien shook his head sadly. "I'm sorry it came to this, Travers. I thought you had the makings of a real trooper. But now it's the guardhouse for sure. No private strikes a corporal in this regiment and gets away with it. Come with me; we're going to see the lieutenant."

I was on the verge of sprinting past him to hightail it into the chaparral and go over the hill when I was stayed by the staccato call of a bugle.

9

" 'Boots and Saddles,' boys! Turn out!" came the cry from the parade ground.

Immediately, the business at hand was deferred. "Somebody clean up McCabe," ordered Sergeant O'Brien. "The rest of you men turn out and wait for orders." We did so, and soon Lieutenant Greer appeared.

"A wire came in from Fort Huachuca, men," he explained to the assembled troopers. "We're to send a patrol south to Bisbee to escort some big tycoon from back east who's in Arizona to inspect his copper mines. George Duncan's his name—owns the Copper King Mine down at Bisbee."

There was a buzz of excitement at this; everyone in the territory had heard of Duncan's operation. It produced most of the copper in Arizona, and its parent corporation, Duncan Enterprises, was expanding into new deposits year after year.

Lieutenant Greer continued his briefing: "Huachuca's got no cavalry available; they're all on patrol out west toward Yuma." He turned to

Sergeant O'Brien. "I want fifteen men and an Apache scout. Bring the greenhorn," he said, nodding at me. "It'll be good experience for him. Get the patrol ready. We'll leave at dawn."

"Yes, sir," answered Sergeant O'Brien with a salute; then he turned and bawled out a spate of orders. They were largely unnecessary, however. The troopers, seasoned campaigners that they were, knew just what to do without being told. They mechanically went through the well-known steps of preparing for a scout, as patrols were known to the troopers. Mules were cut out of the herd and their packs filled and balanced. Shovels, called army banjos by the men, were strapped to the mules in case the patrol should be forced to dig for water. The commissary officer issued rations for ten days—hardtack, bacon, beans, and coffee. Weapons were oiled, ammunition was issued by the armorer, and the mules and horses were groomed and watered. As the sun rose red in the eastern sky, the scout was ready to move out.

As custom dictated, Lieutenant Greer assembled his small command before the flag post outside the regimental headquarters. At the stroke of seven, Colonel Sumner, the sprightly, silver-haired commander of the 7th Cavalry, strode from the headquarters building, and Lieutenant Greer barked the order for the men to dismount.

Colonel Sumner was by all accounts a fine old gentleman, courageous in battle and solicitous of the men's welfare. The veterans in the regiment regaled the newer men with tales of the colonel's exploits against the Plains Indians and more recently against the Apache. In short, Sumner was considered a first-rate soldier by his troops, a rare compliment indeed. As was his wont, he always personally inspected each trooper before a patrol left the post.

"Patrol ready for inspection, sir," reported Lieutenant Greer with a salute, which the colonel returned. With the lieutenant at his heels, Colonel Sumner inspected each man, his arms, his boots, the mules, their harnesses, the labels on the ammunition crates— literally everything there was to see. There was quite a bit to see that morning, and the colonel's sharp eyes missed nothing.

The first thing that caught his attention was the fact that apparently most of the men were recovering from a tremendous bender. Where they had gotten liquor, and how they had found time to consume it during the hectic night, was a mystery to me. As a newcomer I had to prove myself before I was let in on any squadron secrets, so I was as sober as a judge; but the red eyes and staggered gaits of my fellows were unmistakable. Yet Colonel Sumner said nothing, and I concluded that it was expected that the men would get soused the night before a patrol.

Other than me, the only perfectly sober members of the patrol were Lieutenant Greer and our Mescalero Apache scout, He Listens, a runty little heathen whose dark eyes revealed nothing. He Listens was a scarred veteran of a dozen battles, his visage somewhat disfigured by a knife cut across the eyelids that left the right one with a permanent droop. Because of this disability, the troopers called him Droopy.

Nobody had said anything to me about the expected dress for the patrol, so I wore my regulation uniform, with the only departure being the substitution of a wide-brimmed campaign hat—its crown creased to form the "Montana peaks" favored by the cavalry—for my usual kepi. I had expected that the Apache scout would not be in a regulation uniform, and he had not disappointed me. Only his blue coat marked Droopy as a part of a civilized military establishment. The rest of his costume was pure Apache: knee-high moccasins, a breechclout that hung to his knees—so voluminous that it looked like a kilt—and a bandanna of red gingham wrapped around his jet-black hair.

This I expected. What I hadn't expected was that the rest of the patrol would affect similarly bizarre costumes. Some sported chaps, others buckskin shirts worked in intricate Indian designs. Greer wore buckskin breeches tucked into his cavalry boots. None of the soldiers had their sabers; this weapon being deemed unsuitable for field use, it was invariably left behind, locked away in the arms room. To my surprise, Colonel Sumner said nothing about the troopers' uniforms. I surmised that in the field, matters of dress and side arms were very much a matter of personal choice.

In fact, the only sharp words Colonel Sumner had in the inspection were for one unfortunate private whose Springfield's breech was fouled with a residue of gunpowder. This wretch was tongue-lashed unmercifully, sent scurrying to clean his piece immediately, and left quivering thereafter with a final warning to never again attempt to leave the front gate of Fort Grant with a dirty weapon.

The inspection done, the colonel completed his instructions to Lieutenant Greer, bade the men godspeed, and instructed Greer to carry on. Greer ordered the detachment to mount, but before he proceeded any further, we were joined by two latecomers, First Sergeant Richmond and Henry.

This was a surprise to me, but it wouldn't have been if I'd known

that First Sergeant Richmond saw to it that all new recruits from the
25th Infantry participated in a mounted scout in order to get the lay
of the land around the fort; he felt that his soldiers could fight better
if they understood exactly where they were.

Men in barracks talk a great deal, especially about their superiors,
and it wasn't long before I knew quite a bit about Richmond. For
instance, I learned that he had been with the 25th Infantry for about
three years, and that he had transferred from the white 9th Infantry
in order to secure his promotion to first sergeant. The reason for this,
I had been told, was that Richmond had been married while in the 9th
to the attractive young widow of the regimental commissary sergeant.
This lady had acquired a taste for the things a lowly company sergeant's
salary just could not buy. I'd seen Richmond's wife—Ida was her
name—flitting about Soap Suds Row, the quarters of the married
sergeants.

I watched First Sergeant Richmond as he took his place near the
head of the patrol. Although not a cavalryman, he sat his mount well.
Henry was another story; he clung precariously to the back of an ornery
old mule that continually eyed him over its shoulders as though measuring
him for a sudden buck.

"Column of twos, forward, ho!" sang out Greer, and the detachment
galloped out the gate to the tune of "Garry Owen" played by a small
group of bandsmen drawn up on the side of the parade ground. Ida
was at the front gate as we cantered out, waving a kerchief at her
husband and smiling broadly at the troopers, who winked and blew
her kisses as they passed.

"Scouts out!" called Greer once the fort was behind us and we had
passed the cluster of wickiups (tepees) where the squaws of the Apache
scouts resided. Droopy spurred his pony, galloped ahead, and was soon
out of sight. Once on the march, the place of an Apache scout was
generally a half mile to the front or on the flank of the column he
screened. Droopy would gallop back if there was a sign of trouble,
but otherwise he would generally not appear until camp was made in
the evening.

We rode steadily south down the Sulphur Springs Valley, raising
clouds of alkali dust as we went. The troops were in fine fettle, for
there was little prospect of combat, and Lieutenant Greer had a reputation for being a congenial commander. Although he was a recent
graduate of the Dude Factory, as the troopers called West Point, he

was not too much of a martinet, and everyone was looking forward to an enjoyable expedition.

The valley floor was flat and open, and I soon learned that the land was not nearly as barren as I had first thought. We passed numerous small ponds that were home to flocks of mallards and canvasback ducks. In the chaparral I saw wild turkeys and roadrunners, those incredibly quick birds of the Southwest. In the hills on either side of the valley I caught sight of an occasional mule deer, and on the heights in the distance could be seen herds of pronghorn antelope. It was obvious that this land was a sportsman's paradise. Greer evidently agreed, for he sent Corporal McCabe off as an outrider to try to bag a mule deer for our supper. McCabe didn't get a deer, but he did bag an unlucky longhorn steer, which we quickly butchered into portable chunks of steak. Then we hurried along our way.

I say that the steer was unlucky in that McCabe claimed it did not carry a brand and was therefore fair game; but in truth the haunch of the beast, where a brand would be if there were one, was so mutilated by McCabe's knife by the time we caught up with him that there was no telling whether or not the animal was the maverick McCabe claimed.

"Old habits die hard," cracked a veteran private, at which McCabe reddened but held his tongue in the presence of Lieutenant Greer.

By the end of the day we had crossed the Southern Pacific tracks west of Wilcox and were in the shadows of the Dragoon Mountains, a distance of forty miles from Fort Grant. Greer guided his small command into the mouth of a box canyon, where we pitched camp. The pack mules and horses were watered at a small spring we found a short distance up the canyon and then were tethered for the night. This was Apacheria—Apache land. Years earlier these mountains had been the stronghold of Cochise, the legendary Chiricahua war chief, but tonight no hostiles were abroad, so a jolly campfire was lit, and soon we were roasting our steaks over the roaring flames.

After a hearty meal of beef and hardtack, Greer retired a short distance to sleep, and Sergeant O'Brien posted the first guard shift. Since I wasn't one of the guards, I fetched myself a steaming tin mug of blackjack (coffee) and sat with my back to a boulder to watch the flickering flames. McCabe, having eaten his fill, was in a mood for devilment. He meandered in my direction but then noticed Droopy hunkered down on an ammunition case staring into the fire. In garrison, the Apaches rarely approached McCabe because he was

so cantankerous and had a reputation for needling redskins unmercifully. Having a captive audience like Droopy was a rare treat, and
McCabe veered from my direction and squatted next to the Indian.

Sergeant O'Brien, returning to the circle of the firelight after posting
the guards, watched this development uneasily. With him was First
Sergeant Richmond, who was also well aware of McCabe's reputation
as a troublemaker.

"Hey, Chief," said McCabe. "Tough day in the chaparral?"

Droopy didn't even glance at McCabe. His only acknowledgment
of the unwelcome visitor's presence was to move a brown hand slowly
to the top of his knee-high moccasin, where a roll of excess deerskin
was gathered.

"Careful, McCabe," cautioned one of the troopers, "'Pache always
carry Arkansas toothpicks [knives] in those moccasins."

Undaunted, McCabe merely gave an evil grin. "Don't fret none,
boys, 'Pache don't fight at night. Everyone knows that."

An owl hooted from somewhere nearby, and Droopy gave a nervous
glance in that direction.

McCabe cackled. "You think it's a ghost, don't you?"

Despite my better judgment I asked, "What makes you think that,
McCabe?"

"'Cause I knows, tenderfoot. Injuns in general is superstitious, but
'Pache are the leaders of the pack that way. Once the sun goes down
they're afraid of their own shadows. They think there's ghosts afoot
then, and ghosts can steal their souls and keep them from ever getting
to the happy hunting grounds. That's why they don't fight at night.
See, they think if they're killed, their soul will get lost in the dark
or get captured by a wandering ghost. That's why they turn yeller until
the sun comes up again."

"They think they got souls?" I asked, curious now. "You mean like
Christians do?"

"Oh, yes," McCabe affirmed with a grin. "'Pache have got more
religion than a posse of padres. Why, look at that little bag a-hanging
'round Droopy's neck."

In the firelight I could see what appeared to be a small deerskin
sack dangling from a cord attached to a turquoise-beaded necklace
around He Listens's neck. "That there bag is stuffed full with ashes.
They're blessed by a *di-yan*—a 'Pache medicine man. Droopy thinks
that if he loses that bag, the ghosts will wade right in and snatch his

defenseless soul. That's why he'd rather die than part with it. If that ain't religion, I don't know what is."

"Dat's voodoo," offered Henry from across the circle of troopers.

McCabe guffawed. "That's right, nigger. It's voodoo. 'Pache set great store by their magic. Why, see them twisted cords across Droopy's shoulders?"

Now everyone eyed He Listens with interest. Sure enough, there was a braided cord running over the Indian's right shoulder and under his left arm. "Them's his battle cords. 'Pache think them cords is powerful medicine in battle. If you surprise one of 'em without his cords on, he'll hightail it rather than fight. Yep, they're strange folks. Why, I even happen to know they pray to katydids! Just think of it— 'Pache worship damned little bugs."

That sounded a bit preposterous to me, but not to Henry, for McCabe was talking his language now. Intrigued, he pressed, "Hows about witches, Massa, er, Corp'ral McCabe? Does dey believes in witches?"

"And how," McCabe assured Henry. "Don't you never tell any 'Pache to go to hell. We say that to each other all the time, and mean nothing by it. But a 'Pache hearing that would think you were trying to hex his soul. In his mind, that means you're a witch, which means trouble for you because 'Pache burn witches, see? And they don't waste no time about it, either. A witch can kill cattle and small children with a look, and drain a warrior's battle medicine, so they got to be killed quick-like."

Henry whistled in awe, for Droopy's savage demeanor left no doubt that he was a fellow who would stop at no amount of mayhem once he set his mind to it.

McCabe was warming to the attention he was getting from his audience. "Bears," he said apropos of nothing, but then explained further: "'Pache is scared stiff of bears. They think bears are the ghosts of criminals that have been condemned to wander the earth. No, 'Pache won't have no truck with bears. And lightning? Ain't nothing that'll drive 'Paches to distraction faster'n lightning. They'll jump over cliffs to get away from the stuff. One minute they're tough warriors like Droopy here, and the next moment in rolls a thunderstorm and they're a-peeing their britches and wailing their death songs."

The soldiers guffawed, but He Listens looked positively forlorn at these jibes—if that is the right term to describe the smoldering look of hatred with which he greeted McCabe's diatribe. It was cruel to go on so, talking about a fellow right in front of his face like that, and I said as much. He Listens's dark eyes flicked in my direction as I voiced my protest, perhaps understanding my defense of him. But my objection was in vain, for it only drew a withering barb from McCabe in return: "Listen, boys, the tenderfoot's an Injun lover!"

More guffaws until Henry rescued me in turn from their ridicule. "What else, Corp'ral McCabe, what else?" urged Henry, genuinely entranced by talk of magic and superstition.

His enthusiasm elicited a sly grin from McCabe, who rose and went to his bedroll. He came back with his saddlebags and chuckled, "All you boys know how the Injuns fear poisonous critters, right? Like gila monsters and such?"

"What's a gila monster?" I asked.

"A big ugly lizard," explained a veteran private. "It's black with splashes of yaller all over it. You'll know it when ya see one, brother. It's got poison fangs that pack a wallop like a whole nest o' hornets."

"That's right, tenderfoot," added McCabe. "The gila monster's black because that's what color any limb he bites turns. Yep, turns black and drops right off, clean off as if 'twere cut by a surgeon's scalpel."

I shuddered at this image, but McCabe didn't notice, for this line of talk had sent him off on another tangent. "Talking about gilas reminds me, I meant to tell you boys that while I was out hunting today, I was thinking of poisonous critters and such. Then I got to thinking about Injuns in general and ol' Droopy here in particular. I thought how nice it would be if I could bring something back to camp that would let Droopy know how I felt about him. Well, I just got lucky, I reckon, and found something to fill the bill. Droopy, this here's for you."

McCabe turned one saddlebag upside down, causing the headless carcass of a sidewinder rattler to tumble to the dust an inch from Droopy's moccasins. In an instant the Apache was on his feet screaming at the top of his lungs in his heathen tongue. McCabe went white with sudden fear, in part because of the violent fury of Droopy's reaction, but more directly because of the blurring speed with which the infuriated Apache had whipped out a Bowie knife, the point of which he was now waving in the general direction of McCabe's throat.

But before Droopy could get down to butchery, Sergeant O'Brien was between him and McCabe. "He Listens! He Listens!" implored O'Brien. "Don't say it! Don't say it! McCabe's a fool, you know that. Just let it pass."

For a fleeting second Droopy hesitated, then lowered his blade and stomped off into the dark, muttering loudly to himself. Sergeant O'Brien then rounded on the shaken McCabe. "You damned fool! You know better than that. 'Pache fear snakes and never touch 'em. Hell, they won't even eat any animal that they think touched a snake. What the hell's the matter with you, McCabe? Are you trying to get yourself slaughtered? Let me tell you something, partner. If you rile up that scout again, I'll have your stripes. First Sergeant Richmond saw the whole shebang, and he'll back me up if you push me. Ain't that right, First Sergeant?"

All eyes went to Richmond, who nodded grimly.

"Corporal McCabe, you just don't know when to hobble your lip, do you? As far as I'm concerned, your damned cinch is getting frayed," snarled Sergeant O'Brien. "Now get out on guard and stay there until I call you!" Infuriated at the outcome of what he had considered until then to be an evening of peerless entertainment, McCabe sullenly did as O'Brien bid.

As McCabe left, Henry could no longer restrain himself. "Don't say what, Sar'gint O'Brien? What didn't ya want ol' Droopy to say?"

"*Ahagahe!*" said O'Brien in reply. "That's what the 'Pache say when they accept a challenge to fight. When you hear a 'Pache say that, either you or the 'Pache are on the way to the happy hunting grounds most directly."

With McCabe gone, the show was over. "You men turn in," Sergeant O'Brien ordered. "Dawn comes early."

10

We rode all the next day, stopping briefly at the town of Tombstone so that Lieutenant Greer could pay his respects to the local marshal— the army in those days was a key adjunct to the law enforcement effort in the territory, you see—and reached the outskirts of Bisbee at dark. Lieutenant Greer elected to pitch camp outside of town, and we turned in only to awake to a gray dawn.

"Damned peculiar, so many clouds in this neck of the woods," Corporal McCabe pronounced darkly, studying the sky with a wary eye. After a breakfast of bacon, hardtack, and coffee, Lieutenant Greer led the patrol into the awakening town. On the way we passed the hulking works of the Copper King Mine set in a gulch running up the flank of a low mountain. The gulch was crammed with assay equipment, steam engines, and smelters, which led up to the gaping mouth of the mine itself. It was clearly a highly advanced operation; evidently Mr. Duncan had spared no expense to get the most out of his mine.

Although it was barely light when we rode into Bisbee proper, the saloons and gambling dens were already doing a booming business. Roulette wheels graced the wooden sidewalks outside the casinos, and from the windows of the many bordellos "soiled doves" of every race waved gaily to the troops as they rode past. Lieutenant Greer led the column directly to the Bisbee Hotel, where he and First Sergeant Richmond dismounted and went inside. Sergeant O'Brien ordered the troops to dismount, and we lounged in the dusty street awaiting our leader's return.

In minutes Greer was back, accompanied by a trim gentleman impeccably decked out in jodhpurs, a Norfolk jacket, and a Stetson hat. This must be the high and mighty Mr. Duncan, I reckoned. Duncan looked and acted the part of the man of substance and power he was reputed to be. He doffed his Stetson to study the troopers a moment, and I studied him carefully right back. His salt-and-pepper thatch was neatly parted down the middle, and his beard and mustache were carefully trimmed. He was a dandy all right, in his midfifties, if I guessed correctly. He had gray eyes that fixed upon whatever the object of his attention happened to be, a small unsmiling mouth with perfect little white teeth, and the tiniest ears I'd ever seen on a full-grown man. When he spoke at last to Lieutenant Greer, it was in short, clipped tones filled with authority.

"I'll trouble you only for the day, Lieutenant Greer," the grand fellow explained. The accent was Eastern, probably upper-class New York. "I want to look at some rock formations to the northeast of town. Have your command nearby, but there'll be times when I'll want to go off a short distance alone. I think better that way, you understand."

"To the northeast, sir?" mused Lieutenant Greer. "That would be the Pedregosa Range—a haven for rustlers and Mexican bandits who get run over the border by the *rurales*."

"It's a goddamned viper's nest," Sergeant O'Brien muttered under his breath.

Mr. Duncan's tiny ears proved sharper than those of a fox. He fixed Sergeant O'Brien with a glare and snapped, "I know that. That's why I wired the governor for an escort."

Chastened, Sergeant O'Brien wisely held his tongue. Clearly Mr. Duncan was a person accustomed to giving orders and having them obeyed without question. From his commanding demeanor, it was clear that he considered himself the lieutenant's social better and certainly would not countenance second-guessing by a mere sergeant. Judging by Lieutenant Greer's fawning attitude, he seemed convinced it was prudent to toady to Mr. Duncan.

"Of course, sir," Lieutenant Greer said almost contritely. I guessed from this that if they taught classes in bootlicking at the Dude Factory, Lieutenant Greer had passed with flying colors.

For all his dominating presence, it was not Mr. Duncan who held my attention. Instead, it was the lovely green-eyed girl who suddenly strode out of the hotel to join him and Lieutenant Greer. This beauty also gained the attention of my fellow troopers, even those old bachelors who had long ago given up on the notion of female companionship—at least the white variety. She was about twenty years of age, with luxuriant auburn hair gathered into a neat bun beneath a large sunbonnet. Evidently she was coming along with Duncan and the patrol, for she wore a short jacket and a long skirt over riding boots. I eyed her intently. Was she Duncan's wife? Improbable, I decided; the age difference was too great. Besides, she didn't bear herself as though she were the spouse of a great man. A daughter then? Perhaps, I mused.

A stable man trotted out two fine mounts for our guests—a tall black hunter for Mr. Duncan and a dainty bay mare for the girl.

"Allow me to introduce my niece, Alice Brenoble. Alice, this is Lieutenant Greer," said Mr. Duncan.

"A pleasure, Miss Brenoble," said the lieutenant, tipping his campaign hat.

"Alice insisted on making this trip to see the great West," continued Duncan. "I've never allowed her to accompany me on such trips before, but she was so insistent this time, I just couldn't say no. She'll accompany us, of course."

"Of course, sir," said Lieutenant Greer predictably.

"Have one of your men assist her to mount, Lieutenant," commanded Duncan. It was clear to me that Lieutenant Greer himself would have rather assisted this lovely vision into her saddle, but years of deference to authority brought immediate obedience.

"Private Travers," ordered Lieutenant Greer, "post over here and help the lady to mount."

I was moving forward before the words had fully passed his lips, removing my hat as I did. This was fortunate, for I was covered with alkali dust and encumbered by the weapons and "prairie belt" (cartridge belt) strapped to my person. But when my hat was removed, the girl had a clear view of my features, a sight I saw she appreciated by the fact that her green eyes opened wide to gaze into my blue ones. It was evident to me that contact with this lovely creature had just been made.

"Snap to it, man," prompted Lieutenant Greer when our awkward encounter slowed me to inaction for a second. The girl smiled at my momentary distraction and walked to her mare, waiting there for me to hold the stirrup. I obligingly did so as the horse screened us from the others. She lifted the hem of her skirt and put her boot in the stirrup. In the instant before she swung up into the saddle, I caught an intoxicating expanse of pink silk pantalets embroidered with French lace.

Now mind you, I had rolled about in haystacks with more than one willing filly back in Elm Grove: The fairer sex was not terra incognita to Fenny. But never before had I seen such an elegantly attired creature. She caught the direction of my gaze and smiled, not at all offended. Encouraged, I smiled back.

"Travers, today, man, today!" called Lieutenant Greer. The uncharacteristic note of impatience in his voice made it clear to all that he too was entranced by the lovely creature, which caused the dusty troopers to smirk and nudge each other. I also realized that his peremptory tone was calculated to inform the lovely miss that I was a mere lackey, whereas he was an officer and eminently more suitable to be the object of her interest. Up she swung, and seated herself sidesaddle, and I returned to my mount.

Lieutenant Greer took his place at the head of the column with Mr. Duncan at his side. He turned in the saddle to shoot me a peeved look, and then growled, "Forward, ho!"

Off we went, running once more the gauntlet of whores and cardsharps. We cleared the last of the sprawling mine operations scattered about Bisbee and were again in the virgin Arizona wilderness.

Mr. Duncan quickly demonstrated that he intended to roam free of the column, galloping hither and yon, up canyons and draws, as though he were looking for something far more mobile than a sedentary rock formation. Alice, on the other hand, remained more sedate, alternately gazing at the rugged beauty of the scenery unfolding around us and casting furtive looks back in my direction. Whenever I managed to catch her in the act, she rewarded me with one of her endearing smiles. We proceeded in this way until we crested a low rise and suddenly confronted a steep-sided dry creek bed. There Droopy waited for us.

11

As we drew near, Lieutenant Greer called out, "He Listens! What's the trouble?" Duncan, seeing the Apache scout now, spurred back to the column just as Droopy made his report.

"Sign here," grunted the Mescalero in reply, which prompted an alarmed buzz of conversation down the column.

"Silence!" ordered Sergeant O'Brien.

"Many *mesteños*," grunted Droopy.

"Mustangs, sir," interpreted Sergeant O'Brien.

We all eyed the ground. "Maybe twenty," announced Droopy. "Three, maybe four hours ago. Here," he pointed to a scuff on the ground that was undecipherable to me, "is *mexicano*."

"*Bandidos!*" exclaimed Corporal McCabe. Sergeant O'Brien and First Sergeant Richmond exchanged grim looks.

"Bandits?" queried Duncan.

"I'm afraid so, sir," answered Lieutenant Greer. "A large party, too. They must have crossed over from Sonora. They'll do that from time to time to rustle or to rob some isolated settlers or miners. They're a damned nuisance."

I rather thought this news might alarm Duncan, but if anything, it seemed to brighten him perceptibly. "Where are they now?" he pressed eagerly.

Lieutenant Greer looked at Droopy, who merely shrugged and pointed to the looming Pedregosa Range.

"I see," murmured Duncan, gazing intently in the direction that the Apache indicated.

But Droopy wasn't done with the tracks yet, for he pointed to one particular set of horse prints and grunted: "Yaqui."

"A Yaqui riding with Mexes?" pondered Sergeant O'Brien. "Can't say as I've heard of that too often, have you First Sergeant?"

First Sergeant Richmond shook his head. "Nope. Yaquis don't cotton to bean-eaters. Keep to themselves. Nope, don't make sense to me."

The others nodded at this. The Yaquis, a warlike tribe from western Sonora, were a fractious breed. To find one of them riding with Mexican bandits was a mystery, or at least it was until McCabe spoke up.

"Well, there's one Injun that rides with Mexes."

All eyes shifted expectantly to McCabe. Although he was still under a cloud from the previous evening, the fact remained that he was from this part of the country and was familiar with its more odious characters.

"Who?" demanded Lieutenant Greer.

"Pedrolito," replied McCabe.

"Pedrolito?" echoed Lieutenant Greer. "Isn't he the hombre who gunned down Sheriff Jones in Nogales last year?"

"Yep," affirmed McCabe, "the very same."

Now here was some disturbing news. Even I had heard of the outlaw Pedrolito. Gossiping troops back in Fort Grant had told me that he had killed eleven men so far and was one of the most bloodthirsty jackals the frontier had seen in recent years.

"What'll we do now, sir?" First Sergeant Richmond inquired of Lieutenant Greer.

The lieutenant didn't answer immediately. He looked up at the ever-darkening sky and at the lightning flashes beginning to appear over the Pedregosas. Droopy saw them too and seemed to flinch in the saddle. Then Greer looked at Duncan. "What do you say, sir? How much farther?"

Duncan's calm contrasted sharply with the unease felt by the soldiers. "Oh, another five miles should do it, Lieutenant Greer. We're quite close now. I think I'll find what I want up in those hills there." He pointed at the foothills of the Pedregosa Range. "Let's continue, shall we?"

Reluctantly, Lieutenant Greer acquiesced. "Let's cross this one by the numbers, Sergeant O'Brien," he ordered.

O'Brien nodded. This was a perfect place for an ambush, so it was prudent for the command to clamber down the steep obstacle and up the other side in small groups so that one section would always be in place to cover the others with carbine fire should the bandits suddenly appear.

"I'll take the forward section, sir," suggested Sergeant O'Brien, "and then you can send over the pack mules."

"Okay," agreed Lieutenant Greer. That decided, Sergeant O'Brien spurred forward with me, Droopy, Henry, Corporal McCabe, Duncan, and Alice on his heels. We gained the far side of the arroyo without incident and reined in.

"Send on the mules, sir!" called Sergeant O'Brien, and Lieutenant Greer dutifully sent the pack train clambering down into the dry creek bed led by a single trooper.

It was then that an awful rumbling like the roar of an approaching freight train froze everyone in place. Droopy was jabbering in 'Pache now and pointing excitedly upstream.

Then we saw it too. "Flash flood!" screamed Corporal McCabe as a wall of water the height of a barn suddenly boiled into sight around a curve in the arroyo not a hundred yards away. No words were necessary to explain what had happened; the lightning we had seen over the Pedregosas had been accompanied by a sudden downpour on the heights. That rain had been too much for the dry soil to absorb, and the runoff had rapidly poured into the arroyo, swelling into a sudden torrent as it went.

"Save the mules!" Lieutenant Greer yelled as the wall of water hit the hapless animals broadside, bowling them over like playthings, ripping crates of rations and ammunition from their packsaddles and hurling them into the air. The trooper leading the mules simply disappeared in the boiling cauldron of water.

One mule was knocked back to the far side of the arroyo, and it flailed desperately with its hoofs to regain dry land. Lieutenant Greer saw it and spurred down the steep bank.

"Come back, sir!" called First Sergeant Richmond. "Let it go!"

But his warning was to no avail, for Lieutenant Greer leapt from his mount and seized the mule's bridle. He was straining at it and was seeming to make some progress when a second wall of water, fully as high as the first one, pulsed down the now-drenched arroyo.

"Look out, Lieutenant!" cried First Sergeant Richmond, but it was too late. The wall of water passed the spot where Lieutenant Greer had been standing; when it receded, both the mule and Lieutenant Greer were gone from sight.

Alice shrieked, and Sergeant O'Brien gasped involuntarily, "Oh, my God!"

Then a light rain commenced as we eyed the scene of disaster with stunned disbelief. Was it possible that in the span of a few seconds we had suffered two killed and lost our entire pack train? It seemed as though I was in a bad dream, until First Sergeant Richmond's gruff voice rang out and broke the spell.

"Stay put on that side, Sergeant O'Brien," he ordered. "I'll circle downstream for a crossin' point and then come over and get you. Then we're all goin' home. This heah scout is over."

Duncan began to protest this decision, but First Sergeant Richmond was no shavetail lieutenant; his mind was made up and that was that. With a wave of his arm, and without even bothering to acknowledge Duncan's remonstration, First Sergeant Richmond led his diminished part of the patrol off in search of a ford.

"Damn that stubborn oaf!" fumed Mr. Duncan. "Lieutenant Greer gave him his orders. We're to go on until I say different."

"Lieutenant Greer's gone, sir," observed Sergeant O'Brien, but Duncan wasn't listening. Instead he turned his hunter toward the hills and put spurs to its flanks. As it galloped off into the light rain he called over his shoulder, "Wait here for the others, Sergeant O'Brien, and take care of Alice. I'll be back in a while."

"Damnation!" cursed Sergeant O'Brien as Duncan pounded away. "It's his fault that we're in this fix in the first place, and now he's riding off alone even though we've told him this country is crawling with bandits."

"Then let the fool go," suggested McCabe with a snicker. "It would serve his dumb ass right to catch a few rounds of Mex lead."

But lovely Alice, who up to this point had spoken not a word, protested. "Sergeant O'Brien, please, don't let Uncle George go off alone. I don't know what's gotten into him, but I don't think he truly appreciates the danger he's in."

Sergeant O'Brien balked at this. There were two dead men already, and he didn't want to be responsible for any more. But Alice begged and cajoled, and soon her entreaties were too much for O'Brien.

"All right, lady, all right, give me some peace, will you?" He eyed his command. "McCabe, you take Droopy and set out after—" Then he stopped, for a sudden flicker of a smile had crossed He Listens's usually expressionless face. Sergeant O'Brien knew that Apaches smiled only when they smelled the blood of victims, and in that instant he knew that the Indian intended to kill McCabe for the insults McCabe had heaped on him the previous evening. Sending McCabe out with Droopy would just mean three men dead. Since Droopy had to go— he was the only one who could reliably track Duncan—McCabe was out. Sergeant O'Brien's eyes fell on me.

"Travers, you and Droopy go get that dad-blamed fool back here. We'll stay here and wait for First Sergeant Richmond and the others."

I had seen He Listens in action over the past two days and was fully confident that he could track a snowball through an avalanche, so I felt no concern at this order. Besides, the lightning was gone now, and Droopy seemed more composed. "Right, Sergeant," I said and together with Droopy set out after the troublesome Mr. Duncan.

We followed a narrow deer run worn through the chaparral that climbed steadily upward into the hills. The mesquite and yucca of the lowlands soon gave way to juniper bushes and scrubby piñon pines; as we climbed still farther, stands of stunted oak and stately ponderosa pine appeared. Our way was shaded now, and our horses' hooves were muffled by a carpet of pine needles. From the branches a few songbirds called melodiously, and from somewhere I heard the steady drumming of a woodpecker busily boring out grubs from a tree trunk. The forest was so lush compared to the harsh desert below that I became disoriented in the heavy vegetation; I almost didn't notice when He Listens suddenly stopped his pony and raised his hand.

"What is it?" I whispered.

He Listens didn't answer, but instead drew his carbine from its boot, slipped from his mount, tied it to a nearby ponderosa pine, and then padded up the trail on foot. Nervously, I did the same, shakily chambering a round in the breech of my Springfield as I followed. He Listens now slowed to a stalking pace, placing one foot forward, slowly transferring his weight to it so as not to snap any twigs that might be underfoot, and then repeating the process with his other foot. I followed suit, and in this manner we crept forward until we were on the edge of a small mountain meadow. I could hear voices now: Duncan's in English and a strident one in pidgin English.

He Listens advanced to the cover of a clump of junipers and peered into the meadow. I was at his shoulder, and the sight that greeted me sent my senses reeling. Duncan was afoot, palavering with a dismounted band of heavily armed ruffians. From their sombreros and leather chaps worked with inlaid silver, I surmised that they were Mexicans, probably the ones whose trail we'd crossed earlier in the day.

Their leader was a sight to behold; he was an Indian all right—that was evident from his copper features and the thick, tangled mane of greasy black hair that tumbled down his back. He wore a sleeveless leather jerkin over his torso, and a breechclout like He Listens's. The fellow's arms were tattooed with lurid blues and reds, and he sported silver arm bands about each bulging bicep. But primarily it was his pistols that drew my attention; he carried two big Colts slung low on his hips. Each revolver was carried butt forward in its holster, so that the Indian would have to reach across his body to draw the revolvers. I recognized this style as the "border draw" that was so popular among the desperados of southern Arizona, and I instantly realized that this brute was a skilled gunman.

"Yaqui!" hissed He Listens under his breath.

I nodded, having already concluded that I was beholding the dreaded Pedrolito. I strained to hear what appeared to be an argument in the meadow.

"No, gringo!" the big Indian was saying. "That was not our deal. You want protection in Mexico, and I can give it to you. But you must meet the price." In his heavily accented pidgin English, it came out as, "Tha' was no our deal. You wan' protection een Mehico, and I can geeve eet to you. But you mus' meet the price."

"I know we had a deal, damn you!" countered Duncan. "And I intend to keep it. But your price just isn't realistic anymore. Things have changed. Harlock can't get the number of rifles he thought he could into the country. Those damned *rurales* keep finding 'em."

What was all this, I wondered? Rifles? What was Duncan doing up in the hills parleying with this bunch of cutthroats about rifles? The *rurales*, I knew, were the federal police of northern Mexico. But who was this fellow Harlock? This was all damned strange and unnerving.

"It's because of the *rurales* that we need the rifles, gringo," countered Pedrolito. "You knew that when you first sent word to me that you wanted my protection for your copper mines in Sonora. You know that the *rurales* alone cannot give you the protection you need. You must deal with me to do business in Sonora, si?"

So that was it: Duncan's story about wanting to inspect a rock formation in these hills was a damned lie. He had intended to meet with these bandits all along. And from the sound of things, his purpose was to negotiate some sort of guarantee of protection for mining ventures he was planning on the Mexican side of the border. But if he wanted to meet with these pirates, why did he go out of his way to ensure that the army tagged along? I pondered that a few minutes before slowly concluding that Duncan must have expected that this confrontation with Pedrolito might turn nasty, and if that happened he would have wanted as much firepower as possible nearby.

Duncan spoke again. "I understand what you're saying, Pedrolito, and I realize that you must be reckoned with. But what I'm telling you is this: I can get the modern rifles you demand only from Harlock, and he tells me he can't get nearly the number you want. Also, the price for what he can get to you has to go up. That's just plain business, Pedrolito. Now, you understand that, don't you?"

From the furious scowl on Pedrolito's swarthy features, it was obvious to me that he understood no such thing. "I tell you what, gringo. I think that there is no reason not to give me the rifles you promised at the price you promised. I think that you have made a new plan. Si, you and Senor Harlock. You plan to give me only part of my rifles, and then to keep me begging for the rest while you dig your copper from the Sonora mines. That is what I think."

His followers evidently agreed, for they were growling curses now, and one savage-looking fellow festooned with bandoliers demanded bluntly, "¡Maten al gringo!"—kill the gringo!

Duncan flushed red, whether from anger or fear I didn't know, but he was clearly edging back toward his horse.

"Pedrolito, that's crazy!" he insisted. "You know I wouldn't cheat you. I want a good business relationship with you. Honest, I do."

But Pedrolito had a new scheme in mind. "This Senor Harlock and you are amigos, si? He will help you in need, si?"

"Sure, Pedrolito, sure," answered Duncan, a note of desperation in his voice. "That's what I've tried to tell you. He'll help me and I'll help you. Eventually you'll get all the rifles you need."

Pedrolito gave a grin that froze Duncan in place. "That's what I think too, gringo. That's why I think that when I send him your ears, he will keep the deal we already made, si?"

Now Duncan saw the handwriting on the wall; Pedrolito intended to use him as a human telegram to this mysterious fellow called Harlock. With the Mexicans closing in on him, there was no way he could get to his browsing horse before they gunned him down. He was taken and he knew it.

Or at least he was until I edged my knee a little to the left to ease a sudden cramp in my thigh and inadvertently nudged a small log. The log made no sound, but something suddenly gave a low menacing hiss in the brush next to me. Fearfully, I looked down.

Staring up at me with unblinking black eyes was the most horrible creature I had ever laid eyes on; it was a lizard, fully two feet long, with a shiny black hide splotched with yellow-orange. Its great jaws were agape, and it was clearly infuriated at my presence. It was a gila monster! By God, it was as terrible as McCabe had said!

I gagged, the overwhelming fear that shot through me almost forcing me to vomit. He Listens sensed my panic, spied the huge lizard, and flinched, his usually stoic features ashen with fear and his dark eyes nearly bulging from his head.

With another awful hiss, the dreadful lizard advanced, snapping its jaws. It was only inches from my naked hand, and I broke in fear. "Yiiii!" I screamed, leaping from the bushes into full view of the momentarily silent Mexicans.

They faced me as one; pistols cleared holsters and thumbs drew back the hammers of carbines. I realized with a sickening drop of my stomach that in a moment I would be a dead man.

Then He Listens was at my side with his carbine shouldered. He fired once, and a Mexican rolled in the dust.

"*Ahagahe!*" screamed He Listens. At the sound of the dreaded Apache war cry, the Mexicans scattered like quail, evidently expecting a war party to burst from the trees in an instant.

I realized that He Listens could have easily made his escape when I stumbled into the meadow, but instead he elected to stand by me. Was it because I had stood up to McCabe for him? Or was it because I was a Long Knife—a cavalryman—and he wore the blue coat of the Great White Father? Whatever his reasons, I was never so glad to see a fellow as I was to see Droopy's squatty form standing elbow to elbow with me at that awful instant.

This break was all Duncan needed; in a blur of speed I would have guessed was beyond him, he leapt into the saddle and spurred past He Listens and me, galloping straight down the trail we had just climbed.

"Wait for us, damn you!" I railed as he pounded past us with nary a backward glance. The Mexicans, recovering warily from their shock, loosed a ragged volley after Duncan.

That was enough for me; I took to my heels and He Listens did the same. Down the trail we flew to our horses, the sound of hooves behind us telling me that the Mexicans had already mounted. No sooner had we gained our mounts and clambered into the saddle than they were on us, their six-guns blazing.

Fighting back was out of the question; there were too many of them. Flight was the only sane course of action.

I spurred my horse and bent far over its neck to present the smallest possible target to our pursuers. He Listens did the same, reloading his carbine as he rode. We careened down the mountain as bullets flew over our heads, gouging great chunks of bark from the pines along both sides of the trail. Glancing back fearfully, I saw that the Mexicans had gained on us. The nearest was not ten feet behind He Listens, and it was clear that once we reached level ground they would take us. Perhaps sensing the same thing, He Listens suddenly twisted in the saddle and raised his carbine. He fired once, tumbling the nearest Mexican from his saddle, but not before our pursuers unleashed a fusillade in return.

He Listens sagged in the saddle, then fell. His body hit the earth hard and then cartwheeled into the trunk of a huge ponderosa pine with a sickening thud. If he hadn't been dead when he hit the ground, the tree certainly finished him.

But He Listens's sacrifice had not been in vain. His sudden departure from his saddle was enough to unbalance his galloping horse, which slid on the still-wet ground, went down hard on its knees, and then cartwheeled down the mountain behind me. It came to a sliding halt athwart the trail, and the Mexicans, unable to rein in, crashed headlong into this still-living obstacle. Several of them were thrown from the saddle as the others stormed through the undergrowth on either side of the trail to resume the pursuit. The delay gave me just enough time to spur my horse into a small lead as I cleared the pines and galloped through the mesquite and yucca to where Sergeant O'Brien and the others, alerted first by the shots and then by the sight of a panicked Mr. Duncan fleeing for his life and crying out for help, waited tensely by the arroyo.

The Mexicans had fanned out behind me when they reached the open country. Pedrolito was in front astride a magnificent Appaloosa stallion. On they charged, firing as they came. Suddenly before me I saw Duncan halted at the edge of the arroyo, yelling and gesturing to Corporal McCabe. Sergeant O'Brien had time only to get the cavalry mounts into the Rarey position—prone on the ground to serve as breastworks— before I pounded into their midst. Then the Mexicans were on us.

At a cry from Pedrolito, they fired a volley into their prey, loosing hell and damnation all around me. McCabe went down in the first volley, a bullet through his throat. Sergeant O'Brien had time only to empty one Mexican saddle before he too was hit. He slumped to the ground, but his fire had given me time to draw my pistol and to pick up his from the ground. Duncan clambered over the lip of the arroyo and cringed behind a boulder, while Alice sank to the ground and wailed at the death that was breaking over her.

Only Henry stood by my side now; he had escaped injury only because his balky mule refused to kneel like the horses and had conveniently absorbed that part of the murderous fusillade meant for the black man. Now the mule lay riddled on the ground like the horses, and together we fired from behind the wall of dead animals.

Our bullets broke the charge, dropping a Mexican here and toppling a horse there. In the face of our determined fire the Mexicans checked their mad rush, circling instead like a pack of wolves and keeping up a hail of steady musketry in an attempt to silence this last resistance. Bullets threw up puffs of dust at our feet as Pedrolito screamed for his men to charge home. But our shots were too accurate for them, and we could see the Mexicans turning aside whenever Henry or I leveled our guns at a particular rider. Sheltered as we were, we held the advantage for as long as the Mexicans elected to fight from horseback. Their accuracy suffered as their mounts shied from the lead filling the air around them.

Infuriated at his men's sudden shyness, and knowing that the only way to get to Duncan was over these last gringos, Pedrolito leapt from his Appaloosa and charged straight for me, his carbine blazing. It was a Winchester repeater, its stock decorated garishly with brass tacks and totem designs in the Indian fashion. Pedrolito fanned the Winchester's pump action with blurring speed, tearing great chunks of flesh and saddlery from the horse carcass that sheltered me. This stream of fire, washing around me like a swarm of maddened bees, was too much to withstand with my revolvers; all I could do was cower behind the dead horse and wait for Pedrolito to inexorably close the distance between us.

And he did, advancing step by step, secure in the knowledge that any attempt by me to raise my Colts in self-defense would spell my doom. After all, he had a seventeen-shot magazine, and I had almost expended the bullets chambered in my pistols.

On and on he came, so close now I could hear the gravel crunch under his moccasined feet, and I knew that he was just on the other side of the horse and that death was only an instant away. I was frozen by the realization that my life was over. I could think of no way to escape my impending destruction—until his Winchester suddenly jammed.

At first I couldn't believe it; the rugged Winchester rifle almost never jammed. Yet as I cautiously raised my head, there was Pedrolito before my very eyes struggling unsuccessfully to work the pump mechanism. Perhaps the dust kicked up from the battle around us had clogged the breech, or perhaps the speed of Pedrolito's firing had jammed one round against another inside the rifle's chamber; whatever the reason, I was the beneficiary of a miracle.

Pedrolito hurled away the Winchester in fury and went for the Colts strapped to his hips. At this close range I could see the many notches in those gun handles and knew that each one represented a life snuffed out. Seeing my chance, I leveled one of my Colts as Pedrolito drew. The speed of his border draw was quicker than the strike of a rattler but not quicker than my finger on the trigger. Like He Listens, Pedrolito wore an amulet bag around his neck; I fired straight for it.

The Colt roared. Pedrolito slammed to the ground, his pistols sailing from his hands to land harmlessly in the scrub. As the gunsmoke from my Colt cleared, I saw Pedrolito thrashing about on the ground like a wounded mountain lion. But then—incredibly—he struggled to his feet!

I was staggered; was all that hoopla about Injun medicine true? Was this demon indestructible? It was only then that I saw a glint of gold inside the torn bag around Pedrolito's neck and realized numbly that the Indian carried a large gold coin in his medicine bag and that I had simply had the misfortune to hit the coin dead on. My shot had staggered Pedrolito, to be sure, but the coin deflected the bullet before it could penetrate. Shaken by this turn of events, I again raised the Colt and again squeezed the trigger.

The hammer clicked harmlessly. Damn, the gun was empty! Hastily I raised the other revolver to fire, but it too was empty. Now I was truly shaking, for if Pedrolito didn't have powerful war medicine, he was at the very least the luckiest hombre I had ever encountered.

The sound of my hammer hitting on empty chambers was all the encouragement Pedrolito needed.

"Eeeahhh!" he roared, flashing his fighting knife and leaping for me all in the same instant. Desperate to ward him off, I met him with a clubbing blow from the handle of one of my revolvers. The blow was only a glancing one, but it nonetheless was enough to cause Pedrolito to misjudge his stab. I dropped the useless revolvers and seized his powerful wrist with my two hands. Locked in combat, we fell to the ground, rolling about wildly as he flailed at me with his free hand. I did my best to knee his groin while holding the knife immobile.

Henry could do nothing to help me, since it was only his carbine that now held the rest of the Mexicans at bay. We rolled to within a foot of Alice, who screamed anew as she got a good look at Pedrolito's hideous countenance. She cried aloud for God's deliverance.

Now, I'm not the praying type, at least not ordinarily. But at the moment, divine intervention looked like the only way out of the fix I was in. As I struggled with the infuriated Indian, I realized that if my strength flagged before his, I would be notch number twelve. From the petrified look on Alice's face, I could tell she knew that if I went, she wouldn't be far behind. So pray I did: I called on the angels and the saints, and struggled to remember some shreds of prayer that might demonstrate my sincerity to the Deity. But for all of my struggling and for all of my feverish devotionals, it quickly became evident that Pedrolito was the stronger fighter. He sensed it too, for he ceased clubbing me with his free hand and instead clamped it like a vise around my unprotected throat.

Immediately I felt my air supply cease, and despite the fact that I still held him with two hands, he was able to raise his blade to position the point above my chest for another stab at me. When he had gained enough clearance for his purpose, he plunged the killing blade downward with a force that two men could not have resisted. I escaped annihilation only by jerking suddenly sideways so that his blade lacerated my ribs rather than passing between them.

"Eeeyoww!" I cried out in agony as the blade bit into my flesh, which brought forward a dreadful chortle from the murderous Pedrolito. He raised the knife again for a final plunge and might well have finished me off except that I suddenly became aware of his tattered medicine bag dangling just inches in front of me. I momentarily loosened my right hand from Pedrolito's thick wrist, seized the leather pouch, and with a desperate yank snapped the cord holding it to Pedrolito's neck.

"Ahhhee!" he screamed, as though I had physically maimed him. For a fraction of a second the downward pressure of the knife stopped, and I took advantage of his agitation to hurl the bag as far as I could.

It wasn't very far, for Pedrolito's bulk blocked my arm and cut short my throw; the pouch landed only ten feet away. But my purpose was served, for Pedrolito was determined to regain his precious medicine bag before dispatching me. He sprang to his feet and retrieved the bag, tucking it securely into a pocket of his jerkin.

The next part of my plan, however—which was to find a loaded gun during the respite and slay this madman—went awry. Pedrolito had so thoroughly cut off my air that all I could do was lie on the ground and gasp helplessly like a beached catfish. Seeing that I could not move, Pedrolito shifted his knife in his hand and closed in once more for the kill. My head was pounding dreadfully, and I heard a strange music ringing in my ears. Yes, it was definitely music—the music of a distant trumpet filling the air.

A trumpet? My fearful brain struggled to understand what was happening. Was I so near death that a band of angels was swooping down to carry me home? The trumpet blew again, but now I recognized it as a bugle, and it was sounding the charge!

The Mexicans heard it too, for Pedrolito instantly ran for his horse. "¡Vamonos, muchachos!" he cried.

Shakily, I arose. Along the water-filled arroyo swept an advancing line of blue-clad troopers, First Sergeant Richmond at their head. Above the onrushing yellow legs I saw puffs of smoke, proof that they already had the Mexicans under fire. The Mexicans, having no stomach for a stand-up fight with gringo cavalry, were already flying. It was over, by God, and I had survived!

Then I remembered I had a score to settle with that son of a bitch Pedrolito. I saw McCabe's loaded Colt in his lifeless hand and seized it, just as Duncan clambered over the ridge to greet his rescuers, and just as Alice dared to raise her head.

"Pedrolito!" I bellowed.

The fleeing Yaqui halted in midstride, saw the gun, and then leapt contemptuously into the saddle. "You won't shoot me in the back, gringo," he sneered and wheeled his mount to gallop off. Evidently he had dealt with *norteamericano* soldiers in the past and knew that they had an aversion to shooting a fleeing foe. He figured that he would be safe with his back turned to me, so he dug his spurs into the flanks of the big Appaloosa and it leapt forward.

Again my Colt roared. Pedrolito was dead wrong about me; I would have shot him on a Christmas altar in front of the choir after what he had done to me.

Pedrolito turned painfully in the saddle, a look of utter amazement on his face. For a second he tried to speak, but only a bloody froth came to his lips as he slid slowly to the ground and, after a convulsion or two, had the decency to die.

Then the troopers were upon us, scattering the Mexicans to the wind, and Alice was in my arms sobbing.

12

A week later I was still in the hospital. My knife wound was healing nicely, but the regimental surgeon was reluctant to discharge me too early for fear of infection. Hospitalization suited me just fine, since it involved clean sheets, solicitously hovering orderlies, and most importantly, no fatigue details. Why would orderlies be hovering over a mere private? you may ask. The answer was that I was no longer only a mere private. I was now something of a hero. Colonel Sumner had made that clear on my first day back at Fort Grant.

"That was a fine bit of fighting you and that colored boy did, Private Travers. Why, if it hadn't been for the two of you, I shudder to think what would have become of Miss Brenoble."

Well, what could a homegrown Illinois boy say in the face of such overwhelming flattery? Why, only the obvious: "Sir, it was nothing, really."

"Nothing my eye, son. That fight was a damned close-run thing. To top it off, you killed that fiend Pedrolito in single combat. They don't grow heroes any bigger than you, Travers. I've already wired word of your exploit to the territorial headquarters in Phoenix. Why, the governor has personally wired back his congratulations to you."

Here he waved a sheaf of papers at me, one of which I took to be the governor's salutations. I assumed that the remaining sheets were for the others—Corporal McCabe, Sergeant O'Brien, and Lieutenant Greer. All were deceased now, Sergeant O'Brien having bled to death on the ride back. Lieutenant Greer we had found after a search down the arroyo before we returned. Henry had seen it first, a knot of dead mules piled around a collection of smashed tree trunks and boulders. Jutting from the mass of debris and dead animals was a booted foot, and on it was a Spanish spur.

It was a damned ignominious end for a soldier, but I was rapidly coming to understand that life was fragile in this wild land. We had dug Lieutenant Greer's body out of its tomb, wrapped it in a bedroll, and lashed it across the back of his horse for the slow journey back to Fort Grant. Corporal McCabe and Sergeant O'Brien were given proper burials beside the post chapel; Lieutenant Greer's body was sent by rail back to West Point for interment.

"This is big, Private Travers, very big," continued Colonel Sumner. "As for Mr. Duncan, well, I wouldn't be at all surprised if he extends to you some concrete token of his gratitude for what you've done."

It was the mention of Duncan that set me to wondering for the hundredth time since the furious fight just what it was that I had witnessed high in the ponderosa pines before He Listens had met his death. That Duncan and Pedrolito were in bed together was beyond doubt; as best I could piece together the story, their liaison was over a protection scheme that Duncan had tried to concoct for enterprises he hoped to embark upon south of the border. But who was this mysterious Harlock fellow, and how exactly did he figure into Duncan's plan?

When Mr. Duncan did get around to visiting me, I of course put none of my questions to him. In fact I couldn't have gotten a word in edgewise as he puffed and blew about how proud he was of our army, and how fortunate the nation was to have soldiers like me, and other drivel along the same line. Nothing was said of Henry, although as far as I knew, Henry and I were in the same army. I endured Duncan's pompous humbuggery in stoic silence, even when it became quite clear to me that nothing "concrete" would be forthcoming from the wealthy yet parsimonious Duncan. Nothing, that is, until lovely Alice joined her uncle at my bedside.

"Private Travers, you're looking well," she positively cooed. I smiled eagerly in return, for I had missed her. On the long ride back to Fort Grant, Alice had insisted on changing my dressings herself and had been ever ready with a canteen of cool water when the threat of fever loomed. Through it all she had been properly respectful of me, her deliverer, and I had been manfully stolid in return. We had grown close, so it was no surprise that she appeared at my bedside now.

"I'll leave you young people alone, then," said Duncan, beaming with a paternal smile as he betook himself from my sick ward. I watched him go, wondering whether he was busy hatching new Mexican schemes now that Pedrolito was out of the way.

Alice's dulcet tone stirred me from my musings. "Fenny, would you like me to read to you?" Lovely Alice was careful to address me as Private Travers whenever we were in the company of others, but once we were alone it was Fenny, and had been ever since that dreadful day.

"Yes, that would be nice," I replied, eager more for the music of her voice than for the maudlin meanderings of some addlepated novelist.

But Alice had no novel to offer. "The only volumes Colonel Sumner has are the Bible and some dusty old books about war. This is the only one that looks the least bit interesting. It's called the *War Commentaries* of Caesar."

"Caesar, eh?" I mused. "I've heard of him. He was a great Roman general."

"That's right," affirmed Alice, "a great warrior—like you."

I actually blushed at this, not at all displeased at the notion. After all, my father had been a soldier, and perhaps my blood was beginning to tell. And besides, receiving compliments from a colonel and a congratulatory telegraph from the governor was a hell of a lot more flattering to the ego than poling bacon to market on a barge.

So Alice read to me about Gaul and its musty old tribes, which seemed to have had a powerful amount of trouble staying on the reservations that the Romans set them on. According to Caesar, they came boiling out of what was Indian territory back in Europe as regular as clockwork to burn towns and murder settlers. As Alice read, I couldn't help thinking that those Gauls were just like the Indians, and the Romans were like the cavalry. We soon fell into a pattern; Alice would read a chapter while I lay in bed and gazed at her like a lovesick pup, and then she would hand me the book to read the same chapter back to her as she held my hand or stroked my brow.

Caesar was as windy as Duncan, so his book was long; Alice and I couldn't read it in one day, or even several. Since she insisted on finishing the book, she could be found perched on my bed day after day, sitting so close to me that I could smell the sweet perfume of her breath and feel the tender warmth of her ripe form.

Besides reading, we talked a great deal, and in this manner I came to know much about Alice, such as the fact that her parents had died in a yachting accident years before and that she had been raised by her uncle George. Her story was similar to mine in that regard, but the similarity ended when she related how her uncle doted on her and looked after her every whim. That was fortunate for her, since he was one of the wealthiest men in New York. Duncan headed a giant trust called Duncan Enterprises, which invested in everything from mines to real estate. Alice was a very fortunate girl indeed.

I, in turn, told her about my upbringing and obscure roots, and all in all we became close. Duncan was generally gone during these days, off to Tucson one week and Phoenix the next, to tend to his business affairs. That left tender Alice alone with me, enchanting me with her flowing auburn hair and healthy good looks.

Enchanted is perhaps a mite too tame a word to describe my fascination for Alice. The truth was that she set my loins aflame with lustful sensations, and I was prepared to chase after her bouncing bottom shamelessly. Young though I was, I had already learned that although opportunity may knock but once, temptation will literally kick down the door, and Alice was a temptation. I knew I wanted her, and so, like Caesar, I set about a campaign of conquest.

By the second week of playing librarian, Alice had become accustomed to being near me, and her manner was relaxed. On the day I decided to put my scheme into effect, I was propped up by an overstuffed pillow with Alice roosting next to me, droning on about Roman civil wars in provinces I couldn't even pronounce. I suddenly winced and put my hand to my ribs, which were now sufficiently healed to warrant my being returned to duty but for the gratifyingly persistent inclination of the doctors to pamper the conquering hero.

Alice reacted with predictable sympathy. "Oh, you poor dear," she soothed, "are you still in pain?"

I turned to look into those caring green eyes and gave a brave smile. "It's getting better, Alice. You know, having you here with me, well—it's just made things much easier to bear."

Alice blushed and dropped her gaze to the plank floor, gracefully turning her lovely white neck as she did so. For a second I feared I might have been too bold, but to my great delight Alice lifted her pretty eyes and laid a soft hand on my shoulder. "I'm so glad you're healing, Fenny," she purred in her comforting way. "I was so afraid when you were fighting with that horrible Indian that he would . . . hurt you. I realized then that I would just die if anything should happen to you."

"Then it's so, dear Alice," I smiled like a cat watching a bird willingly climb onto its branch. "You do care for me. Oh, I prayed it was so." With calculated boldness, I seized Alice's hand in both of mine as I spoke hotly: "I'm so glad you just up and said it. I want us to be good friends—very good friends."

Alice smiled fondly at me, and with her free hand gently brushed my blond locks from my eyes. "You must get some rest now, Fenny. Soon you'll be feeling better, and then we can talk about all of this calmly."

Rational talk was the last thing I wanted, of course; my true goal was a bout of irrational cuddling with this ravishing creature before her uncle took her off and I never saw her again. "No, Alice," I insisted, a pathetic little whimper in my voice that I knew would melt her heart. "When I'm well I'll be marched out of here and back to the barracks. You won't be allowed near me because I'm a mere private with no prospects. If we're to have any time together, dear Alice, it must be now or never!" I stealthily put my hand in her lap, and after a moment's hesitation, she gave me a trembling smile and put her small hand on mine.

"Ah, there now, Fenny," she said, pulling my head to her ample bosom with her free hand. "Don't you worry so; I have no intention of letting you escape from me so easily."

That was exactly what I was counting on, of course, all thought of my still-aching side evaporating in the presence of Alice's inspiring femininity. As I felt the fullness of her breasts beneath my ear, I plotted my next move and decided to work on her sympathies a bit more before closing in for the kill.

"That's so kind of you, Alice," I breathed into the fabric of her dress where it strained across the bulge of her breasts, the aroma of lilac water filling my nostrils. "But you're just saying that to make me feel better. I've seen your uncle, and I think I understand him. He's a millionaire back east, and you're his niece. Your people have a place in the world, but I have nothing. I couldn't believe for a minute that he'd ever consider letting the two of us continue on as friends once I'm let out of this hospital."

In that regard, I was absolutely right. To Duncan, the very thought of his pretty niece, who had already drawn admiring glances from some of the most eligible beaux in New York, becoming romantically entangled with a hayseed soldier boy was ludicrous. He tolerated her mooning over me only because I had gunned down Pedrolito before the Indian could haul him off to Sonora as a hostage. That act had earned me a bit of forbearance, but only a bit, and as soon as his business in Arizona was done, he and Alice would be gone, leaving this godforsaken wilderness to the savages and the army.

"That's not true, Fenny," Alice scolded me gently. "Uncle George is a decent man who is properly grateful for what you did for us. Why, if I could only explain to him how you feel, I'm sure he would understand. Perhaps he could even arrange for you to visit us back in New York. . . ."

I could see that this conversation was quickly running off course. The only visit Duncan would arrange for me would be a trip to the stockade for molesting his niece. Time was short and the last thing I needed now was for Alice to prattle on about hopelessly romantic happy endings. It was time to take the offensive, I decided.

"Perhaps you're right, dearest Alice," I allowed with forced reasonableness. "Maybe my fears that I'll never see you again are baseless, and I should put them out of my mind."

Alice beamed happily, until I added slowly, "But then, what if you're wrong? What then? These days will be our last moments together for the rest of our lives."

Alice was silent now. My arrow had hit home. "I'm just a country boy, my love, and I don't know about fine manners and such. Why, if I tried to make your uncle cotton to me, I'd be so nervous just thinking about you that I'd make a complete fool of myself. No, it's no use, I'm afraid."

Alice's face clouded over as she considered my bleak ending to our budding romance. Seeing that I had her undivided attention focused on my ruse, I prodded her a bit further into the snare. "I'd like to put on a brave front, Alice, and face your uncle. You know, ask him for permission to visit and all like you suggested. And I will, too, but I'm telling you, just the mention of your name will set me to shaking and it'll all come apart."

I thought I saw tears beginning to well up in her eyes, so I paused to let her feelings run amok a bit before continuing. That was a wise move, for now she gave a little sniffle; I could almost hear the springs of the trap groaning in anticipation. "Unless, that is. . . ." I left the thought hanging in the air.

Alice caught it before it floated to the ground. "Unless what, Fenny? Unless what?"

"Unless, well, naw . . . you'll think it's crazy."

"No, I won't," she insisted fervently. "Tell me, dear Fenny, please."

"Maybe if . . . no, it's not possible," I demurred with exquisite drama, turning away and hoping my prey would push on for the bait.

She did. "What's not possible, my love?" she pressed. "Please share your thoughts with me, Fenny. I must know what you're thinking."

I turned and fixed Alice with my most earnest gaze. "Maybe if, if you could show me how to be close to you, then maybe when I spoke to your uncle I wouldn't be so awkward and nervous. Maybe then I could make a better impression. . . ." I stopped to let the idea sink in.

"I, er, suppose you can't be expected to be calm in presenting your case to Uncle George when you're not, er, completely certain that you have my love," she allowed at length, a throaty note in her voice.

Lay it on, Fenny, thinks I; the fox has its paw caught now! "Then tell me true, dear Alice. Do you . . . could you . . . love me?" I fought to keep my voice from breaking wildly and pressed my head tremulously against her heaving bosom. Her heart was pounding madly and her breath was coming in gasps. There was no mistaking it: The trap had sprung and Alice was caught!

"I could, Fenny," she whispered warmly in my ear. "In fact, I think I might already be in love with you." She smiled down at me fondly, and I smiled back eagerly into the fabric of her dress.

Raising my head now, I put my arms around her supple waist and kissed her tentatively. She put her arms around me and hugged me in return, and then, after a moment's hesitation, she gave me a slight peck on the cheek.

But it was a great deal more than a sisterly peck I was after, you can rest assured. Give me a yard and I'll take a mile. Alice was hardly my first dalliance with the opposite sex; I had developed a precocious and unnaturally powerful attraction to the ladies, and I was already a scarred veteran in the war for their delectable favors. My early conquests in Elm Grove had been pubescent daughters of townsmen, and before long, tales of my flirtations had begun to find their way to the

Judge's scandalized ears. He managed to keep these tales from Aunt Hannah, but as I matured the Judge slowly came to the conclusion that his nephew was an emerging womanizer. Of all my conquests, however, Alice was by far the biggest game I had yet stalked, and if my ears were not deceiving me, she was bagged.

"Then it's true!" I gasped dramatically. "You do love me! Oh, how I prayed it could be so! You've made me so happy!" Surreptitiously I slid a hand up from Alice's waist until it rested on a high, firm breast. I felt her stiffen under my touch and then relax sensuously.

"Fenny, you shouldn't be touching me there," she whispered, unconvincingly. "It's not seemly."

"I can't help myself, dear Alice," I replied honestly enough, my passion starting to get the better of me. "When I'm near you like this, I just lose all control. You're so lovely, so delicious, that I'm lost when I look into your eyes." I gave her breast a gentle squeeze. "Please, Alice, don't turn me away! Don't reject me," I pleaded urgently. And urgent I was, for my member was by now as stiff as a Potsdam grenadier on parade. If I was denied the chance to take Alice this very instant, I was sure I'd be crippled for life.

For a moment more she hesitated and then, with a shuddering sigh, whispered, "I understand, Fenny, I understand. Never fear, I won't turn you away."

I had her! The battle was won and I closed for the kill. I hastily glanced about to see that we were still alone. All was quiet; the orderlies were nowhere to be seen, and the ward was empty except for us.

"Dear Alice, oh dearest Alice," I burbled mindlessly as my trembling fingers clumsily unbuttoned her bodice.

She shuddered delightfully at my touch. "Oh, Fenny," she breathed, seeking my lips with her own moist mouth.

"Alice, Alice," I murmured insanely in her ear as I tugged her dress away and furiously began untying her stays. "You're all I have, dear Alice! Please let me have it."

"Yes, yes," she answered hotly, utterly lost now in her own rampant passion. I undid the last of her stubborn stays and pulled them aside. Two of the largest, most perfect breasts I had ever seen popped shyly into view.

"Oh, my God," I moaned, taking one of her delightful orbs in my hand and tenderly licking its pink tip with my tongue.

"Fenny, my love!" she cried softly at my touch. "It feels so good. . . ." She seized my golden locks with surprising force and thrust my face full into her bared breasts.

"Mmmph!" was all I could say as my mouth filled with her bounty.

"Don't stop now, dearest," urged Alice, reclining on the bed and cupping a breast in each hand. Her green eyes glowed with the light of unleashed lust.

"I won't stop, Alice," I promised as I laid her down and clambered clumsily aboard her, trying not to burst my sutures as I thrust my hips energetically between her parted thighs. "I can't wait for it. . . !" My mind boggled at the thought that Alice had finally surrendered, and her charms were now mine for the taking.

As things turned out, however, I would be forced to wait a while longer to fully savor Alice's charms, for at just that moment the door swung open and in strode Uncle George. In our excitement, neither Alice nor I had heard him thumping across the wide wooden veranda of the hospital and down the hall that led to the ward.

"Private Travers," he began as he entered, "have you seen Alice. . . ?"

The words died in his throat as he took in the scene before him. That I had seen Alice—all of her—was beyond denial. There was an eerie silence in which Duncan's face drained of all color and his mouth fell open. For an awful moment I thought he was going to have an apoplectic seizure on the spot, but suddenly his ashen face flashed a bright crimson.

"What in the name of God is going on here?" he roared with a force that nearly blew the covers off the bed.

"Eeeek!" shrieked Alice, throwing me off in one great heave as she bounded off the bed. In a blur of motion she pulled up her bodice to cover her nakedness and bolted from the room.

Duncan's burning glare fixed upon me: "You, you filthy heathen," he stuttered in rage. "Here I go out of my way to sing your praises to Colonel Sumner, and how do you thank me? By fornicating with my niece under my very nose!" He seized a cane from where it rested against a bunk and, bearing it as a club, he advanced.

"Now, Mister Duncan," I quailed as I painfully edged off the bed and moved carefully out of his range, "it's not what it seems. I can explain everything."

"Explain, hell, you savage!" Duncan growled, hefting his cane menacingly and moving to cut me off as I backed across the room. "I saw everything with my own eyes. You were pawing Alice, by God, and now I'm going to teach you a lesson you'll never forget."

With that he raised the cane and lunged for me. A lantern on the wall was smashed to bits as I easily ducked his awkward blow and danced to a far corner of the ward.

"Goddamn it, hold still!" he bellowed furiously and then, whirling, advanced upon me once more.

Hold still and be pounded to a bloody pulp? Not on your life, I told myself. It was clear that in his rage Duncan was out to kill me.

"Yaaa!" screamed Duncan as he took another mighty swing at me, only to hit air. The momentum of his swing carried him around in a half circle and left him blinking in rage and facing the wrong direction; I politely tapped his shoulder to reorient him.

"Mister Duncan, please, let me explain," I begged in desperation. "Alice and I are in love. She wanted me to speak to you. Honest, it's not what you're thinking. . . ."

He whirled at the sound of my voice so quickly that I didn't have time to duck his swing cleanly. He caught me a glancing blow to the shoulder, knocking me painfully to the bed.

"Silence, you son of a bitch!" he hissed venomously, raising the cane above his head for the death blow. "I'll not be turned from my task!"

I was up in a flash, the specter of destruction galvanizing me into action. I seized the cane, and in an instant we were locked in furious combat. Although I was stronger than he, the pain of my wound told and for a second I thought he might prevail. But with a mighty effort I wrenched the cane from his grasp and hurled it through a closed window. The sound of the shattering glass elicited shouts of alarm from outside and footsteps as orderlies came running.

For a moment Duncan stood before me breathing heavily through his mouth, thoroughly winded. But he was still game. "So you think you can face up to me, hey? We'll see about that."

He raised his fists and closed upon me once more. But this time I didn't scamper off. I had been swung at, insulted, and, worst of all, interrupted just as I was about to enjoy the delectable favors of the most beautiful girl I'd ever lured within groping range. Duncan had taken me by surprise, and it was natural that I should try to appease him, but I was beginning to get damned angry now, so I raised my fists in return.

Duncan's slitted eyes opened wide in surprise, and he halted; he clearly didn't like what he saw. I was a good-sized brute for my age, nearing six feet already and well muscled. And, what was more, the image of what I had done to Pedrolito was still fresh in his mind. For a second I saw him hesitate, then he backed off. Mightily relieved, I lowered my guard.

Like lightning, Duncan lunged forward with a leading right hand. "Take this, you scum!" he roared. But I reacted with rodentlike agility, ducking aside to slip the blow and tripping Duncan as he sailed by. He crashed into my bed and then fell heavily to the floor. I leapt lightly over his prostrate form, flew down the hall, and fled for the relative safety of my barracks. Behind me I could hear Duncan screaming bloody murder: "Run you bastard! I'll have you up on charges before the day is out! You'll not get away with this!"

13

Duncan was true to his word. He went straight to Colonel Sumner for justice; his niece had been deflowered, by God, and he wanted the culprit to swing. Colonel Sumner, however, an experienced old hand, was reluctant to convene a court-martial based solely on Duncan's excited babblings. Colonel Sumner sent first for Alice and then for me. First Sergeant Richmond led the detail that came for me, and after allowing me to get into a uniform, he marched me back to headquarters. He wasn't sure what the matter was, but judging from Mr. Duncan's livid features and Colonel Sumner's stern face, it was a matter of utmost gravity undoubtedly related to some misconduct on my part.

This only confirmed the low opinion that First Sergeant Richmond had formed of me over these months. While every other living soul at Fort Grant was lionizing me, First Sergeant Richmond took a dim view of the fact that I had shot Pedrolito in the back. You see, he was a Southerner, and he had unusual notions about honor. Although he was only a noncommissioned officer, First Sergeant Richmond considered himself an honorable man—a gentleman, even—and a gentleman didn't shoot a foeman in the back. He had a personal code not unlike that of the knights I'd read about in Sir Walter Scott's novel, *Ivanhoe*.

Now don't get me wrong; I have a sort of honor myself. All things being equal I'll try to do the right thing just like any other upright fellow. Also, although I'll never start a fight I can't finish, I'll generally let the other fellow go when he's had enough—if he's a decent sort. But there is a limit to my sense of fair play, a boundary I understandably pass when a mad-dog killer is within clear pistol-range and I have a loaded Colt. If that put me outside the pale of First Sergeant Richmond's concept of honor, well, so be it.

I was ushered into headquarters just as Alice came out of the colonel's office and closed the door behind her. Her face was red, and I could see that she had been crying. "Oh, Fenny, my uncle is simply impossible. He's sending me back east today. He says I can't see you again!"

I smiled bravely for her benefit, although I had no reason to doubt that Duncan meant exactly what he said. I responded comfortingly, "Alice, we can't expect him to talk sense right now. Let him calm down a bit. Things'll work out. You'll see."

Alice stifled a sob, tried to smile, failed, and then ran from me, crying into her well-irrigated handkerchief. I wanted to go after her, but I was stayed when the colonel's door opened.

"Private Travers, march in there and report to th' colonel," ordered First Sergeant Richmond.

I did as I was told. Colonel Sumner was seated erectly behind his polished mahogany desk; I marched to the front of his desk, snapped a salute, and barked: "Private Travers reporting as ordered, sir."

Colonel Sumner returned the salute gravely. Duncan stood off to the side glowering at me. I stared straight ahead and awaited the inevitable assault. It came directly.

"Miss Brenoble told us that the two of you have regards for each other, Private Travers."

"That's true, sir," I replied stiffly. Of course, my regards toward her were rather more carnal than were hers to me, but I didn't think the colonel needed to know that right at the moment.

"You know, son, it's not generally accepted that a young couple become so, er, intimate on such short acquaintance."

This was all Duncan could stand; he had demanded a hangman's noose and all I was getting from Colonel Sumner was an avuncular chat. "Damn it all, Colonel! They're not a young couple! My niece is from one of the finest families in New York. By God, the Duncans go back two centuries in this country. How can you possibly suggest that Alice and this rapscallion are a couple? There's been a crime here, sir, a crime! This man forced himself on poor Alice, and I want to see justice done!"

"That's what I aim to do, Mister Duncan," replied Colonel Sumner, not in the least intimidated by Duncan's bluster. "And to do that, I have to keep in mind the fact that your niece told me in her own words that what you saw in the hospital was not against her will—not entirely, that is. Seems that things did move along at a faster clip than she anticipated, but then, things like this usually do."

"Colonel, I must insist you stop insinuating that there was any fault on Alice's part," demanded Duncan. "The point here is that your private is as randy as a deckhand on a China clipper. He's not fit to be loosed on decent society. He's destroyed Alice's reputation, and for that he deserves to be on a chain gang or worse."

I bore all this silently. I would have been worried if a less self-possessed man were deciding my fate, but Colonel Sumner gave me the impression that he was not overly shocked by the idea of two healthy young people romping on a bed. Yes, perhaps I'd come out of this in one piece after all, I was thinking.

Then Colonel Sumner dropped the other shoe: "If it's the girl's reputation you're concerned with," he suggested lightly to Duncan, "then there's a remedy to cure the harm."

Duncan stared with wide-eyed disbelief. At first he couldn't speak, and it was only with effort that he was able to gasp, "You can't be serious, man! Alice and this . . . this . . ." He glared at me in utter contempt as he struggled for a suitable appellation. "This murderous bumpkin! Why, the very thought is preposterous, Colonel. Totally preposterous!"

Now I was gaping. Was the colonel suggesting marriage? My God, this had all gotten out of hand! An hour ago the only thing I expected from Alice was a frolic under the sheets. Now she was being ballyhooed as a potential mate—and I was not even in the market for one!

But Colonel Sumner saw nothing preposterous about such a match. "Why not, Mister Duncan? She cares for him, and from what you told me of what you saw in the hospital, he cares for her. Marriage usually obtains under those circumstances, does it not?"

"Colonel," thundered Duncan, "marriage only obtains under those circumstances for people of the same social class! Alice is of the highest class; she's a Knickerbocker, by God, a Brahmin of New York. Your private," he said, gesturing at me as though I were a particularly odious insect on display under glass, "on the other hand, is of patently dubious ancestry and questionable blood." I smiled inwardly, thinking that if Duncan knew the truth of my origins, he'd faint dead away. "A marriage under such circumstances is out of the question. Utterly out of the question."

Colonel Sumner nodded his understanding. "Then only a court-martial will answer, sir?"

Duncan nodded grimly; he was finally making headway. "Yes, Colonel, a general court-martial."

The words bore into my skull. A general court-martial was hardly a trial by my peers. Such a court was presided over by the regiment's lieutenant colonel and consisted of a panel of five to thirteen officers. Alarmingly, the Articles of War provided that there could be no enlisted members. I rather doubted that the other regimental officers would be as open-minded about my dalliance with Alice as Colonel Sumner was being.

"Then you'll have one, Mister Duncan. First, the charges must be drawn up by the adjutant and then sworn. After that, there'll be an investigation to see if the charges should be referred to court-martial. Referral would normally be done by myself, but now that I'm a witness in the case—"

Duncan interrupted, confused. "A witness, Colonel? What the dickens are you talking about? I'm the only witness. I'm the one who saw what happened."

"Oh, I quite agree that you are the only eyewitness, sir. But as we both know, there are other types of witnesses." He paused to eye Duncan flintily before continuing. "Such as corroborating witnesses. If Private Travers here were to be tried for despoiling your niece, I would imagine that the gravamen of his defense would be that the conduct was consensual and hence lawful. If that were the case, I would be a witness to the fact that your niece told me she consented to Private Travers's advances."

"Colonel, this is outrageous! Just whose side are you on here?" demanded Duncan.

"Mister Duncan, you told me earlier that you sought justice. Well, I aim to see that you get it. To that end, I take no sides other than to seek the truth. Now, let me continue. Where was I? Ah, yes. Since I would be disqualified from referring the charges to a court, that task would be referred to my higher headquarters, the Department of Arizona in the state capital. That headquarters might well remove the trial to Phoenix, and the trial would necessarily be subjected to a higher degree of scrutiny from the newspapers."

"Newspapers?" echoed Duncan, aghast. "Colonel, I have no intention of making a circus of this thing. All I want is a nice quiet trial here at Fort Grant with a rapid conviction of this scoundrel. Then I'll be on my way and your routine can return to normal."

"I'm afraid I can't guarantee a quiet little trial, Mister Duncan. Once matters like we're discussing are set in motion, they have a way of taking on a life of their own. I wouldn't be surprised if this was a story that was telegraphed from coast to coast. I'm afraid it's a sad truth that the public's appetite for lurid love stories is quite unquenchable."

"Coast to coast, you say?" Duncan was now shaking his head uncertainly. The colonel's blows were beginning to tell.

"If I'm wrong here, Mister Duncan, tell me so. You yourself said that you were a Knickerbocker, a blue blood. Is it erroneous of me to suggest that the newspapers would seize an opportunity to boost their circulation by rubbing your nose in the dirt?"

Duncan was silent now, walking to the window and staring hard at the distant mountains. Then he turned, a defeated look on his face. "What do you suggest, Colonel?"

"Go home and leave this young rascal to me. He'll get to know the inside of the 'mill' for a few months, and by the time he's out, this whole matter will have been forgotten."

"But I can't do that," Duncan protested, almost plaintively. "Alice is ruined if this gets out, especially if it becomes known that she consented to this lout's advances. No man of good family would have her. No, things have got to be made right somehow."

"I agree," seconded Colonel Sumner. "That's why I once more propose marriage as a solution to your problem."

"Colonel, we've just been over this—" began Duncan, but Colonel Sumner silenced him with an upraised hand.

"Mister Duncan, you object to Private Travers because of his class. I'm not unsympathetic to that; it's a fact that must be considered. But there is a way to change the boy's class," he suggested.

Here Duncan was completely lost. "Change his social class? Colonel, that's impossible—a zebra cannot change its stripes."

Colonel Sumner smiled indulgently. "In civilian life, I quite agree with you. But in the military it's not impossible. All this boy needs to be a suitable match for your Alice is a commission."

A commissioned officer? Me? What in the blazes was Colonel Sumner talking about? I wanted to ask exactly that, and it was a struggle to hold my peace.

"A commission, eh? Make him an officer, eh?" Duncan considered this. He looked first at Colonel Sumner, then doubtfully at me, and then back. "How?"

"It'll be difficult, but it can be done. Remember Private Travers's citation for gallantry that I sent forward a few weeks ago?"

Duncan nodded slowly.

"Well, that citation will eventually find its way to the War Department. Every year in the entering class of the military academy there are a certain number of young men who are former enlisted men. They are selected by the War Department for their unusual leadership potential and their academic promise. A list of these young fellows is put together and sent to the president. The president nominates a few, and these lucky few nominees are then accorded what's referred to as a presidential appointment to West Point. What I'm proposing is that we submit young Travers here for a presidential appointment. If he's picked, and if he's successful at the academy, in four years your Alice may have a suitable beau."

Duncan was now paying serious attention. "Leadership potential, you say? How can he show that? After all, the only experience he's ever had in the army is following orders, not giving them."

"A good point," conceded Colonel Sumner, who then countered tellingly, "but don't forget the fact that this boy brought down the most wanted outlaw in these parts. That feat alone will go a long way toward compensating for any perceived deficiencies he may have in actual experience."

Duncan saw the truth in this; I was a certified killer, and the men who ran West Point would understand a character like me. In Duncan's mind I definitely had the raw material from which purveyors of mass destruction are made. Duncan was now eyeing me appraisingly, his gaze beginning to raise the hairs on the back of my neck. My feral instincts told me that I was in deep trouble.

"What you say is true enough, Colonel. He may be a buffoon, but nobody can deny that the boy can fight. But that's only half of what he'll need for West Point. What about the entrance examinations? He'll have to pass them, won't he? Well, I for one don't believe that will happen. Why, just look at this ruffian; it's obvious that he has the brains of a dried cod."

Colonel Sumner eyed me appraisingly. "Hmmmm. Well, looks are sometimes deceptive, Mr. Duncan. Before he died, Lieutenant Greer— God rest his soul—mentioned to me that Travers here was unusually well educated for an enlisted man. He's had twelve years of school- ing. That's right, isn't it, Private?"

At first my mouth protested giving witness against myself, and no noise would come forth. But Colonel Sumner cleared his throat impa- tiently, and I croaked: "Almost, sir; I left school before graduation."

Mr. Duncan beamed triumphantly at this, but Colonel Sumner merely observed, "Graduation from a high school is not a requirement of the academy, Mr. Duncan. The only requirement is that the entrance ex- aminations are passed to the satisfaction of the faculty."

"Colonel, please, let's be honest, shall we," objected Duncan. "Even if I concede that the boy is modestly bright—and that's being inordi- nately generous, I think—those examinations have stymied better candidates than him. What's more, he probably hasn't been around books for months. The point is that he'll never pass the examinations."

This sober appraisal cheered me immensely. That was all there was to it, then. Duncan would just have to mosey off to the East with Alice in tow, and I would serve my time in the mill, and that would be the end of it. A finished chapter in my life. But Colonel Sumner was not ready to close the book just yet.

"I considered that, Mister Duncan, and you're right; if he took the examination tomorrow, he'd fail sure as he's standing here. That's why you need to send him to a preparatory school."

"Me?" stammered Duncan. "Send *him*—the very beast who attacked Alice—to *school?* Now you've completely crossed the line, Colonel!"

But Colonel Sumner was unruffled. "There's no other way. I know of several good preparatory schools in Highland Falls, the small vil- lage just south of the academy. A good friend of mine runs one, and I recommend him. I can arrange for an extended leave for Private Travers for the duration of his attendance. It'll be one of the best investments you ever made, Mister Duncan."

Colonel Sumner had put the matter in terms that Duncan understood. I saw Duncan's eyes narrow to slits as he considered both sides of the ledger. On the asset side, Alice could marry *and* be happy, a rare enough combination of events. On the debit side, there was the risk that Duncan would have to endure my society far into the future. But then on the asset side again, I had no prospects outside the army, and would probably have to follow the colors on the frontier for the rest of my days, and thus I would not be around to darken his threshold. Maybe, he allowed, this young lecher was officer material: After all, only half-wits stand in the open when guns are going off all around them.

These calculations ran through Duncan's brain in an instant; then, his mind made up, he smiled narrowly at Colonel Sumner. "Colonel, you've convinced me. The boy's a natural for a life of soldiering. I'll do my part. You can count on it."

"Fine, Mister Duncan," smiled Colonel Sumner in return. "I think we almost have an understanding. The last person we need to hear from on this matter is Private Travers. Travers, what are your views on Mister Duncan's gracious offer to put you through preparatory school?"

I cleared my throat. I wanted to put my case eloquently, to convince them both with cold logic and soaring oratory that the best course of action was to let bygones be bygones and to return me quietly to my lowly station in life. But that's not what came out; once I opened my lips, only a torrent of whining burst forth.

"West Point? Me? Impossible! First, I'll never pass the entrance examination even if you set a whole battalion of tutors on me. Oh sure, I was in school nearly twelve years, but I'm still nearly illiterate, and no tutor in the world can undo the damage wrought by years of academic indifference. Also, I'm not temperamentally suited to be a soldier. Honest to God, Colonel; my disposition is too delicate. It's true— I swear I joined the army only for the national bounty!"

Colonel Sumner interrupted. "National bounty? What the devil is that?"

"It's a figment of Sergeant O'Brien's imagination, dad-blame his carcass. It's how he lured fools like me to enlist. I'm not a soldier, sir, I'm just a mercenary. Don't send me to the Dude Fact—, er, West Point, sir. Believe me, it'll be a big mistake."

All this outburst did, however, was bring a smile to Duncan's lips.

He was first and foremost a businessman, and he was well schooled in settling thorny financial disputes. If his business experience had taught him anything, it was that a good settlement was like two porcupines rutting: Everyone got hurt a little if the thing was done right. Colonel Sumner's proposed resolution had galled him no end, but my outburst revealed that it promised to be sheer torture for me. And that was just dandy as far as Duncan was concerned.

"Well, Colonel," he chortled, "it looks as though we've got a deal here," and they shook on it. I was dismissed as they set about the remainder of their caballing, straightening up the details for getting me out of Arizona and back east and such.

Distressed beyond words, I trudged out of the office as First Sergeant Richmond eyed me coldly. As I staggered across the parade ground and back to my barracks, my mind reeled at the disaster that had befallen me. No, I told myself, this couldn't be happening. I clung to one slim hope: I would buttonhole the colonel after Duncan left and dissuade him from this insane scheme. Surely we could work out a compromise. True, he was a tough old bird, but he was fair in his own irrational way. Yes, I would get to him right after Duncan left.

Never fear, Fenny, I assured myself, you'll find a way to put this calamity aright.

14

West Point, New York
July 1893
"What's your name, Mister?" demanded the tall, menacing cadet who greeted me as I descended from the horse-drawn tram that had carried me from Highland Falls the short two miles to West Point.

"Why, it's Fenwick Travers . . ." I smiled hopefully, only to be ruthlessly upbraided.

"Wrong, ducrot!" screamed the cadet. "You don't have a first name anymore. Understand?" He thrust his chin directly into my face to emphasize his point. Ducrot, I quickly learned, was a pejorative applied to plebes.

"Y—yes!" I stammered in reply.

" 'Sir'!" he screamed. "You'll address me as 'sir' from now on, ducrot. Do I make myself clear?"

"Yes, sir!" I gulped.

Already I could feel the sweat streaming off my brow in the muggy July air. Needless to say, the Sumner-Duncan combination had proven too formidable for me. After a hurried departure from Fort Grant, I was at West Point, after having completed six months of preparatory school and received a presidential appointment. It was very unusual for any West Point preparatory school to accept a student after the term had begun, and only Colonel Sumner's influence had made that possible. I had been extensively tutored in mathematics, English, history, and chemistry, and was as ready as I ever would be to take the dreaded entrance examination, which would be administered here at the academy on the morrow.

"Get your neck in when an upperclassman addresses you," ordered my tormentor. He pushed his finger against my chin and drove it back toward my collarbone, forcing me to crank my chin against my Adam's apple until I was in the characteristic "brace" position of a West Point plebe. From the corner of my eye I studied the cadet as he stood sneering at me; he was a slender fellow, fair haired and about my height, but with a thin, almost cruel, face. It was not the bluff, honest visage of a soldier like Colonel Sumner, but rather the face of a born intriguer; it brought to mind images of the dandified courtiers who found employment in the European armies of yore. I knew immediately that I was dealing with an exceptionally unpleasant customer.

"I'll bet you're some kind of Yankee, ducrot. I'm right, aren't I?" demanded the upperclassman, his disdain for me obvious in his drawl. Another damned rebel, I thought; I was in trouble now.

"Ummph!" was all I could manage through my constricted larynx.

"I knew it. We've got too many of your type up here already. You can bet I'll be keeping an eye on you. If you've got some funny notion that you actually deserve to be in West Point, you can rest assured that I'll send you packing in short order. In fact, it would be my pleasure. Do I make myself clear?"

"Yes, sir!" I barked obediently.

"Travers, you're one sorry-looking sight. If there's anyone who can straighten you out, it's me, Joshua Longbottom. I'm your platoon leader, ducrot, the person who will completely rule your life for the foreseeable future. And believe me, if I can't straighten you out, I'll damned sure run you out." He chortled maliciously at the prospect of sending me packing.

I stood silently and gazed forlornly at the gray haze wafting over the turgid waters of the Hudson River. I felt as though I had just died and gone to hell.

"What's the matter, son, aren't you enjoying yourself?" laughed Longbottom snidely.

Longbottom took charge of me and marched me smartly over to the administration building. Once inside he escorted me to the adjutant's office and placed me at the end of a short line of other cadet candidates. In time I was ushered in to see the adjutant, a young and very trim officer, who reviewed my letter of appointment. It was a bit out of the ordinary and, as I expected, he spent a good deal of time studying it. He also reviewed my army record as I stood before him, nodding his head, and murmuring, "I see you're a sharpshooter, Mister Travers. That's very commendable."

Things must have been in order, for I was next marched down the hall for a physical examination. That being satisfactory in every respect, I was given an ill-fitting gray uniform, called a plebe skin, to wear in place of my civilian clothes. Next I was taken to a large waiting room to join other cadet candidates who had been found physically acceptable. Now we awaited only the entrance examination to determine if we would join the Long Gray Line.

No sooner had I entered this chamber than I got the biggest surprise of my life: There before me sat Charlie Hobart!

"Fenny!" he cried, springing up to grasp my hand. After a few hours at West Point, I gathered, any familiar face is a welcome sight. I was not quite as gratified to see him, but I remained civil nonetheless.

"I see your pa got you an appointment, Charlie," I observed levelly.

"He sure did," smiled Hobart. "He had to send a $500 contribution to Senator Palmer's last campaign, but he thinks it was a good investment."

"Well, the tuition should be a bargain over Harvard or Yale," I replied noncommittally.

"But you, Fenny, let's talk about you," insisted Charlie. "How did you come to be here? You never wrote or anything after I last saw you in Sent Looey."

My faced clouded over. "There was nobody to write to and nothing to be said anyway," I snapped. "You of all people should know that."

Hobart did, for he flushed red and hastily changed the subject. "I hear that the examination will be the first thing tomorrow morning. Are you . . . well, up to it, Fenny? No offense, but you were never exactly the studious type, you know."

"We'll see, Charlie" was all I said. I had been drilled to the sharpest academic edge I'd ever had, so much so that I was afraid to tilt my head lest some useful nugget spill out of my ear and roll irretrievably away. "Either I'm ready, or tomorrow will be the last you ever see of me."

The following morning we cadet candidates were herded in a shuffling, confused mass into the cadet mess hall. There the three-hour written examination was administered. It was tough, but I immediately saw that my months of preparatory school education had been right on the mark. I simply regurgitated the chemical equations and mathematical theorems I'd been force-fed and found that I was answering the questions quite satisfactorily. History and English were challenging as well, but I found no situation confronting me for which I had not been thoroughly prepared. When the command rang out to cease work, I felt that I had acquitted myself as well as possible in this phase of the examination. Although I was sure that I had set no new standards for academic excellence, I had definitely put a few slugs in the target. All that remained was the demanding and all-important oral examination.

We were tumbled out of the mess hall, formed into a column of fours, and marched off to a grove of trees across from the gray limestone library. Members of the academic board, ancient fellows resplendent in blue swallowtail coats, were seated there. The professors, each one looking as stern as the Almightly on Judgment Day, were arrayed behind a row of desks that had been carried out of doors for this occasion. Each desk was separated from the next by fifteen feet, and at a signal from a professor, a cadet candidate would advance, state his name, and stand at attention. The professor would then select a volume from a pile on the desk before him, turn to a particular page, hand the volume to the young man before him, and order the fellow to read aloud.

As he did so, the cadet candidate was judged on his deportment— his soldierly bearing—as well as his ability to read and project his voice. A fellow found wanting on deportment could be rejected even though he had scored well on the written examination. Similarly, a fellow who scored well on the oral examination could be accepted into the academy even if his written examination scores were only marginal.

I awaited my ordeal in silence, my palms wet and clammy and my throat as dry as the sands of Apacheria. What if I got some obscure text that forced my tongue to trip over my words? I wondered. Or worse yet, what if I had to read from some science textbook? It would be impossible to hold a steady rhythm and show a soldierly bearing while reading material that was totally incomprehensible to me. I would be consigned back to the wilds of Arizona with no chance of ever holding sweet Alice again.

Then I heard my name called. "Mister Travers!"

I stepped forward and awaited my destiny. The professor before me, a wizened old colonel with riveting eyes and a peg leg, handed me a much-worn book. It was opened to the first page. I glanced down at it and at once felt waves of relief flooding over me: I was staring at the first chapter of the *War Commentaries* of Caesar!

"Begin, Mr. Travers," instructed the aged professor in a dry rattle that sounded like the voice of doom.

And begin I did. I boomed out that Gaul, like an insect, had three parts. I rolled sonorously on about the Helvetii, the Suebi, and the Allobroges. I recounted the battle of the Saone River and the ultimate defeat of the perfidious Helvetii. On I orated about the Juras and Cisalpine Gaul and Transalpine Gaul. I was in familiar territory now, you see, and felt more as though I was partaking in a homecoming than enduring an arduous trial with the greatest possible stakes riding on the outcome. Confidence flowed through me, making my voice louder and clearer as I went on. Just as I paused to fill my lungs to expound upon that archfiend Ariovistus, I was interrupted.

"That will be enough, Mister Travers," rasped the ancient pedagogue. "Please accept my commendation on a splendid performance."

I was in, and I knew it; no other cadet candidate before me had elicited such a comment from this fossil. I returned to my place in the formation, serenely confident. At the end of the afternoon, we cadet candidates, accompanied by the drums and fifes of the Hellcats, the academy's bandsmen, were marched back to the "area," the plaza in front of our barracks. Our barracks was known in cadet lore as Beast Barracks, for as cadet candidates we were beasts, not yet part of the corps. Once we were there, the names of those who had failed the entrance examination were called out. As each name was called, that person stepped from the formation, entered the barracks to exchange his plebe skin for his civilian clothes, and prepared to return home in disgrace.

At the end of the roll call, I was still in formation. So was Charlie Hobart. A drum roll sounded, and a color guard marched to our fore, wheeled to face us, and halted. The color guard bore both the national colors and the army flag. The latter was dipped majestically so as to leave Old Glory flying supreme. The superintendent of the academy then materialized as if by magic before us and ordered us to raise our right hands. We did so and, by repeating after him, swore allegiance to the Constitution. Then it was over. I was a plebe. The superintendent departed, the drums and fifes roared out once again, and we new plebes were marched out onto the Plain, West Point's famous parade ground, to the summer encampment of tents, where senior members of the corps eagerly awaited to commence our education as cadets.

15

As I had immediately suspected, Longbottom and his fellow senior cadets, or firsties as they were known, made my life and that of every other member of the class of 1897 pure misery. Once in the tent encampment, we endured endless hours of close-order drill, marksmanship instruction, and foot-numbing marches across the rugged hills of the Hudson highlands. All the while we were subjected to verbal abuse and occasional physical assaults by our cadet leaders. I quickly decided that keeping up with the pack was more desirable than suffering the agony of those poor souls who for whatever reason were branded as slackers. These wretches went through the worst tortures the hazing system could devise. It was not at all unusual to see a plebe marching across the Plain at midnight staggering under the weight of a knapsack filled with rocks.

So I put my nose to the grindstone and kept it there. But despite the feverish pace, I had time to ponder my relationship with dear Alice and her uncle, Mister Duncan. It was the latter who occupied most of my thoughts, for a new notion had occurred to me after I left Arizona Territory. Although I was cool on the idea of marriage, even to as lovely a creature as Alice, I began to conceive the dream that someday I might finagle my way into a posh position within the Duncan business empire. I hadn't the foggiest idea of how to run a business, of course, and didn't particularly care to learn. What I wanted was a post with no real responsibility but one that would nonetheless pay me a salary large enough to allow me to live in the style to which I desired to become accustomed. In essence, what I wanted was a titular position where I could while away my hours gaming, hunting, drinking, and generally being a parasite on the corpus of American industry.

And why not? I thought. After all, Duncan did owe me something for saving his ears from Pedrolito that misty day not so long ago. If it hadn't been for me, he'd still be gathering mildew in some peon pueblo south of the border. Any fool could see that he was worth millions, so he'd never miss a few thousand a year funneled in my direction. In fact, I'd been toying with the idea of raising that very matter with Duncan when the unfortunate brouhaha about Alice made any rational conversation with the tightfisted tycoon impossible.

The worst part of all this was that I was being held incommunicado at West Point. I couldn't leave the grounds: Absence without leave was punishable as a violation of the Articles of War. The thought of rotting away in some stockade didn't appeal to me, so I stayed put. Instead of deserting, I wrote long, soulful letters to Duncan seeking his forgiveness and suggesting a release from my bondage. There were only terse, cool answers, so I tried writing directly to Alice. To my surprise, these letters were returned as undeliverable. I saw Duncan's hand in this and, as summer faded into fall and the first cool breezes began to blow down from Canada, I concluded that Duncan had me exactly where he wanted me: locked up in a monastery from which escape was impossible and where the future promised nothing except hard work and an early grave.

Ironically, however, as events unfolded it became clear that although I had no burning desire to become an officer, the officer corps was rapidly taking a shine to me. It wasn't long before I began to pick up little hints that I was one of the chosen in this martial world.

Even Longbottom, who had taken a visceral dislike to me the minute he laid eyes on me, grudgingly acknowledged my new status before summer encampment concluded. One day he braced my squad against a wall to dress us down for general incompetence and negligence. "When are you 'crots going to get cracking?" he demanded. "You are a disgrace to this fine academy. I'll bet a month's pay that Billy Sherman's bummers were more presentable than you feeble excuses for future officers. Why can't you be like Travers over there? He may not be the brightest thing to ever walk through the academy's front gate, and he wouldn't recognize military tactics if he tripped over them, but at least he looks like a soldier."

And Longbottom was right, by God. I did look every inch the soldier. My large handsome frame, chiseled features, and blond locks fit perfectly the popular notion of what an officer and a gentleman should look like. Attired in a formfitting dress-gray coat, complete with snowy white cross belts, a highly polished breastplate, a glistening black leather shako, and armed with a perfectly oiled Model 1870 cadet rifle, I was a stirring sight to behold. Even veteran officers, who should have known better, were gulled by my martial facade. "A sharp one, that young Mister Travers," they would tell each other when they thought I was out of earshot.

I quickly learned that the warrior caste exalted form over substance: No matter that I didn't have a warlike bone in my body, as long as I looked the part, I would be accepted as the beau ideal of the warrior. So I kept my mouth shut and let those around me—officers, upperclassmen, and fellow plebes alike—adopt me as the epitome of military excellence. In short, I was a natural at this game!

With the coming of fall, the sophomores and juniors, or yearlings and cows in West Point jargon, rejoined the corps. We plebes were released from the summer encampment and assigned to companies in the reconstituted Corps of Cadets. I went to Company C, where I was assigned to Longbottom's squad for the academic year. Along with Longbottom and me, the squad consisted of two mutinous cows who chafed under Longbottom's overbearing authority, and three acned yearlings who lorded it over me and the only other plebe in the squad, Charlie Hobart.

We quickly settled into the rhythm of academics and military ceremonies. On parade fields, where looks were everything, it soon became evident that I had no peer. I was a born flanker, as tall fellows at West Point were known, and was simply smashing in the succession of mass reviews, where gawking onlookers were dazzled by the precise ranks of young stalwarts marching across the Plain beneath snapping guidons and gleaming bayonets. Indeed, as time passed I became widely recognized within the corps as one of the most promising cadets in the class of '97.

Of course, fame always has its pitfalls, as I quickly learned in Major

Elliot's class on military history. Because of my outstanding leadership qualities, I had been designated as the section marcher. As such, it was my duty to march my fellow plebes to the class, get them seated, salute sharply when Major Elliot entered the room, and render an attendance report. All rather mundane stuff, you see, but the section marcher also had to sit right up front under the instructor's nose, and therein lay the seeds of a problem.

It was late afternoon on a raw March day, and Major Elliot was drawing to the close of a long-winded lecture on the Battle of Gettysburg. An unimposing little man with thinning hair and a weak chin, Major Elliot had a lecturing style that was as dry as dead leaves, and his class was a burden to endure.

Suddenly he was finished. "Are there any questions, gentlemen?" he asked primly.

I readied myself for the rush to the door, only to be brought up short by a question from behind: "Yes, I have one!" I heard a voice say.

A groan went up from the bored plebes. I turned to see who the miscreant could be. It was Charlie Hobart—no surprise there. In his first few months at West Point, Hobart had indisputably emerged as the class springbutt, academy jargon denoting that person in every class who seemed to be always raising his hand to ask useless questions and invariably delaying the class's departure in the process. As you can imagine, springbutts drew the ire of their fellows. Hobart, however, hadn't yet gotten that message.

"Yes, Mister Hobart," said Major Elliot.

"Sir," asked Hobart, rising deferentially as he spoke, "do you think that Longstreet's actions on the third day of Gettysburg were tactically sound? Don't you think that if his corps had moved more quickly in support of General Pickett, the charge might have succeeded?"

Eyes rolled at this and cadets surreptitiously made motions as if they were gagging. "Well, there's been much speculation to that effect," allowed Major Elliot, oblivious to the mass ennui around him. "Longstreet's behavior throughout the battle was reticent—he was hardly his usual energetic self, you know. Certainly he showed nothing like the élan he was to show a mere ten weeks later at the Battle of Chickamauga. So perhaps you're right, Mister Hobart. Maybe if Longstreet had moved forward with resolve on that third day, Pickett's Charge might have caused the Union center to give way."

Just then Major Elliot noticed me yawning widely and looking impatiently at the clock on the wall. "Perhaps you'll grace us with your views on this matter, Mister Travers," he said sharply.

"Wha . . . I—er, that is, I'm not sure I was following you there, sir," I stammered, taken totally unawares.

"Gettysburg, Mister Travers," said Major Elliot pointedly. "Longstreet, Pickett, the third day."

I got an unexpected reprieve in which to collect my thoughts when Hobart chimed in, "Yes, Fenny, what's your opinion? Do you think Longstreet lost the battle for the South?"

I cleared my throat, set my course, and plunged forward. "The third day of Gettysburg, hmmm? Well, as I see things, sir, it's totally irrelevant, at least as far as this class is concerned, what General Longstreet did some thirty years ago."

A roar of laughter greeted this and hoots of, "That Fenny, he's a card I tell you!"

I smiled all around with my best devil-may-care grin. Hobart wasn't smiling, of course; he was crestfallen. As the nephew of one of the survivors of that conflict, Hobart took all aspects of the Civil War very seriously.

Major Elliot wasn't amused either. He had served in the Union army and had lost most of his left hand in the trenches outside of Petersburg. For him the war had been a holy crusade, and to hear a callow youth commit such blasphemy in his presence, and within the hallowed halls of West Point to boot, was almost beyond enduring. His pale face turned a dangerous scarlet above the deep blue of his tunic, and for a moment I was afraid he'd burst a blood vessel. He fixed me with a piercing stare and hissed venomously, "Explain yourself, Mister Travers."

I immediately realized that I was skating on thin ice. "Well, it's like this, sir," I explained, the soul of reasonableness. "I don't think it will help any of us to mull over what General Longstreet did in the Civil War."

"What?" exploded Elliot. "You don't think the campaigns of the Civil War won't be long studied and emulated by future generations of American military leaders?"

I'd started out badly; the study of Civil War campaigns, and a deep veneration of the leaders who conducted them, bordered on being a cult fetish at West Point. Most cadets could rattle off obscure details about the life of Jeb Stuart the way children sang "The Twelve Days of Christmas." In the eyes of Major Elliot, I had defiled the holiest of holies.

"In principle, I suppose those campaigns will always be a subject of discussion and may have possible applications in the future," I allowed, defensively.

"Possible applications?" echoed Major Elliot, dismayed.

"But, sir," I insisted, "you must concede that the nature of war has changed greatly since then. Why, the French have invented an automatic rifle that fires so quickly it can mow down attackers by the hundreds. Longstreet never had to contend with anything like that. Also, I read in the newspaper that barbed wire may soon have a military application. If there had been barbed wire at Gettysburg, there wouldn't have been a Pickett's Charge in the first place."

"Newspaper, Mister Travers? From what newspaper did you glean this intelligence?" Elliot demanded, his voice dripping with disdain.

"Why, the *New York Journal,* sir. It was a great article—"

"Soldiers, Mister Travers, don't read newspapers!" thundered Major Elliot. Apparently I had inadvertently stumbled across another of his pet peeves. "I'm surprised at you, Travers. No wonder you're so woefully misinformed on military history. I strongly suggest you cease perusing such unseemly publications and confine your studies to learned treatises by recognized authorities in the field. Is that clear?"

"Yes, sir," I answered placatingly, steeling myself for a sharp riposte at my iconoclastic views. But, astonishingly, the matter of Gettysburg now seemed to have slipped Major Elliot's mind completely. Unbeknownst to anyone in the class, Major Elliot had received other less visible wounds in the war. Specifically, he had taken a nasty gash on the head from an exploding shell at Cold Harbor. The wound had healed, but thereafter whenever Major Elliot was goaded to fury, he completely forgot whatever matter happened to be at issue at the moment. When he cooled down, moreover, he had no distinct recollection of what it was that had infuriated him in the first place. Oh, Elliot would thereafter have a subconscious aversion to me, but he would never be able to recall precisely why.

So I, like my peers, sat there waiting for the other shoe to drop, but it never did. "This class is dismissed. Tomorrow we'll discuss Phil Sheridan's Shenandoah Valley campaign." With that Major Elliot drew himself up and marched out.

As soon as he was gone, life surged back into my classmates, who only seconds before had been shocked into complete silence. They crowded about me shaking my hand and clapping me on the back. "You certainly told him, Fenny," some said, while others whistled approvingly and laughed, "Our hats are off to you, Fenny," and similar banter.

Their acclaim was genuine, though; no cadet, let alone a mere plebe, could deliberately antagonize a commissioned officer without severe retribution. My survival was unprecedented and nothing short of miraculous. Hobart sidled up with his hand outstretched. "You certainly do know a lot about military developments, Fenny."

I ignored his proffered hand; instead, I jabbed him hard in the chest with my finger. "And I know a lot about thrashing loudmouthed little snots, Charlie," I growled.

The other plebes fell back at this confrontation, but I knew that there was no risk of fisticuffs; I had whipped Hobart before and had no doubt I could do it again. The fact that he was now a full head shorter and thirty pounds lighter than I only added to my confidence in that regard.

"I didn't mean anything by it, Fenny!" protested Hobart, backing away in alarm. "I just thought everyone would be interested." The arrogant Charlie Hobart of Elm Grove was gone; he had come to realize that I was the king of the roost here, and he would do my bidding or pay the penalty.

"Hobart, the next time you have a question in this class, you look at me. If I don't nod my head and smile from ear to ear at you, I want you to keep your damned mouth shut, understand?"

"Sure, sure, Fenny, I understand. It won't happen again, I promise," he assured me.

"Good," I huffed, giving a ferocious look around the room at my fellows. I was gratified to see that they were suitably impressed by my gruff demeanor. And with that I turned on my heels, leaving Hobart shaking his head in disbelief that anyone could truly be uninterested in the mental processes of General Longstreet at Gettysburg. Later that same day I took Hobart aside and told him in no uncertain terms that if the story of my illegitimate birth should be circulated around the academy for any reason, he would be the first person I would seek. "Remember that I get vicious along rivers, Charlie," I growled. Recalling the MacFee affair and that I had killed at least one man

already, Charlie gushed his wholehearted assurance of complete dis-
cretion in this matter, his quivering features convincing me that he
would remain silent.

And so the years at West Point passed. My encounter with Elliot
only served to elevate my already-rising stock with my peers. Hobart, far
from being repelled by my boorish behavior toward him, became my
devoted lackey for the remainder of our time at the academy. I dabbled
away at my studies all right, but never managed to rise above the bottom
of the class standings, mainly because the honor code made it so difficult to cheat at West Point. My popularity, however, ensured that my
intellectual deficiencies posed no impediment to achieving higher and
higher cadet ranks with each passing year. After all, I was the only member
of my class ever to have been cited for gallantry in action. By my first
year I was a cadet captain, and the ranking cadet in Company C.

As I progressed in stature, however, no corresponding desire for a
military career blossomed in my breast. The reasons for this were mani-
fold. First, although by nature I could be aggressive indeed if I felt
myself wronged, all the serious brawls in which I had thus far been
involved were essentially personal affairs. I was cold to the notion of
fighting and dying for something as impersonal as the nation or the
flag; if a particular tussle wasn't my personal fight, I wanted no part
of it. Further, despite Major Elliot's injunction, I had continued to read
newspapers, and what I read about wars around the world led me to
conclude that modern battle was certain to be lethal to any participants unfortunate enough to be in range of the formidable weapons
pouring forth from the assembly lines of England, France, and Germany. Thus, as May 1897 approached, the date for my graduation from
the academy, I did some hard thinking about my future after West Point.

There had been no possibility of a peace with Duncan. My few leaves
to Manhattan had been awkward occasions, and Duncan had been careful
to offer me no opportunity for reconciliation. On these occasions I asked
for Alice, only to be told vaguely that she was abroad and had been
for some years. Ironically, the feared damage to Alice's reputation had
never materialized; word of my liberties with her had never filtered
back east. Over the years, therefore, Duncan cooled noticeably to the
notion of a match between Alice and me, and rather than treating me
as a future son-in-law, he seemed intent on distancing himself from
me as much as possible.

I therefore turned my mind to making myself as safe and comfortable in the army as possible. I wouldn't object to a posting in the Quartermaster Corps—perhaps a cushy job in Washington somewhere. That might do, but I had been told that it got awfully hot in the District of Columbia in the summer, and so, after some deep thought, I finally fixed upon an even better solution. I decided to apply for a commission in the Coast Artillery. That corps had billets in New York harbor. The duty couldn't be too terribly difficult, I figured, since there'd be sergeants and privates about to do the real work, and the proximity to Duncan would allow me to resume my unending campaign to worm my way back into his good graces.

Thus, when Hobart popped his head into my room and yelled, "Let's go, Fenny, the assignment list has just been posted in First Division," I was up like a shot and out the door running. We bolted through the area with our hearts in our mouths; that list would affect our lives for years to come.

"I can't wait to see it," panted Hobart at my side. "I hope I get an infantry assignment. My uncle was in the infantry, you know."

"I hope you get your wish," I huffed back with all sincerity. The infantry was just what the little twit deserved.

We arrived at First Division and confronted a milling crowd of gray-clad cadets, all thronging about trying to read the same list. Because of my size I was held to the fringes, but Hobart, being more wiry, was able to slip forward through the press of bodies.

"Can you read it, Charlie?" I cried.

"Yes, yes, I can!" he called.

"Well, what does it say, goddammit?" I demanded in frustration.

"Let's see—Thorton, Toll, ah yes, Travers," he read.

"Where am I going?" I pleaded.

"Great news, Fenny!" he yipped.

"Then it's the Coast Artillery for me?" I cried in relief.

"Even better; you're for the infantry! The 9th Infantry Regiment, Plattsburgh Barracks, New York."

Plattsburgh? My God, that was on Canada's front porch!

"Hold on, Fenny, there's even more great news!" called Hobart excitedly. "I'm being posted to the 9th with you. Isn't that grand? We'll be together for years!"

16

"Hey, Fenny, have you heard the news?" I turned to see Hobart standing in the door of the company arms room. As the company supply officer, I was tasked to count the unit's Krags once each month to ensure that our poverty-ridden enlisted men didn't steal any and hustle them over the Canadian border for a quick sale.

"I haven't heard a damn thing since I came into this godforsaken vault this morning," I replied, more irritated with Hobart than usual since he had just made me lose count.

"It's the battleship *Maine,* Fenny! She's gone down in Havana harbor. This means war for sure!" cried Hobart jubilantly.

"What? War? What the hell are you talking about?" I demanded with alarm.

"War with Spain!" whooped Hobart. "It just came over the wire. Colonel Liscum's called a meeting of all officers at headquarters immediately. Looks like we'll be on our way to Cuba directly!"

"Cuba?" I bawled, thoroughly alarmed. I jumped up and grabbed my fur cap and greatcoat. "Corporal," I called to the armorer, "take over until I get back."

This worthy nodded in my direction and fired a noxious wad of tobacco into the bean tin that served as the spittoon in the arms room. I took this to be a "Yes, sir," and departed with Hobart on my heels.

Halfway across the parade ground we were joined by 1st Lt. Joshua Longbottom, his tall figure ramrod straight as usual. When Hobart and I arrived at Plattsburgh Barracks last summer following our graduation from West Point, we'd found our former Beast Barracks platoon leader already with the 9th. To make matters worse, we were both assigned to the same company—Company A—with Longbottom. Hobart saluted as we joined Longbottom since he was senior to us; I didn't.

"Good morning, Joshua," hailed Hobart. "Did you hear the news?"

"Yes," Longbottom answered curtly as we fell in beside him. Longbottom, Hobart, and I were the junior officers of Company A, which was under the unsteady command of Captain Harris. Longbottom functioned as the second in command and took over whenever Captain Harris was absent. Although we were all commissioned officers now, there was no friendly camaraderie between Longbottom and us, for Longbottom viewed Hobart and me as his inferiors just as we'd been back at West Point, and he tried never to let us forget it. "This *Maine* incident sounds damn dicey to me," allowed Longbottom with uncharacteristic openness as we walked briskly along.

"Come now, Joshua, you can't be serious," exclaimed Hobart. "Why, the Spanish Empire is a rotten melon. If there's war, we'll go through those dagos so fast they won't know what hit them." When it came to holding forth on things about which he knew nothing, Hobart had few equals.

"We'll see about all that when the time comes," replied Longbottom noncommittally. "There's a lot of things that can go wrong in war."

Despite my instinctive aversion to him, I had to admit that Longbottom was a realist; he wanted advancement all right, but that would come only in a successful war. He'd had sufficient time to take the measure of the 9th, and he was none too confident that our fight with Spain would be a cakewalk.

"Oh, pshaw!" countered Hobart. "What could go wrong in a war against Spain? I say we ought to go down to Cuba as soon as possible and settle this thing man to man. It would take only a few weeks at most. Isn't that right, Fenny?" he asked, looking to me for support.

I shrugged my shoulders. "Could be, Charlie" was all I could manage. In truth my mind still spun at the thought of a war that involved me personally. I knew that Duncan would be thoroughly pleased to see me off to some malarial swamp where I could be extinguished by fever or a stray bullet. But I'd be damned if I'd let him get rid of me that easily; I'd resist any effort by the army to drag me off to Cuba. Just how I'd accomplish that eluded me, but I'd find a way somehow.

We reached the red brick headquarters building and clambered up the wooden steps. The front door was open and the large antechamber outside the commanding officer's office was crammed with blue-clad officers chattering excitedly among themselves. We arrived not a moment too soon, for at that instant the commander's door flew open and a sharp cry of "Attention!" brought a measure of order to the room. In strode Col. Emerson H. Liscum, the flinty old Hoosier in command of the 9th, his demeanor as grim as that of Abraham at the altar. Indeed, the snowy hair above his stark features and his flowing white mustache gave him the look of an Old Testament prophet. At his side was Major Whittaker, his second in command, a tall, kindly fellow cursed with the look and clumsy manner of a tamed orangutan. At the sight of the colonel, the excited buzz instantly abated.

"As you all know," commenced Colonel Liscum, "things have heated up in Havana. The addlepated navy has managed to get one of its tubs blown sky high, so it looks like war at last."

A great cheer went up at this.

"Pipe down, you idiots!" snarled Liscum. "Let's see how damned cheery you are after we get to Cuba!"

Silence immediately prevailed again at this rebuke. Liscum eyed us all sharply and tugged at his mustache for effect before continuing. "Now the first question in your little minds, I'm sure, is how this to-do will affect the 9th."

All those around me nodded affirmatively at this; I didn't, since my first question was how this war would affect my own hide. "For starters," continued Liscum, "training will pick up immediately. I've seen so little meaningful activity around this post of late that I believe most of you have forgotten what a rifle looks like, much less how to use one."

We suffered this affront in silence. Anyone assigned to the 9th for more than a few days knew that Colonel Liscum, a caustic misanthrope and a blooded veteran who had won his spurs in the Civil War, was capable of hurling nonstop insults regardless of the company or the subject under discussion. "I've given Whittaker here a list of every martial skill this regiment needs to master in order to quickly become a formidable fighting unit."

Whittaker dutifully waved a sheet of paper over his head, and Liscum continued. "Volley firing. This regiment doesn't know how to fire in volleys. We need to work on timing so that the men in the rear ranks don't blow the heads off the men in the front rank."

Volley firing? I wondered. What need had we of learning how to volley fire with breech-loading rifles? Besides, in order to fire in volleys, we'd have to stand in nice neat lines, which the Spanish could blow apart with their modern artillery. I saw my concern reflected in the furtive looks exchanged by some of the other officers standing near me.

"Close-order drill," Liscum announced next. "The key to volley firing is proper alignment, and there's nothing as effective for instilling an instinct for alignment in troops than close-order drill. I'm going to personally see to it that the 9th becomes the most aligned regiment in the dad-burned army." Or at least the most maligned regiment, I told myself, as Liscum continued forcefully. "So I want mass formations marching to drums. The stiffening effect of drums on the men can't be overestimated. . . ."

By then I had stopped listening. Volley firing, close-order drill, drums—things were going to be as bad as I had feared. The old fool was intent on handling the 9th as though it were on its way to Virginia to raze the Shenandoah Valley anew. What was more worrisome, however, was the number of officers who stood there and nodded their heads in approval at Liscum's discourse on tactics. These dolts had evidently learned well at the feet of Major Elliot and others of his ilk.

Captain Harris, of course, was among these, bobbing his head in vigorous approval at every word uttered by Colonel Liscum. He was a short, rumpled man with an unkempt collection of whiskers sprouting from beneath his bulbous nose in a manner that he took to be a mark of martial ferocity. Harris's hirsute display, however, disheveled and bedraggled as it was, failed to have its intended effect. Instead it gave him the look of a marmot suffering from distemper, an impression that was heightened by the fact that Harris perpetually wore that surly expression affected by the incurably stupid whenever they are raised above their station in life. The purple veins on his nose, engorged from years of heavy drinking, did nothing to ameliorate Captain Harris's thoroughly seedy aspect. I had disliked him from the moment I first laid eyes on him, and during my months here in Plattsburgh Barracks I had no occasion to alter that initial impression. Even Longbottom, a consummate bootlicker, had difficulty disguising his repugnance for Captain Harris.

In short, Captain Harris was a walking mélange of the most objectionable traits possible in an officer; he was loud, vulgar, and possessed of a mediocre intellectual capacity, with a physique to match. Morally he was bankrupt; it was well known that he extorted money from his troopers in exchange for favors like passes and promotions. Moreover, his addiction to hard liquor was fearsome to behold. When Harris got liquored up he was meaner than a Comanche with hemorrhoids. Drunk or sober, he was shunned by his fellow officers and avoided by the common soldiers.

As Colonel Liscum droned on, Harris sidled alongside me; Longbottom and Hobart shifted uneasily in his presence.

"This is it, Travers," he snickered, showing crooked yellow teeth.

"War at last. God, how I've waited for this. Now we'll see just what you're made of, Lieutenant."

Harris would have been tickled to know that I too was wrestling with that very thought at the moment, mindful that the penalty for cowardice in the face of the enemy was death. But I was determined to keep up a brave front, if only to spite Harris. "And perhaps we'll see exactly what you're made of *again,* sir," I countered nonchalantly. I smiled cheerfully at Captain Harris, having discovered by pure happenstance that he became infuriated whenever an intended victim remained calm while enduring one of his sadistic little attacks.

Sure enough, Harris's coarse features began to redden. I could tell from the way his piglike little eyes bored into mine that he had gotten the point of my quip. I was referring to a morsel of information I'd picked up shortly after joining the company. Harris had a habit of regaling new officers with tall tales of his exploits on the frontier during the Indian wars. To hear him brag, you'd think that Harris was personally responsible for bringing the warlike Sioux to their collective knees. So after I'd suffered through a number of his boasting sessions, I had made some discreet inquiries about my illustrious leader. It seems that the regimental surgeon, an octogenarian civilian who provided contract medical services to the army, had been on campaign with Captain Harris in 1890 during the last great Sioux uprising. One day I mentioned idly to the old fellow that Captain Harris had apparently been a great hero of that campaign.

"Harris?" snorted the surgeon. "Is that old dog telling lies agin?"

"Lies?" I asked innocently. "Whatever can you mean?"

"The only warriors Harris ever saw up close were the miserable wretches that real soldiers rounded up and put on reservations," guffawed the surgeon. "I was with Harris at Wounded Knee, and I know how the gallant captain handles himself under fire."

"And how is that?" I pried gently.

"Like a dang lily-livered varmint!" hooted the surgeon, spitting a great wad of tobacco juice onto the floorboards at his feet for emphasis. "I was there when we went to arrest Black Foot, the Sioux war chief. There was a motley band around Black Foot who stupidly put up a fight and we cut 'em down. 'Twarn't much of a fight, though; there was hundreds of us and only a handful of starvin' Injuns. That's why we were surprised—we figured the Sioux would come along peacefully. I guess Harris was surprised too, because at first he pushed up to the front ranks to seize ahold of what he thought was a pack o' whupped Injuns."

"Then what happened?" I asked eagerly.

"Then all hell broke loose, sonny, like it usually does when civilized folks try to reason with savages. One thing led to another and before you could fart there was gunplay. Old Harris, he looked like he was going to expire from anxiety right on the spot. He was a-screaming like a cat on fire and commenced to high-stepping to the rear before the first bodies could hit the ground. I ran for cover, too, you can be sure, but not before I got an eyeful of Harris. He was a-dodging lead like a goose flying over Chesapeake Bay in November—and screaming for mercy all the while. Why, even the Sioux were laughing at him."

"Did he get hit?" I asked.

"Not on your life, sonny," chortled the surgeon. "Harris may look like a sack of meal, but on that day he was too danged fast for those bullets. He stampeded right out of our ranks and dove under a supply wagon in the rear. We didn't see hide nor hair of him until the last of them Sioux was laid out dead on the frozen ground. So the next time your high an' mighty Captain Harris spins his Injun-fighting yarns, you just whittle him down a peg or two with the real story."

And I had done just that. The next time Harris boasted of his Indian-fighting prowess, I asked pointedly: "Tell me, sir, did the manual of arms in 1890 require that officers inspect the undercarriages of supply wagons at the first sound of musketry?"

The malevolent glare this drew from Harris told me my barb had struck home. From that moment on, I was on his list; our relationship quickly deteriorated from mutual disdain to open antagonism.

Suddenly something in Liscum's litany caught my attention. "One more thing, gentlemen," he said. "I've been ordered to select one officer for detached duty in the War Department in Washington, D.C. Apparently the department needs officers to perform administrative duties to prepare the army for deployment to Cuba." Translated, that meant the dozen or so pensioners who normally rambled around the bowels of the War Department had been so overwhelmed by this emergency that there was a distinct possibility the army would never even be able to draw up a plan to get itself over the sea to Cuba.

"Now I realize that every officer in this room wants to be with the troops," continued Colonel Liscum. "It would be a shame for anyone to have to miss out on this truly wonderful opportunity. But I must have one volunteer, or I shall be forced to draw lots. That's all gentlemen. Dismissed!"

Instantly the door flew open and a blue torrent spilled from the room into the chilly air. A good-natured bantering broke out as officers boasted among themselves about whose company would be whipped into shape first while here and there young lieutenants could be seen imploring their captains not to send them off to that awful job in the War Department now that the nation's hour of glory was at hand. Their place was at the front with the troops, they argued.

I, to the contrary, propelled myself against the tide toward Major Whittaker. Like a salmon swimming upstream, I pressed forward until I broke through the sea of humanity. "Major Whittaker, may I have a moment, sir?" I implored, pulling at his sleeve. "I'll volunteer to go to Washington, sir."

He eyed me in his distracted way. "Ah, young Travers," he mouthed. "And how are things in A Company?"

"Fine, sir," I lied easily. "About that assignment to Washington, sir. I'll go."

"Hmmm," intoned Whittaker ponderously as I waited impatiently—now I could appreciate why Colonel Liscum had such little patience with this fool. "Are you quite sure about this, Travers?"

"Absolutely, sir," I beamed confidently.

"But why, Travers? Don't you realize that you might miss out on one of the most exciting moments in our history? After all, times of actual conflict are few and far between, and any career-minded officer would be well advised to ensure that he's been on at least one campaign." He paused and eyed me sympathetically. "I'd heard about your record at the academy, Travers. A very good record indeed. Yes, we were all pleased to hear you were coming to the 9th. So your request to leave now, on the eve of battle, *is* a bit surprising, especially when there are other officers in A Company better suited for this detached duty."

I knew he was referring to Charlie Hobart, who already had a well-deserved reputation as the regimental nincompoop. Then a thought occurred to Whittaker and his simian eyes lit up with concern for me: "Travers, you're not, er, that is, I mean, you're not perhaps unsure about how you'll behave under fire, are you?" Whittaker stretched out a long thin arm and solicitously laid an enormous hand on my shoulder, his sad brown eyes set in a look of paternal concern.

My God, I thought wildly, this monkey's on to me! Was I that transparent? I fought to regain my composure and plunged on. "Not at all, sir, and I must say that I'm deeply disappointed that the thought even crossed your mind! I'd no idea that by answering the colonel's call for a volunteer I would have my honor impugned in this way!"

Whittaker recoiled at this. "I intended no such thing, Lieutenant Travers!" he stammered, his hand distractedly going to the top of his bald pate, making him look for all the world like an ape confronting a snake. "I would never question your honor. Such was not my intent. I merely—"

But now that I had the initiative, I pressed home. "Sir, I only offered my services as a concerned officer. I know that any lieutenant in the regiment would be crushed to leave the 9th at a time like this. For that reason I offered to take the burden on my own shoulders. I intended nothing more."

"Well, that certainly is a commendable thought," answered Whittaker shakily, anxious to leave the subject of my honor. "But what about Captain Harris? What does he say about all of this?"

It was a good question, and it deserved a good answer. Since I didn't have one, I lied again. "I know Captain Harris well enough to be able to say that he'll do what's best for the regiment. Even if that means having me on detached duty."

"Well, that would be very fair-minded of Harris," allowed Whittaker. He was silent a moment, thinking all this over.

I didn't want him to regroup his faculties, so I put a few more chips on the table. "In addition to having Captain Harris's almost-certain approval, I'm uniquely qualified for such a job."

"Oh, how's that, Travers?" queried Whittaker.

"I have an extensive background in the Romance languages, sir," I replied briskly, referring, of course, to the vocabulary of choice vulgarities I'd garnered during my service in Arizona.

"A knowledge of foreign languages is certainly an important asset for a staff officer," agreed Whittaker. He pondered a few more moments and then said, "Very good, Lieutenant Travers. Your request seems in order. I'll speak to Colonel Liscum about it."

I was about to fawn all over Whittaker in abject gratitude when Colonel Liscum swept back into the room. He had on his wide-brimmed felt campaign hat and was strapping on his saber. "Let's go, Major," he ordered. "Time's a-wasting."

"Yes, sir," replied Whittaker obediently, all thought of my entreaty shelved for the moment. He grabbed his own hat from the peg on the door and hurried out on Liscum's heels. I watched him go and hoped he did not completely forget about my request. Breaking the news of my departure to Harris would be the first true joy I'd experienced since I arrived in Plattsburgh!

17

Plattsburgh Barracks, New York
March 1898

"Skirmishers forward! Deploy in open order!" bellowed Captain Harris through his walrus mustache. At once, A Company skirmishers, arrayed in the prescribed thin line for sniping, plodded forward toward an imaginary foe for the hundredth time that day. They swept toward a distant tree line and when they neared it, plopped to their bellies in the snow and went through the motions of reaching for cartridges from their cartridge boxes, loading their rifles, sighting, and firing. "Bang!" I could hear them say wearily each time they squeezed their triggers. Behind them the rest of the company formed two ranks and also went through the motions of firing at nonexistent Spaniards.

The movements looked precise enough to me, but Captain Harris groaned aloud to his lieutenants at what he saw. "They're rusty, gentlemen! Too damn rusty. You can be sure that I don't intend to take an untrained mob that doesn't even know how to align itself properly down to Cuba!" He turned and glared angrily at us junior officers. "Officers, walk the ranks to make corrections!" he barked. "I want even, straight ranks, damnit!"

Listlessly, Hobart, Longbottom, and I ranged along the shivering ranks of troopers, aligning the poor buggers as ordered. We moved a man here and a squad there until Captain Harris was satisfied that the company was "properly aligned to the goddamn manual."

Now, with the faint sun setting in the west and black shadows advancing in the heavy woods around us, Harris at last seemed satisfied. "First Sergeant," he called to First Sergeant Richmond—yes, First Sergeant Richmond—"get 'em up and march 'em back to the billets. Have 'em formed up right after reveille tomorrow for a twenty-mile march."

That had been another surprise in store for me when I arrived at Plattsburgh. First Sergeant Richmond had transferred from the 25th

Infantry when that regiment had departed Arizona during the years I was at West Point. He had rejoined his original regiment, the 9th Infantry, and had come to roost as the first sergeant of Company A. If my elevation over him caused any displeasure, he hid it well; he was careful to comport himself with at least superficial respect toward me at all times. Yet try as he might to hide his true feelings, I knew that First Sergeant Richmond still couldn't abide me. His antipathy toward me, however, was only a pale shadow of the repugnance I knew he felt for Captain Harris and Harris's petty extortion schemes.

"Yes, suh," replied Richmond with a salute and then trudged to the fore of the deployed company. The weary troops eyed Richmond expectantly. "Get to yer feet!" he bellowed, hot steam from his lungs blossoming in the frigid air. The men staggered to their feet numbly. "Fall in!" he ordered. "The last man will be shovelin' shit from the colonel's nag's stall all night!"

Richmond was instantly enveloped in a sea of blue as the fagged troopers scurried into march order to avoid doing extra duty. As soon as the jostling ceased, Richmond ordered the men to shoulder their rifles and was about to march them off when Harris called out, "First Sergeant, what's the name of the last man?"

At this, several fellows who were clearly later than their mates screwed up their faces into pained expressions.

Richmond stopped and stared at Captain Harris, his flat face impassive. At length he spoke. "Can't rightly say, suh. The light's so poor, I couldn't see."

"Damnit!" swore Harris. "That's what I mean. We're too damned soft for war. When you make a threat, by God, carry it out, or these louts won't fear you. I'm disappointed, First Sergeant, very disappointed."

"Yes, suh," drawled First Sergeant Richmond, his stolid face reflecting his utter indifference to Harris's disappointment.

"Get 'em out of here!" ordered Harris disgustedly. First Sergeant Richmond saluted once more and marched his "louts" off into the growing night.

We officers dutifully clustered around Captain Harris, anxious to get out of the biting cold but too deferential by training and nature to quit the field before him. As I unsuccessfully fought to keep my teeth from chattering, I noticed that Harris was weathering the cold quite well—due in no small part to the numerous nips of whiskey he'd sneaked from the flask inside his greatcoat throughout the long day whenever he thought he wasn't being watched. I didn't damn him for drinking on duty—that was common enough, God knew—but I was mightily put out by the fact that he'd not offered me a swallow.

With his belly aglow from all his imbibing, Harris was in the mood for a speech. "As far as I'm concerned, this company is no better trained for battle than it was a month ago. There's no sense of urgency in the men, or," here he glared at us meaningfully, "their leaders."

Hobart looked shocked at this barb. It presaged a poor efficiency rating, which was, of course, the death knell of any officer who aspired to higher rank. Longbottom merely returned Harris's glare coolly and impassively while I grinned like an idiot.

"But, sir," protested Hobart, "that's not fair of you! I for one have tried my hardest to impress the men with the importance of these drills—"

"Then your best ain't good enough, Hobart!" snapped Harris, clearly pleased at having evoked a reaction from at least one of us. "Between your feeble efforts and Travers's constant back-stabbing, I'd be better off with no junior officers in the company than the likes of any of you."

Oh, ho, I thought! So Captain Harris keeps his ear to the ground about me after all! Both Hobart and Longbottom shifted uncomfortably in the face of this public airing of my slanders against Harris. I, on the other hand, was composed, almost serene, in the face of Captain Harris's accusation. With a sly smile, I took evasive action.

"Now, sir," I soothed in a deliberately patronizing tone, "I'm afraid you've been giving credence to groundless tales. I've never been the least bit disloyal to you."

"You're a damned liar, Travers!" fired back Captain Harris. "You didn't hear me stop outside Lieutenant Hobart's quarters last night while you ran me down in front of your peers. I heard you repeat that same stale falsehood about Wounded Knee that seems to fascinate you so damned much."

He had me dead to rights, the bat-eared bastard. But rather than being appalled at being exposed as a liar, I sensed an opportunity. I wanted out of the 9th Regiment, and now seemed like a perfect time to make Captain Harris want to see me off as well.

"You've got me there, sir. It's true I was telling lies behind your back. But it could have been much worse—I could have told the truth!"

Harris's face reddened with fury, and he squared up to me with balled fists. For a second I thought he would strike me, but I felt no fear;

the thought of trading punches with the puny Captain Harris was hardly daunting. In fact, the only man in the company whom Harris could probably manhandle was Hobart. So not only was I not afraid of tangling with Harris, I positively welcomed a tussle. It would be perfect if Harris struck me, for in that case I would demand that charges be filed, and Colonel Liscum would undoubtedly hustle me off to another post—hopefully the War Department—to bury the scandal.

"I ought to knock you flat on your ass, Travers!" Harris screamed.

Hobart was all a-twitter at this unseemly confrontation. "Now, Captain Harris, I'm sure Lieutenant Travers meant no disrespect."

"Right you are, Charlie," I affirmed with a smirk. "I meant no disrespect. What I meant was utter contempt."

Now Hobart blanched, but the shadow of a smile crossed Longbottom's face—whether it was from seeing Captain Harris discomfited so, or whether from seeing my career end, or both, I didn't know.

As for Harris, he was thunderstruck; his mouth moved but no sound came. He pointed at me with an incredulous expression on his debauched face as he fought to regain his power of speech until at last he was able to croak, "Okay, Travers, we'll see what you're made of when we get to Cuba! I know that you want me to nursemaid you through this fight with Spain. When you first got here, I thought you had potential. Colonel Liscum and Major Whittaker told me I was lucky to get you in Company A because of your sterling reputation at West Point and out west. But in the last several months you've given me absolutely no indication that you can soldier. I doubt if you'll bear up when the lead starts to fly."

A belief I tended to share, but of course I said no such thing; instead I remained silent before Harris, rocking on my heels nonchalantly. My smug attitude infuriated him further, as I knew it would, for he screamed hysterically, "I know you're counting on me to save your bacon, Travers! You don't have a manly bone in your body!"

"Captain, please," interjected Longbottom, finally becoming embarrassed at this tawdry scene. "Haven't you made your point?"

"Silence!" ordered Harris, keeping his beady little eyes on me. "One more comment from you and you're on report, Longbottom!"

My needling had nearly unhinged Harris, for he reached under his greatcoat, produced his flask openly, and took a long pull. His face was a dangerous scarlet now from the combination of the biting wind and the whiskey. He corked the flask and tore into me anew. "I've had it up to here with your snide ways, Mister. When we get down to Cuba, I intend to expose you for the cur you are. You'll be on your own, Travers."

With that he abruptly turned on his heels. He almost fell in the snow, but recovered with an effort before staggering off to the bar at the officers' mess. The thought crossed my mind to pounce on him then and there and strangle the stale air out of his lungs. But my strong instinct for self-preservation restrained me; after all, there were two witnesses.

"Damned petty tyrant," spat Hobart when Harris was safely out of earshot. "But, Fenny, you must admit you deliberately goaded him."

I smiled bravely for his benefit and said, "It's the principle of the thing, Charlie. Harris thinks he can damn well run my life for me, and I don't like it one little bit."

Longbottom eyed me with disapproval. "Most captains do tend to run their lieutenants' lives, Travers. That's the way the army functions, something I thought you might have learned at West Point. Now, if you'll excuse me, I intend to retire for the evening. We have an early day tomorrow."

I watched Longbottom march off through the swirling snow toward Officers' Row, knowing he was secretly pleased that I was the object of Captain Harris's wrath: It saved him the trouble of trying to make my life miserable.

What he didn't know, however, was that I intended to settle matters with Harris once and for all. "Charlie, it's been a long day," I said with deliberate calm. "Can I stand you to a drink?"

Hobart readily agreed, so we headed for the officers' mess in Harris's wake. The officers' mess at Plattsburgh Barracks was a large brick structure that housed a dining room and a comfortably appointed saloon. The fare was simple but good, and the drinks were reasonably priced. Since many of the officers were bachelors, the mess was their home, and certain rules of decorum were always observed. For instance, officers did not talk about business in the mess, and one never, ever spoke rudely to or about fellow officers within those hallowed halls.

On a cold night such as this, the favorite spot in the club was in front of the roaring fire in the saloon. On the paneled wall above the hearth were trophies from wars and skirmishes past—swords, flags, Indian shields, and feathered headdresses. When we arrived, Harris was already ensconced before the fire, clutching a half-drained glass of whiskey and holding forth on some Indian campaign in which I was sure he'd never participated.

"Watch this," I whispered to a perplexed Hobart and handed him my hat and coat. I ordered a bourbon and branch water at the bar and then sidled over to where Harris sat.

"There must have been a hundred of them painted hellions pouring over the hill straight for us," he was recounting to a bored captain who pointedly drew his timepiece from his vest and eyed it. "We knew we'd have to make every bullet count. If we wasted our lead, we'd be goners!"

"Fascinating," I gushed from over Captain Harris's shoulder.

Harris stopped short and stared up at me. "I'm surprised to see you here, Travers," he growled. "I'd have thought you'd be at your quarters studying the drill manual, which you've apparently forgotten— or never bothered to learn in the first place."

"Haw, haw!" I laughed easily. "Such a wit."

My interruption gave Harris's captive audience a chance to escape. "Gentlemen, I must be off," breathed the captain with a sigh of relief, springing to his feet. "I bid you good night."

As the captain hurried away, Harris and I eyed each other out of earshot of the others. "Captain Harris," I declared with mock humility, "I came here to apologize. I'm afraid my behavior today was completely unforgivable."

"You'll get no argument from me on that!" snorted Harris, a triumphant ring to his voice.

"And I propose to mend my ways here and now, sir. I'll begin by telling you a sidesplitting joke, which I've been told came from the lips of Colonel Liscum himself."

"The colonel himself, you say?" queried Harris, his interest piqued. Captain Harris was a natural toady, and anything that interested Colonel Liscum interested him.

"Indeed," I assured him.

"Let's have it then, Travers," he demanded.

"Well, it goes like this: I'll pretend I'm knocking at your door. And when I do, you say, 'Who's there?' Understand?"

"I suppose so," groused Harris. "But it sounds like a damn-fool joke to me."

"Not at all," I assured him. "Liscum was quite taken with it, I've been told."

Kissing his well-founded mistrust of me good-bye, Harris said, "Oh, all right, then."

"Very well," I smiled. "Here it goes. Ready?"

"Ready," replied Harris, and he drained his glass.

"Knock, knock," I began.

"Who's there?" said Harris on cue, clearly expecting a punch line. I merely repeated, "Knock, knock."

Perplexed a bit, Harris dutifully repeated the question, "Who's there?"

But I merely led him on further. "Knock, knock," I again repeated.

His short fuse now entirely burned, Harris shouted, "Who's there, goddamnit?"

"Colonel Liscum, you bastard!" I shouted, at the same time lashing out with a straight right that sent the amazed Captain Harris toppling from his chair and crashing to the carpet.

"Umph!" he grunted as he hit, his glass spinning away to shatter on the bricks of the hearth.

Pandemonium instantly broke loose. Hobart was between us, and others were dragging the befuddled Captain Harris to his feet. Harris rubbed his jaw tenderly and blubbered, "He struck me! You all saw it! He struck a superior officer! I want him placed under arrest!"

Outraged looks were cast my way; for a second it looked as though I might be clapped into irons straightaway. But then I put the second part of my plan into action. "Sure I struck him!" I admitted, gesturing disdainfully at Harris. "But any other Hoosier here would have done the same. I couldn't let him stand there and speak ill of Colonel Liscum and all the other Hoosiers in the regiment!"

A gasp went up from the assembly at this accusation.

"What?" squawked Harris wildly. "I never did any such thing!"

Then Major Whittaker was among us. He was determined to get to the bottom of any alleged slander against the irascible Liscum. It would be Whittaker's head if the truth wasn't ferreted out immediately.

"Is what Travers says true?" he demanded of the officers surrounding us. Many merely shrugged their shoulders; they'd been too far away to hear the exchange between Captain Harris and me.

Then Hobart spoke up. "I think Lieutenant Travers is telling the truth, sir. I couldn't hear everything that was said, but I definitely heard Captain Harris mention Hoosiers, and then Lieutenant Travers mentioned Colonel Liscum."

"That's right," chimed in another lieutenant. "Right before Travers struck Captain Harris, I heard the captain mention Hoosiers and then a profanity."

Others began nodding their heads, and Harris was suddenly very much on the defensive. "But that's not what happened at all!" he attempted to explain. "It was all a joke. Travers, tell them, for God's sake!"

He was silenced by a curt gesture from Major Whittaker. "This is disgraceful. Officers brawling in the mess. But even more seriously, a captain speaking disrespectfully about the regimental commander. This will not do," he clucked. "This will not do at all."

"You're damned right it won't!" averred a voice behind us. It was Liscum; he had entered the mess unnoticed during the turmoil I'd created.

"Attention," called Whittaker, but everyone ignored the command except himself.

"So you don't care for Hoosiers, Captain?" demanded Liscum, glowering ominously at the cowering Captain Harris.

"No-no-no, er, I mean, yes, sir," stammered Harris miserably. I smiled inwardly at his discomfiture; I had the bastard properly twisting in the wind.

I decided that it was time to drive in the final nail. "That's not the tone he took a moment ago," I piped up. "Captain Harris said that Indiana boys will cut and run at the first hint of trouble in Cuba."

An angry rumble went around the room. Many of the 9th's officers besides Liscum were from Indiana, as were many of the enlisted men.

"He didn't!" breathed Major Whittaker, astounded.

"Oh, yes, he did," I assured him. "I told him that the colonel was from Indiana, a fact I believe was already known to him. I demanded he retract his scandalous remark, but he refused. Instead he repeated it in a louder voice."

"That's right, I heard it all," added Hobart.

"Finally, sir," I said, pleading my trumped-up case directly to Colonel Liscum, "I couldn't stand it anymore. I struck him." I hung my head in silence at just the right moment to communicate to the others that it was the only thing a real man could have done, implying that they would have done the same had they been in my shoes.

"I see," said Liscum tightly, fixing Harris with such a withering stare that the stricken captain recoiled visibly.

"But he struck me!" whined Harris, nonplussed as to how he had managed to become the goat in this donnybrook. "I'm his superior and he struck me!"

"You're damned lucky I wasn't here, or I would have helped him!" bristled Liscum. "Captain, go to your quarters. I want you out of my sight this instant."

Harris shot me a murderous look but, fearful of Liscum's wrath, did as he was ordered. "I'll see you in the morning, Travers," he muttered as he brushed past me.

When he was gone, I downed my bourbon in triumph. "I'm very sorry you had to see that, sir," I offered solicitously for Colonel Liscum's benefit. "I'd have much preferred that this matter hadn't come to your attention."

Liscum now fixed me with a withering stare; I realized immediately that he was none too pleased with my antics either. "I agree, Mister. I too am sorry I had to witness this sight. But you made that inevitable when you decided to flatten your company commander. Let me tell you something, Lieutenant Travers: In the army, lieutenants don't go around leveling captains. All that's going to save you from a court-martial are the extenuating circumstances of this affair. Ordinarily, I'd read charges against you so fast your head would spin."

I blanched in the face of his fury; perhaps I'd gone too far after all. Then Liscum was silent for a moment, mulling over the matter in his mind. Finally, he spoke decisively: "Major Whittaker, I want Lieutenant Travers out of A Company. Transfer him to another company immediately."

"But, sir," protested Whittaker, "there are no vacancies in the regiment at the moment. He'd be excess wherever I put him."

"There's no helping it," retorted Colonel Liscum. "Besides, there'll be vacancies aplenty after we've been in Cuba a few days."

"Very well, sir," replied Major Whittaker.

Liscum turned to leave, and I saw my future slipping away. I had planned to turn this ruckus into the reason for transferring me out of the 9th. Anything less would not do, especially now that Captain Harris was certain to seek revenge at the first opportunity. So I decided to seize the bull by the horns.

"Wait a moment, sir!" I called. "There is a position in which I'm needed right now!"

"Lieutenant Travers, the colonel's spoken!" gasped Major Whittaker, shocked at my effrontery.

But as unaccustomed as he was to having his final word questioned by anyone, Colonel Liscum nonetheless paused. "And what position is that?"

"Why, the officer you're required to send to the War Department," I replied. "I've already volunteered to Major Whittaker to take that position. I hereby renew that request; the regiment would be relieved of any embarrassment that my presence might cause, and I'd be helping my country in its hour of need."

Colonel Liscum thought this over. In his opinion, any service I might render the nation at the War Department was so insignificant as to be beneath mention. But the second part of my argument held some merit; my continued presence in the regiment would occasion some awkwardness. Sending me off as soon as possible would be a way to signal to the other young lieutenants that it wasn't open season on captains.

"Hmmm," murmured Liscum as he tugged on the end of his ermine mustache. "It would wrap up this matter nicely," he allowed, shook his head as he pondered my proposition, and then spoke. "Major Whittaker, draw up the necessary orders. I want Lieutenant Travers to be our nominee to the War Department."

"Yes, sir," said Whittaker. "I'll have him on his way first thing in the morning."

"Wrong," retorted Liscum. "I want him on his way tonight. He can stay up all night on a train south and rue the day he ever struck a superior officer."

18

Three hours later I was on the train. I was on my way south, all right, but my true destination was Manhattan, not Washington. I planned to find Duncan and beg him to think of some way to get me out of the army. I was in desperate straits, and he was the sole person I knew with the clout to get me out.

By late afternoon I was at Kingston, where I was delayed by a northbound freight. I took advantage of the stop to step down to the platform for a stretch. Newspaper vendors were everywhere, so I bought a copy of the *New York World*. "WAR LOOMS! PEACE TALKS LAG!" screamed the headline. I read further:

Lamps are burning late tonight in Madrid and Washington as diplomats struggle to halt what appears to be an irreversible slide into war. It is clear to all levelheaded men, however, that our grievance with the Spanish Empire can only be settled with the sword, and the sooner the better.

The sun was sinking behind the brownstones of Manhattan when the train rolled slowly into Grand Central Station. My euphoria at having escaped the 9th Regiment was quickly giving way to the cold realization that I was still very much in the soup. If Duncan couldn't or wouldn't help me, I might become a combat veteran in spite of myself.

I secured my valise and made my way outside, where I looked for transport to Duncan's house. The gas street lamps were flickering on, and in their glow I could see numerous trolleys rumbling about on tracks outside the train station. I elected to travel by more traditional means and hailed one of the black hansoms parked by the curb, giving the driver Duncan's address.

Duncan's baronial abode, I knew from my infrequent visits during my years as a West Point cadet, was a sprawling limestone-and-granite monstrosity on Fifth Avenue just north of 70th Street and across from Central Park. I climbed aboard the hansom, the driver waved his whip in the general direction of his nag, and we were off. I sat back in the cab and watched the early evening sights pass me by. I must have dozed off, for I suddenly awoke with a start and peered from the cab at a part of New York that was foreign to me.

"Where the hell are we?" I demanded irritably of the driver. "I said I wanted to go to Fifth Avenue and 71st Street!"

"Whot's dat ya say, boss?" said the cabby, taken aback. "I could'a swore you said West 31st Street."

"I said no such thing, you fool!" I snapped. "Now you've gotten me thoroughly lost. I've never set eyes on this part of town in my life."

I looked about on the dark street. I could see numerous little red lanterns in windows all around me. Then it dawned on me: The cabby had inadvertently taken me to the Tenderloin, New York's infamous red-light district. As I pondered the situation, the thought of Ida Richmond

popped unbeckoned into my mind. It had been a while, I found myself admitting.

"Aw, okay," replied the cabby. "Hold onta' yer britches, an' I'll
run ya upta' 71st Street."

"On second thought," I said, lifting a hand to stop him, "I'll walk.
A little exercise might do me good." I handed him two bits and he
tipped his derby in grudging acknowledgment. When I alighted he set
his nag to a canter and in a moment disappeared around a corner. Oh,
to be young and free in New York, I thought with a smile! And with
the current national interest in all things military, I should be well regarded by the ladies in my perfectly tailored blue uniform. So I snapped
down the brim of my felt Stetson-style hat at a rakish angle and
sauntered down the street. In no time at all, a likely-looking young
lady sailed up the street in the opposite direction. I doffed my hat with
a gallant flourish.

"And good evening to you, miss," I smiled. "Would you happen to
know where a valiant officer off to the Spanish wars might find a lady's
company on a cold winter's night?"

"I'm sure I wouldn't know, sir," she rejoined primly enough, but
the hint of a coquette's smile at the corners of her mouth told me that
I was on the right trail. I surveyed her quickly; she had a smooth, sweet
face and a gentle manner: Perhaps a high-priced whore or someone's
mistress, I thought. Although, to be truthful, she was so bundled against
the cold that I couldn't exactly tell whether or not she was dressed
for the trade. On the other hand, if she was merely an honest citizen,
that would do, too.

"But certainly a lady with as bright an eye as yours must know where
I might go to inquire into obtaining such company," I pressed.

She smiled broadly at this. "Certainly a gentleman as handsome as
yourself doesn't need to seek female companionship. Surely the ladies flock to you."

She said it mockingly, but a note in her voice told me that there
was a backhanded accolade here. I smiled indulgently at her jab and
retorted smoothly, "You're quite right, miss. In fact, unless I'm mistaken, a lady has just flocked in front of my very eyes."

She started to turn around and search the streets. Then, as if suddenly catching my meaning, she smiled with becoming coyness. Encouraged, I pressed on vigorously. "Forgive me if I'm too abrupt, but

in war every moment is precious. Perhaps you might join me for a spot of supper? You see, I've just arrived in town, and I'm quite famished."

She hesitated in the face of my bold advance. "Well . . . well, I'm not sure," she demurred. At just that moment a bevy of trollops sailed brazenly past, the prettiest of whom openly winked with mascaraed eyes at the dashing young military man. That seemed to motivate my new acquaintance. "This is highly unusual," she said hesitantly. "But seeing that you appear to be a gentleman, and war is about to start and all, I suppose it would be all right just this once."

"Then it's settled," I declared heartily, taking her by the arm and starting off down the street. "And where in this neighborhood might we find a decent place to eat?"

"There's a lovely little German place only a few blocks from here," she suggested. "It's Bavarian."

"Fine," I agreed, "Bavarian it is. But forgive me, my dear, I've forgotten my manners. Allow me to introduce myself. I'm Lieutenant Fenwick Travers, United States Army. My friends call me Fenny. At your service."

"How quaint," she cooed. "Fenny, hmmm? Well, Fenny, my name is Esther Waite."

"An exquisite name," I assured her perfunctorily as I hurried her along the sidewalk toward the German place. I was indeed starved, and now I had my after-dinner entertainment in tow. Things were beginning to look up quite nicely. A good meal, a roll in the hay, and then I'd be on my way to see Duncan.

"It must be exciting to be a soldier in these times," Esther bubbled with genuine curiosity.

"The life of a military man is always exciting," I assured her, affecting the stern gravity of an old hand who'd seen a hundred battles. "If there's no savages to suppress, there's an alarm of one sort or another. Over the years, one gets used to that sort of thing, you see."

"My word, I suppose it is quite a dangerous life," she breathed, thoroughly enraptured. "Although I'm surprised that you are such a veteran. You look so young."

I smiled at this. "Looks can deceive," I said with asinine pomposity.

"I'll say," cooed Esther, gratifying deference in her voice. She was easy to con, I saw, a fact that boded well for the remainder of the evening. But just then Esther clutched my arm tightly and stopped dead in her tracks.

"Good evening, Esther," called a rough voice from the gloom ahead of us. Under the glare of the street lamps, I made out a dark figure slouched against a building.

"I told you to leave me alone," squealed Esther, fear and hatred in her voice.

"And I told you the rules of the Tenderloin," countered the stranger. "If you want to work here, you have to pay. And to my way of figuring, you're in arrears, dearie."

"I'm not that sort of girl," sobbed Esther, clearly disturbed at this encounter. "I never have been, and I'll never pay you a cent!"

The stranger stepped from the shadows into the full glow of the lamps. I saw a squat, brutish form packed into a garish plaid suit. His face was flat, with dark eyes that flitted from Esther to me and back again. On top of the stranger's large square head perched a derby a size too small, which he proceeded to cock at a jaunty angle, and then he sauntered straight up to us. His jaw was covered with stubble and his breath stank of cheap whiskey. A lighted cigar glowed red between his thick lips.

"Don't give me that line of crap again, Esther," he chortled without humor. "Any woman who lives here is 'that sort of girl.' Who do you expect me to think your soldier boy is? Your long-lost brother?" He laughed harshly but he wasn't amused, for just then he thrust his face sharply toward Esther's. "Pay up, floozie, or else."

I wasn't amused either. Oh, I wasn't affronted by his calling my companion a floozie; indeed, I hoped he was right on that score. No, the point was that time was short and this reptile was in my way.

"Now see here, my man," I warned him icily. "Why don't you just run along like a good fellow before there's any trouble."

His ferret eyes lighted on me. "Trouble?" he cackled. "I'll give you trouble, greenhorn." Laying a great heavy hand on my lapel, he shoved me violently. His strength was enough to knock me flat on the seat of my pants. "Get out of here while you still can. And stop butting into other folks' business."

I could see that I was dealing with a rough customer, but I wasn't ready to panic yet, for under my greatcoat I was packing my infantry saber. It was a standard-issue, U.S. Army straight-bladed ceremonial sword, designed for use by staff and field officers, and not really suited for heavy combat; but it would be just the thing to deal with this lout. If things got out of hand, I was confident that I could skewer the bastard.

I rose carefully, putting an arm's length between us as my hand sought the pommel of my saber. "This appears to be my business now, partner," I declared, a hard edge in my voice.

"Suit yourself, soldier boy," the stranger growled in reply, squaring up for a rush. I flexed my knees and drew my blade six inches. I eyed his throat above the collar. I'd strike there, I decided, hoping to drop this beast in his tracks with one blow. If not, I'd simply have to hack him until he ran or bled to death. I determined all this quite calmly, you see, for physical combat never troubled me; besides, I was holding all the aces.

But before the butchery could begin, a third party suddenly appeared on the scene. "Ah, up to your old tricks again, Becker!" said the newcomer. "Still trying to squeeze graft out of poor Esther and the other forlorn women like her, hey? I'd thought you'd learned your lesson the last time I exposed your sordid scam in the *Eagle*."

The *Eagle?* I thought. Why, the stranger must be referring to the *Brooklyn Eagle,* one of the small dailies in the city. That meant this newcomer must be a newspaper reporter, I concluded. I eyed him narrowly as he approached. He was thin, with nondescript features, and sported a scraggly mustache, which I took to be his pathetic attempt to ape the great flowing growths that were de rigueur for manly fashion. Although it was cold, the newcomer was thinly dressed; the pay at the *Eagle* was obviously somewhat less than princely. But if the newcomer was truly a reporter, then who was my antagonist, this man he had called Becker? The newcomer had mentioned graft. That could only mean one thing: Becker was a policeman. I was squared off against a member of New York's finest!

"I thought you were out of the country, Crane," sneered Becker. "Heard you were holed up with some fancy writers over in England. If you knew what was good for you, you would have stayed the hell out of New York."

"What?" retorted Crane in mock horror. "And let you and your fellow 'Knights of the Club' rape the Tenderloin? Never, Becker, never! Someone has to tell the city about the depredations of its own police force."

"Well, it sure won't be you, Crane," snarled Becker, who reached into his inner coat pocket and produced a wicked-looking paddywhacker, a lead-weighted blackjack. "I'm running you in, Crane, for resisting arrest and interfering with an officer in the performance of his duties. If you have any objections, you call tell 'em to the desk sergeant. Then I'm coming back for your precious Esther."

With that he lunged for Crane, but the latter nimbly danced out of reach. "Don't be a fool, Becker," taunted Crane. "It's murder you're up to, and you know it'll never work. Even a dumb dick like yourself realizes he can't leave witnesses walking around. Esther here and her soldier friend will sing like canaries!"

Becker paused, then smiled brutishly. "With you gone, Esther will soon be in no position to harm me. As for the soldier . . ." He left the thought unspoken. "Looks like an officer, too. What a pity."

I could plainly see the handwriting on the wall. "I'll just be running along now," I suggested. "I really am late for an appointment, and I'm terribly sorry if I've disturbed you in any way. And, Detective, you needn't worry, I promise I'll forget everything that occurred here as soon as I'm around the corner."

"Not so fast, you," growled Becker, moving closer to me with his paddywhacker gripped firmly in his massive hand. "Officer or no, I think you're about to fall victim to a pack of street rowdies on the prowl. Yes, I think a tragedy is about to occur, if you get my drift." He snickered sinisterly and tensed to spring for me.

I caught his drift, all right. The bastard was about to crack my skull so that he could continue to extort his piddling tribute from the forlorn hooker, Esther. "Now officer, really," I quailed, suddenly losing all stomach for a fight now that I knew Becker was a policeman, "there's really no need for violence. I think you'll find me to be quite reasonable. If you'll just let me go, I'll never breathe a word about what happened here tonight."

"Sure, bucko," laughed Becker harshly, "and I'm the Duke of York." With that he lashed out viciously with the blackjack.

"Yipe!" I shrieked, jumping to one side just in the nick of time. I went to draw my saber, only to have the pommel catch on the lining of my greatcoat. As I struggled to draw my blade, Becker closed for the kill.

At that moment Crane acted. "Damn you, Becker," he shouted, and gave the detective a shove that knocked him off balance for an instant. An instant was all I needed. The blade slipped out of its scabbard and I leveled the tip at Becker's throat.

"Hold, you stinking varmint," I ordered. In the glare of the gas lamps the sword gleamed murderously. Straightaway Becker froze, his eyes locked on my blade. Apparently my saber was somewhat larger than the pigstickers he was accustomed to encountering in street fights in the Tenderloin. "Drop the paddywhacker," I commanded.

Becker did as he was told, but then he made his move. With a speed I would never have suspected he possessed, Becker produced a long stiletto from his waistband and in one fluid movement slashed at my neck. I drew back just as the tip of the blade grazed my chin, and then I struck downward hard with the pommel of my sword against Becker's forehead. He grunted, sagged backward, and dropped his stiletto. I leveled my blade once more at his exposed neck; he was mine!

Like any true bully faced with superior force, Becker turned craven. "Don't hurt me, Mister," he pleaded whiningly. "I'm a copper! A detective! I was only doing my job!"

"Only doing your job?" I sneered. "Since when is murdering citizens part of a city policeman's job?"

"Let me go, Mister, please," begged Becker. "I promise nothing will come of this! I'll never report it to anyone, I swear!"

"That's the first thing you've gotten right yet," I told him levelly. "But the reason you won't be talking about this little incident is because you'll be lying dead right here in this very street." That seemed fair enough to me; the bastard had clearly intended to do me in, and it seemed only fitting that I now return the favor. And make no mistake, I had the stomach for it. If I let Becker go, this wouldn't be the end of the affair. He'd never rest until he tracked me down and did me in. No, there was no going back now; a clean slice, I figured, and the bastard would be a goner. Then the three of us could scatter into the night, each certain to be silent for our individual reasons.

"Say good-bye, Becker," I spat coldly, and then my blade flashed. I intended a quick slash at his neck, but instead the blade caught Becker's heavy jaw and cut a jagged gash across his face. Becker's derby tumbled from his head and with the reflexes of a startled weasel he was up and running.

"Help!" he screamed. "Murder! They're murdering me! Help!" He rounded a corner at full speed and soon his cries were fading into the night. I watched him go, roaring all the while at this high good fun, then scooped up his stiletto, dropped it in my pocket, and gave the blackjack a pitch that landed it on a nearby rooftop. Then I turned to go since any hope of trysting with Esther was now gone.

"Wait a minute, friend," called Crane. "I haven't thanked you yet for what you did for Esther and me. I don't even know your name."

That's all I need, I thought, my name blaring from the headlines of the *Brooklyn Eagle*. "I've no desire to give you my name," I replied tersely. "As you must understand, this incident is closed for me. Good-bye."

"But I need your name for my story. I intend to roast Becker in the morning edition. I need your name to do it up right."

A cab came into view. I hailed it and climbed in. Fresh snow was starting to fall, and the wind was rising. "Fifth Avenue and 71st Street," I called to the driver. "And there's an extra greenback in it for you if you go the whole way at a gallop."

"Your name!" called Crane from the curb. "What's your name?"

"Colonel Emerson H. Liscum, 9th United States Infantry!" I yelled from the window as the hansom pulled away. "I stab detectives and molest hookers every day of the week. I can't help myself, it's in my blood!" I shouted with glee as the horse broke into a canter. In the gloom I saw Crane scribbling furiously on a pad, then we rounded a corner and he was gone.

19

Ten minutes later the hansom pulled up to the curb at Duncan's mansion, an enormous structure with a bewildering mélange of towers, turrets, and buttresses. I bounded up the steps and pulled the bell cord. The door swung open to reveal a dour butler. I gave the fellow my card, and he bowed me into a spacious foyer lined with marble columns. He took my hat, greatcoat, and valise and then retired.

As I waited I wondered what type of reception to expect. After all, Duncan had made it clear on my previous visits that I had worn out my welcome. Any refined person receiving such signals would have never darkened his threshold again. Of course, I wasn't refined, and what's more, I was desperate. The old skinflint was my last hope, and I was determined to brazen out my petition for survival no matter how uncomfortable it made him.

The butler must have announced me promptly, for in a moment I was staring at the scowling visage of George Duncan. For a second my resolve deserted me, and I felt my legs bow, but then I recovered myself and gave him a grin and said brightly, "Mister Duncan, how good of you to see me with no notice."

Despite my hopeful smile, Duncan's scowl remained fixed. I could see I was as welcome as a cave-in at one of his mines. The important thing, however, was that he did not immediately order me out. Perhaps it was my sheer brass at thus invading his domicile, or perhaps it was the sight of me in the full regalia of an officer of the republic. Whatever it was, Duncan was taken aback at the sight of me. Since he was apparently struck dumb, I decided to plunge on.

"Sir, it's so good to see you. I'm sorry I couldn't announce my arrival by telegraph, but things have been so rushed of late."

"Fenwick," he managed to say at last, forcing his jaws to work through sheer force of will. "Yes, well, er, come in, Fenwick, come in." He gestured toward an ornate parlor down the corridor, and I eagerly followed. I was in! He could have summoned a constable, or ordered his domestic to toss me into the gutter, but he didn't. I was to have an audience, I realized exultantly. Perhaps my luck was changing for the better.

He ushered me into the lavishly appointed chamber and said, "Fenwick, sit by the fire. I know you can't stay long, but at least we can get the chill off before you're on your way."

I hadn't said I couldn't stay long, I thought, my mood suddenly gloomy. As I neared the roaring flames in the hearth, a tall, elderly gentleman rose from a divan that until that moment had shielded him from my view. "Fenwick, this is Mister Harlock, an old and trusted business associate of mine," announced Duncan.

I shook Harlock's proffered hand. He was about sixty-five years old, I reckoned, exceedingly slender, and with a shaved pate that gleamed in the firelight. He was attired in a black suit of expensive weave, a costume that, together with his gaunt features, gave him an eery, almost funereal aspect. Without a word, he resumed his seat. An odd bird, I thought, as I moved to the hearth to thaw my backside.

The butler bustled in with a decanter of white wine and a tray bearing exquisite crystal glasses, and then backed out, closing the parlor doors behind him. Duncan poured, and I accepted a glass gratefully. As I sipped, I studied Harlock from the corner of my eye. He sat on the heavily embroidered divan with his hands folded neatly in his lap. With his ashen face, skeletal frame, and elongated neck, he looked like a vulture in a morning coat.

There was no getting around it; something about Harlock made me profoundly uneasy. There was a force, a malevolent aura, around the fellow that made the hairs on the back of my neck rise. What's more, I had heard his name before, but for the life of me I couldn't recall just where. It took me two more sips before it came to me.

Harlock! Why, that was the name I'd heard Duncan mention to Pedrolito years ago in Arizona! Harlock had been Duncan's business partner in the Sonora mine scheme. Just then Harlock spoke.

"So, Lieutenant," he said, the dry rasp of his voice startling me, "where is it the army's posting you?"

Before I answered I tried to place his accent: It was eastern, but he was no New Yorker. No, the tones were too clipped, too terse. New England, I decided; the fellow was an old-line Yankee.

"I'm off to Washington, sir," I replied carefully. "I've been detailed to the War Department."

"I see," replied Harlock enigmatically. He seemed to weigh this information carefully.

"Tell me, Fenwick," said Duncan, settling himself into an overstuffed chair, "will you be going off to the war?"

"Not immediately, sir," I answered truthfully enough. "But when my duties in Washington are completed, who can tell?" It seemed prudent to address the old tyrant as "sir," since I wanted to wheedle something out of him.

"Well, Fenwick, if you're on your way to Washington, what exactly was it that prompted you to grace me with your presence?" asked Duncan. His face had a tight smile, but his voice was pure ice. As could be expected, he had gotten directly to the heart of the matter.

Directness at a moment like this, however, was the last thing I wanted, and so I demurred awkwardly. "Well, er, that is, I thought it would be appropriate to see you en route to my new post. You know, well, with the Cuban situation being what it is, well, naturally, er, one has no idea what tomorrow may bring." I paused for dramatic effect.

To my surprise Duncan laughed heartily. "Why, Fenwick, tomorrow holds another day! It always has and always will, boy."

I knew from his tone that he was on to me. There would be little opportunity here for a private audience to plead my case. Moreover,

I could sense that as far as Duncan was concerned, the sooner I got to Cuba the better. Any begging I intended to do would have to be done right here in front of Harlock. Checkmate.

"I suppose so," I conceded lamely.

"Washington, you say, eh?" said Duncan.

I nodded numbly.

"Well, how about that? Only a short while ago you were off in Pittsburgh, buried alive, as it were. . . ."

"Plattsburgh," I corrected him.

"Whatever," Duncan said with a shrug. "The point is, you've done better for yourself than I would have imagined possible." Then he uttered the words that flabbergasted me. "I'm proud of you, Fenwick."

Proud? Did I mishear the old goat? No, I'd gotten him right. And I had to admit, I did rather look the part of the dashing young staff officer. My natural coloration handsomely set off my dark blue uniform with its gold trim. I'd even started a mustache, since facial hair was all the rage then, especially ferocious-looking handlebar mustaches. Suddenly I was hopeful again; had Duncan's feelings toward me changed somehow?

"Why, thank you, sir, thank you," I stammered. "I'm most gratified to hear you say that."

"And I'm sure you'll serve your country as well in the future as you have in the past," he added.

"Of that you may be sure," I replied. By which I meant I'd gotten by on my wits and fists in the past and I intended to do so in the future.

"Oh, I am," smiled Duncan right back at me, taking a sip of his wine. Then he winked at me and I knew nothing had changed; he was still able to read me like an open book.

The evening droned on interminably. Harlock and Duncan talked of currency exchange rates and trade matters, which were absolute Sanskrit to me. I sipped my wine and thought of ways to raise my plight with Duncan short of throwing myself abjectly at his feet. But years of business experience had developed in Duncan an un- canny ability to adroitly avoid unwanted petitions whenever it suited him; he completely ignored my numerous meaningful looks in his direction. At last we all rose and went into the dining room—yes, Duncan deigned to feed me, as amazing as that may sound—where I took a desultory meal, and as supper drew to a close I took my leave. I was beaten, and I knew it. All I wanted now was to find a room where I could get forty winks and then ponder my predicament afresh in the morning. Clearly Duncan was not about to initiate an open-ended stay on my part.

"I won't detain you," said Duncan briskly as a bevy of maids cleared the table. "There must be urgent affairs that require your attention. So I'll bid you farewell."

All eyes were upon me; it was clear that my visit was at an end. There was no sense in railing against Duncan for his coldhearted ways. If I survived this war, I might still need him in the future.

The butler brought me my greatcoat and saber. I put them on in the foyer and, turning, said, "Well, I'm off. It's been a pleasure making your acquaintance, Mister Harlock."

"Farewell, Lieutenant," said Harlock. "I shouldn't be greatly surprised if our paths crossed again someday."

Duncan gave Harlock a queer look but held his tongue. Then I was ushered to the door with the same firmness shown to a snake-oil peddler, and my valise was thrust into my hand. There were some more lukewarm good-byes at the door, and then Duncan planted a firm hand in the small of my back and propelled me out.

Perhaps it was the finality of my exit, or perhaps it was the unnecessary hand on my back as I passed his portal, but whatever it was I was suddenly incensed by Duncan's unfairness. This was damned fine hospitality, I fumed. Why, I was being given the old heave-ho, and right in front of Harlock to boot. Angered, I lashed out the only way I could: "Oh, and by the way, is Alice still under your roof?"

"That's none of your concern!" snapped Duncan angrily. "You just forget about Alice and worry about yourself. That's one memory that should be left to die!" With that he slammed the door in my face.

It was still snowing. I put on my hat and turned up my collar. So, I thought, after five years the scandal still lived. I turned and walked down Fifth Avenue. I had gone only a few blocks when I heard a whispered voice. "Psssst! Over here!"

Alarmed, I turned to see a figure beckoning to me from the alley that ran between two brownstones. "Who's there?" I demanded fiercely, hiding the sudden fear I felt. Had I been trailed here by that brute Becker? My hand went to my saber.

"Alice!" came the reply.

And so it was, by God! I hastened over to the shadows. "Alice, my darling," I said, catching her in my arms and giving her a great squeeze.

She gave a squeak and struggled from my grasp. "You haven't changed a bit, Fenny."

"Oh, but I have," I laughed. "I'm naughtier than ever!"

"Fenny, you're incorrigible," scolded Alice, but her eyes danced with animal excitement. It was evident that she would not be at all averse to picking up our intimate acquaintance where we had left off. "Why didn't you write or call on me over the years? You knew I was here."

"But I tried," I protested. "My letters to you were returned, and when I did visit I was told you were abroad. Believe me, Alice, I tried to contact you."

She was silent a moment; evidently she knew her Uncle George well enough to suspect that what I was saying was the truth. Then she asked worriedly, "Are you off to the war?"

"Not if I can help it," I replied with a broad grin, but I could tell from her frown that her worry was genuine, and my bluster did nothing to dispel it.

"When are you leaving New York?" she asked urgently.

"I don't really know," I replied truthfully. "It could be a day or two, or it could be longer." What I didn't say was that in light of the evaporation of all my hopes for rallying Duncan to my cause, I was seriously considering desertion.

"But what about tonight, Fenny? Where are you staying?"

That was a damn good question, and from the gleam in Alice's eyes I could tell that she was motivated by more than idle curiosity. I quickly tried to think of some suitable accommodations nearby.

"The Fifth Avenue Hotel," I decided at length. "It's just south of Central Park." The Fifth Avenue Hotel was the gathering place for West Pointers whenever they were in town. The reason for this was in part because it was a swell place in its own right, but another major reason was because it was just down Broadway from the Hoffman House, a fashionable dining establishment renowned for the huge murals of Rubenesque nudes that decorated its saloon. "Go there as soon as you can slip away tonight, okay? The door to my room will be open."

"Oh, yes, sweet Fenny!" Alice breathed, and gave me a moist kiss on the lips to seal our bargain. Then she slipped out of my arms and disappeared into the night.

Humming a jaunty tune, I caught a cab and soon arrived at the Fifth Avenue Hotel. I checked in and was shown to a modest yet comfortable room. Several hours later Alice quietly slipped into bed beside me and we renewed our relationship at the point at which it had been so abruptly terminated years earlier.

20

It was nearly dawn when the knock came at the door. "Get up, Lieutenant Travers! I've got to speak with you this instant!"

"Who's that?" screeched Alice, instantly awake and clutching the bedclothes to her bare breasts.

"How the hell should I know?" I bellowed, instantly awake with her. I leapt from the bed buck naked and looked out the window. It was four stories straight down with no fire escape!

The pounding at the door came again. "Open up, damnit! It's Crane!"

Crane? How the hell had he learned my name and what did that meddling snoop want with me?

I pulled on my trousers and opened the door a crack. Crane stood alone in the hall. I opened the door wider. "What's this all about, Crane?" I demanded.

Crane could see Alice, still half-naked, and his eyes widened. "Sorry, old man," he apologized. "I had no idea you were entertaining. But you've got to get out of here and right away."

"Just hold your horses, Crane," I snapped. "I'm not so sure I want to go anywhere just yet."

"You will if you know what's good for you, my friend," he insisted. "Your life won't be worth a plug nickel if you stay in this town much longer. It's Becker—he's on your trail. He's got the whole force out looking for you."

"So what?" I bluffed. "It's his word against mine. In a court of law, the word of a military officer is bound to carry a lot of weight."

"That's true, if you ever get to see the inside of a courtroom," countered Crane. "I don't know what you've heard about our guardians in blue, Travers, but very few people charged with assault on a copper in this town ever get to trial. They turn up dead instead, usually killed while trying to escape, if you get my meaning."

I got it. "Let me get my things," I answered hastily. I dressed in my uniform, which was the only clothing I'd brought, wishing fervently that I had an inconspicuous set of mufti to slip into instead. I strapped on my saber and, as an afterthought, slipped Becker's stiletto into my boot. Then I kissed the perplexed Alice good-bye and hurried off after Crane. As I bounded down the stairs I could hear her wailing plaintively, "Don't leave me here, Fenny!"

"I'll write, dearest!" I promised as I hurried after Crane.

We paused in the lobby as Crane peered about furtively. "Do you have anywhere to go?" he asked.

I thought for a moment. "I suppose so. I can go to Washington. I've got orders to report to the War Department."

"Splendid," replied Crane. "I'll join you."

"What?" I cried. "Now see here, Crane, I don't know you from a hole in the ground, and it suits me just fine if things stay that way. You're not coming along with me, and that's final."

"Don't be a fool," scoffed Crane. "I have to get out of town, too. Becker wants me as much as he wants you. If I'm taken he'll beat me until I tell him where you've run off to. And that won't take long, my friend, since I have an extreme aversion to pain."

"Goddamn!" I stormed. "Just what I need, a pet reporter tagging along with me. I can't believe this."

"Well, Travers, don't forget that this pet reporter was the one who warned you that you were in danger," rejoined Crane, clearly irritated now.

"Don't get uppity with me, Crane," I hissed in return. He was a damned nuisance, all right, and I didn't at all care for his company, but at the moment I could think of no alternative but to bring him along. "Okay," I conceded at length, "you can come with me to Washington. But once we get there, we go our separate ways. Understand?"

"Perfectly," he answered loftily, offended by my ingratitude. We turned to leave, when suddenly I was hailed by the desk clerk. "I say, sir, are you Lieutenant Travers?" he asked.

Crane and I froze. "Who wants to know?" I demanded gruffly, ready to fly should the bastard call the law on us.

"Please don't take offense, sir," quailed the clerk, alarmed at my demeanor. "I just wanted to tell you about a telegram that came in about an hour ago for you. I didn't send it up right away because I thought you'd be sleeping."

He handed me a folded sheet of paper. I scanned it quickly; it was not good news:

Travers, F.
2 LT, INFANTRY

DISREGARD PREVIOUS INSTRUCTIONS STOP
PROCEED IMMEDIATELY BY ANY MEANS AVAILABLE TO PORT
TAMPA, FLORIDA STOP REPORT TO HQ, V CORPS FOR FURTHER
INSTRUCTIONS STOP
WAR DEPT
WASH, DC

I must have paled noticeably, for Crane asked solicitously, "Anything the matter, Lieutenant?"

"I'll say," I muttered. Then, more crisply, I explained, "I'm being sent to Port Tampa. That's a likely staging area for an invasion of Cuba."

"How exciting!" gushed Crane. "This must mean that war is near. How perfect. Where there are troops, there's bound to be good copy, and the *Journal* will pay top dollar for any story about Cuba."

"I thought you worked for the *Eagle*," I said.

"Technically I do, but, er, the pay's meager for the sort of muckraker stories I've been writing lately. The *Journal* is much more generous, I've heard, and, well, I've been a bit short of cash."

I gave him a stony look at this bit of information. "Well, don't expect me to pay your fare down to Tampa."

"Not at all, Travers," replied Crane with a disingenuous attempt at indignation. "I don't accept charity from strangers."

"Good," I replied, mollified.

"But we'll be much better acquainted by the time we get to the station," Crane chirped brightly.

Damn him, I thought. He was nothing but trouble, and a born panhandler to boot. But I put him out of my mind for a second. There was something about the telegram that bothered me.

I turned to the desk clerk. "How did Western Union know I could be reached here? I don't recall giving anyone in the army that information."

"Beats me, Mister," replied the clerk with a shrug.

I looked carefully at the address on the outside of the telegram. It had been sent to Duncan's address. That was reasonable; I had taken to listing him as my next of kin in my official records. Oh, I know that seems strange, but whom should I have listed? Certainly not Uncle Enoch. But how did Duncan know to send it on to the Fifth Avenue Hotel? The only explanation was that he applied his knowledge of my personality to the problem. He knew I'd head for the most reasonable accommodations available that could be reached with the least expenditure of energy. Bull's-eye, I thought, awed by his deductive powers. No wonder he was rich.

"Let me check the street before we step out," suggested Crane.

"Okay," I replied, more than pleased to let him stick his neck out as far as he pleased. I waited in the lobby, standing behind an elevated shoeshine chair and trying to look as inconspicuous as possible. I thought I'd succeeded when a liveried coachman entered the lobby and looked directly at me. He was turned out magnificently in a morning coat of forest green velvet, fawn breeches, and gleaming Wellingtons, all of which was set off with a black silk top hat. He must charge a fortune for his fare, I thought in wonder. To my surprise he marched right up to me.

He doffed his hat and asked, "Lieutenant Travers?"

Flustered, I stepped from behind the chair. "Yes, what is it, my man?" Crane must have hired him, I thought, and then sent him to me for the fare in advance.

To my surprise, the coachman produced a small wrapped package. "A gift to you, sir, from Mister Harlock. He sends his warmest personal regards along with it."

A gift? From Harlock? He hardly looked the Father Christmas type. What in the blazes was going on? I wondered. But on the other hand, one never looked a gift horse in the mouth. "Well that's very kind of Mister Harlock, very kind indeed. You must give him my thanks," I said.

"I shall, sir. Mister Harlock also said I'm to be at your service for as long as you're in the city."

Well, that's damned convenient, I thought. "Very well," I agreed, springing at the opportunity, "take me to Grand Central Station straightaway."

The coachman gave a curt nod of his head and led the way to the curb where his rig stood. It was a majestic brougham, lacquered in red and green and bearing the coat of arms of the newly completed Waldorf-Astoria Hotel. If Harlock was staying there, he was quite well off indeed, for the use of the Waldorf's coaches was reserved for the privileged few who kept suites there year-round. Then I wondered if it might not have been Harlock who had found me at the Fifth Avenue Hotel, and not Duncan as I had first suspected. It was possible. Those hooded eyes I'd gazed into in Duncan's parlor held limitless cunning. My curiosity about Harlock waxed anew.

Just then Crane returned. "No sign of the dicks yet," he huffed, his breath labored from his patrol. "I saw a beat cop but drew nary a glance. I'd say that Becker is relying on his fellow detectives to run us down."

I gave the empty street a quick once-over. "That's encouraging, but we can't rely on it. Besides, Becker's had hours to sniff out our trail. My friend here has volunteered to take us to the station," I said, gesturing at the coachman. "Get in."

Crane looked quizzically at the opulent coach. "I see you run with a posh set, Travers," he said, impressed, and then climbed in. I clambered up on his heels, and in moments we were cantering through the morning streets. Settling back in the soft leather seat, I unwrapped my unexpected gift. It was a small liquor flask, apparently fabricated of solid silver, nestled in a unique alligator-skin case. Imprinted into the leather was a pattern. I held it up to the light for a better look; it was the silhouette of a clipper ship, the quintessential symbol of a New England Yankee.

I had been right about Harlock after all, I decided. I hefted the flask appreciatively. Harlock intrigued me all the more. Why would a gent of apparently independent means want to cultivate the friendship of a penniless junior officer? God knows that Duncan would never have made nor approved of such an effort. There had to be a motive for such unprovoked largess, I knew, but at the moment it remained a mystery to me.

Crane whistled appreciatively at the flask. "There's a pretty how-do-you-do. Let me know if you're of a mind to pawn it—I've had a bit of experience in that field."

"No surprise there," I retorted dryly. "After all, you did say you were a newspaper reporter." And then a thought occurred to me.

"Tell me, Crane, just how did you find out who I was?" I demanded. "I never told you my name."

He chuckled lightly in reply. "Ah, that was the easy part, Lieutenant. First, I didn't for a second believe that you were this Colonel Liscum. You're too young to be a colonel. So I merely asked Esther what name you'd given her. You used your real name, too. Very, er, indiscreet."

He was right, and the thought of him being right angered me, so I brushed aside the point and pressed, "Even if that's so, Crane, it doesn't explain how you were able to find me at the Fifth Avenue Hotel. Did you tail me?" Of course, everybody else in the world had seemed to be able to find me there, but I wanted his story anyway.

"No, I didn't tail you. I wasn't able to; you took the only available cab. No, I found you with a quick bit of investigative work, Lieutenant Travers, the sort of thing a reporter does every day," Crane explained, rather enjoying discussing his trade. "You see, you're an officer, which to me means that you're probably a West Pointer, too." This didn't impress me; almost every officer in the regular army hailed from the academy. Crane continued, "That immediately made me think of the Fifth Avenue Hotel, as that's where army men seem to stay when they're in town." This bit of reasoning made me sit up, since almost no civilian other than a relative or date of a West Pointer would have filed away such a trivial detail. "I checked with the night clerk and voila, there you were."

Maybe Crane was a competent enough reporter after all, I allowed. Intrigued by the fellow, I decided to plumb his knowledge further. "Do you know George Duncan?" I inquired.

"*The* George Duncan?" he queried.

Deciding that there could be only one, I answered, "Yes."

"Why would that be of interest to you, Lieutenant?"

My interest was simple; Crane was the sort of fellow who probably had the dirt on all the major figures in New York, and I wanted to know what he knew about Duncan. But I decided to be somewhat indirect on this subject. "Duncan and I are, well, associates of a sort; we met out west some years ago. I rarely get to New York, as you can imagine, and so I'm naturally curious about the great man's reputation in his own town. So, I repeat, do you know Duncan?"

"Not socially, I can assure you," laughed Crane, pleased that his sleuthing had caught my interest. "However, a few years back I lived in the Bowery. I was doing a little serious writing, you see. You may have seen some of my works. One was particularly suitable for a soldier such as yourself. It's about the Civil War."

"Can't say as I have," I sniffed; the Civil War was understandably not one of my favorite topics.

"Well, whatever," he continued blithely. "The point is that during those years I supported myself by selling articles to tabloids. One story I wrote was about a spectacular blaze in one of Duncan Enterprises' sweatshops over on the East Side—"

"But I thought Duncan was a mine magnate," I interrupted.

"George Duncan is the head of a huge trust," Crane informed me. "He owns mines, factories, textile operations, even a few small railroads. If it makes money, it interests Mister Duncan. Well, back to my tale. A real barn burner, that one. Dozens killed."

"How disgusting." I grimaced with distaste.

Crane merely smiled. "Perhaps for the participants. But not for me. Lurid headlines put bread on my table, Lieutenant. But the beauty of that particular blaze was that it allowed me to run a series of stories. I did personals on the workers and another story on the building itself. It was a firetrap. Then there was a series on the corrupt officials who failed to cite Duncan's building as a firetrap. Oh, it was a muckraker's paradise. You know, I could say that Mister Duncan made me what I am today."

That was hardly a resounding endorsement, I thought, giving this lettered vagabond a sideways glance. "Crane," I said, tiring of his upbeat vivaciousness at this ungodly hour, "if you spent the night searching for me, you should be bushed. But you look quite fresh. What's your secret?"

"Ah, you guessed," he replied, giving me a big wink. He pulled a half-drained bottle from his coat pocket. It contained a viscous, murky brew. Crane popped the cork and took a huge swig. "Ahh!" he gasped blissfully. "You?" he offered, holding out the bottle. "Care for a nip?"

I squinted at the label in the dim dawn light. "Doctor Munro's Opiate Elixir," it read. My God, the man was an opium fiend! "Not on your life!" I cried, fending off the bottle with my raised hand. "My brain's fried enough without imbibing of that witches' brew."

"Suit yourself, Travers," Crane responded, smiling blissfully as the tonic reached his brain and worked its magic. A look of serene repose came over him and he fell silent.

We bumped along over the cobblestones for half an hour as Crane drooled over himself, obviously lost in some fantasyland. At length we pulled up to the station. "Out we go, Crane," said I, propelling my groggy companion from the coach.

I alighted to the pavement and warily eyed the crowd around the station. The coachman dismounted and approached.

"Will there be anything further, sir?" he inquired unctuously.

"Thank you, no. We'll see ourselves to the train."

"Indeed we will," gushed Crane, his face florid. "But we can't leave without awarding you a suitable gratuity, my man." Crane ostentatiously fished about in his trouser pockets. "I say, Travers, I seem to have left my cash in my other suit. Could you spare a dime?"

"Damn," I grumbled, handing the coachman a dime.

The coachman eyed the thin coin as though I'd just deposited horse dung in his gloved hand. "You're really too kind, sir," he sniffed frostily.

I ignored his sarcasm. After all, he was used to a better set than us. "Let's go, Crane," I growled. "Let me know if you see anyone who looks suspicious," I added, hoping silently that his sense of sight was still functioning.

We slipped into the crowd and made our way to the ticket counter without incident. I bought two third-class tickets to Tampa via Charleston and Atlanta. Our passage secured, we went to the platform on the lower level to await the arrival of our train. It was not long in coming; in a few moments the platform was engulfed in great clouds of steam as the locomotive pulled slowly into the station. All was well, I thought, until Crane suddenly clutched my sleeve. "We've been spotted, Travers!" he whispered urgently.

"How? Where?" I demanded, scanning around me through the steam.

"That fellow over there," hissed Crane with a jerk of his head, his torpor thrown off by the sudden proximity of danger. He indicated a thoroughly dangerous-looking Irish tough lounging against a pillar some twenty feet away. From his ragged clothes and the stubble on his chin, I'd have picked him for a derelict rather than a detective. Besides, he seemed too young to be on the force. No more than eighteen years of age, I'd say.

"That's a lawman?" I asked in disbelief.

"No. That's Willy Delaney," whispered Crane. "He's a snake. When he's not housebreaking, he makes a living as a snitch. He knows me, Travers— I've written stories about him. The law won't be far behind now."

"Damnit," I swore under my breath. "Now what do we do?"

"Oh, no," groaned Crane, "here comes the law now!"

I followed his gaze. It was Becker coming along the platform, a thick bandage plastered to his face where I'd slashed him. He must have personally staked out the train station as our most likely escape route. "We're in for it now!" wailed Crane. "Becker's won after all!"

Not if I had anything to say about it. I hadn't schemed my way out of Plattsburgh Barracks only to spend the next few years in prison. Becker suddenly stopped; enveloped by the steam, he couldn't see us clearly, yet he sensed that something was up. He gazed suspiciously from Delaney to us and then back to Delaney, who laid his finger alongside his nose and nodded toward Crane and me.

I instantly resolved to fight and feverishly pondered my choice of weapons. I couldn't use my saber: That would only tie the deed to me. Then I remembered. I had Becker's stiletto in my boot! In an instant the blade was in my hand and I was leaping for Becker. The blade flashed, and Becker fell to the platform, gushing blood and howling like a dog under a trolley's wheels.

Before Delaney could blink, I shoved the bloodied stiletto into his hands. "Whaaa . . . ?" was all he could utter as his jaw fell open slackly.

Only now did bystanders peer my way through the billowing steam. "Murder!" I bellowed. "He's murdered a policeman! Help me, someone! Help me!"

For a second Delaney stood rooted to the spot. Then a woman screamed and a man shouted, "Catch the murdering son of a bitch!"

"Holy muther o' God," roared Delaney in despair, and in a blind panic bolted from the platform.

"After him!" I yelled. "Don't let him escape! That's Willy Delaney, the archfiend! He's killed a policeman!"

In a flash the cry was taken up and the platform emptied as the crowd set off in hot pursuit. In the hubbub, Becker was left thrashing about in the welter of his gore.

"You . . . you killed a man!" stuttered Crane in disbelief, the mist of the opium-induced haze in his brain having vanished with the flash of my blade.

There was no time to debate the niceties of my action; instead I propelled Crane unresistingly onto the train as it began to pull out of the station. With one hand I hauled him to a seat and sat down beside him. The train was largely empty; most of our fellow travelers were hotfooting it after the woebegone Delaney.

"Travers," ranted Crane, "you're a murderer!"

"Hold your tongue, or I'll do you in too, Crane!" I snarled viciously. "Don't blame me for what happened back there. If I hadn't met you, none of this would have happened! You can blame that dead copper on yourself. And don't worry about Delaney; if he hangs for this, I'm sure it'll be the only unselfish thing that miscreant has ever done in his life. So hold your peace, Crane, and don't breathe a word of this to anyone. If you do, I wouldn't be surprised if you never get to Tampa. Get my drift?"

"I get your drift," gulped Crane as the train emerged from the shadows of the station and accelerated across the Hudson.

21

Two days later we were in Tampa, the gathering place of V Corps under the command of Gen. William ("Pecos Bill") Shafter. I quickly gave Crane the slip, confident that he'd hold his tongue. He'd emptied so many opium elixir bottles along the way that he could barely remember his own name, let alone what had happened back in New York two days before. Looking about the vast encampment, I spotted a multistory structure towering over the rows of tents in the direction of Tampa Bay and headed toward it. I could make out a handsomely painted sign proclaiming it the Tampa Bay Hotel. Below that was a smaller hand-painted sign reading, "No Dogs or Enlisted Men Allowed."

I surveyed the place appraisingly; it was a rambling structure with a distinctly Moorish decor. Arabic arches were everywhere, and silver minarets adorned the roof. A large, comfortable porch, shaded by a graceful canvas awning, ran around the entire perimeter. Long-tailed parrots, colored in vivid emeralds and crimsons, perched on the roof, squawking and flying about as they pleased. The Tampa Bay Hotel was a lush oasis in an otherwise-sandy wasteland. Without further ado, I pushed through the hotel's swinging doors and into the cool, yawning darkness within.

The lobby was crowded with officers pleading for accommodations. A fair number of low-looking types in mufti also buzzed about the place. Reporters, I concluded. Rooms must be scarce, I thought, for on the divans and chairs in the lobby sprawled sleeping officers from a dozen different regiments. I dismissed the problem of securing lodging from my mind; first, a stiff drink was in order. I marched into the saloon.

I ordered a double bourbon and branch water, downed it in two gulps, and ordered another. Refreshed, I looked about with renewed interest. I was clearly in the nerve center of V Corps. The dining salon adjoining the bar was crowded with jovial parties of officers and their ladies, the tables groaned under appetizing entrees of fresh seafood, and good wine flowed freely. Much heartened by the cheerful atmosphere surrounding me, I dared to hope that war might not be the dreadful experience I had feared.

With my thirst slaked, I turned my attention to my growling stomach. I noticed that a table had become vacant in the dining area, so I dodged past the overwhelmed maitre d' and sat down. I gestured to a harried waiter.

"What's fresh?" I asked the overworked fellow when he finally arrived.

"The pompano, sir," he replied. "We received a shipment on ice from the Atlantic coast just this morning."

"Then the pompano it is," I said decisively. "But I'm hungry as the dickens. What appetizers can you bring me while I'm waiting?"

"Let me check, sir. There might be some scallions in cream sauce," he replied.

"That would be just the thing!" I exclaimed, smacking my lips. "Send them along, by all means." In no time the good fellow was back with my scallions. He set down the plate before my watering mouth; but before I could set to, a hush fell over the room.

I looked up to see the great bulk of Gen. Shafter, the exalted commander of V Corps, lumber into the room.

"Carry on, damnit," rumbled the general at the silence that greeted his entrance.

As the conversation cautiously resumed, I watched as Shafter made his way to a reserved table. Walking through the crowded room was no mean feat for him; he was just under six feet tall but appeared to weigh at least three hundred pounds. He surged through the densely packed diners like a whale among minnows, shoving people and tables aside as he went. Clearly, I thought wryly, Shafter was a great man in the fullest sense of that term.

"Excuse us, excuse us," his lackeys apologized in his wake as Shafter's enormous stomach knocked floral arrangements into Key lime pies and spilled mint juleps into starched laps.

With great exertion Shafter finally reached his table and sank into a chair with obvious relief. From where I sat I could see great rivulets of perspiration cascading off his fleshy face and pouring down his collar. It was apparently all he could do to walk to his meals. My God, I thought, is this the warrior who'll lead us to victory?

No sooner had his enormous bottom hit the chair than Shafter commenced the serious business of getting himself fed. "What's the soup du jour?" he demanded querulously of his entourage. Immediately an exquisite aide snapped to and marched off to find the answer to this pressing question.

Shafter hefted a menu petulantly and eyed it. "Where's the lunch menu? This is the damned breakfast menu," he whined in a peculiar, high-pitched voice. It had none of the commanding tones one associated with a conqueror.

Immediately a bright young captain set off in search of the proper menu. Supervising these antics was a familiar face: It was Major Elliot, by God, my plebe military history instructor! Only, to judge from the silver oak leaves on his epaulets, it was now Lieutenant Colonel Elliot.

Shafter's mewling tone and rotund form gave him the appearance of a giant, mean-tempered child. This juvenile look was underscored by the fact that Shafter eschewed the stiff, high-necked collars of the regulation officer uniform. Instead he wore an open, civilian collar, with a white linen choker wrapped about the folds of fat where his neck should have been. The effect was that of an overweight toddler in a school uniform. It appeared that Elliot was the chief baby-sitter; from where I viewed things, he had his hands full. I fervently hoped that McKinley had been right in anointing this obese buffoon as the leader of a mighty corps.

Turning to my appetizer, I was just setting to with zest when suddenly a shrill squeal brought me up short. "What are you trying to tell me, Colonel?" demanded Shafter. The object of his wrath was a suddenly ashen Lieutenant Colonel Elliot. I knew immediately that the topic was food, for the general's face had assumed a porcine expression, his little eyes slitted and his delicate, full lips drawn into a scowl that revealed small, irregular teeth. It looked for all the world as though Shafter was about to eat Elliot.

"S-s-sir," stammered Lieutenant Colonel Elliot, obviously terrified, "there simply aren't any scallions available!"

"No scallions, no scallions," mocked Shafter. "Surely you are mistaken, sir. There must be scallions because I desire scallions. Haven't I made that clear to you?"

"B-b-but, General, the chef assures me that there are none to be had," quavered Elliot miserably.

"I want scallions, damnit, Colonel, and you'll get me scallions," screamed Shafter at the top of his lungs. The room was shocked into silence at his outburst. "All of you get out of here and scour this miserable camp until you find me a plate of scallions!"

At once his staff bolted from his side, running out the front door of the hotel and scattering to the four winds in search of the elusive vegetables. The thought of a bevy of staff toadies rooting for onions like so many French peasants cheered me immensely. I popped a scallion into my mouth and chewed it contentedly.

His wrath vented for the moment, Shafter subsided into his chair like a spent volcano. His treble chin vibrated from the force of his outburst, and his great stomach sucked air from his exertion. "Is there no one around me who's the least bit competent?" he grumbled morosely to himself.

Then it hit me; my course became blindingly clear! It was one of those moments in war, I realized in retrospect, which makes an ordinary man suddenly stand out from his fellows. In the deafening silence around me, I slowly rose. Shafter's piglike eyes immediately fixed upon me. There was no going back now, I told myself; I picked up my plate of scallions and approached the seat of power.

"Sir," I oozed with the innate smoothness of a French pimp and, not waiting to be acknowledged, plunged on. "I couldn't help but hear that you were having difficulty in obtaining scallions. It would give me the greatest pleasure if you would accept mine." With a flourish I set the platter before him. His eyes fastened on mine, and I fought not to reveal the trembling I felt in my bowels.

Suddenly he spoke. "What's your name, son?"

"Travers, sir. Second lieutenant, infantry."

"Regular army, eh?"

"Yes, sir," I answered snappily.

"I knew it," wheezed Shafter. "There's just something about a regular that marks him as different from all of these damned volunteers."

Probably the sunlight shining through the hole in his head, I thought, my face frozen in an inane smile. By this time Elliot had stolen back to his liege lord's side. He gaped incredulously; there was no doubt he remembered me. Shafter seized a fork with a surprisingly dainty fist and crammed a scallion into his mouth. He gave one mighty chew and swallowed.

Instantly his attitude changed, and he became the soul of convivi-
ality. "Most kind of you, son, most kind. Splendid eating, splendid."
Shafter's moods were obviously regulated by the proximity of forage.
"You seem to manage things a great deal better than my staff." He
shot a meaningful look at Elliot, who gazed uncomfortably off into
space.

"Tell me, Travers," queried Shafter between bites, "what's your outfit?"

"I haven't one, sir," I answered truthfully. "I'm detached from the
9th Infantry with orders to report to Headquarters, V Corps. I arrived
only a few hours ago."

"Is that so?" mused Shafter, shoving another forkful of scallions
into his maw. He chewed thoughtfully for a moment. "Tell you what,
Travers," he rumbled when he had swallowed enough of his onions
for his tongue to work again, "why don't you come and work for me?
God knows I can use people who can get a job done."

Elliot cleared his throat as a signal that he desired to protest Shafter's
decision. It was bad enough I had graduated from the academy; but
to have me on the general's staff with him was too much for Elliot to
endure. "Sir, if I may be heard," insisted Elliot. "There's no position
available on the staff. Besides, there's a critical need for officers in
the line regiments."

"That's not news," shot back Shafter. "But one officer more or less
won't matter the slightest. If the staff is full up, make him my aide."

"But, sir," protested Colonel Elliot. "You already have an aide."

"Then he'll be my assistant aide," ordered Shafter.

Colonel Elliot fell silent in defeat and glowered at me, but I beamed
happily in response. "Sir," I chirped to Shafter in my most obsequi-
ous manner, "there's nothing I would like better."

"Then it's settled," announced Shafter with finality. "Colonel, cut
the necessary orders. Glad to have you with us, Travers. Report to Colonel
Elliot as soon as you're settled in."

I drew myself up impressively, shot Shafter a snappy salute, about-
faced, and marched straight back to my table, where I promptly ordered another bourbon, downed it in one gulp when it arrived, and
congratulated myself that all those hours spent studying tactics at West
Point had not gone to naught—I'd just won my first engagement of
the war!

Later that afternoon I prowled the docks of Tampa. I found a local
fisherman, a Creek Indian, and arranged for the fellow to paddle up

nearby streams every morning for as long as the V Corps remained there to gather up a basket of wild onions. He was to deliver it to me in the Tampa Bay Hotel in exchange for his fee of ten cents per trip. Between the high cost of onions and a bar bill that I knew would soon go through the ceiling, I could only hope the fighting broke out before I went bust.

22

Two weeks later I was just finishing breakfast and looking forward to another day of careful indolence when I glanced up to see Crane coming through the hotel lobby straight for me. "Travers, old man, where have you been keeping yourself?" he hailed.

I noticed that Crane had a stranger in tow, an immaculately groomed fellow with an air of grandeur about him. Out of an abundance of caution I arose and smiled heartily.

"Oh, here and there, Crane," I replied evasively, for one never knew when Crane was seeking alms. "And yourself?"

"Holed up in a flea-infested garret near the shore, working my backside off. The *Journal*'s buying my copy as fast as I can write it, which is good of course, but I've never labored so hard in my life."

"Come now, Crane. Since when has the life of a reporter involved labor? I'd say it's more like telling lies for pay, wouldn't you?"

Crane grinned, mirthlessly. "That it is, sometimes. But right now there's so much going on, there's no need for lies." Then he recalled his companion. "But I forget myself. Let me introduce Richard Harding Davis. *The* Mister Davis," he added, emphasizing the article meaningfully. "Mister Davis is the correspondent for the *London Times*." Noting my unimpressed look, Crane went on to ensure that I understood I was in the presence of an august personage. "Mister Davis is probably the most famous reporter in the world today, Travers."

Then why the hell is he traipsing about with you? I wanted to ask. But ever since I had landed on the general's staff I had made it a habit to be nice to everyone I met—at least until I had determined whether they could hurt me or not—and so I flashed the newcomer the winning Travers smile and said smoothly, "A great pleasure, Mister Davis," and then threw in a white lie: "I've heard so much about you."

We shook hands heartily; manly handshakes were absolutely necessary under such circumstances, I'd come to learn, so I let Davis have
a knuckle-cruncher. He didn't wince; this dandy is tougher than he
looks, I thought. In contrast to the spindly Crane, Davis was a tall,
well-made fellow with bright eyes and an intelligent face.

"The pleasure is all mine, Lieutenant Travers. But do call me Dickie.
All my friends do." He spoke in the beautifully modulated tones of a
trained orator. Davis was clearly a class above Crane and the other
newspaper hacks I had met. "Stephen here has been telling me all about
you."

"Tell me, er, Dickie, why would I be of any interest to you?" I asked
cautiously.

"Ah, you're too modest, Travers," smiled Davis. "I like that in a
man. You see, you're a symbol of the new age in America; a West
Pointer on the fighting edge of America's quest for empire. That makes
you a member of America's ruling class, and my readership finds all
that very interesting."

A member of America's ruling class? I wondered. Me, a bastard
from Elm Grove? As for being a West Pointer, that hardly made me
special, either. Why, Davis couldn't swing a dead cat around this room
without hitting a score of them. No, that wasn't it, but I sensed that
Davis wasn't quite ready to get to the point yet.

I shrugged. "I suppose so. But there's got to be a limit to the drivel
people are willing to read about."

Davis laughed. "I quite agree with you, Lieutenant Travers. Most
of what's being written now *is* drivel; but then, that's what we reporters
are stuck with until the war starts."

"Right you are, Dickie," agreed Crane. "At the moment, in fact, I'm
pondering just what drivel to write about for my next column."

"Why not write a piece on these European military observers,"
suggested Davis, nodding at the gaggles of foreigners wandering aimlessly
about the lobby clad in the military regalia of most of the major powers
of the continent. "In fact, there's a likely subject for a story over there."

I followed his gaze to where a muscular brute wearing a *feldgrau*
Prussian service uniform stood. The man's spiked helmet was tucked
crisply under one arm and his jackboots gleamed in the sultry air.

"A captain, or *hauptman* as the Germans say," explained Davis. "And
that broad red stripe down his trouser leg marks him as a member of
the general staff. That's a gentleman with a future, I'd say."

"Hmm," mused Crane. "I'll explore that idea, thank you."

"Oh, you're more than welcome, Stephen. The fact is, I could use some fresh subject matter for my column as well. And you, Lieutenant Travers," he added, turning to me, "might be in a position to assist me in that regard."

"Oh?" I asked. "And how could I help the most renowned journalist in the world?"

"Simple," smiled Davis. "You're on General Shafter's staff. I thought you might be able to arrange an interview for me."

The request didn't surprise me. After only a few weeks in Tampa, I was recognized on sight by American and foreign officers I chanced to meet. I rather liked the attention; it placed me several notches above ordinary lieutenants, and buoyed my already-inflated opinion of myself. Also, my new status had allowed me to secure a comfortable room in the hotel. But my pleasure turned to consternation when newspapermen tried to use me as a stepping-stone to Shafter. Every time I ventured into the hotel lobby, I was set upon by these jackals for some bit of news about our military plans, or the general's health, or some other nonsense.

"I don't think that's possible, Dickie. The general's terribly pressed at the moment. Troop movements and all. I'm sure you understand."

That was all true enough, of course, but I might have also added that Pecos Bill was thoroughly resentful of the lambasting he had taken from the press for alleged incompetence. Talking Shafter into granting Davis an interview would be about as easy as convincing Shafter to skip a meal, and Shafter had not skipped a meal in living memory.

"A pity," clucked Davis, clearly miffed at my failure to jump at the chance of being an intermediary between himself and Shafter. "Although in truth, Lieutenant, my sources tell me that the general has hardly been a blurof motion lately. In fact, the word is that Shafter is almost completely paralyzed at the thought of the daunting task facing him."

Davis was right on the mark there. From what I could see, Shafter was terrified of the responsibility that had been thrust upon him. In fact, in my opinion, Pecos Bill should have been relieved for incompetence, but for the moment I decided to play the role of the loyal little staffer. "Paralyzed is he, Dickie? Come now, that's a little strong, isn't it?"

"Perhaps, but it's the truth, Travers," retorted Davis.

I smiled benignly at this, for Shafter was in a fix, you see. There's a rule of war that says there are two types of generals. One type is offensive and the other defensive. It's hard for an offensively minded general to fight defensively, but it's positively disastrous for a defensive general to fight offensively. Shafter was a defensive general; indeed, his very physique, with its vast bottom and low center of gravity, cried out: "I shall not be moved." Asking Shafter to mount a lightning attack against the Spanish was like asking a walrus to fly.

Clearing my throat, I gingerly phrased my reply. One never knew what a reporter would print, after all, and I had no desire to be dislodged from my comfortable berth by a slip of the tongue. "I think the truth is that General Shafter is a very concerned leader who likes to carefully consider each step that he takes," I explained gently to Davis. "Such a temperament does not make for rapid progress, but it makes for sure progress."

I could see from his dubious expression that Davis was unconvinced. "Very well, if the general will not see me, he must assume all responsibility for any inaccuracies that may occur in my columns. He must understand, of course, that I shall continue to feature his actions, or more accurately, inactions, in my column whether or not he grants me an interview."

I was certain that a frank exchange of views with Davis was the last of Shafter's concerns right about now, but I didn't tell that to Davis. Instead, I promised, "I'll tell the general of your request at the earliest opportunity, Dickie." Eyeing the lobby clock pointedly, I announced with what I hoped sounded like regret, "I must be off, gentlemen, or I'll be late for the daily staff briefing."

With a nod of my head I excused myself and hurried away to the suite of rooms on the mezzanine level that served as Shafter's operations center.

23

Although I had come to dread the daily staff briefings because they bored me to distraction, I was glad to have an opportunity to escape Crane and Davis. The meeting had already begun when I arrived; I slipped inside and settled among the other officers ringing Shafter as he held court at a large polished oak table. I quickly saw that he was in his usual form.

"I simply don't see how this is all supposed to get done!" whined Shafter to nobody in particular. "Honest to God, I don't. There aren't enough trained troops, not enough uniforms, and not enough artillery or small arms. For God's sake, I don't even have enough ships to get this corps over the sea to Cuba!"

Across the table from him were brigadier generals Lawton and Kent, the commanders of Shafter's two infantry divisions, and Brigadier General Bates, who commanded an independent brigade. They nodded calmly at this outburst, for it was old news to them. Although I was a newcomer to the staff, I had already heard this litany a dozen times; Shafter tended to repeat his woes like a Dominican father fingering his prayer beads.

"Colonel, what was the status on the available shipping today?" demanded Shafter, looking at Elliot.

"Five transports are at anchor, sir," answered Elliot. "Fifteen more are steaming for Tampa now and are expected any day."

"Twenty transports aren't enough to carry this corps across Tampa Bay, let alone to Cuba," complained Shafter peevishly. "I need forty, by God. I've already told that to Secretary Alger."

"We've been assured by the navy that additional transports will arrive shortly," said Elliot carefully.

"That's what the navy said yesterday and last week! I can't move my forces across the Florida Straits on empty navy promises," snorted Shafter, his jowls mottled with anger. "The War Department doesn't understand that simple fact. They keep pressing me for progress, but the truth of the matter is that I'm stuck here until I get some support from the navy." He pounded the table in frustration, and then demanded of Elliot, "What's the situation with the canned rations, Colonel? Have we stockpiled enough for operations in Cuba yet?"

Elliot cleared his throat. "No, sir, not yet. We have a week's worth of rations here. There's another two weeks' worth on the sidings in Atlanta, but the freight cars necessary to move the food haven't been released from Chickamauga by General Miles." General Nelson A. Miles was the commanding general of the army and Shafter's direct competitor for martial glory.

"Damn Miles!" raged Shafter, his bloated face flashing crimson at the mention of his nemesis. "He's deliberately hampering me, trying to make me look like a nincompoop so that the War Department will relieve me and he can step into my shoes here. If he wasn't so damned keen on running for the presidency, he might be more inclined to act like the military leader he's supposed to be. I have half a mind to wire McKinley and tell him I'm so hamstrung from all quarters that any operations against Cuba this year are impossible. If we continue to stumble forward like this, lots of soldiers are going to get hurt unnecessarily, mark my words. And you can bet I'm not going to take the blame, no sirree," he vowed to the assembled officers, who eyed him wordlessly.

The truth was, Shafter was right on all counts. Miles was undercutting him, and McKinley had no grasp of the complexities entailed in an invasion of Cuba. McKinley wanted a tidy little fait accompli that would not involve Miles and would be concluded well before the next presidential election. The problem was that the forces necessary to make a rapierlike strike at Cuba didn't exist, and it was Shafter's unhappy lot to have to create them from scratch.

So Pecos Bill was in a tight spot, and we all knew it. For some men elevated to the heights of responsibility, pressure is like a tonic that allows them to overcome formidable obstacles. For others, like Shafter, too much stress snuffs them out like a candle in a hurricane. Sighing deeply, Shafter took out his timepiece. "Half an hour to lunch," he announced dejectedly. "We may as well go over the maps again."

Aides scurried to spread a large map of Cuba on the great oak table. Shafter rose and bent ponderously over the map, planting his hands on the table to steady himself. The staff gathered behind him in a close knot. I caught a glimpse of the diminutive octogenarian, Maj. Gen. Fighting Joe Wheeler, the commander of Shafter's cavalry division, fast asleep in a straight-backed chair on the far side of the room, his ermine beard flowing down his chest. Wheeler was V Corps' token Confederate. He'd been a general in the South's losing effort, and McKinley was clearly trying to mend regional fences by placing this son of Dixie in a position of authority in the war against Spain. But Fighting Joe's best fighting days were clearly behind him: Since being on the staff I'd noticed that Wheeler took late-morning naps regardless of what the rest of the world was up to. I prayed that most of the fighting in Cuba took place in the afternoon.

"Colonel Elliot," Shafter inquired, "what do we know about the location of the Cuban rebel forces?"

"We know that they've been routed from the vicinity of Havana and that most of western Cuba is firmly under Spanish control," answered Elliot. "The rebels exercise some degree of dominion over eastern Cuba, primarily from Santiago to the eastern tip of the island, Punta de Maisi. Their chief is a fellow named Garcia, and he's reputed to be the most effective of the rebel leaders. As to their location, strength, and arms, however, we can only guess."

"I take it, then, that none of the agents we sent to contact the rebel chiefs have yet reported back?" queried Shafter.

"Not yet, sir," confirmed Elliot.

"Damn!" swore Shafter. "This is a hell of a fix! I'm ordered to land in Cuba, but nobody can tell me if I'll be met by an army of allies or a motley crew of beggars who'll be just as big a problem for me as the Spanish."

Elliot had no reply; he knew that Shafter was right on this score.

"What about the beaches near Santiago?" demanded Shafter. "Has the navy examined them yet? Which ones are suitable for a landing?" Santiago, on the south coast of Cuba, was Shafter's objective. He hoped to capture that strategic port and then march overland to Havana.

Silence again from Elliot at first, and then he mumbled apologetically, "Er, the navy has not yet conducted any reconnaissance, General."

"Not yet?" roared Shafter. "Just look at this map! It tells me nothing about the condition of the coast! I could be landing this army in deadly surf for all I know. The navy promised me full cooperation when I took this command, yet all I've gotten out of them so far are excuses and delays." He was dangerously red now and paused to sputter his indignation. "Goddamn them!" he bellowed furiously, pounding the table with the flat of his hand for emphasis.

His exertion was so great that he immediately and violently broke wind, passing gas into the packed ranks of officers around him. Knees buckled and men gagged as the stench raced through the room like exploding shrapnel. I got a whiff, turned on my heels, and marched out of the room, on the way out passing Fighting Joe, who was mercifully asleep and oblivious to the odor enveloping him. All that needs to be done to dislodge the dagos from Cuba, I thought as I departed, is to tow Shafter into Havana harbor in a dinghy. After a few days, his flatulence is certain to drive the proud dons to their knees.

24

I paused in the lobby to ponder my next action. My duty day was at an end, so I decided that a little refreshment was in order and marched into the saloon. I found an empty stool in a dark corner, and ordered a double bourbon.

"Lieutenant Travers?" I turned to see an elderly lieutenant colonel of volunteers, drink in hand.

"Yes?" I replied, adding as an afterthought, "Sir?"

"Lieutenant Colonel Terrence Quinlon, 71st New York Volunteers, at your service, bucko," he said, extending his hand.

"Pleased to make your acquaintance, sir," I mumbled without enthusiasm as we shook. What did this fellow want? I wondered.

Quinlon read the uncertainty in my expression. "I've heard from Mister Crane that you're a protégé of the great Mister Duncan," he said. "Is that so, lad?"

I cringed at the mention of Crane's name, and then at the question. How could George Duncan possibly be connected to this fellow? Alarmed and suspicious, I decided to answer the question with a question. "Are you acquainted with Mister Duncan, sir?"

The old fellow laughed gaily. "No, unfortunately. I've never met the dear man, I'm afraid. But I know of him; he's one of the lions of Tammany Hall, I can assure you, a credit to New York and the salt of the earth. One of the shining lights of our great metropolis."

If that statement was accurate, it was a sad commentary on the caliber of New York's citizenry. I caught a broad Hibernian brogue in Quinlon's voice and pegged him as an upstart bog-hopper who somehow had wangled a commission. I studied the Irishman anew. He had a typically florid Celtic face capped with a mane of ginger hair speckled with gray near the temples, a pug nose, and craggy cheekbones set off by bright blue eyes. All this topped off a compact, wiry build that gave him the appearance of an overgrown leprechaun.

My drink quickly arrived, and I raised it. "Well, here's to you, Colonel, and to old New York," I toasted, taking a long swallow. Quinlon raised his rye in reply, drained it easily, and set his glass on the bar.

"'Tis a blistering hot day out there, lad," he said genially, then rapped on the bar and called out, "Bartender, more of the same poteen, straight up." Turning to me again, he laid a hand on my shoulder and proclaimed, "Fenwick, me boy"—he'd learned my first name, probably from Crane—"I can't tell ye how pleased the lads in the 71st were when I told 'em ye were down here."

I smiled noncommittally and took another sip. My instincts screamed that I was being approached, and that the touch was coming momentarily. I had Quinlon pigeonholed already; he was probably one of the army of papist politicians who were forever courting the old-line Knickerbockers like Duncan as the New York Irish moved slowly from the tenements to the halls of power. I mused about how much it must have galled a patrician like Duncan to rub elbows with slavering Fenians like Quinlon and derived no small amount of pleasure from the thought.

"It's a regular ye are, if I'm not mistaken, Lieutenant?" ventured Quinlon.

"Right you are, sir," I replied evenly.

"I knew it!" he chuckled. "West Point, right?"

"Right again," I confirmed.

Now Quinlon's face assumed a grave expression. "'Tis a shame, though, the way we poor volunteers are treated down here, Fenwick," he clucked sadly. "We're only doing our duty, of course, and we want no different treatment from that accorded the regulars. So there's no reason for the hellish suffering we've endured, lad. There's nary a drop of clean water to be had, and the food is enough to kill a heathen Injun dead."

Here it comes, I told myself.

"So I says to myself, Quinlon, who do ye know who could help the boys out in these troubled times? Certainly none of them holier-than-thou regular officers in my division. Then I heard that the general, bless his soul, had elevated ye to his staff. Saint Bridget be praised, says I, young Travers will be the savior of us all. Sure and he's the favorite of the greatest man of our fair city. He won't let us down."

I drained my drink. For a moment I toyed with the notion of asking Quinlon just how many onions his men needed, but I thought better of it. Just then, however, we were interrupted by another officer of volunteers, a bantam of a fellow with a jutting chin and a pince-nez perched on his nose. He marched straight up to Quinlon, pushed his face into the Irishman's, and demanded imperiously: "Quinlon, you old son of a bitch, what are you doing here while your men are out languishing in the sand?"

Quinlon recoiled from the newcomer like a rat from a terrier. Recovering himself with an effort, he stammered, "Lieutenant Travers, allow me to introduce Lieutenant Colonel Roosevelt, First Volunteer Cavalry."

"They're called the Rough Riders, and you damned well know it, Quinlon," snapped Roosevelt. "Bartender, a schooner of beer."

I had heard of Roosevelt, of course, as had everyone in camp. He'd run unsuccessfully for mayor of New York some years back on a reform platform. The whole nation knew the story of the Rough Riders he'd raised, and by all accounts Roosevelt was determined to return from this war drenched in glory. As a war hero he would no doubt have a much better chance of becoming New York's mayor.

Roosevelt eyed me aggressively, his bristling mustache twitching with nervous energy. His attempt to stare me down was futile; I was a full head taller than he, which forced him to crane his head up just to make eye contact with me. Defeated, he gave up the game. "You're with Shafter, aren't you, Lieutenant?" he demanded accusingly. There was none of the deferential tone to which I had lately become accustomed.

"Yes, sir, I'm one of the general's aides," I answered, not liking at all Roosevelt's confrontational airs. In fact, I had a strong urge to shove the little prima donna down on the seat of his pants, but years of servility, ingrained during my stay at the Dude Factory, prevailed. "Lieutenant Travers, at your service," I added, somewhat stiffly.

"A bloody mess here, Travers," grumbled Roosevelt irritably. "No one seems to know what they're doing, and my men are out there without adequate food or water."

Roosevelt's tone was unrelentingly biting, but I had no intention of rising to his bait. If Roosevelt wanted onions, I could help. But if he thought I was going to engage him in a debate about the clumsy handling of this expedition, he was out of luck.

"There've been some logistical shortfalls," I admitted breezily, "but none that couldn't be expected to occur in an undertaking of this magnitude."

"That's not the point!" shot back Roosevelt. "What I want to know is just what Shafter's going to do to fix these deplorable conditions. It's no secret that some people in high places are already calling for his relief, and with cause, I say. My God, a warehouse clerk would be sacked if he caused a fraction of this mess."

"Things will improve as soon as the corps crosses over to Cuba," I soothed him, with no factual basis whatsoever for my assertion.

"That is, if we ever get to Cuba," Roosevelt retorted. "Personally, I think this corps is going to dry up in this hellhole and simply blow away. The Spanish'll win this war without firing a shot."

Just then I was wishing that Roosevelt would blow away when he fortunately spotted a table full of correspondents. Showing the instincts of an inveterate candidate, Roosevelt let his feet begin moving him in their direction even as he finished his dialogue with me. "Travers," he observed tartly in parting, "this affair is a damned disgrace, I tell you. It won't be long before what's going on down here becomes a public scandal, and I'm just the man to get the ball rolling in that direction."

With a curt tip of his hat, Roosevelt sauntered off to the reporters, who bobbed up and down at his approach like excited puppies at a bitch's teats. It was clear to me that Roosevelt was determined to emerge from this war as a winner, whether or not V Corps ever budged from Tampa.

"I can't stand that bastard," muttered Quinlon as Roosevelt left. "Him and his damned sanctified attitude. It's as though he's the Almighty's personal representative on earth, come to lead us all back to the garden. And to think the deceiving creature had the unmitigated gall to run for mayor! It would have meant the end of civilization in New York had he been elected, I tell ye."

Or at least civilization as Tammany Hall knew it, I thought. Quinlon continued to grouse quietly to himself, and if there had been another decent bar in Tampa I would have excused myself. But there wasn't and I wasn't going to let myself be run off by this old ward heeler.

Suddenly the room brightened as a beautiful apparition appeared at the saloon's entrance and scanned the room intently as though searching for someone. She was a breathtaking golden-haired beauty, wearing a flowing white summer dress and a delicate sky blue bonnet adorned with sweeping white ostrich feathers. She looked in my direction, smiled, and approached.

I froze, afraid that any sudden movement on my part would frighten her away like a startled doe. All heads turned to follow her progress across the room.

To my amazement, she stopped right in front of Quinlon! "Father, where have you been? I've looked all over Tampa for you," she said admonishingly, and then planted a peck on Quinlon's wizened cheek.

25

"Fiona, darling," said Quinlon, "I was just on me way to meet ye. I only stopped off a minute to speak with Lieutenant Travers here. Army business, ye understand," he added gravely. Turning to me he said, "Lieutenant Travers, may I introduce me daughter and the light o' me life, Fiona."

"Charmed, miss," I said, rising. "Your father and I were just discussing the logistical arrangements of his regiment."

"Pleased to meet you, sir," smiled Fiona as she eyed me appraisingly. She was quite a stunner; her blond tresses set off her blue-green eyes and creamy complexion to perfection. It was simply amazing that an old troll like Quinlon could have begotten such a lovely specimen.

"Father, you promised to take me down to the waterfront," she gently scolded. "You know that a reputable young lady simply can't stroll about an army encampment unescorted."

"That I do, colleen," conceded Quinlon. "But I'm a trifle busy today. After all, there's a war on, ye know."

"Perhaps I may be of assistance, Miss Quinlon," I interjected amiably. "I would be honored to escort you. My duties for the day are finished, and I'd like nothing better than the pleasure of your company."

"Well, I don't know," hesitated Quinlon, giving me a sidelong look. But I could see that Fiona was delighted at the prospect of being squired around camp on the arm of a tall, handsome young officer. Quinlon was giving the matter some thought; indeed, if he had truly known me as well as he let on, he'd never let Fiona be alone with me as long as she was in Tampa. On the other hand, he probably attached some weight to the notion that regular officers were supposed to be perfect gentlemen, not to mention the fact that he'd be loath to get on my bad side and thus sever the only connection he had to Shafter. In the end, the politician in Quinlon prevailed over his fatherly concerns. He arranged his face into a benign smile and said, "Sure and be off with the both of ye. And Fiona, don't be pestering the young gentleman with your eternal questioning. For once in your life do some listening."

"Of course, Father," she promised, beaming at me.

I offered her my arm with a courtly bow, and together we strolled into the bright sunlight outside. I steered my pretty charge off to the bay, where a flotilla of craft lay at anchor.

"Isn't it all so exciting?" breathed Fiona. "Everything and everybody here is so alive compared with the way things are back in stuffy old New York."

"Tell me, Fiona, whatever could have compelled a lovely lady such as yourself to forsake the comforts of New York for an unlikely spot like this?" I asked. We were walking in deeper sand now, and Fiona leaned on my arm for support. I felt the pleasant pressure of her soft and lithesome body.

"I'm on a bit of a holiday, you might say, Lieutenant," she explained.

"Fenwick, please," I insisted.

"All right, Fenwick," she said. "When Father was commissioned in the regiment last month, he left me with nobody to stay with. You see, he's been a widower for years. I couldn't bear the thought of being packed off to some awful girls' college, so I talked Father into letting me take a commercial position until the war's over. I'm to start with a brokerage firm on Wall Street as soon as the army leaves for Cuba and I return from Tampa."

"A woman on Wall Street? That's a bit unusual, isn't it?" I queried, more because I knew that she expected to hear it than because I cared. I've always believed that women should work—the harder the better, too.

"Yes, it is," she laughed. "But Father has always encouraged me to make my way in the world. Besides, I'm only going to be a secretary, so it's not so shocking. But the important thing is that Father doesn't lock me in a dusty old apartment until some twit of a boy appears to ask for my hand. Since I have no taste for higher education, a commercial position for me, at least for the present, suits him just fine."

"How enlightened of him," I observed. And how convenient, since Fiona's position would relieve Quinlon of the burden of clothing and feeding her. Although I had short acquaintance of Quinlon, I hesitated to ascribe a benevolent motive to anything he did. "Tell me, Fiona," I asked, changing the subject, "what would cause your father to seek a commission in the first place? I would think that an old—er, that is, a man his age would not particularly care for the rigors of a campaign."

"Oh, I'm sure that Father isn't looking forward to the hardships of war, Fenwick," she replied. "But he was in a situation back in New York that was rapidly growing impossible." She paused, deciding whether to burden me further with her father's woes. I hoped she'd decide not to, but unfortunately, I have the type of face that makes women feel they can confide in me, and Fiona was no exception.

"Father had a good position with the city water commission," she continued. "Oh, he'd never get wealthy, but we were comfortable. Unfortunately, Father's tenure was tied to his ability to deliver the vote for his Tammany Hall ward boss on election day. In years gone by, this was never a problem. But then that awful man Roosevelt, with his muckraking ways, ran for mayor. He was the police commissioner then, and he stormed around the city ranting about corruption in high places. He appealed directly to the voters to throw off what he termed the chains of Tammany Hall. In the end Roosevelt lost, but Father's ward bolted the machine and voted for Roosevelt. From that day on, Father was out. There's no appeal from that sort of decision, so when the war came along Father used every last bit of pull he had to get his commission. The army is only temporary for him, of course, and I hope that when this dreadful war is over something better for him will turn up."

"I'm sure it will," I assured her, not bothering to mention that the sort of trouble that could turn up in Cuba might make Quinlon's troubles back in New York seem like child's play.

We arrived at the waterfront and stopped to rest beside Tampa's main pier, which jutted out into the bay. Hundreds of troopers from the Quartermaster Corps were stacking mountains of supplies that would soon be loaded onto the invasion transports. I watched the poor bastards sweating in the brutal heat and had a momentary stab of compassion for them. But then I remembered that every man here was a volunteer—there were no conscripts in this army, you see—and I laughed out loud.

"What amuses you, Fenwick?" asked Fiona, smiling. Although we'd been together only a few minutes, I could tell that a mutual attraction was stirring.

"Oh, nothing really, my dear. It's just a fine day to be alive and to be able to laugh."

She smiled. "Yes, I think I understand. Although it's a tragic time for so many people, I've never felt so free. It's wonderful."

Suddenly there was a mighty cheer from the direction of the encampment. Troops were throwing their hats in the air and firearms were discharged. We heard shouting from man to man, and like wildfire the word spread. "Victory at Manila Bay! Dewey has sunk the Spanish fleet! We didn't lose a single ship or man!"

If that were true, I realized, it would be an accomplishment of epic proportions! Why, the Philippines would be at our feet! All around us men laughed and slapped each other on the back. This war was off to a spectacular start!

"Oh, Fenwick, isn't it simply too good to be true? The Spanish swept from the sea by our valiant navy! And the war has only just begun!" cried Fiona. She flung her arms about me in an unexpected outburst of emotion and hugged me violently. I felt her breasts pressed enticingly against me and returned her embrace eagerly.

"Don't you think this is all so exciting?" she asked coyly, looking up at me.

"Indeed it is," I agreed warmly. "I feel so grand I want to kiss someone."

"How about me?" she asked quietly, her blue-green eyes wide.

By way of an answer, I kissed her hard on the mouth. Now here you might criticize me, and call me to task for so quickly forgetting dear Alice back in New York. Make no mistake, my affection for Alice was undiminished. She was sweetness, she was light, she was womanhood incarnate. All in all, Alice had but one fault: She wasn't in Tampa.

26

Tampa Bay Hotel, Florida
June 1898
"Up and at 'em, my dear," I said, pulling the covers from sleeping Fiona. "Get your lovely backside up before the halls are filled with people."

It was false dawn, and as had become her custom over the past few weeks, Fiona spent the evening with me but, for the sake of decorum, retired to her own room before the hotel stirred. I didn't give a damn for propriety, but if it meant keeping Quinlon from interfering with our trysts, I'd shoo Fiona out.

"So soon?" she mumbled drowsily. "It seems like I just got here."

"Well, you didn't," I laughed. "Now get up. If we expect to keep our little situation going, we mustn't get careless, right, dear?"

She sat up and stretched. "I suppose not. Father would have an absolute fit if he knew what we were up to."

"I can imagine," I said, hopping out of bed and getting dressed. "I've got a busy day ahead of me, Fee. There's the general's onions to rustle up, you know. That should keep me occupied until noon. Then, of course, I've got to drink at the bar and tell lies until dinner. There's no rest for the weary, I'm afraid."

When Fiona was dressed I popped my head out into the hallway to ensure that the coast was clear and then gave her a farewell kiss. "Off you go, my dear. I'll see you tonight."

"Good-bye, dear Fenny," she breathed in that delightfully husky bedroom voice of hers, giving me a kiss in return. She slipped out the door and was gone.

I waited a decent interval and then went downstairs to get breakfast in the dining room. There was nothing like a night of romping under the covers with a willing filly like Fiona to work up a man's appetite. I found a table and ordered a stack of flapjacks. The waiter brought coffee, and I was taking my first sip when who should stride in but Colonel Liscum of the 9th Infantry. At his heels like a faithful hound was Major Whittaker.

I squirmed uncomfortably; the 9th had been in Florida for about two weeks now. Liscum had been surprised, to put it mildly, that I was at V Corps and not in Washington as he had been led to believe. Now that the 9th was here, he wanted me back with the colors. But, as I had learned from Hobart the other day, there was another nettle under Liscum's saddle.

"Fenny," Hobart had told me when I rode over to A Company while it was conducting target practice in a clearing in the palmetto jungle ringing the encampment, "you're in deep trouble with Colonel Liscum."

As he spoke he enviously eyed my impeccably tailored khakis, gleaming boots, and the handsome hunter I had cut out from the herd reserved for corps staff. My carefully creased campaign hat was tilted so as to accentuate my fair features and now-magnificent blond mustache. All in all, I was a rather smashing figure of a man as I sat my mount easily and rested my fingers on the grip of my Model 1878 Colt. It was a .45 caliber—big enough to stop anything, human or animal, likely to cross my path.

"Over what?" I asked innocently. Around us, prone troopers popped off rounds at straw targets as we spoke. Generally they hit what they aimed at, but after all these were regulars.

"It's about that night up in Plattsburgh when you floored Captain Harris," Hobart explained. "Liscum went back to check your official records. He found out you were appointed to West Point from the regular army, not Indiana. He also knows that you hail from Illinois. He's convinced you pulled a fast one on him, and he's none too happy about it."

"How's that?" I challenged Hobart. "I never claimed to be a Hoosier that night as I recall."

"Maybe," conceded Hobart, "but Liscum feels that was the impression you deliberately gave. And he's mad as hell about it."

Now here was Liscum barely twenty feet away scanning the crowded room for a table! I became suddenly aware of the three empty chairs at my table. My God, he might join me, and then there was no telling where things might lead, I realized. Just then I saw a familiar face; it was Crane, and he too was searching for a place to alight.

"Crane!" I called hurriedly, "over here. Sit down and have a bite, old friend." Crane sauntered over and plopped down. That left two chairs, and I saw Liscum eyeing them. But he also eyed Crane's loud plaid suit and notebook and pegged him correctly as a newspaperman. Liscum would rather have had breakfast with a mob of half-breed goat herders than with a reporter; he marched off.

"How have you been, partner?" I asked, feeling expansive because of the narrowness of my escape. "Could I stake you to breakfast?"

"I'm afraid not, Travers," replied Crane morosely. "My stomach's been giving me absolute hell lately."

That was hardly surprising. Indeed, I was amazed that Crane could even arise in the morning, given the quantity of opium elixir he habitually swilled. "Then have some coffee, man," I offered heartily.

But it was more than Crane's stomach that was making him feel blue. "Tell me, Fenny," he asked, "when is Shafter going to get this show on the road? Everyone is tired of sitting in this vermin-infested hellhole."

Everyone but me, apparently. I merely took a sip and said blandly, "Oh?"

"Mark my words, Travers, things are coming to a boil," continued Crane. "McKinley's had about all of Shafter's procrastination he can stand."

My breakfast arrived, and I went at it with gusto. "Come now, Crane,"

I chided, "you newspaper fellows have made up so many rumors about Shafter's imminent relief that you've come to believe them yourselves. Take it from me, Shafter's not leaving Tampa until he's good and ready, and I don't see that happening for months."

Just then Colonel Elliot stormed into the dining room. He was searching for me and knew just where to look. "Lieutenant Travers, on your feet!" he barked. "The general's given the order to board the transports. We're going to Cuba at last!"

"Oh, no!" I groaned.

"Yippee!" yelped Crane, jumping up and scampering out the door past startled diners. "It's on at last!" he screamed as he ran across the beach and headed straight for the telegraph office.

27

Pandemonium broke out instantly in the camp; tents were struck, herds of horses and mules were rounded up from the brush, and the troops were formed into regiments and began to surge toward the dock area located at the end of a railroad spur.

Foremost among the agitators trying to board any available vessel was Lieutenant Colonel Roosevelt and his Rough Riders. "Give me a damned ship, b'gad!" he roared to nobody in particular, hopping about on his bandy legs like a frog in a frying pan. "I'll not be missing this fray, I tell you! Especially not for the want of a piddling boat."

Then he spied me lounging on the pier. "Travers!" he called. "Get me a boat, man! You're close to that whale of a general of ours. For God's sake, do something!"

"I'm afraid my hands are tied, Colonel," I countered airily, giving a languid shrug of my shoulders. "You'll just have to wait until Colonel Elliot makes transportation available to your regiment." In truth, I couldn't care less about Roosevelt's political ambitions or the greater glory of his precious Rough Riders.

"Goddamnit!" swore Roosevelt vehemently. "That's just like a staff officer for you—absolutely useless!"

He had my number, all right, but I nonetheless assured him disingenuously, "I'd like to help, sir. I really would. But General Shafter has a plan for embarkation. You should wait for the vessel that's been assigned to your regiment."

"I'd sooner believe that cows can fly than Shafter has a plan to get us to Cuba," shot back Roosevelt. "And if you won't help me, Travers, I'll find someone who will." With that he stormed off down the crowded pier to belabor some other poor staffer. I watched his antics with great satisfaction for ten minutes or so until he'd screamed himself hoarse and had just about given up, when the steamer *Yucatan* pulled up at dockside. The manifest prepared by the corps staff indicated that the 71st New York was to board the *Yucatan,* and indeed Quinlon's boys were forming up a short distance away.

Roosevelt quickly took in the situation and had a sudden flash of inspiration. He shouted instructions to some of his officers, and in a few moments a large herd of horses belonging to the Rough Riders was driven by wranglers directly between the *Yucatan* and the 71st New York. Then the Rough Riders, who had been lounging near the dock, conspicuous in their all-khaki uniforms, cavalry yellow epaulets, and the gaudy unit pins fastened to their campaign hats, suddenly arose as one man and ran pell-mell for the gangplank the *Yucatan* was lowering. The cavalrymen clambered aboard in minutes, and as the last of them cleared the gunwales, the wranglers put whips to the horses and drove the herd to the dock as well. There, cavalrymen manning booms with slings attached began swinging the bewildered beasts aboard one after the other. By the time Quinlon and his men had pushed past the bucking and snorting horses in their path, the Rough Riders had the gangplank up and were jeering the furious New Yorkers. Above the din stood Roosevelt on the deck of the *Yucatan,* hands on hips, shouting, "Bully! Bully!" each time a squealing mustang was hauled over the rail.

Quinlon, beside himself with rage, stormed down the pier directly for me. "Travers, just what the hell is going on here? That ship is reserved fer *my* regiment, damnit!"

"I realize that, sir," I answered, "but there appears to be a misunderstanding with Colonel Roosevelt." I gestured up at the mustachioed maniac capering on the deck above us.

"Misunderstanding me sweet arse, bucko!" retorted Quinlon angrily. "That pompous bastard Roosevelt stole this ship from me and I want it back!"

I had no intention, however, of undoing what Roosevelt had wrought. If I forced the Rough Riders off the *Yucatan,* I would have Roosevelt right back here on the pier yelling in my ear.

"Sir, I've no authority to order anyone off a steamer. If you must protest, Colonel Elliot's right over there," I said, pointing to where Elliot was similarly besieged by irate regimental officers who, like Quinlon, felt themselves wronged in the loading process.

"We'll see about this, laddy," huffed Quinlon ominously, and he stalked off toward Elliot. In the end it turned out that I'd done Quinlon a great service, for no sooner had all thirty-two steamers been loaded and assembled in the middle of Tampa Bay than a cable was received from Secretary of War Alger instructing Shafter to remain at anchor indefinitely. As their comrades swung miserably at anchor only a half mile away, the fortunate stay-behinds erected tarpaulins against the sun and availed themselves of the cool drinks hawked by the itinerant vendors who clung to the army the way ticks cling to a dog. Soon banjos were strumming as the beached troopers serenaded their ship-bound fellows with endless choruses of the popular song sweeping the nation, "There'll Be a Hot Time in the Old Town Tonight!"

By sundown the order to stand down was verified, and the stay-behinds marched from the docks back to their old bivouac areas. When I reached the hotel, I picked up my key at the desk and made my way upstairs to my room. Although V Corps had been stood down, I was certain that the delay would be brief. I therefore intended to put my remaining time in Tampa to the best possible use, which to me meant bedding Fiona as often as possible. With that happy thought I swung open my door.

The sight that greeted my eyes left me speechless.

"Who are you, Mister?" yelped a frightened, middle-aged fellow, jumping up from my bed as I entered. I was rooted to the spot in amazement. I recognized the intruder as one of the corps chaplains, a Methodist minister if I remembered right. And there on the bed was Fiona, the bedclothes pulled up to cover her bosom, her mouth wide with astonishment.

The minister hopped into his trousers, gibbering, "Don't shoot, Mister, don't shoot! Are you her husband?"

For a moment I couldn't move; I hadn't even thought about shooting anyone until he mentioned it. My hand moved to the Colt strapped to my waist. Should I shoot him? Her? Both of them?

With a titanic effort, I decided what to do. "No," I calmly explained, "I'm not her husband. He's down in the saloon. But he knows you're up here with her. I came to warn Fiona that he's gone to get a revolver."

"Oh, dear God!" moaned the distraught cleric.

"It's not too late yet," I offered solicitously, warming up to my part in this ad hoc charade. "You can still slip out the back entrance before he returns. Her husband doesn't know your name, so if you go now and keep your mouth shut, this might all blow over."

"Oh, thank you, thank you," sobbed the chaplain abjectly. "That's what I'll do." And without so much as a fare-thee-well to the terrorized Fiona, he was out the door and scampering down the hallway, no doubt thanking the Almighty for his deliverance as he went.

"And now for you, my dear," I growled, turning to Fiona who shrank even farther under the covers.

"Please, Fenny, please," she mewed piteously. "I didn't want to; he forced me!"

I laughed at her gall. "Forced you? Why, that old man couldn't force a canary into a cage." Leaning over her, I hissed ominously, "He didn't force you, Fiona. You lured him up here, didn't you, you little trollop?"

So saying, I lunged for the bed covers and pulled them violently away, leaving Fiona completely naked to my gaze. At a complete loss as to what to do, and frightened out of her wits, Fiona turned over on her belly and clasped her hands over her head. Seeing my opportunity, I struck her a resounding blow with the flat of my hand across her comely buttocks.

"Yeee!" screamed Fiona, instantly hopping up to all fours and scuttling away to avoid further punishment. Stirred beyond control at the sight of her voluptuous body so wantonly displayed, I ripped off my uniform.

"What are you doing?" she asked with a quavering voice.

"Doing, my dear?" I answered. "Why, I'm merely availing myself of the services our friend the chaplain so charitably relinquished." With that I seized her wrist and threw her down roughly on the bed. As my bulging member slid home, Fiona's fear vanished and her ardor rose.

"Oh, Fenny," she sighed, "I missed you so much."

"Missed me?" I echoed incredulously. "Why, I left your side only this morning."

"But, my dear," she cooed, "when you're in love, every day seems like a year."

Oh, sure, she's in love, I thought—with the whole of V Corps. My shy little maiden had turned out to be a wanton strumpet! Nonetheless, I was no longer furious; a trollop she might be, but at least for the time being she was my trollop.

Unfortunately, I was to have the pleasure of Fiona's fickle company for only a few days longer. On June 14 another cable arrived from Washington, directing Shafter to once again proceed with the invasion. By this time a sufficient number of vessels was on hand to embark the entire corps. The troops on shore were quickly loaded and, after a tender farewell ride with Fiona, I, along with Pecos Bill and the rest of the staff, was ferried by lighter out to the steamer *Serguranca*. Soon the entire armada raised steam and sailed majestically out into the broad swells of the Gulf of Mexico.

28

In four days our flotilla steamed down the west coast of Florida, through the astonishingly clear waters between the Dry Tortugas and the Marquesas Keys, and then sailed east by southeast along the length of the north coast of Cuba. We rounded the eastern tip of the island, and slipped into the indigo waters of the Windward Passage between Cuba and Haiti. There we were joined by the Atlantic fleet, commanded by Admiral Sampson from aboard his flagship, the USS *New York,* and on the fifth day out we dropped anchor twenty miles west of Santiago. From the bridge of the *Serguranca* I studied the shoreline through binoculars. A jungle-covered bluff, green and lush, rose steeply from the sea. The land appeared deserted until I spotted a wisp of smoke— a campfire, I figured—wafting up into the morning air through the dense jungle canopy. Plainly, someone was waiting ashore.

In short order, Shafter, Elliot, myself, a few other staffers, and our marine escort were lowered in a launch and were pulling for shore. From my position in the prow I could see that small boats had been lowered by the USS *New York* as well, and these were racing to join us. I knew enough about the infighting between the army and the navy to know that one of these bore Admiral Sampson, who had stood upon protocol and insisted on being present at any meeting at which the landing of V Corps was discussed.

As we neared the chalk-white beach, figures filtered out from the jungle and hailed us. By the time the launch crashed through the surf to beach itself, the welcoming natives had grown to a crowd of several hundred people, many of them shouting and dancing in joy at our arrival.

"Have a care!" called the stalwart marine captain in charge of our escort. "There's a tremendous riptide on this coast. Watch yourselves getting ashore."

"Give the general a hand!" called Elliot from his place beside Shafter. At once army officers and marines sprang forward to drag our corpulent commander ashore. I stood aside to make room for them.

"Be careful, you fools!" bellowed Shafter as he was hauled bodily from the launch. "I'm no sack of oats!" Grimly clutching their protesting burden, the officers and marines went over the side and plowed through the surging foam.

"He's slipping!" cried a major as the current threatened to pull Shafter from his grasp.

Pecos Bill, completely unable to assist with his own landing, cried helplessly: "Don't let me go, boys! For God's sake, hold on! I'll drown, I tell you, I'll drown!"

"Steady, men, steady!" Elliot called out above the roaring surf. But the current was stronger than all of them put together, and for a moment it looked as though Shafter would be swept out into the shark-infested Caribbean Sea. Apparently sensing that the human elephant slowly settling into the depths in front of their eyes was the *americano comandante,* the Cubans surged into the spray en masse and dragged the sputtering Shafter onto the beach.

Satisfied that the general was on firm ground and would be no impediment to my disembarkation, I took off my boots, hurled them ashore, and waded to the beach. Once safely on dry ground I carefully rebooted myself, slapped the clinging sand from my trousers, and stood there eyeing the growing number of Cubans dancing about happily on the beach. Shafter sprawled nearby on the sand, heaving and blowing like a beached whale as he tried to catch his breath. About this time Admiral Sampson's party, clad in whites and looking like they were off to a cricket match rather than to a war council, splashed ashore. Then orders were shouted, a squad of marines hauled Shafter to his feet, and we formed ranks and prepared to meet Garcia.

Immediately a snag developed; Garcia, too, wanted to stand on protocol. He insisted that he receive Shafter and Sampson in his camp, which was perched on the crest of the two-hundred-foot hill to our immediate front. This raised the question of how Shafter, who had difficulty merely perambulating around the dining room of the Hotel Tampa Bay, was going to negotiate this formidable obstacle.

When told of the problem by Colonel Elliot, Shafter exploded. "You tell that pipsqueak to get his brown ass down that hill immediately! Who the hell does he think he is, demanding that white men come to him?"

"There *is* a matter of protocol here," murmured Admiral Sampson at Shafter's side. "After all, it is his country."

"Not yet it ain't!" snapped Shafter peevishly. "That's why we're here in the first place. You can climb that damned hill if you want, Admiral, but I'm not going to. Besides, if it wasn't for the navy whispering in McKinley's ear that Spain was a pushover, things would never have come to this pass."

"Well, I never," gasped Sampson in outrage, drawing himself up to his full height and stalking off, his coterie right on his heels. As he went he muttered in scandalized tones about damned impudence and how he wasn't about to be dressed down as though he was a callow ensign, and by a damned army general at that. It was insufferable, by God, and an affront to his dignity. Shafter merely snorted in dismissal at this feather-ruffling, but the fact of the matter was, Sampson was in the right and Colonel Elliot felt obliged to say so.

"The admiral's right," insisted Elliot, only to draw a gimlet eye from Shafter. Undaunted, he continued, "It probably is correct for you to go to Garcia. It's only a point of etiquette, General; what harm can it do?"

"What harm can it do?" roared Shafter. "Are you daft, man? Take a look at that bluff! I'll die of a stroke before I'm halfway up. It's all well and good to be polite, Elliot, but not if it's going to cost me my life. Either Garcia comes down from his damned mountain or I'm going back to the ship."

Elliot made the problem known to the Cubans with sign language and a smattering of Spanish. After much babbling and gesticulating, a solution was found. A diminutive burro was led from the jungle to the now-perspiring Shafter. A dozen strong hands lifted Pecos Bill onto the sturdy little beast, and without further ado, the procession, with Sampson in tow, ascended to Garcia's camp.

We reached the crest and passed through a wall of dense foliage into a pleasant clearing dotted with tall palms. There another several hundred Cubans milled about and, like their fellows who had greeted us on the beach, they were mostly Negroes and mulattoes.

A wizened old codger with dark, Indian-looking features stepped forward. He was dressed in plain linen, but from the ornate saber that hung from his belt, and from the obvious respect accorded him by the other *insurrectos*, I could tell that this clearly was Garcia. He promptly greeted Shafter in an effusive volley of Spanish. I could only make out parts of it: something, I thought, about Shafter's mother being a particularly fecund sow. That couldn't be right, I quickly realized, and recognized that we were facing a language barrier. For a moment we were stymied until the Cuban ranks parted and a gorgeous black-haired senorita with fiery brown eyes stepped forward.

"Beloved Shafter, Calixto Garcia Iniquey, *comandante* of the *insurrectos* of Cuba greets you," she announced melodiously.

By now Pecos Bill had dismounted and, still red and puffing from his ordeal, answered, "Major General Shafter, United States Army." Behind him Admiral Sampson coughed delicately, expecting to be introduced as well. Shafter ignored him.

Garcia flashed a toothless smile and, doffing his straw sombrero, made a sweeping bow to Shafter.

Shafter responded after a fashion by doffing his pith helmet and curtly bobbing his massive head in the general direction of the Cuban. With the preliminaries out of the way, Shafter got down to business. "Tell your general that I would be most obliged if he gave me his understanding of the location of his forces and those of the Spanish," he told the girl.

A quick-paced dialogue transpired between the lady and Garcia. As Shafter awaited Garcia's reply, my eyes roamed her revealingly clad body. Apparently the whalebone corsets and other prim fashions of America and Europe were unknown in this country. The senorita was wearing a sheer blouse, worn off the shoulder, which happily displayed a daring bit of décolletage. Her dark skirt ended above the knees and her feet were bare.

When the senorita had gotten Garcia's response, she let us have it.

"We have five thousand *insurrectos* within one hour of this camp. In Santiago Province, between here and Santiago de Cuba, there are another ten thousand. *Los españoles* have twelve thousand regulars in Santiago de Cuba, with small garrisons in the towns along the coast. These garrisons will not fight, but will only observe and report to their leader, General Linares. Linares is in command of all the troops in Santiago Province, and he has another twenty-six thousand soldiers to throw into the battle."

Her English was heavily accented—she pronounced "general" as "h'eneral," for example—but the liquid tones of her voice played upon my ears like music. In fact, her voice was so sweet that I completely ignored the hard facts she was relating to Shafter.

"Ask your general where he recommends I land my army," Shafter directed the girl.

At length she replied to Shafter. "My general begs to inform you that the beach at Daiquiri meets your needs. It is east of Santiago; just far enough away so as not to be watched closely by *los españoles,* but also close enough to be within marching distance of the city. One day's march at most. *Los españoles* are not at Daiquiri now, so your army may come ashore without fear."

Shafter nodded, looking at the ground as he digested this intelligence. I knew from his daily briefings that Daiquiri was among his possible landing sites.

"General," interjected Admiral Sampson stiffly, "I have no reliable charts of that area. I recommend we land closer to Santiago, where the tides and the currents are better charted."

Of course I saw the old salt's intent right off. His charts of the Daiquiri coast were no less reliable than the rest of our charts of Cuban waters. In plain truth, *all* our charts were next to useless. What Sampson was doing was putting the navy on record as opposing the landing site. If the landing failed, it would be Shafter's fault alone, not Sampson's. I smiled; I'd been able to discern the true purpose of Sampson's protest in the blink of an eye. Perhaps a military career was for me, after all!

"Admiral, I appreciate your counsel as always," replied Shafter without meaning it. "But Daiquiri it will be."

Our lovely interpreter relayed this exchange to Garcia, who grunted, spat a great brown wad of tobacco juice on the ground, and then grasped Shafter's hand. On that signal a fiesta broke out, and Shafter was invited to sample various delicacies that had been prepared for his enjoyment. Since the Cubans were now speaking Shafter's language, there was no further need for an interpreter. I caught the senorita's eye and nodded meaningfully toward the edge of the clearing, then strode off in that direction without looking back. When I was well clear of the festivities, I turned. She had followed.

"Senor, I welcome you to Cuba," she said with a dazzling smile that revealed perfect teeth. She pronounced the name of her country as "Cooba."

I doffed my campaign hat smoothly and gave her my most winning smile in return. "It is an honor to come to the aid of your great nation in these troubled times," I announced grandly.

The girl apparently believed me, for she smiled rather than laughed, which, of course, encouraged me further. "I'm glad to see you are pleased, senorita. Tell me, what is your name?"

"I am called Marguerite, senor," she said, not at all shyly, and I guessed that Marguerite was experienced in clandestine meetings under the palms. I certainly hoped so; the outlines of soft flesh under her clothes offered the promise that my stay in Cuba would not be devoid of carnal pleasure. "I hope you will not think me too bold for speaking with you like this," she added.

"Not at all, my dear," I assured her warmly, for I rather like my ladies on the forward side, you see. "But allow me to introduce myself. My name is Fenwick Travers."

"Feenweek?" she ventured, mangling my moniker horribly.

I smiled hugely now, like a cat would smile at a sparrow that had just flown in the window. "Yes, I know it's hard."

"Feenweek," she repeated softly.

"Close enough. I think you should know, Marguerite, that I think you speak my language very well. I find capable women like yourself to be very attractive."

She smiled demurely. Message received, I thought. "Senor, you are too kind," she whispered, almost timidly, and batted her lustrous eyes at me.

My heart was thundering now, and I smiled back droolingly; not half as kind as I intend to be, my dear, I vowed silently as I edged closer to my quarry and got a clear view down her ample cleavage. My early surmise was correct; the lady was bare as a baby's bottom under those clothes. I stirred at the thought. "Have you been with General Garcia very long, Marguerite?" I asked.

"For *cinco años,* Feenweek," she replied, giving a little giggle as she struggled with my name. Then, turning serious, she continued. "My family was butchered by *los españoles*. Without Garcia, I do not know what would have become of me."

You'd probably be playing the role of leading lady in some dago bordello in Havana, I thought, giving her an appraising look. Marguerite was a very handsome woman. Her dancing brown eyes captivated me, glowing warmly with promises of tantalizing intimacies. But there was something else in those eyes, I knew; it was a hint of a smoldering passion that I suspected could turn into a blaze of jealous rage if ever she was crossed by a lover. "Tell me, Marguerite," I asked, "where did you ever learn to speak English so well?"

"Oh, gracias, Feeny, but I do not speak the English so well. You are too kind. I was taught on my father's hacienda before the revolution. He required each of his children to learn a tongue other than *español*. I am indebted to him for his wisdom."

"A very farsighted man, indeed," I said sincerely. If not for him, I would be reduced to trying to seduce Marguerite using sign language alone.

"Lieutenant Travers!" called Colonel Elliot from the center of the clearing. "We're leaving. Say adios and let's get moving."

Damn the luck, I thought. I had hoped that Shafter would have tarried for hours once the Cubans rolled out their cuisine. Putting the best face on the situation, however, I gave a gallant bow and said, "I must go now, senorita. Speaking with you has been a great joy for a weary soldier."

"And a joy for this senorita, too, Feeny. *Vaya con Dios*." Bowing once more, I turned and joined the tail end of the column, which was snaking back down the hill to the beach. The surf had subsided a bit, making Pecos Bill's reembarkation a little more manageable, although a brawny marine dislocated his shoulder in the process. A short time later we reboarded the *Serguranca,* and thirty minutes after that were under steam, destination Daiquiri.

29

The fleet arrived off Daiquiri during the night, and at first light Shafter gave the order to commence operations. Shafter, Elliot, and I were on the bridge of the *Serguranca* when the blue peter, the pennant signaling the order to open fire, was hoisted up the yardarm. Immediately, guns on the battleships and cruisers roared. As we peered through binoculars toward the silent beach, we could hear the screech of shells hurtling through the air, and then geysers of earth exploded on shore: The war was on!

Shafter watched this for a few moments and then ordered, "Send the troops ashore." Although there was allegedly a disembarkation plan, the unbridled confusion that unfolded before Pecos Bill's eyes was mind-boggling. Steam launches sped erratically among the transports while barges filled with troops went ashore whenever and wherever the mood seized them. Through his binoculars Shafter could see inexperienced sailors and irate wranglers hauling terrified horses up from the holds to the decks of the ships and then dumping the creatures unceremoniously into the sea. The panicked horses bobbed about in the waves until they could be persuaded to paddle for shore. From my vantage point at Shafter's elbow, I could see several horses heading determinedly out to sea.

"Colonel Elliot!" Shafter screamed furiously. "Get the staff into boats and get that disaster organized! Do you hear me, man? Get this landing organized or I'll have your head!"

I wasn't sure if Shafter was speaking in a figurative or culinary sense, but I decided not to stay around long enough to find out. I rushed down to the main deck and hurried over to the rail, where a group of tars had tethered a steam launch and stood about waiting for orders.

"Lower away there, boys," I ordered. The sailors did as they were told, and we all hopped into the boat as it descended. As soon as it settled upon the waves, one tar started the boiler, and we pulled away from the *Serguranca*. Colonel Elliot appeared at the rail above as we steamed off.

"Come back here, Travers!" he yelled. "That's my boat!"

I pretended not to hear him, but instead settled back to enjoy the morning. An amphibious landing didn't happen every day of the week, and I intended to watch this one from a front-row seat. Besides, I'd be damned if I'd follow Elliot around all day jumping at his every beck and call like a puppy on a chain. My plan was to lark about until the army was ashore and Pecos Bill had himself under control once more.

It was an eventful day indeed, for all around me the water was filled with craft of every description either heading for shore crammed full of troops, or else empty and heading back to the transports for another load. The soldiers were exhilarated at being freed from the confines of the transports, and a carnival mood had descended upon them. Jovial bantering echoed across the water, and there was a sense of good clean fun being had by all. Many sang the newest ditty that was all the rage:

> O Dewey was the morning
> Upon the first of May
> And Dewey was the Admiral
> Down in Manila Bay;
> And Dewey were the Regent's eyes
> Them orbs of royal blue
> and Dewey feel discouraged?
> I dew not think we dew.

"Steer for the *Yucatan*," I ordered the helmsman on a whim.

"Aye, aye, sir," replied this worthy. As we neared the *Yucatan* I could see that the transport was disgorging its livestock. Two struggling troopers hauled an exquisite Arabian mare to the rail and heaved her into the brine. I recognized the beast; it was one of the two mounts that Roosevelt had brought with him from Long Island. To the horror of all, the mare hit the waves with a great splash and was seen no more.

"Shark bait," grunted the helmsman behind me.

Roosevelt, watching from the bridge, was agog. "You bungling fools!" he bellowed. "Don't you know how to unload a horse? You've killed my mount, you bastards! I'll see that you both swing for this. Now use a hoist to lower the horses into the water like you're supposed to, or I'll throw the both of you over the side!"

The two troopers, used to such eruptions from their peppery leader, merely shrugged their shoulders and stood looking at the bridge until Roosevelt's outburst subsided. A group of officers appeared behind Roosevelt, called him into conversation, and then the whole lot of them stepped inside the bridge. The minute Roosevelt disappeared, the two troopers seized his second Arabian roughly, brought it to the rail, and heaved it over the side. Happily this creature soon reappeared at the surface and began swimming strongly for shore. I already knew that our troopers were not in awe of the Spanish; now I knew they were not in awe of their officers either.

The fun continued in a similar vein all morning, and I was having a thoroughly good time until one of the tars interrupted me. "Pardon me, sir, but the coal for the boiler is running low. Should we head back to the *Serguranca?*"

I had no desire to confront Colonel Elliot so soon after stealing his launch, so I replied, "Please be good enough to put me ashore first. Then you're free to return to the ship." Since we were only a few hundred yards offshore, in a matter of minutes the tars ran through the surf, deposited me on the beach, and took their leave.

The town of Daiquiri, I soon found, was no more than a ramshackle collection of thatched huts set haphazardly along a single mud street. Despite the naval gunfire, I saw little damage; in fact, the only evident casualty of the thunderous bombardment was a dead pig lying in the quagmire that was the main street of this woebegone place.

I spent the rest of the day wandering aimlessly around the beachhead, calling encouragement where it was not needed and generally making a nuisance of myself. Nobody seemed to mind—after all, that was what staff officers were for. In time, despite my assistance, the invasion got itself sorted out, and by late afternoon things were humming along smoothly indeed. As the sun set, my thoughts turned to supper and a place to bed down.

That's when the strains from a distant guitar caught my ear. The music came from a bungalow up on the hillside. Intrigued, I approached. When I arrived at the bungalow, I found a party that had evidently been underway for some time. Drunken American reporters and officers lurched about wildly, toasting the gods of war with purloined liquor. Intermingled among them were some equally besotted Cubans.

"Travers!" cried Crane as I entered. "Have a drink, old man."

"Don't mind if I do, Crane," I replied cheerily, accepting the bottle of dark Cuban rum he thrust into my hand.

"Ain't it wonderful?" gushed Crane. "This is the beginning of a new era of Cuban-American relations, I tell you. It's the first step toward creating a spirit of fellowship between our two nations."

I couldn't resist a riposte at this nonsense, so I took another swig from the bottle and retorted, "Oh, is it now? You wouldn't think so, judging from some comments I've heard made by some regular officers, who shall remain nameless."

My barb struck a nerve. "Eh? What's that they're saying, Travers?" demanded Crane, not at all pleased by my refusal to wallow in his maudlin pool of brotherly bonhomie.

"They say we're going to annex Cuba," I told him flatly. "Make it part of the United States. This war really won't be any different than the wars against the Indians. First, we send in the army to pacify the bastards, and then settlers begin arriving. In fifty years, Cuba will be as American as Ohio."

"That's impossible," protested Crane. "What about the Teller Amendment? It was tacked onto McKinley's declaration of war. It says that we are forbidden to annex Cuba."

"What's a piece of paper mean?" I snorted derisively, taking another swallow of rum. "When the casualties are counted, people are going to damn well ask what we sacrificed our troops for. And when they do, they won't be so anxious to give up this piece of real estate."

"Any annexation of this island will take place over my dead body," huffed Crane.

I smiled wickedly. "You may be right on that point, Crane," I quipped. "After all, there's much fighting still ahead, you know."

As Crane paused to ponder his own mortality, the urbane Richard Harding Davis saw me from across the room and angled in. "I see you've found the rum, Travers," he drawled, giving me his polished smile.

"That I have, Dickie," I replied. "Smooth stuff, but a mite too sweet for my taste."

"But serviceable, nonetheless," pronounced Davis. Turning to the assembled throng and raising his voice to fill the room, he called, "I think a toast is in order, gentlemen. To General Shafter, our valiant leader!" he said, his voice oozing sarcasm.

"To Pecos Bill!" roared the revelers, raising their glasses and bottles. The Cubans looked perplexed by the outburst, but smiled good-naturedly nonetheless. They were clearly determined not to offend their saviours.

"Say, has anyone here seen the general recently?" asked Crane rhetorically.

Gales of laughter went up at this. It was common knowledge that Shafter had signaled ashore a few hours ago that he would spend the evening aboard the *Serguranca*.

"It seems that Pecos Bill doesn't believe the scouting reports that say there are no dagos to be found in this neighborhood!" roared a red-faced captain of artillery. Again the company had a hearty laugh, and it was plain that Shafter was well on his way to cementing his reputation as a buffoon in the hearts of his men. Of course, I could scarcely care less; it was all McKinley's fault for sending an overfed boy to do a man's job.

I drank good-naturedly with the others and was roundly admired for it. My companions mistook my profound indifference to their slanders of our chief as high good sportsmanship. So I played the role of the loyal but understanding aide to the hilt and raised my bottle freely.

"Gentlemen, to Cuba!" I cried, offering a toast.

"To Cuba!" they chorused drunkenly. Upon hearing "Cuba" the *guerrilleros* were on their feet in an instant, shouting madly, "*¡Viva, Cuba!*"

From nowhere a trio of guitarists appeared and began strumming the heady tunes of Cuban nationalism. Slender young senoritas were quickly appropriated, and unrestrained dancing and lechery broke out. Not bad for an off-the-cuff remark, I congratulated myself.

Suddenly a familiar face appeared; it was Marguerite, from Garcia's camp! She was twirling across the floor in the arms of a beefy major of engineers. Seeing me, she disengaged from his lewd grasp and ran to my side.

"Feenweek!" she cried ecstatically. "I am so happy to see you! I am glad that *los norteamericanos* are here in Cuba. It is a dream come true for me."

"And looking at you is like a dream come true for me," I replied smoothly. I searched her eyes and saw that the blush on her cheeks was more than just patriotic ardor; unless I was greatly mistaken, the little gal was in heat and had eyes only for me!

I reached for her hand, but instead she flew into my arms and hugged me fiercely. "I rode all night with Garcia to be here," breathed Marguerite. "Garcia wants to fight at the side of your brave general."

That should be quite a trick, I thought, since Shafter had no intention of fighting anyone if he could help it. But reality was obviously not what Marguerite wanted to hear, and so by way of an answer I lifted her off her feet and kissed her forcefully on her full lips. As I suspected would be the case, she did not resist, but instead returned my kiss passionately.

"Feenweek, let us dance together and be loco," she whispered in my ear.

"A splendid idea, my dear!" I cried. I grasped her about her slender waist, and we joined the surging crowd of frolicking fools in an uninhibited Cuban fandango. We danced madly and drank freely, both of us aware that this would be an evening to remember. Marguerite's flashing eyes promised an athletic interlude in the hay as soon as I could contrive to slip off with her. By midnight I was aroused to the point of bursting. With a gallant bow I offered her my arm, and she took it most readily. Quickly we slipped out the door and into the cool night.

"Oh, Feenweek, we must not," she giggled—for form's sake, I suppose, since she made no move to stop me. This was like waving a red cape in front of my eyes. From what I had felt of her firm, finely muscled body, I knew that if she did not care for my little proposition, she was quite capable of wiggling out of my grasp and making a fight of it.

Kissing her smiling face, I whispered in my best border Mexican, "*¡Viva los bravos norteamericanos!*"

"*¡Viva* Feenweek!" was her throaty reply, and she sought my lips and kissed them passionately. Feeling the rising heat from her body, I led her into a thicket and quickly came upon a small clearing. I laid Marguerite on the ground and stretched out languorously beside her. I kissed her tenderly once or twice, and then got down to business. As I expertly pulled her blouse up and over her head two perfectly formed—and surprisingly large—breasts popped into view. Barely able to contain myself, I squeezed them lovingly while planting passionate kisses on Marguerite's parted lips.

Her breathing was coming in great gasps and she was moaning urgently. "Oh, Feenweek," she crooned throatily, "*eres un animal.*"

Oh, it was I who was an animal, eh? And what about her? Her skirt was up above her hips and her strong legs were wrapped so tightly around my middle that I couldn't have gotten away even if the thought had occurred to me. But getting away was the farthest thing from my mind; I struggled furiously to get my trousers lowered so I could service my willing partner.

"*Mi amor, mi amor, qué animal,*" sighed Marguerite beneath me. She was mine, I knew; her ripe fruit was mine for the plucking. But my trousers refused to yield. Goddamn them! I raged silently. A man couldn't get shed of these army britches without a crowbar!

Then a voice boomed out in the darkness: "Lieutenant Travers, come out of there this instant!"

I froze; it was Colonel Elliot!

"I know you're in there, Travers," Elliot called again. "Come out here this instant or I'll have your commission for this."

Now even Marguerite comprehended the fact that we were no longer alone. She ceased thrashing about and snatched her blouse to her exposed bosom.

What to do? I thought. I felt rather like a schoolboy caught smoking corn husks behind the barn. At first I thought about ignoring the bastard, but then decided that since he had walked within a few feet of my rutting ground he probably had a good idea of where I was and what I was up to. Oh, I could appear tomorrow and deny being anywhere near the bungalow, of course. It would only be Elliot's word against mine, and so I was not worried about a court-martial. But I could be summarily tossed off Shafter's staff and sent back to the 9th Infantry just in time for the shooting to start. What would be the allegations? I hurriedly thought. Conduct unbecoming an officer? Attempted rape? Making a general nuisance of myself? Whatever tack he chose, I was certain that Elliot was capable of producing a damaging tale to lay before Shafter.

I made up my mind; I would have to cut my losses and haul myself out of the bushes as Elliot demanded. I arose quietly, adjusted my uniform, and, gazing down on Marguerite, whispered, "Adios, Marguerite. I shall be in Cuba for many more nights."

She blew me a silent kiss in return and slowly lowered her blouse to reveal her lovely breasts. Damn you, Elliot! I silently stormed. But duty called, and so, my farewells said, I marched out of the clinging underbrush to confront the bristling Colonel Elliot.

"Just what do you think you're up to, Mister?" he demanded harshly.

"Sir, you mistake my purpose entirely," I replied levelly.

"What? Mistake your purpose?" he snorted. "Don't tell me you're denying you were in the bushes with one of those Cuban tarts. Everyone I talked to in the bungalow says you left with a senorita, Travers."

"Oh, she had to run along, sir. This is a Catholic country, you see, and unescorted young ladies retire early."

"Are you telling me you were not with a woman, Travers?" demanded Elliot.

"Precisely, sir. You see, I had merely sought a little solitude so I could offer up a prayer for the success of our arms."

"A prayer?" exclaimed Elliot, taken back. He had expected craven whining and tearful promises that I would never sin again. But prayer from me was something so unexpected that Elliot appeared stupefied by the very thought of it. Nonplussed, he muttered uncertainly, "I had no idea you were the praying type, Travers." He looked into the bushes a time or two as if hoping to see a half-clothed floozie who could put the lie to my protestation of religious communications, but nobody stirred in the brush. At length Elliot growled, "Come along, Lieutenant. If you have any influence up there, you're going to need it."

"Yes, sir," I murmured meekly as we started down the trail to the beach.

As Elliot marched off purposefully, I stole a glance back. Marguerite stepped into the moonlight, naked from the waist up, and blew me a dreamy kiss.

30

Any fears I might have had about Colonel Elliot running to Shafter with tales of my dalliance vanished with the events of the following day. I awoke to discover that large bodies of infantry and dismounted cavalry were in motion. The troops were moving westward along the coast toward Siboney, five miles from Daiquiri. A track ran inland from Siboney, which, if one followed it long enough, would eventually lead in a circuitous way to the rear of Santiago's defenses.

But under whose direction was this movement occurring? I wondered. Certainly not under Shafter's; decisive action such as this was beyond him. I grabbed a steaming tin mug of Cuban coffee from a nearby camp stove, drained it in great quaffs, and, being careful not to rouse Colonel Elliot, who lay sleeping in a nearby supply wagon, set off after the marching columns.

I requisitioned a roan from the herd reserved for corps staffers, saddled it, and rode west along the coast. At first I passed regiments of dismounted cavalry from Major General Wheeler's division, the men shuffling along under the weight of their Krags, blanket rolls, haversacks, canteens, and the Mills cartridge belts strapped about their lean waists. Once past the cavalry I encountered infantry: General Lawton's men.

After an hour of hard riding I found the head of the column. Brigadier Gen. Henry Lawton and his staff were halted astride their mounts in a banana grove just on the far side of Siboney. The town, like Daiquiri previously, had been deserted by the Spanish—but not long before, because cooking fires smoldered everywhere, and a Spanish flag still fluttered over the largest hut in the town. Clearly the dagos had been here only hours earlier, and in considerable strength.

Lawton was a lean, weather-beaten veteran, with a full, droopy mustache that gave heightened ferocity to his fiery eyes. Lawton and Shafter went way back together; they had both soldiered in Arizona pursuing the cunning Apache Geronimo. But they had never become close; and in fact Lawton was Shafter's temperamental opposite: Whereas Shafter wanted to advance cautiously and avoid serious fighting if possible, Lawton wanted to rush pell-mell after the Spanish, and if necessary bring them to bloody battle.

Lawton recognized me as I cantered up and saluted. He took the cheroot from his mouth, blew a great puff of blue smoke, and demanded with his characteristic directness: "News from Shafter, Lieutenant?"

"No, sir," I replied. "There's been no word from General Shafter since yesterday, as best I know. The last I heard he was still aboard the *Serguranca*."

"No surprise there!" laughed Lawton harshly. "I'm amazed he even deigned to budge from Tampa." Guffaws came from his staff at this witticism.

Assuaged by the fact that I had not brought orders from Shafter to halt, General Lawton ignored me and resumed his conversation with his officers.

"The scouts are back, General," a major reported. "They say that the Spanish are probably forming inland of here for a counterattack."

"Counterattack?" scoffed Lawton. "Why, just look around you, man. The enemy has skedaddled from here. There's no fight in him. No, they don't mean to counterattack; they mean to put as much distance between us and them as fast as they can."

His officers eyed each other at this but said nothing.

"Push the regiments inland as fast as they arrive from Daiquiri," Lawton ordered. "I have the Spanish on the run and I aim to keep things that way."

Push inland? I thought. That was news; I knew from staff meetings that I had attended on the *Serguranca* following Shafter's meeting with General Garcia that after V Corps landed, Shafter had a vague notion to seize Siboney with one division so as to protect the main force at

Daiquiri. That force was to be a shield between the enemy and Shafter's main force while Shafter made up his mind about what to do next. From what I was hearing now, however, the tail was beginning to wag the dog. Lawton's decision to move to Siboney without orders was probably a laudable initiative; moving inland in force, however, was something else again. Lawton evidently had the bit in his teeth and was running with it. I felt compelled to weigh in with the voice of reason from on high.

"I'm sorry, sir, but do you have orders to move beyond Siboney?"

All eyes immediately swiveled toward me. Lawton tossed his cheroot into the dust at his mount's hoofs and studied me levelly. "Of course, not, Travers. If I had to wait for orders from Shafter, it would take ten years to capture Cuba. I aim to get it done a mite sooner than that."

What he said was true enough. In all likelihood, no attack order would ever issue from Shafter's headquarters until circumstances forced him to act. So I tried another approach. "How far past Siboney do you intend to move, sir?"

"Oh, not far at all," Lawton replied evasively. "You needn't worry about me, Travers. It's not like I'm about to seize control of the campaign." He had astutely zeroed in on my concern, you see. "All I want to do is ensure we're not too exposed should the enemy suddenly get feisty. Besides, there's no place for the troops to dig in around here," he explained, gesturing to the relatively flat sandy environs of Siboney. "We'll be safer and have more room to maneuver in the hills inland a mile or so from here."

"Seems like a logical plan," I conceded.

"Damned right it is," affirmed Lawton with the pride of authorship. "General Kent agrees with me, too. His division is right behind me. I'll screen to the west and north as he moves up. Once his division is in Siboney, I'll send word for General Wheeler to close up with the cavalry division. When we're all concentrated here, the Spanish will never dislodge us."

"But Kent's division is not behind you, General Wheeler's cavalry division is!" I exclaimed, fear suddenly clutching at my guts.

"Goddamn!" swore Lawton. "Wheeler must have gotten wind of our plan and decided to spoil it! That old, unreconstructed rebel has been so uppity since he's been allowed to legally bear arms that Kent and I never tell him what we're up to."

"If Wheeler's not part of your plan, sir, then I'd wager a month's pay that he's got a plan of his own up his sleeve," I said. "The regiments from his division that I passed on the way here are coming as fast as they can march."

"That damned fool better not do anything to jeopardize this expedition, or I'll personally pump him full of lead," vowed Lawton. "Let's find out what the bastard's up to."

With that he spurred his mount into a gallop, and his staff and I pounded along after him. We rode up a low rise that gave a sweeping overview of Siboney, where we reined in. From here we could see Lawton's regiments dutifully taking their places in the heights above the town. But columns of dismounted cavalrymen were marching through these regiments and up a dirt track that led into the jungle and eventually to Santiago. On their flank, along the main road to Sevilla—the next town inland from Siboney—other columns were turning inland as well, disappearing into the dense foliage. Apparently Wheeler had in mind an advance consisting of two parallel columns, one along the dirt track and one along the main road.

Lawton snapped open a spyglass and studied the columns. "Yellow bandannas, all right. That's dismounted cavalry—Wheeler's men. But that mob up front on the trail has polka-dotted bandannas. That's Roosevelt's outfit. What do they call themselves? The Cowpokes, ain't it?"

"The Rough Riders, sir," a staffer corrected him.

"Damned foolish name," growled Lawton, "especially as they're dismounted. But even on foot they're moving quick," he allowed, his voice betraying the anxiety he felt. "Looks like Wheeler's hell-bent on pushing on to Santiago."

"Someone's got to stop them, sir," I burst out, fear getting the better of me now.

Lawton was peeved at this—lieutenants don't tell generals what to do—and he was about to administer a proper tongue-lashing to me for my presumption when a colonel spoke up. "He's right, sir. If the Spanish hold the jungles inland in any strength, they could wipe out Wheeler before you could go to his support. If that happens, there's no hope of taking either Santiago or Cuba."

Lawton considered this a minute; the thought of Wheeler being annihilated was undeniably gratifying, but then his military reason reasserted itself. "Goddamn that Wheeler!" he fumed. "Why didn't he have the common decency to die after the war like Lee did?" Turning in his saddle to me he ordered, "Travers, find General Wheeler and see if you can slow him down. My staff and I will redeploy my division so that I can support him in a hurry if he runs into trouble. Understand?"

I thought about this a second, trying madly to think of a tactful way to tell Lawton that I was not particularly eager to get close to an organized, heavily armed European foe that might be inclined to defend itself, but Lawton roared: "Ride, man, ride!" and swatted the roan's rump with his hat.

In an instant I was flying down the rise on a runaway mustang. "Yes, sir!" I called over my shoulder, trying to put the best face on my discomfiture, and then I turned my full attention to the panicked horse. "Stop, you damned nag, stop!" I cried, jerking on the reins with all my might. The roan fought me for a few minutes until it was winded and then slowed to a jerky, high-strung trot. Its nerves were shot, whether by Lawton's slap or by its absorbing my fear, I didn't know. All that was certain was that I could not prance along a jungle track in combat on a horse ready to bolt at an instant's notice. Besides, a horseman would be an obvious target for a Spanish sniper, so I dismounted and tethered the roan to a stump.

From the trees crowding the trail on either side, wood cuckoos called sweetly, and the mighty hum of uncounted insects filled the air. Although it was only midmorning, the oppressive heat of Cuba in the summer was already rising. I caught up with the lead group of advancing cavalrymen after a bruising hike through thick jungles, which cleared the last cobwebs of the night's debauch from my head. I was among the Rough Riders, and up ahead on the trail I spied Lieutenant Colonel Roosevelt proudly astride his remaining mount, Little Texas. No fear of snipers for him, I noted; the little prig probably didn't believe that any Iberian sharpshooter would have the effrontery to tumble him out of the saddle. Since he appeared to be the ranking officer in the lead, I decided to see if he might be persuaded to slow the pace a bit.

Roosevelt saw me coming and hailed me derisively, "Glory be, it's Shafter's aide. Who says you never see staffers in the front ranks?" His men laughed hugely at my expense.

I grinned disarmingly. "The front ranks, sir? Then there must be some mistake. I didn't know the cavalry division had been given the van position. I'm sure that would be news to General Shafter."

"Our commanding general would be better informed of troop dispositions if he were here on land, rather than bobbing about in the ocean, out of touch with the war," retorted Roosevelt fiercely, turning aside my barb.

"Perhaps," I allowed. "But in any event, one night out of touch with events can be easily rectified," I observed mildly.

If Roosevelt got the veiled threat, he didn't let on. "Talking about nighttime, I heard about that party those reporters threw last evening—Davis and that crowd. And I've heard that a certain young lieutenant registered the first major conquest of this campaign." He cackled uproariously at his own humor, and tugged his walrus mustache in mirth.

But I was in no mood to serve as a pincushion for his needling, so I got to the point: "Just where are your Rough Riders headed, sir?"

"Why, after the enemy, of course," he replied matter-of-factly. "A course of action, I might add, which seems not to have occurred to our commanding general or his staff."

I could have assured him that it would never have occurred to this staff officer. "Do you have the lay of the land up this trail?" I inquired uneasily. It wouldn't have astonished me to learn that Roosevelt was blundering ahead in the blind.

But he surprised me. "Yes, indeed. Colonel Wood was able to secure a relatively detailed map from our Cuban friends. This trail runs parallel to the main road for a few hundred yards more. Since the main road had to ascend a steep ridge and run through a narrow defile off to our right, General Wheeler wanted our column to follow this trail, which runs along the ridge top. That way, if there's an ambush—which seems unlikely—we'd be in place to flank the dagos. We're nearly parallel to the crest of the defile now, and just up ahead the trail will rejoin the road at a place called Las Guasimas. Once we're through the jungle here, the country opens up and there's a high road to Sevilla. As you well know, Travers, Sevilla's the most likely staging point for an attack on Santiago itself, and the regiment that takes that place is likely to be mentioned in dispatches."

Ah-ha, I thought, Roosevelt smells glory up this trail. Getting him to slow this advance was going to be about as easy as calming a miser in a bank run. I decided that the best approach with a pigheaded fellow like Roosevelt was an indirect one, and accordingly, I engaged him in small talk until I found a suitable opportunity to diplomatically urge him to halt, or at least slow down.

"Damn pesky insects hereabouts," I remarked casually, slapping at a passing mosquito.

"B'gad you're right there, Travers," agreed Roosevelt. "I took a scorpion from my bedroll this morning that had to be six inches long. Foulest thing I've seen since those plug-uglies Tammany Hall sent to break up my rallies during the mayoral race!" he said with a braying laugh.

"Z-z-zing!" A larger insect whizzed over my head, followed closely by another. I slapped at them irritably; that last one was close enough to take my ear off.

"There must be a swarm of bugs in this jungle," complained Roosevelt, fanning the air with his hat as his mount danced skittishly.

Suddenly a trooper not five feet away threw up his arms and slid to the ground. A bright stream of red gushed from a small, neat hole in his forehead.

"Those aren't insects!" bellowed Roosevelt. "They're bullets! We're under attack!" As if to punctuate his warning, a huge flock of cuckoos took wing from the branches above us, flying madly from the killing zone.

Before I could move, Roosevelt vaulted off his mount, hit the ground with a thud, and rolled into the underbrush. All around me Rough Riders dove for cover as Mauser bullets filled the air. With a desperate leap I landed in the brush not far from where Roosevelt crouched.

"Ambushed, b'gad!" he fumed. "Travers, can you see them?"

Of course I couldn't; I had my head pressed to the ground, where it was going to stay until the shooting stopped. "No," I answered faintly, "they must be camouflaged."

All around me I could hear soldiers calling nervously to each other. Cries of "Do you see 'em?" and "How many are there?" floated through the dense green foliage. The fire increased in volume, shredding the guasimas trees and showering bark and leaves upon the pinned-down troops. Here and there heavy branches, dislodged by the fusillade, crashed to the ground, and moans from the wounded filled the air.

"What'll we do, Colonel?" men called to Roosevelt. "We can't stay here. We'll be shot to pieces!"

"Let me think a minute, boys, let me think," stalled Roosevelt. I peered up to see him looking nervously down the trail to the rear and then in the direction of the Spanish fire. Why, the little martinet was thinking about retreating—flat-out skedaddling—I realized in an instant! His thoughts of sweeping the craven dagos before him were gone; all Roosevelt could think of now was how to save the hides of his vaunted Rough Riders. Around us I could see individuals here and there anticipating a retreat by slowly inching backward in the direction of Siboney.

As inexperienced in large-scale warfare as I was, I realized that Wheeler's entire advance teetered precariously on a fulcrum of raw fear. Then Roosevelt opened his mouth to give the order to fall back, and I could see his lips trembling.

But no sound came from him; instead from our rear came a sudden roar of voices. I raised my head ever so cautiously and beheld a phalanx of Negroes clad in army blue running up the trail from Siboney. At the sound of the firing, they must have rushed to Roosevelt's aid from the main road, I realized. As they came on, their front ranks fired over our heads toward where the Spanish lay, the gaudy red and white cavalry guidon fluttering above their heads announcing them as the 10th Cavalry—the famed Buffalo Soldiers of the Indian wars. Regulars, by God; I sighed with relief!

The Negroes rushed boldly up to the point where the Rough Riders were pinned down, then fanned out into the brush on either side of the trail and began pushing forward toward the unseen foe. The more audacious among the Rough Riders, chagrined at being saved by their social inferiors, were on their feet now and using their Krags to bring a withering fire to bear on the hidden Spaniards.

Sensing that the crisis had passed, Roosevelt sprang to his feet. "After them boys!" he barked, regaining his poise. I watched him intently from the cover afforded by the rotted trunk of a fallen guasimas tree. Heartened that he did not immediately topple over dead, I too stood up.

"Splendid, yes, splendid!" cackled Roosevelt as his regiment surged forward again. "Don't let them re-form now. After them!" The sound of firing still filled the air, but the reports I heard were the throaty roars of Krags and an occasional Sharps carbine; the deadly zinging of Mauser bullets was gone.

"Good job, sir!" I bubbled. "You've got 'em on the run now. Congratulations."

The little bantam rather liked my ready alteration of events and turned to beam at me, the sunlight glinting off his pince-nez giving him a maniacal air. "Yes, a bully good job!" he readily agreed. "A bit tricky at first, but the men were superb under fire! Bully!"

It was clear that he'd recovered his sea legs, as it were, but caution had been born in the man at last, and I decided to strike while the iron was hot. "It might be wise to clear out those snipers and then halt to await some more support. I'll speak to General Lawton about having Kent's division come up."

"Yes!" Roosevelt concurred eagerly. "Support's just the thing. We don't know that these dagos aren't just a ploy to draw us on. Yes, by all means send up the infantry. And guns, Travers, we'll need cannon, too."

"Very good, sir," I replied. "Guns and reinforcements it is. I'll be off at once," sounding for all the world like a waiter at Sherry's taking a lunch order.

"Yes, don't waste an instant now," urged Roosevelt, smiling with sudden geniality. Ordinarily, a sea change in emotion like this would have taken me a while to understand, but not this time. You see, I understood the little puffer's convoluted mind; in Roosevelt's view, he and I had been under fire together— blooded as it were in a successful battle—and therefore we shared the bond of veterans.

I saluted and turned to go when a second horde of frenzied Negroes suddenly rushed up the trail. It was another squadron of the 10th Cavalry, every bit as inflamed as their comrades had been. At their head rode Fighting Joe himself, mounted on a magnificent sorrel and waving a wicked-looking cavalry saber over his head.

"Come on, boys!" he screeched. "We've got them damn Yankees on the run! Forward for the bonny blue flag!"

Roosevelt's mouth gaped and his pince-nez popped off his nose as he gazed in astonishment at this spectacle from a past war suddenly brought to life. The Africans loping along behind Wheeler, oblivious to the inanity of the scene, pressed forward after the "damn Yankees."

"That man's a lunatic," I heard Roosevelt shout as I turned and hurried to the rear.

31

Four days later, convinced that the action had died down, Pecos Bill had himself ferried ashore and hauled overland by burro to the new headquarters at Sevilla. With his hand on the reins of operations once more, the campaign slowed to a snail's pace. With his presence also came the rains. A dreary pattern of overcast days and soaking nights soon developed, and the campaign degenerated into a nightmare of drenching misery. Hand in hand with the rains came disease: Malaria and yellow fever stalked the army, and soon more men were incapacitated from sickness than from enemy fire.

It was on such a rain-drenched afternoon that I next saw Charlie Hobart. I was in the headquarters, which had recently been moved closer to the troops at El Pozo, seated under an open-sided tent on a camp chair, ostensibly copying orders for dispatch to the divisions, but in reality idling away the hours and surreptitiously taking swigs of potent Cuban rum from the flask Harlock had given me. I was operating under the theory that the only way to ward off the sickness around me was to keep so much alcohol in my bloodstream that no illness could possibly gain a foothold. I might still fall ill, but I'd be so drunk I wouldn't give a damn.

"Hobart, old chum," I called, barely recognizing the bedraggled figure in a rain slicker splashing across the immense puddles between the headquarters tents. "Come in and dry off."

Hobart gratefully stepped under the canvas. He looked a sight: He'd lost ten pounds since I'd last seen him, and it had been days since he'd shaved.

"It's hell out there, Travers," gasped Hobart after he swallowed a swig from my proffered flask. "Liscum's gone; he put Major Whittaker in charge of the regiment. Now Whittaker's ailing with fever, so the senior captain is in charge. If we don't fight the Spanish soon, we won't have any soldiers left."

"Where's Liscum?" I asked, surprised.

"With the black regulars of the 24th Infantry." Just as the black 9th Cavalry was the sister regiment of the black 10th Cavalry, the 24th Infantry was the sister regiment of Henry's black 25th Infantry. "All of their white officers were stricken, and officers had to be stripped from other regiments to fill those gaps. The 9th had two field-grade officers, so Colonel Liscum was detailed to the 24th. God help those poor niggers."

I agreed silently. Liscum could barely stomach white troops; he'd surely make life a living hell for blacks, but then, the 24th had probably seen worse commanders over the years. "The fever's that bad then?" I asked sympathetically.

"The fever and hunger, Travers," replied Hobart. "The food is terrible. We've been getting canned beef that's absolutely rancid. I mean thoroughly putrefied. The troops call it 'embalmed beef.' They throw it to the dogs and the Cuban camp followers. The only way for them to keep body and soul together is to forage off the land."

"It's been bad all over," I commiserated perfunctorily. Hobart's gaze wandered to the slices of ham on the table before me and his eyes narrowed.

"It's not what you think," I hastened to explain. "That's just, well, some good fortune actually. The navy had some extra victuals and sent them along. To help out any way they could, you see. It's not an ordinary thing at all. Here, help yourself," I said, offering the ham to Hobart.

He grabbed it like a starving man and swallowed it before my eyes. I didn't think it wise to tell him that Shafter relied on the navy for all his victuals and we always ate high on the hog at headquarters; Hobart probably wouldn't see the plain good sense in that arrangement at the moment.

"Don't worry, Charlie," I said lamely, "things'll be better when we toss out the dagos and liberate Cuba. You can be sure of that."

Hobart eyed me a bit sullenly. "Toss out the dagos, indeed. I say let 'em keep this damned place, Fenny. We came here to help the *guerrilleros* fight, not do all the fighting while they sat on their black backsides. The closer you get to the shooting, the fewer Cubans you'll see. That is, until you pitch camp. Then you'll see throngs of the beggars howling for the beef the troops won't eat. They'll steal the boots off your feet if you nod off to sleep, I tell you. Why, I've never seen such disgusting people—no wonder the Spanish hated 'em. The only wonder is that the dons have resisted our invasion at all. I'm surprised they're not in the streets greeting us with tears of joy. Now they can abandon this misbegotten island and leave it to us."

It's a pure wonder what a few days of war will do to rearrange one's priorities, I reflected wryly, and felt like telling Hobart so, but thought better of it and decided to change the subject. "Tell me, Charlie, what brings you to headquarters? Surely this isn't just a social call."

"You're right, Fenny. We had a ragged Cuban rider approach our pickets a few hours ago. Said he had a message for our 'heneral.' It was a note scrawled in broken English on greasy parchment. Captain Harris thought it was a prank. But it looked like intelligence on the enemy, so we roused Major Whittaker long enough to look at it. Whittaker finally decided that I should bring it here. We're hoping that it might put the spurs to Shafter to either fight or pack up and go home. We can't just sit around like we've been doing."

He handed it over. I read the flowery script.

Beloved Shafter,
Los españoles have leaved Manzanillo. Soon come they. 8,000 of the line. To Santiago come they.

Vaya con Dios
Garcia

Beloved Shafter, eh? By Christ, wasn't that exactly how Garcia had greeted Shafter back in the *guerrillero* camp? Hobart was right; this was the genuine article!

"Good God, Charlie!" I exclaimed. "If this is true, it means that the dagos are sallying out of Manzanillo to rescue Santiago! Let's see, Manzanillo is three days' march west of Santiago on the coast. If they get eight thousand more troops into Santiago before us, we'll never dislodge them."

"That's what Whittaker said," nodded Hobart, licking the grease from his fingers and hungrily looking about for something else to eat.

"When did you say you got this?" I pressed.

"This morning. Can't be more than a day old," he answered.

"I've got to show this to Shafter," I decided instantly. This might indeed be the thing to finally galvanize him into action. I tossed Hobart the flask. "You can have the rest, Charlie, but leave the flask on the table when you go. It has a special significance to me, you see. And give Captain Harris my fondest personal regards."

I threw my rain slicker over my shoulders, jammed on my hat, and splashed over to the operations tent, where Colonel Elliot was going over the latest troop dispositions. "Colonel, I've got something the general should see. This was handed to pickets of the 9th Infantry by an *insurrecto* courier. I think it's genuine."

Elliot hastily read the note. "Damn!" he swore. "This looks like very bad news indeed, Travers. Follow me."

Without another word he marched over to Shafter's tent, identified by a scarlet pennant upon which were emblazoned the two white stars of his rank. Elliot knocked loudly on the wooden post by the entrance.

"What is it now?" whined Shafter from inside.

"It's Colonel Elliot, sir. I've got to speak with you at once."

"Can't it wait, man?" protested Shafter. "It's too cussed hot for me to think about anything right now."

"I'm afraid it won't wait, sir," replied Elliot, stepping into the tent. I followed on his heels and beheld the ludicrous sight of Shafter seated on a camp chair, naked to the waist, with his feet immersed in a tub of cold water. Rolls of fat hung over his belt, and wet towels were wrapped around his shoulders.

"Oh, I'm sorry, sir," apologized Elliot, taken aback. "I didn't realize you were bathing."

"I'm not, you fool," spat Shafter venomously. "I'm trying to stay cool and ease the gout in my feet at the same time. Well, now that you're here, what is it?"

"Lieutenant Travers brought me a crucial message," answered Elliot. "The Spanish are reinforcing Santiago."

Shafter stood bolt upright in the tub of water, his gout forgotten. "They're doing what?" he roared.

"This message was received a few hours ago," explained Elliot hastily, handing the note to Shafter, who quickly scanned it.

"Blast it!" rumbled Shafter. "Does this troop strength at Manzanillo seem accurate?"

"Very close to what we estimated, sir," Elliot assured him.

"With those eight thousand troops, the Spanish can hold Santiago indefinitely," Shafter said in despair. "What's more, if the Spanish ever move their garrison in Havana to Santiago Province, it might be our turn to be on the run." A look of defeat came over his face, and I knew instantly what was on his mind: Retreat! Pecos Bill was thinking about hightailing it back to the ships. Elliot saw the look, too.

"Of course, any defensive maneuvers are politically out of the question, sir," Elliot observed tautly. "One backward step would guarantee that General Miles would be instantly named to command this expedition."

The mention of Miles's name snapped Shafter out of it. "Then what can we do, Colonel?" demanded Shafter.

"We can move on the city of Santiago this very day and seize it before the reinforcements arrive," replied Elliot with bracing firmness. "Also, we can send a message to Garcia telling him to rally all the *insurrectos* in Santiago Province. They should harry and divert the reinforcements to give us as much time as possible to finish off General Linares's forces in Santiago. Once we take the city, we can bring direct artillery fire to bear on the Spanish fleet lying at anchor there. The enemy will have to either run for open water and face Admiral Sampson, or be sunk in the harbor. With a victory like that, the wind'll go out of the dons' sails, and you'll be hailed as a second Dewey."

Shafter rather liked that. Yes, he'd be lionized and perhaps given command of the entire army in Miles's place. Ah, but wouldn't that be sweet? I could see him thinking, a dreamy expression coming over his gross features. But then his visage clouded over as reality intruded once again.

"We can't do that, Elliot," he protested. "There are no plans drawn up and not enough ammunition stockpiled yet. Most of it's still sitting on the beaches at Daiquiri and Siboney. No, an attack on Santiago is out of the question until we're thoroughly prepared."

"But you've got no choice, sir," insisted Colonel Elliot. "If those reinforcements slip into Santiago before we attack, we will fail no matter how well prepared we are. And don't forget the climate, sir. It's on the side of the Spanish; fever is already stalking the troops. If we delay too long, you might not have any army left to command."

Shafter fell silent; he knew that Elliot was talking sense. His choices were clear: Either act immediately or give up all hope of successfully concluding the campaign and become known in history as an incompetent blunderer. He pouted, and then exhaled heavily. "Very well, Elliot," he said reproachfully, "I want all the division commanders here at once for a council of war—Kent, Lawton, Bates, and Wheeler."

"Wheeler's ill, sir," replied Elliot. "He's down with fever. General Sumner is commanding in his stead."

"If Wheeler's still breathing, I want him at that meeting," demanded Shafter. "Carry him on a stretcher if you have to. If I have to make a decision, I want every commander to approve it. If I sink, we're all going under."

Two hours later the key commanders were assembled as ordered under a great sheet of canvas stretched to keep the elements out but to let in the humid breeze. The rain had auspiciously slackened and the clouds parted somewhat, gracing the meeting with

intermittent sunshine. Shafter sat in his extra large camp stool per-
spiring heavily even though he was in his shirtsleeves. All the others,
except Wheeler, stood.

"Gentlemen," intoned Shafter ponderously, "I've received intelligence that shows the Spanish to be reinforcing Santiago. I expect those
reinforcements to arrive in two days, maybe one. We can't allow
the city to be reinforced, and the only way to prevent that is to seize
it now."

"Well, that's obvious," retorted Lawton, refusing to be deferential
in the great man's presence. "That's why we ought to get off our duffs
and take the place."

Shafter shot him a peeved look, but Lawton stared right back,
undaunted. Lawton might be an unimaginative by-the-book martinet,
but you had to admire his nerve, I thought.

"That, General Lawton, is why I called this meeting," snapped
Shafter icily.

"Hallelujah!" cried Wheeler from his litter, where he had been
deposited by a team of bearers. "It's about time we saw some fire around
heah. Why, if Marse Robert had been leadin' this heah invasion, we'd
a-taken Santiago last week and been knockin' on the front door of
Havana right now."

"Thank you for that insight, General Wheeler. I'll remind you,
however, that Robert E. Lee lost his war, something I do not intend
to do," Shafter replied acidly, drawing muffled guffaws from Lawton
and Kent. Score one for Shafter.

"I heard that, damn you!" snapped Wheeler testily. "I want you damn
Yankees to know that y'all woulda never won that there war if it weren't
for all them furriners and nigras y'all drafted. If it had a-been jus'
you agin' us in a fair fight, you varmints would need a passport to
visit Richmond."

Shafter merely snorted contemptuously; Wheeler's fever was making him more cantankerous than usual. Besides, Shafter had his hands
full with this war—he didn't have time to fight the Civil War all over
again with Wheeler. "Be that as it may," Shafter grunted dismis-
sively, then changed the subject. "Now, gentlemen, I want to hear your
thoughts on my proposal."

"I'm for it," announced Lawton without equivocation. "We came
here to fight the bastards. Let's get on with it."

Kent demurred. "I don't want to be too rash. After all, we don't
know much about the Spanish defenses around the city."

"Oh, piffle!" hooted Wheeler. "The only reason we don't know anything about the Spanish defenses is because we've been a-settin' on our rumps instead of git'n to the front and scoutin' like we should."

"Still, we must know what we face before we act," insisted General Kent stubbornly. "Otherwise, we court disaster."

"To sit heah is courtin' disaster, you fool," retorted Wheeler caustically. Kent's cheeks reddened at this and his hand reflexively dropped to the pommel of his saber, but Lawton laid a hand on Kent's and shook his head sternly.

"Why, look-a me," continued Wheeler. "When we landed, I was fit as a fiddle. Now I'm a sick old man. And I'm not the only one. Hundreds of my boys are down with the danged fever, too. I say attack now, while we still can!"

"I'm with Wheeler," agreed Lawton. "Let's move on Santiago while we can."

"I agree," piped up Bates, the commander of Shafter's independent brigade.

All eyes turned to Kent. "I'm still not so sure" was all Kent could muster in the face of their resolve.

"Neither am I," began Shafter, but at a furious look from Colonel Elliot he hastened to add, "but I'm prepared to order an immediate advance on Santiago nonetheless. I want it clearly on the record, however, that I do so only under protest, and because the majority of the division commanders present feel that this is the proper course of action."

"Praise Gawd for victory!" Wheeler bellowed exuberantly. Then the ex-Confederate cavalryman let out a great rebel yell. Shafter's hair seemed to stand on end at the sound of it.

"Gentlemen," intoned Shafter, "we move at dawn."

32

Aguadores Ford
July 1, 1898
As the first light peeked over the eastern hills, the gringo army went forward up the road to Santiago. Lawton's division was ordered to swing north of the line of march to take the Spanish blockhouse at El Caney, one of the outlying forts guarding the landward approaches

to Santiago. Meanwhile Kent's and Wheeler's divisions, the latter under the command of Sumner, went straight west toward Santiago. Elliot posted me with Kent's division in the van because of my "proven steadiness" in the fight at Las Guasimas. When I joined Kent's division, it was spread out in long columns that were fast approaching the San Juan River, a placid stream running from north to south. The road forded the river at a place called Aguadores Ford, cut through a woods, and then ascended a low defile between San Juan Hill and Kettle Hill. On the far side of those heights was Santiago and the Spanish fleet.

I rode toward the San Juan River and reined into a grove of banana trees a hundred yards short of the ford. Just as I settled in to watch the show, who should I see swinging by but the 71st New York. Old Glory was flying above them, and the men were singing a bawdy ditty about a tumescent fireman and a willing matron. At the head of the dusty blue-clad column was none other than Lieutenant Colonel Quinlon himself, mounted on a stringy nag and singing at the top of his lungs along with his men. You would have thought they were off to a lodge meeting rather than a battle.

"Fenwick, me bucko!" hailed Quinlon when he caught sight of me. "Sure and it's good to see ye, lad! 'Tis a fine day fer a battle, don't ye agree?" Since the enemy was nowhere to be seen, Quinlon evidently thought it was safe to get his Irish up.

"And it's good to see you, Colonel," I said good-naturedly.

An ominous rumbling suddenly reached our ears from the north. That had to be Lawton's troops at El Caney. Shafter had estimated that it would take Lawton no more than ninety minutes to reduce El Caney, and thus I was not unduly concerned about the distant cannonade. Then the first round from the Spanish artillery fell far off to our left, blowing a mud hut into a mist of fine dust. Another shell fell harmlessly far off to the right.

"Look, Fenwick," laughed Quinlon, pointing at the dust from the last blast. "The dago artillery is searching fer us, but they haven't a clue where we are. This is going to be easier than we ever imagined. We'll be on top o' them before they know we're there."

No sooner were the words out of his mouth than his world turned upside down. Just to our rear, a giant hot air balloon popped out of the trees and, tethered to the earth by long ropes, began to rise into the sultry morning air. The balloon belonged to the Signal Corps, and it was being used to send aloft a team of signalmen to locate the source of the Spanish artillery fire and then signal that location to our batteries by semaphore. Our batteries in turn would bring counterbattery fire on the Spanish and silence their guns.

It was a good plan and might have worked except that the Spanish gunners were no fools. As soon as this unexpected apparition appeared above the trees, they seized upon it as an aiming point. In seconds a stream of shells began falling on the hapless 71st. The first round blew a drummer standing twenty paces from Quinlon into liquidy red clumps.

"Holy Jesus!" screamed Quinlon, his horse bucking crazily in the crash of shells. "They're murdering us!"

"What'll we do, sir?" called an ashen-faced captain. "If we stay on this road, they'll kill us all!"

"It's that goddamned balloon!" screeched Quinlon. "It's drawing fire down on our heads! We've got to get the damned thing away from here!" Quinlon didn't say how this was to be done, and none of his men ventured to take on the task. In fact, the whole herd of them looked stunned by their baptism of fire.

Whatever his many faults, Quinlon wasn't a total coward. Sensing that his regiment was losing heart without so much as having seen a single Spaniard, he urged them on. "Push on, buckos! Push on! For ol' New York!" Brave words these, but the damage was done; first one and then another of the New Yorkers went to ground, refusing to budge. Quinlon's command dissolved before his very eyes into a mass of frightened fugitives.

Quinlon was distraught. "Oh, fer th' love o' God, don't disgrace yerselves, men! Go forward! Go forward!" He laid about with the flat of his sword until his frightened nag bucked him and sent him sprawling ignominiously into the dust.

Regaining his feet, Quinlon pleaded, "Men, don't do this! You'll be laughin'stocks!" He appeared ready to say more in the same vein when a shell struck his now-riderless horse, decapitating it. The headless carcass had not hit the ground before Quinlon sprinted to the guinea grass and dove in, his nerve shattered beyond repair.

Of course, I was already under cover by this time, my own abandoned mount having galloped crazily to the rear. At the impact of the first shell I'd vaulted from my horse and hotfooted it to the shelter of a nearby mango grove, all thoughts of advancing instantly banished from my mind.

I had just about decided to crawl to the rear as unobtrusively as possible when the staccato notes of a bugle split the air. Down the road from El Pozo appeared a thin skirmish line of troopers sweeping forward toward me. Through the smoky haze hugging the ground I could make out polka-dotted bandannas; it was the Rough Riders. Hooting derisively at the prone New Yorkers, the men of the 1st Volunteer Cavalry swept across the San Juan River firing their Sharps carbines and Krags as they went. In their midst rode Roosevelt, splendidly indifferent to the carnage around him.

"Bully! Bully, men!" he cried at the top of his lungs. The little rooster actually seems to be enjoying himself, I thought. As the Rough Riders swept by, I saw my opportunity; I would go forward with them, rather than risk running a gauntlet of steel in escaping to the rear.

I saw Quinlon cowering in the grass, and since I was going forward, I made sure I had an audience. "Quinlon! Quinlon!" I cried.

He lifted his head and eyed me fearfully.

"I'm going forward with Roosevelt! You've got to bring your regiment up in support!" How he was going to accomplish that, I had no idea—and I wasn't staying around to find out.

"But we can't move, Travers!" he protested plaintively. "Ye can see that with your own eyes. It's impossible!"

Maybe his boys weren't moving, but yours truly was. I was on my feet in a flash and scampering across the shallow, muddy waters of the San Juan. Here and there a body bobbed grotesquely. The sight of dead men drove me to even greater speed, and I crashed blindly into the undergrowth on the far shore, tripping over the jungle vines that snaked willy-nilly along the ground. I tripped, got up, ran, and tripped again. This time I fell on something soft and yielding. Cautiously, I looked down. I was sprawled on the dead body of Colonel Elliot! He was on his back, staring at the branches above him, a neat, round Mauser hole in his forehead.

"Arrgh!" I gagged reflexively, nearly emptying my hardtack breakfast all over the poor bastard. Elliot was still warm; he must have bought the farm only seconds before I stumbled upon him. Evidently he had been with the Rough Riders when they went by while I cowered in the guinea grass with the 71st New York.

I rose in shock and again stumbled blindly forward through the clinging underbrush. The smoke from the artillery detonations and brushfires all around me was so thick that I lost my bearings. I simply pushed forward until I saw shadows filtering through the haze. I stopped and listened. They were Americans! It was the Rough Riders again! Gratefully I went to them and dropped to one knee, exhausted.

"Hold on, boys," I heard a sergeant call. "Stay in the wood line and get under cover. Don't move until we get the word."

I tried once more to get my bearings. Up ahead the woods turned abruptly into open savannahs that rose to high, grass-swept hills. Any further advance would be in the open, right into the very teeth of the Spanish guns. I realized from the maps I'd studied that the heights before me were the San Juan Hill fortification complex, the outlying ramparts guarding the landward approaches to Santiago. To the rear I could hear the roar of the unabated Spanish artillery fire; to my immediate front was Kettle Hill, Spanish infantry clearly visible on its crest.

I felt a claustrophobic panic welling up inside of me—I was trapped! In all directions I saw only death and destruction.

"I'm hit!" screamed a nearby trooper, spinning to the ground with a bright red gusher of blood jetting from his thigh. I looked up at Kettle Hill; muzzle flashes lit the trench line on the crest of the hill. The dagos were peppering us with Mauser fire. I had to seek shelter!

Thoroughly shaken now, I ran back into the underbrush whence I had come, only to trip over something again. I was fearful to look down at what it was, lest I find Elliot's cadaver following me around the battlefield. But I forced myself to rise, turn, and look. By Christ, it wasn't Elliot; it was Crane!

"Hello, Travers," called Crane cheerily, a dreamy look on his face. He was sitting with his back to a tree casually sketching the scene around him, completely oblivious to the crash of battle. I had tripped over his outstretched legs. "Having a good time?" he inquired with the complete insouciance he emanated whenever he had a bottle of his opium elixir under his belt.

His jarring calmness in the midst of the madness all about me must have snapped my reason, for I gave a couple of great gasps like a landed catfish and then sobbed tremulously, "Crane! What are you doing? My God, you don't mean to tell me that you're sitting here drawing while men die all around you? Why, are you mad, man?" And then the inanity of it all suddenly struck me as hilarious. "Haw, haw, haw!" I roared.

"Sitting here drawing with the world exploding around you! Oh, that's rich, Crane, quite rich!" I howled idiotically.

Crane looked at me silently through the narcotic fog that enshrouded his brain, enough awareness about him to be concerned that I'd finally gone over the edge. "Travers, are you . . . all right?" he asked.

"All right, Crane? Why, I've got half the Spanish army shooting at me, our own balloons giving us away so that the enemy can shell us, and you ask if I'm all right? One of us is out of our goddamn minds, Crane, and I'm not sure who it is!"

Just then a great blast blew me off my feet and stretched me out senseless. When I came to, Crane was hovering solicitously over me.

"What happened?" I asked groggily.

"A Krupp hit one of the Rough Riders' supply mules, Travers. I'm afraid it made quite a mess."

I felt a dull stab of pain in my flank. "I'm hit!" I croaked.

"It appears you are, old man," Crane agreed dreamily, glancing down at me.

I touched my side and felt a warm liquid. I raised my hand before my eyes. It was covered with red goo! Oh God, I was a goner!

Then I blinked and noticed that the goo was also brown in places. Brown? I thought, puzzled. What the hell was going on? I put my finger to my lips. It tasted like blood mixed with beef gravy! And that's precisely what it was; when the mule exploded, it showered the woods with unopened tins of beef it had been carrying in the pack strapped to its back. A burst tin had slammed into my side, bruised my ribs, and lacerated the skin to boot. I'd be stiff for a while, but I would certainly live.

Crane helped me to sit. "Cheer up, Travers," he consoled me, "you'll get a medal for this."

I grunted in pain. "No thanks, Crane, I already have my badge, and it's quite red." Without further ado, I staggered to my feet and left Crane strangely silent, staring after me.

Mauser bullets were now hissing through the woods all around the Rough Riders, but fortunately the fire was high. The Spanish, unwilling to expose themselves to our fire, were merely pointing their Mausers over the lip of their trenches and pulling the triggers. The resultant fire sailed largely over our heads, with only occasional rounds falling on the tree line where the Rough Riders were congregated. This meant that it was actually safer to be in the open near the foot of Kettle Hill than to be hidden in the woods. Slowly, therefore, the Rough Riders emerged from the foliage into the grassy area to their front.

The thought of deliberately exposing myself to enemy fire was anathema to me, but the physics of the situation had an undeniable logic. Fighting to hold down my gorge, I joined the Rough Riders spread across the grass in a line facing the heights.

Spotting me, Roosevelt immediately rode over on Little Texas and eyed me with concern. I looked a sight; my uniform was torn and dirtied, and my entire left side was covered with blood and boned beef juice. "Travers, you're wounded," he barked. "Go to the rear at once!"

But there was no way I could be induced to enter that fire-swept zone to my rear merely to seek medical aid that I would never survive long enough to benefit from anyway. "Begging the colonel's pardon," I retorted, struggling to keep a quaver out of my voice, "but my place is here, and here I will stay."

Roosevelt eyed me sternly, mulling over my words, and then growled, "Well, bully, young man, bully," nodding his head with vigorous approval as he spoke. "I'll see that Wheeler mentions you in dispatches—No strings attached this time."

I smiled wanly and lurched off to an unoccupied clump of guinea grass, where I promptly collapsed. I looked to my side, only to see a prone Negro grinning at me.

"Goo' mawnin' t'ya, sah," this worthy greeted me, as cheery as you please.

"Good day, soldier," I replied sullenly. A black regular, I thought; Roosevelt's troops must have become hopelessly intertwined with the regular cavalry squadrons in the confusion of the battle. Glancing around me, I saw Negroes liberally interspersed with the white Rough Riders. It appeared that the cavalry division had made more social progress in the past thirty minutes than the nation had made in the past thirty years. Bully, I thought.

"Dis heah a bad pass," grunted the Buffalo Soldier at my side. "We needs t'git on dat dere hill." He nodded toward the heights of Kettle Hill above us.

The fellow was right, for the battle had suddenly reached a climax. Our artillery had fallen silent, but the Spanish guns still boomed away on the hills above us, and the Spanish marksmen were becoming more active than ever. The key to the battle was clearly Kettle Hill. As long as the dagos held it, they could pepper us with impunity.

But it didn't look as though anyone was making any attempt to take the height. If we weren't going to fish, shouldn't we cut bait? I thought. Once more I looked nervously to the rear.

"Well, looky dere!" exclaimed my dusky companion. "Dem's de coffee grinders! Deh's done brought up de coffee grinders!"

Looking in the direction he indicated, I lifted my head just high enough to see a section of horse-drawn Gatling guns gallop out of the woods from the rear, unlimber, and commence to lay down a lethal grazing fire in the direction of the Spanish on the summit.

"Let's go, boys!" someone nearby yelled. "Let's kick the hell out of those bastards!"

"Yeee-hah!" whooped a Rough Rider near me. "We got those Mexicans corralled, now let's go brand 'em!" As dazed as I was, I was nonetheless rational enough to doubt that anyone would willingly join such a rash assault up the hill.

But I was wrong; all around me individuals and groups of soldiers got to their feet and started climbing toward the enemy.

"Bully, men! Bully!" cheered Roosevelt as he saw them go, waving his sword to encourage them onward.

Then the entire body of troopers gave a great roar and went forward. Their activity quickly attracted the attention of the Spanish defenders, and soon the grass all around me was alive with whizzing bullets. I was on my feet in an instant, scampering after the assault troops.

"Wait for me!" I screamed above the din to nobody in particular. The Gatling guns continued to put hot lead on the crest when, to our utter amazement, the Spanish began to desert their trenches! As I approached the crest I saw a large frame structure with a heavy metal kettle hanging from the rafters. Inside this scant shelter stood some diehard defenders, but the cavalrymen were cutting down these last Spaniards as fast as they could shoot.

"Ah haven't had this much fun since we shot coons in Memphis!" cackled a white trooper, coolly working the bolt of his Krag, oblivious to the fact that the soldier firing at his side was as black as the ace of spades.

"Wahoo!" whooped the Rough Riders as the last Spaniard scampered away. "They're on the run now!"

Instantly the troops—black and white—were up and running after the fleeing enemy. "After 'em, boys, after 'em!" called Roosevelt. "Don't let 'em rally!" He spurred Little Texas onward and took up the chase down the far side of Kettle Hill and toward the distant height of San Juan Hill, his men at his heels. Already I could see lines of skirmishers from the 24th and 9th Infantry of Kent's division to our left ascending San Juan Hill, and behind them even more formations of blue-shirted infantry. The game was clearly over for the dons.

Exhausted beyond belief, and weak from loss of blood, I was in no condition to join the pursuit. I painfully climbed the rest of the way to the top of the hill and collapsed in a deserted trench. No sooner did my head touch the earth than I started to doze off. As my head swam dreamily, a totally random thought suddenly floated to the top of my consciousness. During this entire day of battle, I had completely forgotten to draw my revolver from its holster!

33

It was evening when I awoke. I was lying flat on my back with a throbbing pain in my side, gazing at a night sky blazing with a luminosity I had never seen in more northern climes. Perhaps, I thought worriedly, I'd been wounded much more seriously than I'd earlier believed, and the reason for the stars' brightness was that I was much closer to them than ever before in my sordid little life! Panicked, I struggled to sit up, and then rose to my feet. Despite my light-headed dizziness, I concluded that I hadn't yet passed over the River Jordan. Vastly relieved, I set off to explore my surroundings.

I wandered about in the dark for some time, searching for a familiar landmark upon which to orient myself. But the terrain looked different in the gloom, and I finally had to admit that I was totally lost. I decided that the way to the rear was down, so I descended the slope with as quick a tread as I could manage.

With the realization that I was lost and totally alone came the accompanying realization that there might be Spaniards abroad in the night as well as Americans. Fear began to well up in me and I started at every noise, no matter how slight.

I was literally tiptoeing through the grass when a whisper came out of the shadow. "¡Alto!"

Spanish, I thought fearfully. Expecting a bullet from the dark at any second, I froze.

"*¿Quién está ahí?*" the voice demanded.

"*¡Americano!*" I squeaked in reply. Why then, of all the times in my life, I chose to tell the truth, I shall never know. But my forthrightness saved my life.

"Amigo!" came the reply, perceptibly less hostile now. Out of the shadows stepped a group of figures, all armed. There were about a dozen in all, and I concluded that I'd stumbled upon a band of *guerrilleros*. They seemed friendly enough, but I was on my guard.

Suddenly I heard a familiar voice. "Feenweek!"

It was Marguerite, by God! Before I had time to react, she rushed into my arms and smothered me with kisses. I struggled to break the surprisingly strong grip she had on me; didn't the little hussy realize we were surrounded by the enemy?

"Stop it, Marguerite!" I whispered urgently. "Try to control yourself, girl!"

She tittered giddily, oblivious to our danger. "Don't be alarmed, Feenweek. You are safe."

I tried to control my terror; I'd be damned if I'd let her laugh at my lack of intestinal fortitude. Besides, something told me she liked the strong type, so I needed to buck up straightaway. "I have no fear, my dear," I assured her, screwing my face into what I hoped was a dazzling smile. "I'm only concerned that we might draw attention and your safety might be compromised. Keeping you safe is the most important thing to me."

My charade of calmness did the trick, for she released me with a final kiss. "Oh, Feenweek, you are so kind," she purred.

"Only to especially lovely ladies, my dear," I assured her, truthfully enough. This brought a squeal and another passionate hug, and although fondling Marguerite was high on my list of priorities, now was neither the time nor the place.

"Marguerite," I insisted, "I must be getting back to the American lines. Perhaps you and your friends could point the way for me."

"Si, Feenweek," she replied and then turned to jabber with a burly fellow who hovered nearby watching me suspiciously. He was a lovely sight all right, with a scarlet bandanna wrapped about his head, a black patch over one eye, and a single gold earring. He looked for all the world like a buccaneer from a Robert Louis Stevenson novel. I caught a note of protestation in his voice; I suspected he was sweet on Marguerite himself. As they bantered back and forth, I studied the other

Cubans. I noticed many of them carrying two or three Mausers or Krags slung over their shoulders. It was evident that our *insurrecto* friends— so conspicuously absent during the battle—were abroad under cover of darkness picking the battlefield bare.

At length Marguerite turned to me and said, "Si, Feenweek, I will guide you back to your *compadres*. I will rejoin Jesus"—I took this to be a reference to the pirate—"and the others later." There was a last exchange in Spanish, and the other Cubans padded off into the night, no doubt to cache their loot. I noticed that the pirate Jesus eyed us sullenly as he left and fingered the wicked-looking machete that hung from his belt.

Then we were on our way, with Marguerite setting a punishing pace for a full thirty minutes. Yet friendly lines were nowhere to be seen, and I was fast wilting from hunger and the effects of my wound. "Marguerite," I huffed, "we must rest."

"Oh, my poor Feenweek," she commiserated, "you must be tired from the battle, no?"

"It's my side," I explained with what I hoped was just the right note of manly dismissal in my voice. "I'm afraid I was wounded earlier. It's nothing really, but it does fatigue me."

"Oh, my poor darling," she warbled with concern, feeling the dried beef sauce on my tunic. "Marguerite will help her Feenweek."

With that she pulled me into the bushes and pushed me to the ground. Without another word she disappeared into the night. I was content to let her go, for I was too exhausted to give chase. I must have dozed off, for I awoke with a start to find Marguerite at my side once more, this time with a canteen of water. Was she gone for hours or only minutes? I wondered. I was finding it hard to keep time straight in my throbbing head. But I knew I was thirsty, so I drank deeply.

"Ahh!" I gasped gratefully, my thirst slaked.

"Poor hombre," clucked Marguerite. "Let me see your wound. I can rinse it."

I lay back contentedly as she got my tunic opened and sponged off my battered and lacerated ribs. In a short while I was reasonably clean and trussed up with strips Marguerite had torn from the bottom of her skirt.

My immediate needs taken care of, I became pleasantly aware of the weight of Marguerite's breasts upon my torso. "I have missed you, my little vixen," I whispered in her ear.

"Vixen? What is a vixen?" she retorted playfully, not drawing back when I enveloped her in my arms.

"A vixen's a fox, Marguerite. And that's what you are. My little fox."

"Si," she breathed in my ear. "I am ready to be your little fox, Feenweek."

She kissed me back passionately, fully as randy as I. Three was my lucky number, and this was my third try at Marguerite, I realized hopefully. In a flash I had her shirtwaist off and had hoisted her skirt well north of her hips. She was naked underneath, and in the moonlight I savored the lush curves of her glorious thighs.

"Oh, Feenweek," she sighed warmly as my hands roamed about her with license, "I need you badly."

"And I need you, my dear," I assured her with equal passion. I was speaking the truth, for I was bulging with urgent anticipation. Not bothering to strip for my conquest of Marguerite, I raised up enough to lower my trousers, rolled her on her back, and mounted her.

"Oh, Feenweek," gasped Marguerite sensuously as I slid home.

"Oh, yes!" I sighed, settling in for a vigorous ride. And ride I did, bouncing the poor girl's bottom off the soft earth. We rocked along merrily to the accompaniment of the chirping crickets, until I could contain myself no longer. My movements became more frantic, and with each thrust of my loins Marguerite moaned blissfully.

"Feenweek, *mi amor!*" she murmured over and over again. I sensed she too had reached the point of no return, for her slender legs were locked around my waist and her buttocks were beating the ground with the rapidity of a Gatling gun firing at full bore.

"Oh! Oh! Oh!" I grunted as, with a feeling of pure ecstasy, I released into her. The thunderous rush of blood to my head became a loud banging sound as Marguerite clung to me even tighter, releasing herself with powerful shudders. Then, spent, she relaxed and released me.

I rolled off her and took a deep breath. For the first time in my life I had actually heard fireworks going off during the dirty deed! The trouble was, I could still hear them. Fireworks? By God, it wasn't fireworks, it was gunfire!

I scrambled to my feet with my trousers still at half-staff, instantly alert. There were rifles going off all around me and figures running everywhere. What's more, from their white uniforms and straw hats, I realized they were Spaniards! I was surrounded by the enemy, by God!

Without so much as a by-your-leave to Marguerite, I hitched up my britches and took off at a dead run for the nearest hill—in the same direction that most of the dagos happened to be traveling. I realized instantly that they were launching a counterattack, and I raced along with them, trying to regain our lines before they discovered me in their midst and gunned me down.

High-stepping like a farm boy through a creek filled with cotton-mouths, I crashed through the front ranks of the Spanish as they crouched to fire. "Out of my way, you bastards!" I screeched wildly, knocking one flat on the ground and scattering the others in ter-ror. Remembering my revolver, I yanked it from its holster and blazed away madly.

From their fearful, wide-eyed looks at me as I rushed past, it was clear that the dagos thought they were surrounded! Their nerves, like mine, were shot. Some threw down their arms and stood with their hands raised; others scampered back from where they had come. But stopping to take prisoners was the last thing on my mind, you can rest assured. I tried to scream "Help! Help!" but the sound that came out was more like "Eeee-yiii!"

Flying up the heights, I leapt over strands of barbed wire and, with my last ounce of strength, vaulted a low parapet of sandbags near the crest and crashed to the bottom of a trench. All around me the dark was split by muzzle flashes as American sentries hurled lead down upon the Spanish attackers. How I was not hit by their fire was beyond me. Thoroughly blown, I lay in the soft earth at the bottom of the trench and heaved great sighs of relief.

Suddenly, I was seized by the scruff of the neck and hauled to my feet by a powerful trooper who obviously thought he'd just captured an insane dago. "And just what the hell do we have here?" he growled fiercely, holding a Bowie knife level with my Adam's apple. Only then did he notice the rank on my collar. "Oh, sorry, sir," he grinned sheepishly, relaxing his vicelike grip. "Are you okay?"

"Y—yes," I managed to cough, forcing the air through my con-stricted throat. "But don't worry about me. Get back to your post." Which was my way of saying, don't stand there gawking at me; start pouring fire down that hill so the Spanish don't pile in on top of me and haul me right back out of here again.

"I say, Travers," came a familiar voice from down the trench line. "That was bully, sir, simply bully!"

It was Roosevelt, making his way down the trench line toward me. Roosevelt? I thought. Why, I'd come to roost right back with the Rough Riders. "That was one of the boldest actions I've witnessed so far in this war!" effused Roosevelt, coming up to me and pumping my hand vigorously. "I thought the Spanish would be in amongst us in a few seconds, but when you came bursting from their rear, the whole yellow pack of them skedaddled!"

At Roosevelt's side was another officer, a full colonel. "Very impressive," agreed this fellow.

"Lieutenant Travers, let me introduce you to Colonel Leonard Wood, the commander of the Rough Riders."

I recognized the name. I knew that Wood, as a regular, had been put in charge of the 1st Volunteer Cavalry, with Roosevelt as his second in command.

"My pleasure, Travers," said Colonel Wood. "You may rest assured that General Shafter will hear of this night's work."

I forced myself to smile calmly; if Shafter got a full report of my night's work, he'd surely succumb to a stroke.

"Travers, you never cease to confound me," went on Roosevelt. "Why, when I saw you stomping and bellowing your way to the top of this hill, I said to myself, that's no little twaddle of a staff officer. No sir, I said, that man's a bear, a ram, a . . . er, er," stammered Roosevelt as he struggled for some suitable animal totem.

"A bull moose?" I suggested, not at all surprised that a mind as primitive as Roosevelt's would naturally gravitate to atavistic symbols.

"Yes, b'gad, a bull moose!" agreed Roosevelt exuberantly. "Just so, like a bull moose."

I was frightened, cold, and hungry, and I had damned little patience for any further babbling from Roosevelt. "Sir, if I may be excused," I said. "I've got to get this wound attended to."

"Wound?" asked Colonel Wood, concerned.

"Why, the lad's a bloody mess!" exclaimed Roosevelt, just now noticing my tunic. "Travers, don't tell me that you've been running about wounded like that since I saw you this morning?"

"The poor fellow's had no medical attention all day?" asked Colonel Wood, concern evident in his voice.

"Oh, it's just a nick I got crossing the San Juan River," I assured him with affected modesty. "It's been field-bandaged, but I think I ought to have a doctor look at it."

"Of course, son, of course," agreed Wood, quickly telling several troops to escort me to the regimental surgeon.

As I hobbled to the rear, I could hear Roosevelt muttering to himself as he gazed vacantly out over the parapet. "A bull moose—b'gad, yes; there's a ring to it!"

34

Two days later I was completely myself again. I'd had plenty of rest, my wound was disinfected and professionally bandaged, and I had managed to secure a fresh uniform and linen. I was pronounced fit and returned to duty, which for me, of course, meant doing as little as possible. Idling was made easier by the passing of poor Elliot and the fact that Pecos Bill called me into his tent to present a citation and to tell me I had been mentioned in dispatches to the War Department. That had boosted my stock immeasurably with the rest of the staff, as you can well imagine. And so I was seen as something of a sacred cow—the general's boy, as it were—and everyone gave me a wide berth, which guaranteed that I could do pretty much as I pleased.

I was feeling fine—so much so, in fact, that I decided to take a stroll up to the front. It would be safe enough, I figured, now that the shooting had simmered down. Indeed, since the charge up San Juan Hill, there had been no real fighting in the area. Taking a hearty swig of potent rum to ward off fever, I set off straight up the road to San Juan Hill and soon was standing on the crest gazing down on the red-tiled roofs of Santiago. Beyond the buildings I could see the placid waters of the harbor where lay the dark hulks of Admiral Cervera's fleet. Those men o' war were a sobering sight, I can assure you.

Not too far away a solitary figure in black stood, taking in the same scene. Seeing me, the fellow ambled over. "Lieutenant Travers," he said, "so good to see you again."

The somber visage before me was unmistakable: It was Harlock, by God, right here in Cuba! "Why, Mister Harlock," I stammered, more startled than I cared to show. "I had no idea you were with the army, sir."

"I'm not," he replied, giving me a wintry smile that seemed quite an effort for him. "I'm here on private business. I heard that Mister

Hearst was coming here on his private yacht, so I arranged passage with him."

"Mister William Randolph Hearst?" I asked, awed.

He nodded.

"I see," I said, not really seeing anything at all, but instantly recognizing that Harlock was very well connected indeed if he could "arrange passage" with Hearst. "When last we spoke, sir—at Mister Duncan's, if you recall—I never did have the chance to ask you what your business was. What sort of private enterprise could you have in a godforsaken place like this?"

Harlock laughed indulgently, with the air of a man who often has his line of work questioned by others. "Actually, I'm in the import-export business, Lieutenant."

"The import-export business?" I wondered aloud. "The only things Cuba can export are sugarcane and rum, and the market for those commodities is quite depressed at the moment. As for imports, why, just take a look around you. These people don't have two red cents to rub together. Oh, they'd like to get imports, I'm sure, but they'll never be able to pay for them. How can you do business in an atmosphere like this?"

"Oh, terms of payments have a way of working their way out, Lieutenant," replied Harlock vaguely, his eyes suddenly hooded.

"But payment for what? What sort of commodity can there be a market for in war-torn Cuba?" I pressed.

Harlock looked almost dreamily at the horizon. "Hardware, mostly," he said absently. "And souvenirs."

Hardware? Souvenirs? I had to confess, I didn't understand the man, and there were clearly aspects of his trade that Mr. Harlock was not about to reveal to me. But Harlock had been generous to me before, and there's nothing that makes me come around wagging my tail for more than someone's unrequited generosity, so I decided to change the subject and let Harlock know I was suitably grateful for his gift.

"I never properly let you know how much I've enjoyed the flask you sent. What with my rush to be off to Tampa and all," I explained lamely, but then continued. "Nonetheless, it's come in handy, and I thank you for your generosity. I only wish I could reciprocate in some way," I said, not really meaning it at all, but it was the sort of nonsense one was expected to mouth at such times. I wanted to go on and ask him how he had deduced that I would stay at the Fifth Avenue Hotel that night after I'd left Duncan's house, but I thought this question might cause him to view me as completely guileless, so I held my tongue.

"Think nothing of it, my boy," answered Harlock, but then added enigmatically, "You shall have ample opportunity to show me your appreciation if you're of a mind to."

What the hell did that mean? I wondered. I was about to ask Harlock exactly that when we were interrupted by the sudden blasts of many ships' whistles. All eyes turned to the harbor below where, to our amazement, great black clouds of coal smoke began to belch forth from the stacks of the Spanish warships. In the space of a few minutes, the entire enemy fleet weighed anchor and began to move purposefully toward the mouth of the harbor—right into the maw of the waiting American fleet!

"They're making a run for it!" screamed a sentry nearby.

"Yes! Yes, they are!" hooted another in agreement.

As I watched through my glasses, the four battle cruisers that made up Admiral Cervera's fleet steamed south until they were out of sight around the Punta Gorda. Only the black clouds in the air above the point betrayed their location to us. Suddenly our ears caught the distant rumble of large-caliber guns; Admiral Cervera had been spotted by our navy and the chase was on!

At once I bade farewell to Harlock and hurried back to the telegraph office adjacent to Shafter's headquarters, where I followed the day's events. A desperate running battle unfolded as the Spanish debouched from Santiago Harbor into the waiting guns of the vastly superior American fleet. In a matter of hours every Spanish vessel was either sunk or run aground. When the sun set that fateful day and the last gun fell silent, no Spanish flag flew over any colony anywhere from the Caribbean to the Sulu Sea. The age of American empire had commenced!

Of more immediate consequence to me, however, was the fact that all Spanish resistance in Santiago immediately collapsed. The following day the garrison sued for terms, and on July 14, 1898, General Shafter marched his army through the open gates of the city. The war was over without another shot being fired!

35

Havana, Cuba
September 1899

Ah, Havana in September. Yep, it was more than a year after the fall of Santiago, and I was still in Cuba. You see, following the Spanish surrender, the volunteers, along with most of the ailing regulars, had been packed off to a temporary camp on Montauk Point on Long Island. There they'd been properly fed and issued the tropical uniforms that had never reached them in Cuba—and for which they by then had no earthly use—before being sent back into civilian life with the thanks of a grateful nation. Wounded regulars had been evacuated, too, including Colonel Liscum, who'd been riddled with shell fragments during the attack on San Juan Hill. The rest of us, reinforced by so-called immune regiments, had been sprinkled about Cuba as an army of occupation, much to the displeasure of the *insurrectos*. Our erstwhile allies wanted us gone as soon as the last Spanish flag was hauled down, but the War Department decided to keep a military presence until the natives showed some capability for governing themselves. Since that promised to be some time in the middle of the next century, we regular officers were detailed off to garrison duty around the island.

In recognition of my exemplary service, Shafter posted me to Havana, which was considered a bit of a plum assignment. I was nicely ensconced in a small villa located within the walls of the Fortaleza de San Carlos de la Cabana, the main fortress guarding Havana harbor. The fort was on the east bank of the Canal del Puerto, the waterway that connected Havana Bay to the south with the Straits of Florida to the north.

My duties generally involved nothing more extensive than signing paperwork allowing shipments to enter and leave the harbor, a sort of customs official if you will, since the harbor remained under American control. My spacious office adjoined my living quarters, through which I could slip out when I was tired or just plain randy, and whence I availed myself of the numerous small ferries that plied the Canal del Puerto to carry me over to the quays of La Habana Vieja—Old Havana— where the nightlife was fast and furious. Compared to Plattsburgh Barracks, Old Havana was paradise!

It became even more so as the result of a little arrangement I entered into as September drew to a close. I was lounging about my office in the Fortaleza de San Carlos de la Cabana (which is quite a mouthful, so we Yanks called it simply Fort Sam Carl), ostensibly laboring over a monthly tonnage report but actually counting down the hours until the end of the day and getting mildly rummed up in the interim, when suddenly there was a knock on my door and my orderly announced a visitor. I looked up just in time to see Harlock step into the room.

"Why, Mister Harlock, what a surprise!" I greeted him. "I haven't seen you in months. I'd supposed you left Cuba long ago." I rose, we shook hands, and I showed him to a leather-upholstered chair positioned beneath an oil painting of some long-dead conquistador. I took a seat behind my desk and studied him with undisguised curiosity. Despite the heat of the day, I noticed that he was attired in his customary somber hues.

"As you can see, Lieutenant, I'm still here. I haven't yet completed my business," he replied crisply. His blue eyes fixed on me calmly, and I could tell this was no social visit.

"I see," I countered noncommittally. Something about Harlock's presence here warned me to be on my guard.

Harlock gazed about the office, I think approvingly, although his face was such a wizened mask that it was hard to tell. "You're looking well, Travers," he said at length. "I daresay this army life quite agrees with you."

I smiled in acknowledgment and gave the end of my mustache a twirl; nothing pleased me more than to have others see me in the lap of privilege. My office was impressive, by God. It had belonged to the chief assistant to the former governor-general of Cuba and was filled with a costly collection of teak furniture and Moorish rugs. "Well, the truth of the matter is I'm doing quite nicely at the moment, thank you." Harlock's innuendo that I was an important cog in the military machinery overseeing Cuba pleased me no little amount and I fairly purred in satisfaction before him. I offered Harlock a cigar from the humidor on the desk; when he declined, I selected one, lit it, blew a great blue cloud of smoke toward the lofty ceiling, and eyed him levelly. "Now tell me, sir, to what do I owe the pleasure of this visit?"

He was unexpectedly direct. "I'm here because I think you and I can do business together."

"What type of business?" I asked guardedly, fully aware that Harlock was used to dealing with men of affairs like George Duncan. Unless I was careful he'd be sure to gobble me up in any business deal like a shark swallowing a minnow.

"It concerns my, er, souvenir business, Lieutenant. Yankee Clipper Limited," he answered.

Yankee Clipper Limited? I'd never heard of it, but I recalled that the outline of a clipper ship was imprinted on the flask Harlock had given me. "What about your souvenir business?" I asked.

"I need a way to ship my souvenirs out of Havana," he replied.

"I'm sure that will pose no problem," I assured him blandly in the pseudohelpful bureaucratic tone I affected in the course of my customs duties. "Simply present your freight for inspection at the customs house. There are soldiers there for that purpose. They'll give your shipments a quick once-over and, if everything's in order, they'll issue you bills of lading. You can bring those to my office to be signed; after that you're cleared to load your freight. It's really quite simple, you see." I smiled cheerfully, waiting for the old fellow to thank me profusely for my learned discourse on the customs system, pump my hand gratefully, and be on his way.

But Harlock didn't smile. Instead he cleared his throat and asked pointedly, "What if I did not care to have my shipments . . . inspected?"

"Not inspected? Really, Mister Harlock, that's quite out of the question. All cargo has to be inspected. . . ." I fell silent as it finally dawned on me what Harlock wanted. He'd come to talk business, all right. I leaned forward on my desk, took another puff of my cigar, and flicked the ashes into an empty shell canister that served as an ashtray. "Mister Harlock, let's be frank, shall we? What precisely is the nature of the souvenirs you handle?"

"Rifles and sidearms," he answered flatly.

"Rifles and sidearms?" I echoed in alarm, sinking back in my chair. Why, of course, I thought as I cursed myself for my denseness. Here I had been laboring under the impression that Harlock was Duncan's partner in essentially legitimate enterprises like mining in Mexico. I had dismissed Duncan's and Harlock's involvement with guns and with that bandit Pedrolito as being merely prudent business practice in a wild place like Sonora. But now I saw my mistake: Gunrunning wasn't a sideline for Harlock; it was his main business, and now, obviously, he was in Cuba to exploit this new market. The pieces were certainly falling into place. It was clear why Marguerite and her *compadres* were picking the battlefield clean of weapons after the battle of San Juan Hill. Those weapons were not intended for the use of the *guerrilleros*. Instead they were to be sold to arms merchants like Harlock for profit. That would also explain Harlock's presence in Cuba in July, just when it appeared that Spanish rule was about to end. He was on the scene to line up suppliers before his competitors could interfere. Apparently the time of gathering was at an end and the time of shipping had come.

"Is there some way you might help me with my, er, shipment difficulties, Lieutenant Travers?" he prodded, quietly but firmly.

"It's hard to say," I demurred, deciding to let the old buzzard stew a bit. "After all, if I understand what you're proposing, it's probably a violation of Cuban and American law." I caught the vaguest hint of concern in Harlock's eyes, and for a second I knew he was wondering if he had misjudged me.

"A violation of law is a problem only if it's pursued by the authorities, Lieutenant," he countered, cool as you please. "I repeat, is there some way you might help me in this matter?"

He wanted a straight-out answer, that was plain, but I didn't intend to be buffaloed into giving him one straightaway. After all, I held the cards here, by God, so I toyed with the bastard some. "It depends. Whose weapons are we talking about and where are you shipping them to?"

"The weapons are mine, bought and paid for. I can produce bills of sale if you insist. As for their destination, I'm afraid that's privileged information. It doesn't concern you, and"—here he leaned over the desk and stared me straight in the eye—"believe me, you really wouldn't want to know."

I eyed him levelly for a few moments, and he continued to meet my gaze with that steely stare. He was a nervy old bastard, I had to admit. He was buying up weapons gathered from the battlefields of Cuba, probably at bargain prices, and shipping them off to some new war zone. I'd wager he was turning a handsome profit on his little operation, and the scent of profit drew me like a bee to a flower. At length I reached into my desk and, by way of a reply to his proposition, produced the silver flask he'd given me months ago. I fingered the clipper ship imprinted on the leather cover, then uncorked the flask, took a sip, and gave Harlock a wink.

Harlock broke into a bleak smile. "Excellent," he rasped.

"Oh, I wouldn't be so certain of that," I smiled back, hungrily. "The services you require will be expensive, Mister Harlock." Harlock didn't blink at this; I suspected he had been through similar bargaining sessions in the past.

I was right. "I realize that, Lieutenant Travers," he countered, completely unperturbed. "What's your price?"

God, he was a cool one! I'd do well to be careful with him, I reminded myself. "I want a retainer of two hundred dollars per month, whether you ship in any given month or not. That's for overhead, you see. And one hundred dollars for each bill of lading I sign." I tried to appear as calm as Harlock, but I sensed I wasn't succeeding. My guts began sliding all over themselves so badly that I felt as though I was about to spill my lunch onto the polished teak desk.

"One hundred dollars a month and fifty dollars for each bill signed," countered Harlock sharply.

"One seventy-five and seventy-five," I shot back, fighting hard not to cave in under his withering gaze. "You have your nerve, Harlock. Sailing in here to ask me to break the law and then dickering over the price like a Cuban fishmonger. It's all very irregular, I tell you." Only my losses at the gaming tables kept me from tossing him out on his ear. Those losses had been so severe, and I was so much in arrears, that I suspected the only reason I hadn't already had my throat slashed in some back-alley ambush was because of my close association with now–Brigadier General Wood. But it was clear that I'd have to come up with the money soon.

"One hundred fifty and sixty, and not one penny more," Harlock announced with finality.

I decided not to press the old miser further. "Done," I said with a broad smile that was not returned. Harlock merely rose and offered me his gnarled claw. "Good day to you, sir," he said simply. My brave facade did not fool him, I realized. He knew exactly who was in charge. "My agents will be in touch with you directly."

With that he reached into his coat, drew out a purse, fished about in it for a moment, and produced two fifty-dollar gold pieces. He placed them on the desk before me and declared, "A down payment, Lieutenant." Without another word, he planted his derby firmly on his head and left.

I sat back, put my booted feet up on my desk, and took another pull on the flask. So I had been bought, by God! And by a conniving gunrunner at that. Funny to say, but when I had first laid eyes on Harlock I'd pegged him for a mortician. But then I suppose a gunrunner—a merchant of death as it were—was a close cousin to a mortician. I eyed the heavy gold pieces on my desk and smiled.

I suppose a word is in order about how I, a commissioned officer and a West Pointer to boot, could allow myself to be bought like that. Well, the simple truth was that in my view the only customs laws that were going to be broken were Cuban laws, and I had never signed on to uphold Cuban laws. Besides, the term *Cuban law* was a bit of an oxymoron anyway; those people sucked in corruption with their mothers' milk and thereafter practiced it with every breath they took; thus my little backsliding would hardly matter in the long run. So I was a corrupt official, and by the blazes, it felt damned good. A steady source of income with little or no work! Things were looking up, I congratulated myself. With that, I closed up shop for the day and sauntered off to my digs in the villa to commence the evening.

You see, Marguerite was in town and was gracing me with a visit. With the end of the war, she and her band, who all hailed from Mariel, near Havana, had migrated back to their home precinct. I saw them occasionally skulking about the docks. Jesus, the ferocious pirate, hadn't forgotten me; he hurled me looks of pure hatred whenever our paths chanced to cross. And occasionally, like tonight, Marguerite would show up on my doorstep for a stay of a day or two.

I opened my door quietly and was blessed with a rear view of Marguerite bending over the hearth fire. She was busily engaged in cooking one of the spicy rice dishes that so captivated the locals. I stole up behind her and, looping my arms wide, caught a ripe breast in each hand.

"Yiiii!" she yelped, jumping a foot in the air, sending rice and water crashing into the flames.

"Feenweek!" she screamed. "Let go of me, you animal!"

"Of course, my dear," I said obligingly, releasing her while in the same movement whipping her blouse over her head and completely off. She crossed her arms in front of herself and smiled seductively. "Feenweek," she complained unconvincingly, "I won't have you stripping me whenever your loins are on fire!"

"Of course you will, Marguerite," I corrected her. "You will because you can't help yourself. Your passions are every bit as uncontrollable as mine. That's why you're drawn to me, my love. You're just like me." I kissed her deeply, and she did not resist. I drew her to my bed, sat her down gently, shucked her out of her skirt, tore off my uniform, and in minutes we resumed our now-familiar Santiago minuet. In hindsight, I can't say that Marguerite was the prettiest damsel I've ever bedded, and she was far from the daintiest, but the fiery little filly was head and shoulders above the competition when it came to sheer enthusiasm. Our rice repast totally forgotten, we rocked along gently toward the blissful release we both craved so keenly.

36

Havana, Cuba
March, 1900

"Two pair, eights high," I announced, laying my cards on the table. I was in a smoke-filled cantina not far from the Plaza de San Francisco, two hours into a high-stakes game of five-card stud. Three hundred gold dollars were on the table, and four pairs of beady eyes were fixed on my cards.

"Beats me," muttered a burly major of artillery with a foul body odor, looking wistfully at his share of the pot.

"And me," echoed a sallow Signal Corps captain across the table, folding his cards and calling it a night.

I eyed the two others expectantly: a new infantry shavetail fresh from the academy and a seedy old surgeon. The shavetail shook his head, chagrined by the size of his losses, and put down his cards. The surgeon eyed me sullenly, no doubt wishing he would someday come across me wounded on a battlefield. Then he too folded and I raked in the pot.

"Boys, I thank you," I smiled with the easy grace of a winner. "Whose deal?"

Late 1899 and early 1900 had been a banner time for me. I whored, wined, and gambled in capital style, as I was doing at the moment. I was welcomed for the big spender I was wherever I went. Ah, it was grand. Harlock's shipments went smoothly, and there was never a question about the Yankee Clipper consignments that left Havana with documents signed by me. I wondered at times if the harbormaster himself had not been bribed, and concluded that Harlock had most probably seen to that detail as well; he did appear to be thorough.

I saw Marguerite from time to time, whenever she and her band of scavengers were in town to sell the rifles they'd collected from the hills. When Marguerite wasn't around, I lavished my attentions on the lovelies of Havana. Indeed, postwar life in Havana was so soft that it was called bordello duty by us stay-behinds.

The artillery major cut the cards twice and began dealing with a shotgun delivery that scattered cards rapidly across the table. He couldn't play poker worth a damn, but his dealing was a work of art. My fellow gamers, except for the new lieutenant, were all old roués like myself who had their own dark motives for staying in steamy Havana. They were generally good for their chits—except for the surgeon, who was a complete wastrel and a deadbeat—and they lost often enough for me to find them interesting. I was settling down to my next hand with relish when a familiar figure strode through the swinging doors of the cantina. It was Quinlon—and he was in uniform!

He spied me immediately. "Ah, Travers, me lad!" he cried heartily. "I've been looking fer ye all over this pesthole of a town. At last I've found ye."

"Colonel Quinlon," I said, not looking up from the table, due partly to my lack of respect for the man, and partly to my lack of trust for the band of jackals I'd fallen in with. I'd already caught the surgeon cheating, and threatened to blow his brains out if it happened again— which was why my loaded Colt was on the table pointing in his general direction. I needed to treat these boys damned firmly, since they howled to the heavens whenever they caught *me* cheating.

"Gentlemen," I announced, using the term in its broadest possible context, "may I introduce Lieutenant Colonel Quinlon, late of the 71st New York Volunteers."

The company guffawed loudly at this, and Quinlon flushed a deep crimson. The tale of the cowardly 71st was common knowledge in the army. Indeed, the whole skulking regiment had been sent home in disgrace soon after the Spanish surrender. But why was Quinlon back in Cuba now, and in uniform to boot? I would have wagered that the old party hack would have been mustered out long ago. "So what brings you to Havana, Colonel?" I inquired with studied disinterest.

"Fenwick, lad, I'm just off a steamer from New York. I saw Mister Duncan some weeks ago, and the lovely man was looking simply splendid," replied Quinlon, evading my question. But I did glean from his response that Duncan was still dancing to the tune of Tammany's jig. Quinlon hurriedly continued, "He even offered his congratulations on me appointment as a regular."

"A regular what?" I shot back.

"Why, a regular in the United States Army, bucko," said Quinlon, grinning hugely.

"I don't believe it!" I cried, so aghast that I dropped the smoking Havana from my lips. "My God, that would take an act of Congress!"

"Right ye are, lad," agreed Quinlon brightly. "It's called a private bill, and one sailed through that great legislature of ours with me own name on it. Ain't it a grand country?"

The table had fallen silent; my fellows, rascals though they were, had all seen battle, with the exception of the young lieutenant. The thought of Quinlon being admitted to their fraternity was roughly akin to someone expectorating on the floor in a first sergeant's office; it just wasn't something you expected.

"How in the name of God did you manage to wangle that?" I asked incredulously.

"Oh, it took a lot o' doing, bucko," confided Quinlon mischievously. "But I noticed at the end o' the war that the regular army was getting bigger, not smaller as ye might have expected. It all has to do with them savages out in the Philippine Islands. Seems they're objecting to becoming our latest collection o' niggers, the damned ingrates. As incredible as it seems, they feel that they should be an independent nation! Have you ever heard anything so asinine in yer life?" he asked with a roar of mirth, oblivious to the fact that home rule for his fellow bog-hoppers in the Emerald Isle was an equally ridiculous idea to their English overlords.

The company at the table laughed uproariously at the notion of little brown beasts anywhere wanting to govern themselves. Even the high-yellow whore sitting on the knee of the big major tittered, no doubt considering herself an honorary member of the Caucasian race because of her frequent dalliances with white officers.

"It's that bandit Aguinaldo that saved me hide, Travers," explained Quinlon.

"Who the hell's Aguinaldo?" asked the major as he peered up from his cards, adding as an afterthought, "sir."

"A leader of the Filipinos," answered the surgeon, unobtrusively palming a dollar from the pot as he spoke. "Fought in the rebellion against the dons out there, I think."

"That's right," concurred Quinlon. "Seems th' bugger has been running amok in them damned islands."

"Archipelago," the surgeon corrected him, raising me the gold dollar he had filched when Quinlon distracted us.

"I'll see you," I said, tossing a dollar in the pot.

"Exactly," continued Quinlon. "Even the great MacArthur himself, God bless his Celtic soul, can't seem to lay his hands on the elusive monkey. So I says to meself, yer country has need o' ye again, Quinlon. So, here I am." He looked about him as if expecting a round of applause; instead, the big major belched loudly.

"How good of you," I observed evenly. Knowing Quinlon, there obviously was more to this story than he had revealed.

"Thank'ee, lad," acknowledged Quinlon, "but it's the least I can do to uphold the honor o' the Anglo-Saxon race in these troubled times." This was a complete non sequitur: The old leprechaun didn't have an ounce of Anglo-Saxon blood in his veins. If I'd had to guess, I'd have said that Quinlon had rallied to the flag to escape the prospect of eternal unemployment in New York.

"But why are you in Cuba? This ain't the Philippines," challenged the major, dropping the "sir" now that he was getting Quinlon's range. Familiarity does breed contempt, I noted. As he waited for his answer, the major bucked the pot another dollar and everyone followed suit.

"Ah, but it's right ye are," agreed Quinlon cheerily. "I'm en route to Manila by way o' the Horn. I stopped in Havana to drop off some dispatches entrusted to me in Washington." He hefted a heavy leather attaché case and patted it lovingly. "War Department matters," he added with a knowing wink. I eyed the pouch; nobody in his right mind would entrust Quinlon with anything of importance. It must be routine correspondence, I concluded—assignment orders and such. But such information could be useful, I knew.

"I'm out," said the lieutenant dejectedly.

"Fold," grunted the surgeon, throwing down his cards disgustedly. That left me and the redleg. I had a pair of fives showing. The major eyed me narrowly; I took a deep pull on my cigar and eyed him right back.

"Anything in that case for General Wood?" I asked Quinlon idly. "I'd be glad to make the actual delivery if you want." Which meant I'd like to find out if any of the papers Quinlon was hauling contained information that I could peddle to Harlock. I had learned that Harlock liked to stay well informed, you see.

"Why, yes," replied Quinlon. "I'm supposed to deliver the pouch to his headquarters. D'ye know General Wood?" he asked eagerly. Something told me that above all else, Quinlon craved access to the army high command, of which Wood was a charter member. But I couldn't guess Quinlon's motive.

"Know him? Why, man, we're practically blood brothers. He and I got to know each other very well in the heat of battle on San Juan Hill. We're quite thick," I assured Quinlon.

"I raise you three hundred dollars," announced the major, shoving three tall stacks of ten-dollar gold pieces to the center of the table. The lieutenant whistled involuntarily, glad that he was out. Even Quinlon stopped talking for a moment.

I switched my attention back to my antagonist. He had a pair of nines showing against my pair of fives, and he might be holding another pair, but so was I. Another pair of nines—one up and one in the hole. Maybe he was bluffing, I mused. I studied him carefully, but his small, feral eyes revealed nothing. Well, if the bastard wants to try his luck, I thought, let him.

"I'll see you," I grinned brightly, pushing my stack of coins to abut his. A gasp went up at this; the loser was undeniably going to be completely bankrupt.

"Two pair," I smiled, flipping over my nine card.

"Three nines," the major announced with a gap-toothed grin, flipping over his own hole card. "I win, son."

"Hold on, there!" I cried. "That's five nines on the table! The deck's rigged! You can't win with a loaded deck!"

With a blur of motion that would have made a striking rattlesnake look lethargic, the major whipped a double-barreled derringer from the top of his boot and leveled it at my heart. "Are you saying I cheated?" he demanded menacingly.

"Why no," I said, gulping nervously, careful to keep my hands above the table and away from my Colt. "I'm just saying that someone slipped an extra nine in the deck." The surgeon studiously eyed a cuspidor across the room. "The only fair thing to do is to play the hand again."

"I never read any rule that says that," retorted the major flatly. "Three of a kind beats two pair every time. I win—any argument?" he asked, cocking back the hammer of the derringer for emphasis.

I shook my head slowly and he uncocked the pistol, jammed it back in his boot, and scooped up his loot. I was bust!

Dejected, I stood up and put on my hat. "Gentlemen, the hour grows late. Colonel Quinlon, good night. I must be off; duty calls at first light." What I really meant to do was to find a whore who would let me into her bed in exchange for my IOU, which was generally good in this town now that I'd been paying my bills. There was nothing like a good romp with a harlot to get one's mind off reverses at the gambling tables. It was the best therapy in the world, as I well knew from past experience.

"Must ye be off, lad?" asked Quinlon anxiously, pulling at my sleeve. "I thought we might talk about the good old days over a bottle, then maybe tomorrow ye might arrange an introduction fer me to see General Wood, what with ye so high up in his estimation and all."

Ah, so that was it, I told myself. It was all clear now: Quinlon had managed to worm his way back into the army because of the trouble out in the Pacific, and now he was doing his best to avoid being shipped there. No doubt he wanted a comfortable billet in Havana until he had enough seniority to nail down a pension. Well, I wasn't in the mood to help him at the moment, even if such assistance had been in my power to give.

"I'd love to, Colonel," I lied, "and I'll see to it as soon as I have a free moment, whenever that may be. But the duties of an administrator are crushing, I'm afraid. Your request will just have to wait."

"Don't go, lad," he pleaded. "I also wanted to tell ye about Fiona. She's due to arrive the day after tomorrow."

I stopped in midstride. "Fiona? Here in Havana?"

"Aye, bucko, right here," he answered with a smile.

"Perhaps, er, my pressing duty might be postponed awhile longer," I relented hastily. "Let's relax a bit, shall we?" I took my seat back at the table and slapped the major's mulatto bitch on her saucy rump. "Get the colonel a chair," I ordered, relighting my Havana.

She rose sullenly to do my bidding. Judging from the scowl on her puss, I suspected that her attitude on the Filipino nationality issue had just changed radically. As Quinlon took his seat, I looked about brightly at my gaming fellows and said, "Deal me in."

"Let's see the color of your money, Lieutenant," growled the major inhospitably.

"Why, it's sitting there in front of you!" I proclaimed, miffed that my credit should be questioned by these ne'er-do-wells. I'd always honored my chits in the past. At least eventually, that is. "Don't tell me you're going to try to keep me from winning back my stake."

"There, there, Travers," soothed Quinlon, "let me help ye." He laid twenty greenback dollars on the knife-scarred table.

"Sir, you're a true leader of men," I smiled, quickly scooping the cash out of his reach. "Cards!" I demanded, and the major obligingly dealt. "Bartender," I sang out, *por favor.* Drinks all around! On the colonel!"

"Travers—" Quinlon started to object shrilly, but I cut him off with a wave of my cigar.

"There's no point in arguing, sir. It's an old Cuban custom. The first time you come into a cantina, you buy a round. When in Rome, as they say."

My cronies grinned openly at this malarkey, and Quinlon angrily clenched his teeth but paid up. We all raised our glasses to him as he squirmed irately in his chair.

"Here's to the 71st New York," I toasted with a straight face.

"God bless 'em," echoed the surgeon. "Salt of the earth."

Out of the corner of my eye I saw Quinlon empty his glass in stony silence. He knew he was being ridiculed, but I didn't care. Let the bastard stew, I thought, drawing my cards and hoping for a change in my luck.

37

Three days later I was sitting behind my desk with my feet up, contentedly lazing away the afternoon. Scattered about on the desk were various reports I'd been ignoring and the leather attaché case Quinlon had eventually entrusted to me. I hadn't yet perused its contents, and had no intention of delivering it until I had done so. After a year and a half in the tropics, you might say I had adopted a rather relaxed, almost Latin, attitude toward life. Besides, prompt attention to paper-work was never one of my strengths. Suddenly a knock on the door interrupted my reverie.

"Come in," I called absently.

The door opened slowly and there stood Fiona looking as lovely as she had when last we parted. "Fenwick!" she called delightedly, running to me.

"Fee—!" I exclaimed, rising. I was cut off by her rushing around the desk and into my arms and kissing me passionately. I could see that she intended to pick things up right where we had dropped them!

"Oh, Fenny," she breathed when at last we separated, "I couldn't bear to be away from you a moment longer! When Father told me you were still in Cuba, I just had to come down to see you!"

"Darling, I can't tell you how pleased I am that you made the voyage!" I said, delighted. "You know there's never been anybody but you," I assured her, keeping my voice as earnest as I could and letting my hands roam freely over her body as I spoke. Subtlety, I knew from experience, was lost on dear Fiona.

"Is that true?" she asked coquettishly.

"On my word as an officer," I vowed solemnly.

But Fiona had been with too many officers since her Tampa days and she was doubtful. "Oh, I wish I could believe you, Fenny," she replied. "But that's not as important as the fact that we should never part again."

Never part again? I thought. That was absurd, of course. The poor desperate girl was making an all-out effort to nail me down good and proper. She must be getting her first case of the spinster jitters, I concluded, but if vows of eternal fidelity were her price for a roll in the hay, by God, that's what she'd get.

"Fee, dearest," I cooed into her ear, "rest assured I'll never leave you. I promise." Cocking an eye toward the door, I asked, "Er—did your dear father come along with you?"

"No, he took my bags to the hotel for me. I don't expect to see him until this evening." She gave me a hungry look.

"I see," I said, leering right back and slipping from her grasp long enough to kick the door shut. Safely alone with Fiona, I embraced her once more. "Oh, how I've missed you, my dear," I breathed in her ear, giving the lobe a gentle nip for effect.

She giggled, not at all displeased. "Fenny, you haven't changed at all."

"Oh, but I have, my love, let me show you," I suggested hotly, all the while tugging at my belt. A daylight tryst was on my mind, you see, right there in my office. There was little danger of discovery, for my duties were so minimal that I hardly ever had visitors.

Fiona knew exactly what I had in mind; her eager hands quickly undid my buttons and, before I knew it, I was standing with my trousers around my boots and Fiona kneeled before me to apply her considerable talents to my elongated member. It was a quaint little practice of hers, one that she never failed to observe whenever we had a few moments together. But frankly, my sport was bareback riding, and although I was happy to let the girl enjoy her ritual, I yearned to get her sweet bottom into bed, or at least into an easy chair. So I hastily looked around for a suitable piece of furniture upon which to take Fiona.

As if sensing my thoughts, she said, "Oh, Fenny, these clothes are so confining. I can't move in them."

"Then let's get you out of them," I suggested helpfully.

"You devil," she smiled impishly. Standing, she doffed her bonnet, tossed it to the middle of the floor, and then shucked off layers of skirts, petticoats, and stays, throwing them one after the other onto the bonnet in a growing pile of feminine unmentionables.

As she struggled with her attire, I idly eyed the valise on my desk. I opened it and leafed through the envelopes within. One caught my eye; it was addressed to me. I tore it open and removed two folded documents.

The first was a promotion list, and I was on it! Great news; I'd been elevated from second lieutenant to first lieutenant. It couldn't have happened to a finer man, I congratulated myself. Yes, a fitting gesture on the part of the army. Very thoughtful of them indeed.

"There," announced Fiona, standing completely unclothed before me. She was a true vision of loveliness.

"Marvelous," I exclaimed, entranced by her beauty.

Smiling seductively, she advanced. "Now let me continue getting acquainted with you, my love."

She knelt before me once more and returned to her task with renewed energy. Her touch was exquisite, and her flicking pink tongue wrought a blissful agony. She was so skilled in her art that I realized I would climax in seconds unless I forced myself to think of something other than my throbbing manhood. Looking down, I saw the second document on the desk. I opened it and read:

Dept. of War
Wash., D.C.

20 Dec. 1899

1LT Fenwick Travers, Infantry, Regular Army, currently assigned to the Dept. of Cuba, is hereby directed to report to the
United States Legation in Peking, Empire of China. This order
shall constitute authority for 1LT Travers to arrange passage aboard
any available American flag vessel bound for China. In no event
shall 1LT Travers depart later than 15 April 1900.

s/ the Adjutant General
United States Army

"Oh, no!" I whimpered, my knees sagging. Fiona smiled up at me,
clasped her hands to my bare bottom and squeezed ferociously, then
went right back to her work, more than a little puzzled to find me
suddenly somewhat limp. Not one to quit, Fiona redoubled her kissing
and licking. I barely felt her, though; instead I forced myself to concentrate. What could I do? Where could I turn? I'd been bamboozled,
by God, lulled into thinking I was safe there in Havana when in fact
I was very much in danger. The last thing I needed at the moment was
a panting woman, albeit a pretty one, hanging onto my hindquarters
and sucking on me as though she were a calf and I the cow! I had
to get away somehow and mull over this debacle. Obviously, my going
to China was out of the question. There had to have been some mistake.
I had to see Harlock; I was much too valuable to him to lose. He'd
help me in my hour of need!

Suddenly, the shock of it all overcame me and I collapsed into my
desk chair. "You poor boy," grinned Fiona lewdly, thinking her min-
istrations had overcome me. "You just sit there and let me help you
relax." With that she opened her mouth wide and ducked her head
between my parted thighs to finish me off.

It was at that moment that there was a single knock on the unlocked
door and then it swung open. It was Quinlon!

"Fenwick, me lad, I'm so glad I caught ye alone before Fiona gets
here," he began, entering the room uninvited. "I've been meaning to
ask ye fer that introduction to General Wood—"

He stopped in midstride, staring puzzled at the disheveled heap of
clothes in his path. Although it looked like no more than a mass of

laundry someone had simply dumped there, on the very top was unmistakably a frilly pair of women's pantalets.

"What th' bloody hell's going on here?" he demanded.

"Father!" squeaked Fiona, popping up from behind the desk.

"Fee!" bellowed Quinlon. "What's this blackguard done to ye?"

I was on my feet now, desperately hauling my trousers up. "Now wait a minute, Quinlon!" I pleaded fearfully, and then added inanely, "Don't go jumping to any conclusions!"

Quinlon's jaw dropped when he saw my flaccid pink seducer swinging limply before me. There was clearly only one conclusion to be drawn here and Quinlon drew it. "Ye vile beast!" he roared, clumsily hauling his .45-caliber Colt revolver from its holster. "I'll kill ye fer this!"

Holding my trousers up with one hand, and stretching the other one imploringly toward Quinlon, I begged piteously, "Don't shoot, for Christ's sake! There's an explanation for all of this! It's not what you think!"

"Ye can do yer explaining to the devil!" he stormed, drawing an inexpert bead on me.

As bad a shot as Quinlon was, he couldn't have missed at that range. The barrel loomed like the muzzle of a cannon, and I would have been a dead man but for the fact that at that very instant Marguerite and her rogues, including Jesus, the pirate, strode into the office with my distracted orderly on their heels babbling helplessly, "I tried to stop 'em, sir, honest I did, but they wanted to see you. . . ." Then he looked from me to Quinlon and fell silent.

Marguerite's eyes immediately went to the revolver. Her beloved "Feenweek" was in danger! "No!" she screamed, lashing out at Quinlon's gun arm with the speed of a cat. The revolver roared, but the bullet sailed a fraction of an inch past my head. It smacked into the whitewashed wall behind me, blowing the oil painting of the somber conquistador from its moorings and showering me with a fine white powder of plaster dust.

"Eeek!" shrieked Fiona, her reason completely unhinged by the gunplay. She leapt from behind me, where she'd cowered as soon as Quinlon had slapped leather, then scampered away from my side and ran out the door of the office, leaving my orderly staring after her in stupefaction. "Father! Father!" she bleated as she ran, "he made me do it! He made me do it!"

Now Marguerite's jaw dropped. She took one look at Fiona, breasts and buttocks bouncing as she ran screaming from the room, and reached into her blouse to produce an elegant little derringer. Her eyes were blazing with insane Cuban fury, and I knew instantly that she would see me dead before she shared me with another woman.

"Feenweek, I will kill you!" she screamed, and then fired.

But the moment she'd bellowed, I had gone into motion, grabbing up the papers on my desk and darting for the door to my quarters. Her bullet slammed into the wall directly behind the spot where I'd been standing only an instant before. In a blur of movement, I ran through my living area, scooping up my campaign hat and pistol belt as I ran. Without breaking stride, I dove headlong out a half-opened window. Luckily I was on the first floor of the villa and was able to open my arms to break my fall as I hit the soft Bahama grass outside. I rolled twice, leapt to my feet, buttoned my trousers, jammed on my hat, strapped on my pistol, and shoved my orders into my trouser pocket.

Forcing myself to concentrate, I frantically cast about in my mind for some way to salvage this disaster. The barracks! I thought hopefully. There'd be some troops there whom I could dragoon into serving as an ad hoc police force to put down this riot. I sprinted off in that direction.

From the window behind me Quinlon's voice called sternly, "Travers, stop or you're a dead man!"

Stopping was out of the question, of course, but dodge I did. His big Colt roared and I felt a brush of air as a near-miss whistled so close to my head that I swore it nicked the crown of my hat! If Quinlon had gotten only half this worked up during the war, I thought, he'd be a general instead of a washed-up hanger-on.

Suddenly I spotted trouble up ahead. Marguerite and her band had run out the main entrance to my office when I bolted, and were sprinting around the villa to head me off. They were between me and the barracks and closing fast. I looked around in desperation; the only route of escape was out the front gate of Fort Sam Carl. As I debated whether I should allow myself to be ignominiously run off a military post in broad daylight or make a stand, my pursuers made my decision for me. Jesus, brandishing a wicked-looking machete, snapped out an order. The Cubans unslung their rifles, dropped to kneeling firing positions, and began shooting at me.

"Great jumping Christ!" I yelped as hot lead slammed into the trunks of palm trees around me.

"Kill him! Kill him!" screamed Marguerite. Hell hath no fury, I thought bitterly, as I scampered off toward the front gate, zigzagging all the way. I knew that my only hope was to sprint for the Canal del Puerto and hope there was a fast ferry that could carry me over to Old Havana. With the canal between me and my pursuers, I would be safe. I flew like a madman to the bank just as a steam-driven launch was casting off for the far side. I leapt aboard and, after a spirited discussion with the pilot, who demanded a few pesos, I hunkered down behind the gunwales for the short journey. Marguerite and her fellows spilled through the gate of Fort Sam Carl, saw the launch heading for the far shore, and took immediate action. They quickly commandeered another launch at gunpoint and in seconds they too were putting out for the opposite shore. This race was clearly far from over.

There was only one course of action left, I thought desperately: I would try to lose my pursuers in the rabbit-warren maze of streets of Havana's barrio. I would have to rely on my knowledge of those back alleys, gleaned during many nights of surreptitious lechery, to throw off the chase. It was the only edge I had left. As soon as the launch touched the seawall on the far side of the canal, I leapt out at a dead run, scampered south on the Avenida del Puerto, and ducked into a narrow alleyway. Behind me I heard the hue and cry as Marguerite and her fellows clambered up the seawall at my heels.

I ran like a cat on fire, turning this way and that. I thought I was actually succeeding in losing them, but then Marguerite changed her tactics. She began screaming something in Spanish as she ran. The crowds lounging on the balconies and in the doorways along the narrow streets began to take notice of me. Something was going on, but under the circumstances I could hardly stop and ask someone to translate. People were glaring at me and several spat at my feet as I scampered past. What the hell was happening? I wondered fearfully.

"Priest beater!" muttered a shriveled old fruit vendor in heavily accented English as I sped past his kiosk, throwing a rotten mango in my direction for emphasis.

So that was it! Of course, I realized in an instant—that was one of the few maledictions that would rouse the somnolent populace of this latter-day Sodom. If Marguerite had called me a murderer or a rapist, these seasoned cosmopolitans would have merely sat back and enjoyed the footrace. But drubbing one of their closed-minded priests was apparently their last remaining taboo. Behind me I heard many more footfalls. Glancing over my shoulder, I was appalled to see that several hundred people were hot on my tail. My God, I realized, it was a lynch mob! If they took me, they'd pull me limb from limb and ask questions later. Clearly, there'd be no refuge in the barrio!

The harbor was my last hope. I had to get away from Havana before this mob took me, or my stay in Cuba would be no more than a bloody postscript in history. A trip to China, which only minutes before I deemed to be completely out of the question, was suddenly a very appealing prospect. I ran like a deer through the Cuartel de Campeche section of the town, past the stately Glesiay Convento de la Merced, until I rounded a corner and saw the tall masts of many ships tied up at dockside. I was at the docks of Alameda de Paula, and not a moment too soon. My legs were like rubber and my lungs burned with each breath. I was at the end of my tether. I knew I had to find shelter soon or I was a goner.

Then I saw it! Up ahead, past a row of squat Cuban fishing trawlers, lay an oceangoing steamer. On its highest mast flew the Stars and Stripes! If I could reach her I'd be saved. As I bolted toward the steamer, I was heartened to see great black clouds of coal smoke gushing from her funnel: She was putting out to sea! I put on a last burst of speed, a physical feat that I thought was beyond me after my months of nonstop debauchery. Behind me a fair portion of Havana's population was pouring across the dock area screaming for my blood. A shot or two rang out, telling me that Marguerite was still with the pack.

I reached the gangplank and clambered aboard without a pause. A few tars sat about on great coils of rope gazing at me curiously.

"On your feet!" I ordered. "Get that gangplank up this instant!" They looked from me to the howling mob and back, and then they sprang to, hauling up the gangplank just as Jesus reached it and began climbing up.

The sailors hesitated and looked at me. "Dump the bastard!" I ordered brusquely.

"You heard the officer," grunted one of the men stolidly to his companions. They gave the gangplank a shake or two, sending Jesus unceremoniously spinning into the fetid waters of Havana harbor. He didn't come up again. Marguerite and her gang in the crowd scowled furiously, but they were loath to use their weapons on the tars, especially in front of so many witnesses. As inconspicuously as possible, I cowered behind the unsuspecting sailors.

The crowd wasn't shy, however, and they unleashed a volley of imprecations and mangoes up at the deck, where I stood trembling. Their jabbering was drowned out by the great "Whoooot!" of the ship's whistle, and then the hawsers were cast off. The gap between the dock and the ship widened, and we were off. Once I was safely out of rifle range, I lifted my hat and blew Marguerite a kiss. She shook her clenched fist at me in return. Then the ship shuddered as her boilers built up a head of steam and we swung about gracefully in the Bahiade de la Habana, turned north, and sailed majestically through the Canal del Puerto and into the Straits of Florida.

38

Once we were safely clear of Havana, I ran to the first mate and learned I was aboard the SS *Brighton*. The *Brighton*'s course called for a stop at the Falkland Islands for coal, and then she aimed to swing around the Horn and up the coast of Chile, take on coal once again in Santiago, and then head for the Philippines by way of Hawaii. Armed with this information, I pondered my own course. I wondered if the Falklands had telegraph communications with the mainland. Perhaps I could get a wire through to Harlock before I was carried out of the Western Hemisphere.

As things turned out, however, I didn't have to wait to get to the Falklands to send my wire. One of the ship's officers took ill as we plowed through the Atlantic swells off the coast of South America, and the captain set a course for Rio de Janeiro to seek medical assistance. By the time we reached Rio, however, the sick officer was dead and several of the passengers were down with the same symptoms. We were forced to lay over in port a full week until the victims of the malady either expired or recovered.

I took advantage of this unexpected port call to send a telegram to Harlock at the Waldorf-Astoria in New York. I anxiously paced the gritty floor of the telegraph office awaiting his reply. When it finally clattered in, I took it in trembling hands and read it carefully.

DEAR TRAVERS STOP CONGRATULATIONS ON PROMO-
TION AND NEW ASSIGNMENT STOP BEST WISHES AND
REGARDS STOP HARLOCK

That was all? No voicing of concern? No promise of succor? By
God, from the tone of his reply you'd have thought I'd sent him glad
tidings instead of notification of a disaster of the first magnitude! The
bastard was throwing me to the dogs, plain and simple. He must have
extracted all the firearms he needed from Cuba, and now that the
operation there was no longer profitable I was expendable.

I vowed I'd show that cur. I'd write to the War Department at once
and expose his slimy dealings before the evidence was all destroyed.
My rational side immediately rejected such a course of action; the first
one to swing would be poor Fenny. I had enough character flaws as
it was, I decided, without adding suicidal impulses to the list.

Damn, I was over a barrel! I had been grievously wronged, but there
was no practicable way to seek justice. Calming down with difficulty,
I realized I would simply have to ride out the gale winds of fate and
see where I was when they subsided. Looking on the bright side, I
told myself that at least China was peaceful. There was no fighting
there, as there was in the Philippines. Perhaps a quiet billet in the
American legation until the Philippine war was over wouldn't be as
bad as I had initially thought. Once the Filipino unpleasantness was
resolved one way or another, I could return home and sniff about for
some way to make a living with minimal labor. Perhaps after my faithful
service to Harlock, he would put in a good word for me with his business
connections. Or maybe take me on himself, eh? Now that was an
intriguing possibility, I thought.

So when the captain of the *Brighton* sent word for the passengers
to reembark to continue the journey, it was a subdued yet hopeful Fenny
who resumed the passage to the Orient. We were at sea the better part
of a month before Diamond Head hove into view, and we stopped at
Oahu for a few days for provisioning.

Three weeks later we made landfall in Manila Bay. There I was able
to book passage on the *Lotus Pearl* for the last leg of my voyage. On
the first of June the *Lotus Pearl* rounded the head of the Shantung
Peninsula and entered the Yellow Sea. We dropped anchor off the
mouth of the Pei Ho River, where lighters met us to ferry passengers

and cargo to shore. I was taken to where a forlorn collection of weather-beaten huts stood on the bleak beach. From the strand I gazed upon the massive bulk of the Taku forts, the protectors of the Pei Ho River. Since the Pei Ho ran more or less directly from the Yellow Sea to the imperial capital, Peking, the forts had been built here by the Chinese to discourage foreigners from making seaborne assaults on their seat of power.

Once my baggage had been brought ashore, I motioned to a waiting coolie who kowtowed and then trotted off to return with a rickshaw. The coolie piled me and my bags into the rickety contraption and then set off at a trot over the cinder path to the Tangku railway station some two miles distant. I knew enough about China from the missionaries I'd met on the *Lotus Pearl* to know that at Tangku I would entrain for Tientsin, a major commercial center some thirty miles upriver. At Tientsin I was to transfer to the Peking train to complete my journey, a further distance of about eighty miles.

The trip went well enough until we reached Tientsin. The town was awash with a gibbering mass of Chinamen, who blocked the tracks as the train pulled into the station. The natives seemed to cover the ground in all directions as far as the eye could see. These buggers badly wanted a ride out of this town, I could plainly see. But why? Had some great disaster befallen them?

The train screeched to a halt and the crowd surged toward it. But a thin line of soldiers appeared at a trot. They were East Indians in turbans, probably British colonial troops. They set to with great truncheons and in minutes had beaten flat the most insistent of the Chinese and cleared the others from the rails. As I alighted, the station was eerily silent. I spied an official-looking fellow in a blue conductor's uniform and hailed him.

"Hey, partner," I asked, "when does the Peking train leave?"

Seeing that he was being addressed by a military officer, the fellow popped to attention. He too was an East Indian. "Ah, sahib, there can be no train to Peking. Spirit warriors have cut the track."

"Spirit warriors? What the hell do you mean?" I asked, perplexed. "And call me sir, not sahib."

"Yes, sahib," said the trainman, bowing as he spoke. Years of close contact with Europeans had taught him to be extremely deferential in the presence of whites.

"Now tell me straight out, why can't I take a train to Peking?" I demanded.

The fellow writhed as though in physical pain; relaying disappointing news to a white officer was the height of unpleasantness for him. "Spirit warriors! Spirit warriors!" he tried to explain, rolling his eyes in desperation at my apparent density.

We were getting nowhere fast, I could see. "Friend, I can't understand what you're telling me until you stop speaking gibberish," I insisted, which only set the conductor to visibly trembling at his ineptness in conveying his point to me.

"Hold on there a minute," called an American voice from behind me.

I turned to see a youngish, nattily dressed gentleman striding down the station platform toward me.

"Hoover," announced the newcomer. "Herbert Hoover. I take it you planned to travel on to Peking?"

39

"Damned glad to meet you, Hoover," I said in greeting, and then, remembering my manners, added, "I'm Lieutenant Fenwick Travers, United States Army." Hoover amiably offered his hand and I took it. Then a thought occurred to me. "Say, you're not a missionary, are you?" Most of the Westerners aboard the *Lotus Pearl* had been simpering missionaries who reminded me of Uncle Enoch at his unctuous worst.

Hoover laughed. "No, my business is not China's soul; it's her capital. I've been retained by a European firm to oversee construction of its investments in China, mines in particular. I'm an engineer, you see."

Noting our congeniality, the relieved conductor vanished gratefully into the crowd. "Tell me, Hoover," I asked, "what's the holdup in getting to Peking, and what's all this nonsense about spirit warriors?"

"What the conductor was trying to tell you is true, Lieutenant," explained Hoover. "The trains can't get through to Peking because the tracks are blocked. It seems that China's secret societies have decided to launch an uprising against all the foreign devils, which is the term they use for us Westerners."

"Secret societies? Uprising? Why, this is all news to me!" I exclaimed. "I was told that things were peaceful here in China."

"That's no longer true, I'm afraid," Hoover replied. "There's been trouble brewing for some time now, but we Westerners mainly hoped it would just go away. Unfortunately, hostilities have gotten out of hand—to the point where it's not safe to venture far from Tientsin without an armed escort."

"My God!" I moaned. "Are you saying China's a war zone?"

Hoover smiled and replied, "Not quite yet, Lieutenant. I'm just saying that at the moment some Chinese hotheads have got the bit in their mouths and are running about the countryside making things unpleasant. In the meantime, why don't you come and stay with my wife and me until you're able to move on? She'll love the company. It's so seldom we have visitors from the States. What do you say?"

"There doesn't really appear to be any choice," I conceded glumly. But then I decided to brighten up and enjoy my stay in Tientsin as much as possible. Putting on a bright face, I raised my chin and smiled heartily at Hoover. "I'd be delighted to be your guest."

"Splendid," said Hoover with a smile. He turned and called, "Fu Chou!" An ancient coolie, clad only in a loincloth and straw hat, padded over to Hoover, bowed and smiled at me to a fare-thee-well, and then, judging that proper deference had been shown to this new white personage, straightened up expectantly.

He had to be sixty years old if he was a day, I judged—although a life of unrelenting exertion made him look a hundred—and he was the skinniest fellow I'd ever laid eyes upon. In fact, he looked like a chicken that had been plucked, stretched, and taught to walk erect.

"Yes, Honorable Hooer?" the old codger inquired, the "v" sound being beyond his palate.

"Get this officer's bags, will you, Fu Chou?"

"Yes, master," the venerable coolie said with another bow. He handled my small bag well, but the large one was completely beyond his strength to budge. He gave a few feeble tugs at it, but it appeared that if he persisted he would simply dislocate his shoulder to no effect.

"Here, let me get that, partner," I offered.

Fu Chou bowed and stepped aside. In this fashion we made our way along dirt streets to the extreme southern part of Tientsin, which Hoover called the foreign settlement, a tiny enclave surrounded by high mud walls that abutted the much larger walled native city to the north.

Westerners were not allowed to wander freely in China, you see, but were instead quarantined in enclaves like rabid pit bulls. They were allowed to interact with the Chinese masses only at certain designated trading houses, so little noncommercial contact between the races occurred.

"Tell me, Hoover," I asked, "whatever possessed you to come to a hellhole like this?"

"Engineers go wherever the trade takes them, Lieutenant," he explained patiently. "The farther away from the States I went, the more I found that a younger man would be entrusted with meaningful responsibilities. After all, the only true satisfaction in life is doing a hard job to the best of one's abilities, wouldn't you agree?"

"I, er—that is, of course," I blustered in what I hoped was a convincing manner.

I must have succeeded, for Hoover hardly paused; talking about dedication and self-sacrifice seemed to inspire him immensely. "I eventually found my way to China. The amount of building that needs to be done to bring this land into the modern world is simply staggering."

"Yes, I can see that," I allowed. From what I'd observed since landing, it looked as though the place had changed little since the time of Confucius.

"Ah, here we are," announced Hoover, rounding a corner on a narrow street. We stopped before an abode that was larger and more solidly built than the native houses we'd passed along the way. Although its architecture was clearly Chinese, the place was a passable imitation of a Western cottage. "Lou," Hoover called as we entered, "I'm home!"

We stepped into what appeared to be a combination kitchen and dining room, where a pretty white woman greeted us. "Berty, there's someone here to see you," she said. Then spying me, she added, "Oh, I see we have more company."

"Allow me to introduce Lieutenant Travers, United States Army," said Hoover. "Lieutenant, this is my wife, Lou. I've invited Lieutenant Travers to stay with us until the tracks to Peking are cleared, dear."

"At your service, Mrs. Hoover," I said, doffing my campaign hat gallantly.

She eyed me quickly, and I knew enough about women to tell immediately that Lou liked what she saw. "Lieutenant. Charmed to meet you. But you must call me Lou," she insisted gaily, extending a soft white hand.

"Then Lou it is," I agreed with a slight bow. She was a winsome-looking number; I would have expected a more drab mate for a sensible drone like Hoover.

"Berty," prompted Lou, nodding her head toward an interior doorway, "you must come along. You have very important guests waiting for you in the parlor."

"I'll just wait here," I suggested politely, hoping that some lackey might take pity on me and bring me food and drink in the meantime.

"Not at all, Lieutenant," insisted Lou. "This will involve military matters. You probably should be there."

Military matters? What could she mean by that? But I held my tongue and dutifully followed the Hoovers into the next room.

"Berty, this is Admiral Sir Edward Seymour, the commander of all allied forces in Tientsin," said Lou, gesturing to a vigorous-looking fellow with a Prince Albert beard, resplendent in a heavily braided and beribboned coat of navy blue set off by a heavy saber dangling from his belt. Clustered behind Admiral Seymour were a gaggle of other Britishers, some navy and some army, judging from the khaki and blue tunics.

"Admiral Seymour, you honor me with your presence," said Hoover, offering his hand to the admiral, who took it.

"Your servant, Mister Hoover," said Sir Edward.

"And this, Admiral, is Lieutenant Travers, United States Army," said Hoover, indicating me. "He's en route to the American legation in Peking."

"Sir," I said, firing a stiff salute at the old sea dog. I figured that a little bit of the old snap-to might be in order at a moment such as this. Representative of the United States and all, you see.

"Welcome to China," intoned Seymour, with the slightly patronizing tone that any flag officer uses when addressing an underling. "If you like action, young man, I think you'll find China to your taste."

"That sounds capital to me, sir," I piped up, beaming idiotically. I expected that Admiral Seymour, like all senior officers I'd ever met, believed that all good junior officers were essentially suicidal.

"And how exactly may I be of assistance to you, Admiral?" inquired Hoover.

"I'll get right to the point, Mister Hoover," replied Sir Edward. "As you know, the Boxers have cut the rail and telegraph lines to Peking. Right before the telegraph was cut, however, I received a message from

Sir Claude MacDonald, the British minister in the capital. He informed me that the foreign legations are besieged, and he requested military reinforcements. I intend to move north to Peking, reopen the rail line, and deal severely with any Chinese who resist. I have been given command of all French, Russian, and Japanese troops in Tientsin. I plan to embark them, along with my own British troops, onto five trains. We'll move north along the tracks to Peking, demolish any obstacles along the way, and eventually lift the siege of the foreign legations."

"Siege?" I blurted. "I haven't heard about any siege. And what are these Boxers you're talking about?"

"Of course, Leftenant," said Sir Edward. "If you've been at sea, all of this must come as quite a shock to you. The Chinese have risen from here to Peking. They're led by a sort of religious sect called the Fists of Righteous Harmony. We call them the Boxers for short. They've laid siege to the Legation Quarter of Peking, where all the Westerners reside. I'm not at all sure how long they can hold out without reinforcements. The Chinese have rallied in surprising numbers to the standards of the Boxers, mainly because they think the Boxers have magical powers. But in reality they're no more than queued rogues who are disturbing the public peace. I intend to give them a whiff of grapeshot, if necessary, to calm them down."

"What's the Chinese government's position on the Boxers?" asked Hoover.

"Oh, they're another shifty lot," retorted Sir Edward. "In public they're silent, and I understand there's a lot of confidential diplomatic traffic from the empress deploring the siege. But for my money, I think the old lady is straddling the fence, hoping secretly that the Boxers humiliate us enough to give her almost-defunct government a bit of legitimacy."

"All this is interesting," said Hoover, "but I fail to see how I can help. After all, I'm an engineer, not a soldier."

"Precisely," agreed Sir Edward. "I need a fellow with a working knowledge of steam engines to fortify my locomotives. I need them sandbagged and steel-plated if possible, so that they'll be proof against musket fire in the event we're ambushed. Captain Jellico and Commander Beatty here," he said, gesturing to two blue-clad officers, "both of the Royal Navy, have volunteered their services as well. With your help, I hope we can complete this project speedily."

"I'll be glad to do whatever I can," Hoover assured him.

"I knew you wouldn't let us down," said Sir Edward, pleased. He took his pith helmet from a sideboard where it lay, and fidgeted about with it so as to signal that the conference was over. "I'll be off now, Hoover. I intend to move as soon as those trains are properly protected. Rest assured, we won't put up with the effrontery of these Boxers a second longer than is absolutely necessary."

He donned his headgear, and with a slight bow to Lou, marched out with his coterie on his heels. Then, as an afterthought, he stopped and turned back to me. "I say, Leftenant Travers, what service have you seen?"

"West Point, class of '97, sir, and the Cuban campaign," I answered smartly. I didn't mention Arizona; I doubted that one of Her Majesty's admirals would be much impressed by the fact that I had personally ventilated the outlaw Pedrolito.

"Cuba, eh?" pondered Sir Edward. "Any staff work there?"

"Yes, sir," I replied slowly with a sinking feeling in the pit of my stomach, the point of his questioning now dawning on me. "I was on General Shafter's staff."

"And you Americans actually won that war, isn't that so?"

"Er, I believe that's correct, sir."

"Excellent," observed Sir Edward dryly. "Then there's a place for you on my staff. Would you be so kind as to report for duty as soon as the trains are prepared?" With that he turned and marched off, not deigning to wait for my reply.

"Well," I quipped, sounding outwardly cheerful, "it looks like I've been drafted!"

"And so have I," chuckled Hoover. "Lou, fetch the lieutenant something to eat, won't you? I'm sure he's starved. In the meantime, I'm off to the railway station to get started on this project. The sooner I'm finished, the sooner the admiral can put down this infernal insurrection, and the better off we'll all be." So saying, he set off in Sir Edward's tracks.

"Lieutenant Travers, please, come into the kitchen and make yourself comfortable," invited Lou.

"I'd feel a whole lot more comfortable if you'd call me Fenwick," I smiled at her.

"Then Fenwick it shall be," she said, smiling sweetly in return.

She led me into the kitchen, where I unbuckled my gun belt. Fu

Chou materialized and I handed it to him to hang on a peg on the wall. He took it with a bow and treated it with the reverence accorded an object of deep veneration.

I took a seat at the table as Lou clapped her hands and called for the house girl. A lovely young Chinese woman appeared and set a steaming bowl of noodles and spiced vegetables before me. At her appearance, Fu Chou's face clouded over, and he withdrew from the kitchen, bowing all the way. I took a tentative taste. "By jiminey, this is first rate," I said gratefully. "Herbert's a lucky fellow to have a woman who can cook like you."

Lou blushed at the compliment but forthrightly confessed, "I can't take the credit, I'm afraid. Liu Chi here is our cook, and she's proven to be a master chef. There's a lot we can learn from these people."

"Maybe so," I allowed, setting to with gusto as I eyed Liu Chi appraisingly. It had been a long journey from the coast and I was starved. But when I got my hunger out of the way, I just might turn to this little Chinese filly for a down-home welcome, I thought. Liu Chi eyed the floor studiously and smiled demurely as I ate. She was tiny, as were most of the women I'd seen thus far in these parts, and quite pretty. I couldn't see much of her beneath her floor-length gown, but if her body was only half as comely as her face, she'd be a rare treat in bed. I did see enough, though, to realize that her feet weren't bound, as was the custom for most of the ladies in this barbarous land.

"Now I see why you and Herbert have been able to endure the Orient so well," I said to Lou. "I had no idea the fare here was so exquisite."

"Oh, it wasn't always so," countered Lou. "Liu Chi is a very recent catch, I'm afraid. She was referred to us by a friend in the American legation in Peking. Our cook before her was quite unsatisfactory; meals tended to be real trials."

"I see," I said, downing another mouthful. "Well, all's well that ends well, eh? But tell me, Lou, how does a pretty lady like you get along in a wild place like this?"

She blushed immediately at the compliment. "Oh, thank you, Fenwick," she murmured, no doubt thinking I was just being courtly. But the fact of the matter was, I was as randy as a shipwrecked sailor, and at that moment the proximity of a lovely lady like Lou was almost intoxicating. I tried not to openly leer at her as she explained. "Berty and I met at Stanford University. When I graduated we married, and I've been following him around the world ever since. So I'm a seasoned traveler, you see, and when he got this opportunity, I was only too happy to travel with him to the mysterious Orient."

"I'll say it's mysterious," I agreed. "Who's this empress the admiral was going on about?"

"The Dowager Empress," answered Lou. "She's the last of the Manchu dynasty that's ruled China since 1644."

"Manchu?" I queried. "Aren't they all Chinese, though?"

"No, they're not," Lou corrected me. "The Manchus were tribesmen from Manchuria to the far north. They're ethnically distinct from the Han Chinese, just as Scandinavians are distinct from Italians. So the Chinese have been under foreign occupation for many years now."

"I'll be damned," I mused. Then remembering my company, I stammered, "er—I mean, how about that?"

Lou laughed easily. "Oh, don't be embarrassed, Lieutenant; I've heard worse."

I imagined she had in this wild land. "How does the Dowager Empress fit into this Boxer uprising, then?" I pressed.

"She and her dynasty have been watching the increasing Western presence in China with unease ever since the Opium War. As far as we know, she hasn't openly sided with the Boxers yet, but the very fact that they've been allowed into Peking at all is evidence of at least tolerance toward them by the empress."

"But why seize diplomats?" I asked. "Don't the Chinese understand that would mean war?"

"Perhaps," answered Lou. "But the Chinese have traditionally viewed all other nations as backward heathens who respond only to force. And, since the European powers will probably accept nothing less than complete capitulation from the Boxers, I doubt that this affair can be settled peacefully. Besides, even if the Boxers were to try to avoid confrontation, I rather doubt that Sir Edward would let them off the hook without at least some fighting."

"You've got a point there," I conceded glumly. From what I'd seen of Sir Edward, he appeared hell-bound to use the current troubles as an opportunity to enshrine himself in the pantheon of British heroes with the likes of Clives and the Duke of Wellington. "But don't worry, Lou," I consoled her. "If there's any fighting, it won't amount to much. From what I've seen of the Chinese, they're no match for white men."

If I'd thought otherwise, I would never willingly have climbed aboard one of Seymour's trains.

"Let's hope so," she said fervently.

I finished my meal with relish. "That was simply delicious, Lou. But I'm exhausted from my travels. I wonder if I might impose upon you further and ask for a corner to curl up in?"

"Certainly, Fenwick," she said, smiling. In two shakes of a China girl's tail she had me installed in a cool loft on a down-filled mattress, where I promptly dozed off.

40

I had an excellent sleep and spent most of the following morning chasing Liu Chi, whom I'd taught to call me "Fenwi," around the Hoovers' kitchen. It was a surprising thing, though—whenever I had the little vixen in my grasp, she would suddenly squirm away and send me crashing into the pots and pans! Either I was becoming exceedingly clumsy of late, or Liu Chi was using some art to fend me off.

I never did learn the truth of the matter, for by noon word came that the locomotives had been prepared as Admiral Seymour desired and the expedition was ready to roll. By the time I arrived at the railroad station, things were well under way; United States Marines, British bluejackets and soldiers, Japanese, and an odd lot of Austrians, Italians, and French—some two thousand troops in all—had been loaded on the cars, and the locomotives had a good head of steam up and were ready to go. I saw Sir Edward a short distance away on the station platform in the midst of a group of officers, both British and other nationalities. I hurried right over and reported.

"Good morning, sir," I said, saluting crisply.

"Good to see you again, Travers," the admiral replied, returning my salute perfunctorily. "You'll be in the command car with me, directly behind the lead locomotive." He pointed at the locomotive and accompanying coaler directly to our front. The windows of the command car were sandbagged, and on the roof was a parapet of sandbags and hastily welded sheets of metal. The barrels of machine guns and rifles bristled menacingly through embrasures in the parapet. "You'll hold

yourself ready to carry messages as necessary and to perform other
duties as assigned."

"Very good, sir," I said, stepping back. I hope none of these duties
involves leaving the relative safety of the train, I thought to myself.

A harried subaltern in the uniform of the Welsh fusiliers hurried
up to report. "Sir, Colonel Gibson's respects! The troops are all on
board and prepared to roll."

"Very good," pronounced Sir Edward portentously. "Gentlemen, shall
we?" He waved at the command car and the whole pack of us clambered aboard to a rousing chorus of train whistles, and the trains slowly
crept away from the station. The route was lined with cheering European noncombatants.

Inside I settled down on a hard seat by a sandbagged window. I
fervently hoped that this whole affair involved nothing more than racing
up the tracks blasting at anything that didn't kowtow in our direction
in order to impress the natives that we meant business, rolling triumphantly into Peking in time for supper, and sending out bombastic victory
telegraphs to the rest of the world. A bit nervous at the prospect of
imminent fighting, I carefully drew my Colt and checked each chamber to see that it was loaded and that I had plenty more cartridges available
in a pinch.

I was interrupted by a voice with a heavy German accent. "Is that
seat taken?" I looked up to see a big brute of a fellow in the *feldgrau*
uniform of the German Empire and sporting a pith helmet.

"No, not at all," I said, slipping my Colt back into its holster. "Please
be seated."

The German sat down heavily and introduced himself. "I am *Hauptman*
Von Arnhem, at your service." I could see that he wanted to click his
heels but couldn't from a sitting position.

"Pleased to make your acquaintance," I replied. "Lieutenant Travers,
United States Army."

"*Ja,* I know that," countered Von Arnhem.

"You do?" I said, my curiosity aroused. Why a foreigner in China
should know me was most puzzling. "May I ask how?"

"You were in Tampa in 1898. I was there, too," he answered
gutturally.

I studied him carefully now. Then it came to me: He was the big
Prussian I'd spotted in the Tampa Bay Hotel. The one who was always
lurking about with the Jappoes! "Ah, yes," I murmured, "you do seem

familiar." What was this fellow's game? I wondered suspiciously. He seemed to pop up in all the world's trouble spots. "Have you been in China long, *Hauptman?*"

"More than a year now," he replied easily. "I am posted to the German legation in Peking. I was fortunate enough to be in Tientsin on business or I would have been the object of this rescue, *nein?*" He gave me a thin smile that accentuated a cruel dueling scar running down the right side of his face. It gave him an almost barbaric appearance.

"Tell me, *Hauptman,*" I asked, feeling oddly compelled by his forceful presence to make small talk, "are these Boxers in your opinion religious fanatics or merely political malcontents?"

"A little of both, I suppose," he replied. "The Fists of Righteous Harmony are named after the clenched fist, which is the symbol of their movement. The Boxers have both religious and political overtones. The basic reason for their existence is a widespread belief by the Chinese that Westerners are exploiting their land. Which, I must agree, is true!"

He roared so heartily in amusement at this that he forced me to smile politely. "Well, it does seem to be a vast market with an endless supply of labor," I observed, merely stating the obvious.

Von Arnhem nodded, unimpressed. "The Chinese government, headed by the Dowager Empress, either cannot or will not challenge us Europeans openly. So, mysteriously, the Boxers appear to sweep us from the land. I do not think they will behave themselves until the empress herself sees that we mean business."

This all seemed more serious than I had first imagined. "But why should the Chinese think that the Boxers can force us foreigners out of China when all their past efforts have failed?" I asked worriedly.

Von Arnhem laughed again, this time harshly. "Not *all* their past efforts have failed, my friend! The White Lotus Society was able to drive out the corrupt Mings centuries ago. And that is where the religious part of this affair comes in. The Boxers are convinced that an army of eight million spirit soldiers will descend from the sky and help them in this war. While they await the spirit soldiers, the mortal Boxers wear these—" Von Arnhem paused as he produced a small piece of yellow paper from his tunic pocket and held it flat in his palm for me to see. On it was painted a small, manlike stick figure in vermillion paint. "This is a talisman that they believe will ward off our bullets."

I stared at it in silence a moment. "How very grim and mysterious," I said. "How did you come upon it?"

"Ah, simple," he explained. "It was pinned to the tunic of a Boxer I shot last night. Straight in the head," he said, smiling wickedly as he put his index finger to his temple and made a cocked-hammer motion with his thumb. I flinched involuntarily. "This paper is supposed to ward off bullets, but it did not work for that Boxer." He chortled.

I digested all this information in silence. I did not for a moment doubt that Von Arnhem was capable of cold-blooded murder. This, coupled with the broad red stripe down the side of his uniform trousers that designated him as a member of the vaunted German Imperial General Staff, warned me to keep a wary eye on him.

Since the train had been chugging along for a goodly while without the slightest hint of trouble, I decided to go aloft. I excused myself and made my way to the rear of the car, outside to the platform, and up the ladder to the roof. Peering through the cinders being shot back by the smokestack, I beheld an impressive array of firepower. Lounging against the protective sandbags were a collection of ferocious-looking Don cossacks and some capable-looking British infantry manning Hotchkiss guns mounted on traverses that allowed them to be trained in any direction that circumstances might require. Before me was the locomotive and the coaler; to the rear was a long line of cars, many of them similarly sporting jury-rigged parapets aloft. Farther aft I could plainly see the smoke from the funnels of the other four trains in our expedition, the last one of which included some stock cars for the mounts of our tiny cavalry contingent. Also to the rear I could make out the steel risers of the railroad trestle that spanned the Pei Ho at Yang T'sun. We'd clattered over the Pei Ho several minutes earlier.

I spied Captain Jellico and carefully made my way over to him along the pitching roof. "No trouble yet, sir?" I asked pleasantly.

"Not yet, Leftenant," he replied stiffly, letting me know by elevating his nose in the air, as though he had just caught a whiff of bilge water, that he was quite surprised a subordinate officer would have the effrontery to speak without first being spoken to. Apparently Jellico viewed himself as very much the captain on his bridge, and as such he took a dim view of idle conversation with a mere ensign.

"Ah, very good," I said approvingly, "very good, indeed." I sidled away from "Captain Bligh" as quickly as I could and found myself an inconspicuous niche from which I could watch the countryside roll past. Everywhere were dreary little mud villages and the ever-present massive earthen dikes that were so much a part of the Chinese landscape. The farmers I saw plowed their fields behind impassive bullocks, not bothering to look up at the armed host passing so near. If any single impression was forming in my mind about China, it was that of a huge seething mass of people in ceaseless motion but never going anywhere. The poor beggars were hopelessly rooted in the past, I realized, and if Sir Edward had anything to say about it, he'd slip them back a few more centuries for good measure.

Suddenly the train began to slow, and all eyes peered forward anxiously. I spotted the problem right off; about four hundred yards up the track a rail had been torn up.

Sabotage, by God! What the hell were we going to do now? I wondered fretfully. "Missing rail forward!" bellowed a beefy British noncom manning one of the Hotchkisses. The train screeched ponderously to a halt, safely short of the missing rail. Behind me I could see that the other trains were slowing as well.

"Pioneers forward!" ordered Jellico sharply from his perch, drawing his sword as though he were getting ready to repel boarders. "Be quick about it, lads!"

A squad of Royal Engineers dismounted from the car behind us and ran forward on the double, carrying a spare rail with them. The Britishers were quickly joined by a platoon of bandy-legged Japanese infantry, and the lot of them set to with a will. I anxiously scanned the brush alongside the track, expecting an ambush at any moment. But, praise the Lord, the repairs were quickly made without incident, and our party hurried back to the train. Maybe the heart had gone out of the Chinese after all, I thought hopefully.

Jellico gave the word and the train rolled forward once more. We had gone another half mile when the same noncom sang out again. "Rail missing forward, sir!" Again we stopped and the repair party went forward. I took the stop much more calmly this time; if the Chinese wanted nothing more than to trade rails with us, this was a game we could play and win. But as I idly watched the work progress, all hell suddenly broke loose. From out of the bushes on either side of the work party emerged a horde of screaming Chinamen.

"Boxers!" roared the British noncom, and instantly the Hotchkisses spoke.

"You may fire at will!" ordered Jellico grandly, waving his sword. He seemed a bit miffed at the Tommies, who tended to fire first and ask permission later. Then he sternly faced the fray and struck a martial pose, looking for all the world like a latter-day Nelson at Trafalgar.

At the first rush, the pioneers had thrown down their tools and fled pell-mell down the track. Some Japanese had grabbed up rifles and fired futilely at their assailants until they'd been taken and hacked to pieces before our horrified eyes. The Hotchkisses, however, quickly got the range and began to bowl over the charging Chinese like toy ducks in a carnival fun shoot. As soon as it dawned on me that the Boxers had no hope of cutting through the terrible fire ripping their ranks, I relaxed and enjoyed the fun.

"The little buggers is done for!" exulted a Tommy at my side. Apparently the Boxers agreed with him, for as suddenly as the assault had started, it ended. Sixty black-clad bodies sprawled on the tracks before us, and streams of Chinese fled through the millet fields all around. Unnoticed by me in all the excitement, Von Arnhem had mounted the car and was standing at my side.

"Cease fire!" ordered Jellico. The Hotchkisses fell silent.

"So much for the dreaded Boxers," I laughed cheerily.

"They are not Boxers," said Von Arnhem grimly.

"Not Boxers!" I exclaimed. "What the hell do you mean?"

He eyed me impassively. "Boxers wear red sashes in battle. Always. These men wear no red sashes."

I looked down at the corpses scattered on the tracks. He was right; there was not a red sash to be seen.

"These are peasants," concluded Von Arnhem. "The countryside is rising to help the Boxers."

41

I digested this silently. If what Von Arnhem said was true, the rebellion had evidently grown in scope, which was of course ominous. On the other hand, if all the Chinese were capable of doing militarily was charging headlong into machine-gun fire, I was not going to get worked up about the situation.

The tracks were again quickly repaired, the carcasses of our dead were hauled aboard, and soon we were chugging purposefully toward Peking once more, the troops much heartened by having splattered the first warlike Chinese they'd encountered all over the countryside.

The remainder of the day passed uneventfully, and by nightfall we were only thirty miles from the capital. Sir Edward was wary of a night advance, however, and called a halt. A picket line was thrown up around the lead train while the trailing train was dispatched back to Tientsin to replenish our ammunition supply. This last feat was accomplished mainly as a result of one of Hoover's suggestions. The engineer had recommended that each train have two locomotives attached; one fore and one aft. They could thus speedily reverse direction without the benefit of a turntable should the need arise. As our resupply train roared away into the dark, the expedition settled down for a night's rest in the cramped cars with the expectation that victory would be ours on the morrow.

Before dawn, however, I was roused by the sound of a blasting whistle. I hurriedly made my way out of the car and leapt to the ground, where Sir Edward was already standing in a tight knot of officers peering back along the track in the direction of Tientsin. A mounted orderly galloped out of the gloom and blurted his report. "Sir, Colonel Gibson's back with the resupply train! He says there's a whole Chinese army dug in on the far side of the Pei Ho at the steel railroad bridge at Yang T'sun. The devils have cut us off from Tientsin!"

"Cut off?" bellowed Sir Edward, indignant at the thought of the wogs actually offering him organized resistance. "Surely Colonel Gibson can fight his way through."

"Begging the admiral's pardon," replied the orderly, "but Colonel Gibson says that this is not just a rabble of farmers. They're imperial banner men with cavalry and artillery."

"Imperial banner men, you say!" echoed Sir Edward, concern registering in his voice. Banner men were the empress's own troops.

Here Captain Jellico piped up. "Sir, it's not advisable to remain strung out along this track if there are imperial forces in our rear. We'll have to fall back on Yang T'sun and deal with the situation there."

I agreed completely, but Sir Edward hesitated. The thought of giving up the relief of Peking caused him heartache, but on the other hand, he wasn't anxious to be the next "Chinese" Gordon of the British Empire. "Very well," he said reluctantly. "Sound recall."

Bugles rang out and the pickets hurried back in. As the blood-red sun rose, the entire expedition raised steam and scurried back down the rails to Yang T'sun before that town fell to the Chinese. We pulled into Yang T'sun about noon, and Sir Edward ordered the trains gathered on a series of sidings near the center of the town with the troops manning a defensive line along the Pei Ho facing the Chinese on the far shore. I, along with Sir Edward and the rest of his staff, hurried to the bluff overlooking the river. Von Arnhem joined us there.

"Well, there is the enemy," Von Arnhem announced almost joyously.

"Oh, my God!" I murmured involuntarily as I viewed the immense host arrayed against us. The far bank was crawling with troops—countless thousands of them. "Let me borrow your binoculars, *Hauptman*," I asked, fighting unsuccessfully to keep a quaver from my voice.

"Certainly, Travers," he said jocularly. "Feast your eyes!"

The deranged bastard seemed to relish our predicament. I focused the lenses and what I saw across the way was far from cheering. I counted the dragon-toothed banners of at least thirty regiments and watched fearfully as cannons, of archaic design but sinister-looking nonetheless, were rolled into position and trained on the vital railroad bridge. The bridge itself was undamaged, but hundreds of *Ten nai,* the feared Manchu Tiger Men, clad in yellow turbans, black-and-yellow–striped tunics, and yellow shields emblazoned with horrific faces, were firmly ensconced upon the bridge and were protected from our fire by sturdy wicker redoubts filled with earth. To add insult to injury, clouds of fierce-looking cavalrymen swarmed along the far bank hurling imprecations at the hated foreign devils.

"Who are those barbarians?" I asked Von Arnhem, pointing at the horsemen.

"Irregular cavalry. Muslims from Kansu Province," he answered. "They serve with General Tung Fu-hsiang, who is in the service of the Dragon Throne. We are facing *Pa chi,* Travers. Manchu banner men. A large portion of the Imperial Army is here."

I peered through the glasses again. Those damned Muslim riders looked like real trouble; lithe brown bodies, black-turbaned heads, and, worst of all, late-model carbines strapped to their saddles. Thank God the river was between me and them!

"Look there," announced Von Arnhem suddenly, pointing to a hillock on the far side of the river. I trained the glasses to where he was pointing and saw a brilliantly garbed figure surrounded by an escort of lancers clad in sky blue robes. "That is Prince Tuan, a crown prince of the realm,

Travers. He is the youngest son of the Dowager Empress, and some say the most dangerous man in China. His guards are called the Glorified Tigers."

"A crown prince?" I echoed, agog. "Why, that means. . . ."

"Correct," said Von Arnhem calmly. "The Dowager Empress has chosen sides. She is with the Boxers."

This was a damned unwelcome bit of news! I studied Prince Tuan and his entourage through my field glasses. "A rough-looking bunch of hombres," I allowed appraisingly.

"Oh, that they are," Von Arnhem assured me firmly.

Even without the gaudy attire of the Glorified Tigers, the sheer pageantry on the other side of the Pei Ho was almost beyond belief. I saw tunics of every conceivable hue under the sun, most of which had the imperial black dragon emblem prominently displayed. Spears, swords, and halberds were much in evidence, and everywhere exquisite banners—some square, some rectangular, but all bordered with stylistic dragon's teeth—floated sullenly in the summer air. The effect was of being lifted bodily out of the twentieth century and deposited in the twelfth!

"Gentlemen," announced Sir Edward gravely, "retreat through that horde is out of the question. We are hopelessly outnumbered."

"Then shall we defend here?" queried Captain Jellico bluntly.

"Absolutely not," answered Sir Edward. "If the Chinese have any modern artillery on that side of the Pei Ho, there'll be no part of our lines they can't hit. They'll slowly pound us to pieces."

Jellico grunted at this. As a battleship man, he could understand the lethality of big guns. "Then what are your orders, sir?" he asked calmly.

"We'll leave the trains here in Yang T'sun and retreat down the Pei Ho to Tientsin."

"You mean on foot?" I fairly yipped in alarm. Sir Edward eyed me as one would a young puppy that's just soiled the parlor rug.

"Yes, Leftenant. If you knew the history of this land, you'd realize that the Pei Ho was the route followed by the allied force that marched on Peking in 1865. That tells me that a force the size of this expedition can march down its banks."

"What about our supplies and wounded?" inquired Captain Jellico, ever the practical professional.

"We'll take them with us," replied Sir Edward. "Gather up all the sampans on our side of the river. We'll tow them along with us as we fight our way to Tientsin. Also, gather up all the oxen in Yang T'sun. We'll need them as draft animals."

Jellico nodded at this, satisfied.

"Gentlemen," announced Sir Edward solemnly, "if we expect to get this expedition back to Tientsin, we'll have to do our duty to the fullest. I know you won't let me down."

With that the meeting broke up and we set about preparing for the trek back to Tientsin. Sampans were expropriated without payment and lined up along the riverbank. The troops were deployed so as to best protect the march: cavalry to the front and rear, infantry in the center with the Hotchkiss guns being manhandled along as best as could be managed. When all was in readiness, the railroad bridge was destroyed by our pack howitzers, which dropped it and a couple of hundred screaming Chinamen into the Pei Ho. Then bugles rang out, drums began to beat, and we marched south.

42

As soon as Prince Tuan divined our intentions, he reacted accordingly. He kept the bulk of his army on the far side of the river, shadowing us as we marched toward Tientsin. He also slipped forces across to our side to harass us as we went. As the numbers of Chinese on our side of the river grew, so did the possibility that they'd soon be numerous enough to make a serious rush at us. Only the steady fire of the marines and bluejackets held them at bay.

We trampled through the rice paddies and millet fields for nearly a week, gaining a few miles in the day and then fighting off probes all night, getting sleep as best we could. I learned then what masters the Chinese were of what many years later we'd call psychological warfare; they'd ring our lines at night banging on gongs and firing rockets into our ranks. The rockets sprayed sparks that stampeded the pack animals and set the men's already raw nerves even further on edge. The only satisfaction we got was when a well-aimed shot sent one of the monkeys sprawling in the mud.

By twilight on the seventh day of this running fight, it was clear to every man in the column that we could go no farther. Our ammunition was dangerously depleted, and the wounded were so numerous that our progress had slowed to a crawl.

I was trudging along behind Sir Edward, eyeing the river and wondering at my chances of slipping off downstream alone in the night when a halt was called far up ahead. Sir Edward trained his glasses on a large edifice looming ahead in the fading light.

"What's that thing?" he demanded.

The staff hastily consulted its maps for an answer. "The bloody thing ain't on the maps, sir!" came the reply.

"Blasted charts!" spat Sir Edward. "How can I properly fight a battle when I don't know where the shoals and reefs are?"

Von Arnhem spoke up. "It is the Hsiku Arsenal. It stores most of the imperial ordnance south of Peking."

Sir Edward eyed Von Arnhem disdainfully. Prussians just naturally stuck in his craw. And Von Arnhem seemed to personify the worst traits of his countrymen: He was both arrogant and efficient. "An arsenal, eh?" mused Sir Edward. "Then it's bound to be heavily defended."

"Not so," declared Von Arnhem flatly.

"Eh? What's that you say? Not defended? Explain yourself, sir," demanded Sir Edward, unaccustomed to having his conclusions questioned by a mere captain, and a Prussian at that.

"If the arsenal were heavily defended, Admiral, we would not have gotten this close to it. There is probably a company of infantry there now, nothing more," opined Von Arnhem.

Sir Edward mulled this over a moment; what the Prussian said made sense. If the Chinese had had a sizable force in the place, they would have hurled it at us to pin us down so that the main army could cross the Pei Ho and finish us off. But how did this Von Arnhem know so much about an imperial arsenal in the first place? "I say, my good fellow," asked Sir Edward, "have you ever happened to have visited this Hsiku Arsenal?"

"*Ja*," answered Von Arnhem impassively, not volunteering a shred of information about the circumstances of his visit. But Sir Edward didn't have time to probe further into Von Arnhem's relationship with the Chinese. He had an imperial horde hot on his heels, and if he didn't get under cover quickly, he'd have no command left.

"Are those walls defensible?" demanded Sir Edward.

"They will withstand anything the Chinese can fire at us," Von Arnhem assured him.

"Then the arsenal it is," declared Sir Edward, his mind made up. "Captain Jellico," he ordered, "we must have that arsenal. See to it at once!"

"Very good, sir," replied Jellico, hurrying off to take care of the matter. In a few minutes the pop-pop of musketry drifted to our ears, and in the last glimmering of light I could make out a party of bluejackets storming the great gate of the arsenal.

"Sounds like a damned close fight," observed Sir Edward fretfully, eyeing Von Arnhem with uncertainty, the yellow flashes from muzzle blasts clearly visible in the dark. Then suddenly the firing ceased and a great huzzahing broke out. "Sounds like we've got it," ventured a fusilier major.

"Too soon to tell," muttered Sir Edward uncertainly.

Within minutes, however, a galloping horseman reined in out of the dark with the word—Hsiku Arsenal was ours and fairly won!

"Excellent!" cried Sir Edward. "Give Captain Jellico my regards and order all the troops inside the arsenal. We'll make our stand from within its walls!"

This made perfectly good sense to me. We'd simply hold fast until enough Western troops arrived in China to tip the military balance in our favor. That shouldn't take too long, I figured; then they could march up the Pei Ho and rescue us. We could then make our way to the coast, and our rescuers could proceed on to Peking and finish the job that we had set out to do, namely relieve the foreign legations. Of course if the foreign legations happened to fall in the meantime, well, that couldn't be helped. We'd done the best we could, and now we were flat blown. As we filed into the imposing arsenal, I was in relatively high spirits. I'd done my bit, by God; it was some other fellow's turn to play the hero.

Even when Sir Edward called a council of war later that evening, I saw no cause for alarm. My serenity, however, abruptly vanished when I learned the meeting's purpose.

"Gentlemen," Sir Edward began, "our troops are now well positioned to fend off the Chinese. Within these walls we are secure."

"Amen," I seconded, but quieted down when I drew withering glares from others around me. The silly fools were down in the mouth, I saw, no doubt because they thought they'd somehow failed in their duty to reach Peking.

"But we must now think of the diplomats in the capital city," continued Sir Edward. "They can't last long without relief. That means we must break out of Hsiku Arsenal as soon as possible."

Break out? Was he insane? Had he already forgotten that we'd been run into this place by at least thirty thousand screaming Chinamen, who at this very minute were squatting on their haunches not a half mile away, whetting their blades and hoping for a chance to separate our heads from our shoulders?

"I've decided we must get word of our predicament to Tientsin. I'm certain that additional troops must have arrived there since our departure," explained Sir Edward. "If they can join with us, we can defeat the enemy currently belaboring us, and then, united, we can drive on to Peking."

A great huzzah went up at this, scaring the living daylights out of me. I realized that my fellows, Britishers mostly, weren't nearly as defeated as I. That meant they were dangerous, both to me and the Chinese. Sir Edward paused dramatically and then looked out over his assembled officers. "Gentlemen, do I have any volunteers to ride to Tientsin tonight?" Instantly everyone around me raised their hands; secure in the knowledge that Sir Edward would never see my hand among the many, and shamed at shirking so conspicuously, I raised mine also.

"Thank you, thank you all," said Sir Edward, visibly moved by the loyalty of his officers. "However, I cannot afford to spare a single officer who is exercising direct command over troops. And our naval officers are not trained horsemen, so I cannot accept their kind offer." He paused. "That leaves only our gallant comrades in arms—Leftenant Travers of the United States and *Hauptman* Von Arnhem. Gentlemen, are you game?"

I almost fainted. Only my tall riding boots held me erect. Things were taking a dangerous turn here. I had come to China under the impression that it would be a quiet berth where I could while away the days until the unpleasantness in the Philippines blew over. Finding that China was in the midst of a bloody rebellion had been unsettling. Finding that I was to be locked in combat with hordes of screaming heathens, however, was nothing short of a nightmare. This wasn't my war, and I wanted no part of it. Now Sir Edward was proposing that I embark on a suicide mission. It was almost beyond bearing, and I was about to tell him so when the sharp crack of jackboot heels clicking together stayed my tongue.

"*Ja, mein Herr!*" boomed out Von Arnhem. All eyes now turned to me.

"And you, Leftenant?" asked Sir Edward quietly.

"I would love to go, sir," I lied bravely; but I added hastily as scattered applause started to break out, "however, I hesitate to act without instructions from my government. The last I heard, my country was friendly with China. I certainly don't want to provoke an incident because of a rash act on my part."

"Provoke an incident!" sputtered Sir Edward. "Good God, man, at this moment your legation is under siege by these pagans! I fail to see how any act on your part at this point could widen the rift that presently exists between Imperial China and all the Western nations. Now see here, Travers, if you don't care to go, simply say so. I'll find somebody with the courage to take your place."

Sir Edward didn't seem a terribly perceptive fellow, but he'd just expertly called my bluff. From the quizzical looks I was now drawing from those around me, I knew I had to backpedal quickly or risk censure in perpetuity. "Sir, you quite mistake my motive," I hastily protested. "If you're quite certain that by accepting this mission I won't be compromising America's relationship with China, I'll be glad to volunteer."

"I give you such assurance," replied Sir Edward. "And gentlemen, thank you. You'll leave tonight as soon as the moon sets. Good luck and godspeed."

Shortly after midnight we slipped out of the arsenal on borrowed cavalry mounts. Our party consisted of Von Arnhem, myself, and a Don River cossack specially selected for his knowledge of the terrain between Hsiku Arsenal and Tientsin. Our plan was simple: We'd ride due east from the arsenal along the near bank of the Pei Ho, hoping that most of the imperial forces were still on the far side, then cross over to the south bank and ride hell-for-leather in a wide circle until we reached Tientsin. To ensure that we would not fail because of tired mounts, each of us led an extra horse.

We passed uneventfully through our pickets. Keeping the river to our right, and giving a wide berth to the glare of the many watch fires the Chinese had lit on the far bank, we traveled in an easterly direction for five miles. Then our cossack guide halted and we reined in behind him. He listened intently to the night sounds around him and then, satisfied, turned toward the river. We gingerly picked our way down the muddy bank and waded our mounts into the slow current.

We were in midstream when the cossack turned and whispered something to Von Arnhem.

"What did he say?" I whispered, fearing that the fellow had smelled danger.

"He says to keep our arms and ammunition dry. There might be trouble on the other side," answered Von Arnhem.

"*Ja,* er—I mean, yes," I whispered back. I drew my Colt from its holster and pulled my carbine from its saddle scabbard, holding them both high as I crossed. We clambered out of the river on the far side and clattered across a rocky embankment into a stand of bamboo. There we reined in and listened for any sound of the enemy. Holding his finger to his lips as a signal for us to remain silent, the cossack slipped off his mount and disappeared into the brush to have a look about. He returned minutes later indicating with hand signals that the way was clear. He swung up into the saddle as lightly as an Apache scout, and the three of us set off at a gallop to the south.

In China, of course, one doesn't just ride in a straight line to one's destination; the lay of the land simply doesn't allow it. After centuries of intensive agriculture, the Chinese had transformed their land into a patchwork quilt of little fields and rice paddies bounded on all sides by huge earthen dikes. Thus we were forced to follow the line of the dikes, the tops of which were beaten hard from the footfalls of uncounted thousands of Chinese. It wasn't that much different from New York, I concluded after an hour or so; one followed the grid of the streets and the avenues, rather than walking through the buildings to get to one's destination.

We rode hard along the tops of the dikes all night, but we were still four miles from Tientsin when the sun rose. We'd continually rotated mounts at the urging of the cossack, but I could tell from the labored breathing of the beasts that it would be touch and go whether we rode or walked into Tientsin.

Suddenly Von Arnhem broke the silence. "There! To our left!"

My head swung in the direction he pointed. Silhouetted against the rising sun was a dark knot of riders. They were traveling along the top of a dike parallel to the one we were on, but separated from us by a good quarter of a mile.

"Who are they?" I shouted.

"Kansu Muslims!" shouted Von Arnhem in reply. "They must have been with us all night!"

I squinted into the sun. He was right; the riders all sported black turbans. It was those damned steppe wolves! My mind raced as I took in the danger. As long as they stayed where they were, they posed no immediate threat. If they crossed over to our dike along one of the connecting dikes we passed every so often, they'd lose a quarter of a mile on us, a distance they'd never make up if their mounts were as blown as ours. So what was their game? I wondered. Did they mean to merely shadow us, or did they have something more sinister in mind?

Suddenly I saw their plan. "Look, up ahead!" I yelled to Von Arnhem.

He looked back at me over his shoulder and nodded grimly; he had seen the trap. We were galloping full tilt toward a steep-sided canal that was perpendicular to the dike along which we rode. The only way across the canal was a narrow wooden bridge located almost midway between our dike and the one on which the Kansu Muslims were riding. It meant that both parties would reach the canal and then turn toward each other to race for the bridge! If they got there first, we were dead men.

The cossack reached the canal and without any hesitation veered to the left, riding parallel to the canal while flogging his panting mount mercilessly. Von Arnhem and I did the same, but as I peered forward over my mount's mane, I saw that the Muslims had reached the canal too and were galloping straight for us, firing their carbines as they came.

"Someone has got to stay at the bridge once we get over!" I screamed to Von Arnhem.

"Ja!" he agreed hoarsely. As we neared the span two central thoughts played in my mind: First, I hoped that Von Arnhem didn't think that I had volunteered for the job; and second, I tried to remember if the cossack had given any indication during the night that he understood either English or German!

We pounded forward, the bullets from the Muslims' carbines filling the air around us. I buried my face in my horse's mane and prayed that neither Von Arnhem nor the cossack went down, for surely the animal would trip over them, sending me into either the canal on my right or the rice paddy on my left. Then the wooden planks were under the horse's hooves and all three of us were on the bridge!

Suddenly, before my astonished eyes, I saw Von Arnhem rise up in his stirrups and strike the cossack a resounding blow across his shoulders with the flat of his saber. The cossack tumbled to the planks as both Von Arnhem's mount and my own vaulted over the man. On the far side Von Arnhem reined in, but I spurred on for dear life. As

I looked back over my shoulder, I saw the Prussian toss the stunned cossack a carbine and then a bandolier of ammunition. Then Von Arnhem let out an insane cackle and spurred his horse after me.

What a cold bastard, I thought, at the same time heartily glad that the cossack was where he was! I half expected the poor forsaken bastard to begin pouring lead into us as we fled. I'm sure the thought occurred in that dim mind, but at the last moment his feral instincts reasserted themselves, and he turned stolidly to face the onrushing Muslims, his blood enemies. He methodically began to cut them down as they came. As good a shot as he was, the Muslims could have bowled the cossack over had they come at him in one great rush. Thankfully, however, self-preservation got the better of them, and they scattered for cover and began to return fire. He was a dead man, I knew, but he'd bought us valuable time.

"Travers!" Von Arnhem shouted, "halt!"

"What for?" I called back, at this juncture quite leery about ever letting Von Arnhem within striking range of me again.

"Change horses, Travers," Von Arnhem exhorted, "or you'll never get to Tientsin alive!"

The bastard was right, I reluctantly concluded, so I reined in. With a rapidity born of fear, I pulled my saddle and bridle from my blown mount, threw them onto my other horse, and sprang onto the animal's back. As I did so, I suddenly realized that the firing at the bridge had ceased!

I turned to urge Von Arnhem to hurry, and found him saddled up already. No doubt, I thought, he was an expert equestrian along with all his other talents. We spurred on and within the hour galloped up a gentle slope overlooking Tientsin. We halted and scanned the panorama below us; what we saw was not encouraging.

"Look!" cried Von Arnhem. "There is the Boxer army in the native city!" He pointed to the northern end of town: From the walls of the native city flew the same kind of dragon-toothed banners we'd seen at Yang T'sun days earlier.

"What do we do now?" I asked helplessly.

"We ride for the foreign settlement!" he exclaimed, pointing at the southern end of the city. "It has its own walls, and I do not think the Boxers can take it by storm!"

"By God, you're right!" I agreed, spotting the Union Jack fluttering proudly from the walls of the foreign settlement.

It was then that we heard the hoofbeats behind us. Turning in the saddle I saw them cresting a low ridge behind us. It was the Kansu Muslims! There were fewer of them—the cossack had evidently sold his life dearly—but still more than enough to annihilate Von Arnhem and me.

Von Arnhem spotted them at the same time. "What do we do now?" I wailed. We were in a steel trap from which there seemed to be no escape.

"We ride, Travers!" sneered Von Arnhem, the proximity of danger seeming to strangely exhilarate him.

"But what about them?" I demanded, pointing to the groups of Boxers on the plain below between us and the foreign settlement.

"We ride between them," retorted Von Arnhem, as calm as you may please. You would have sworn from his serene demeanor that we were discussing nothing more threatening than the obstacles on a steeple-chase rather than a real-life dash through ranks of bloodthirsty fanatics. "The Boxers have no modern weapons like the Kansu riders," he explained, then added lightly, "but they use their swords to inflict the 'Death of the Thousand Cuts.'"

"A thousand cuts?" I gulped.

"*Ja,* but don't worry, Travers," Von Arnhem said, laughing harshly, "I have never yet seen a man last past five hundred."

He's unbalanced, I shuddered—a stark raving lunatic!

"Let's go, Travers!" roared Von Arnhem. And then we were off, careening down the slope and onto the plain below. In the wink of an eye we were among the Boxers, dodging left and right as they swung at us with great, curved scimitars and jabbed viciously at our mounts with wicked-looking pikes. These bastards sported red sashes, I saw; they were the real thing. If I fell now, the end would be horrible!

Ahead of us, the walls of the foreign settlement loomed larger, and it appeared that we'd easily gain the ramparts before the Boxers gathered enough strength to stop us. I saw a gate slowly opening and rode straight for it. Then my mount slammed to the ground, hurling me to the hard-packed earth with sickening force. Stunned, I rose groggily to my feet, only to see Von Arnhem and his mount crash to the ground also. Instantly I realized what had happened. The fiendish Boxers had dug camou-flaged foot traps all over the plain to trip unwary men and beasts. Now the entire Boxer camp, thoroughly aroused by our antics, was bearing down on us, with their great swords glittering in the sunlight, screaming for our blood as they came.

I took one look at the onrushing mob and all thought of assisting

Von Arnhem vanished. The devil take the hindmost, I thought, and began hotfooting it for the gate ahead, only to see it slowly closing before my very eyes!

Great Holy Christ; were they abandoning me? It couldn't be—I hadn't come eight thousand miles just to be the first man to live through all one thousand cuts!

Then hope sprang up anew. "Over here!" called an English voice from atop the wall as a crude rope ladder was lowered from the ramparts. I dashed straight for it and began clambering up, with a chorus of limeys urging me on from above. "You can do it, old chap! That's it! Come on!"

Oh, how I climbed—I clambered up like a monkey with its butt on fire! Glancing down, I saw Von Arnhem starting up below me. I didn't think any man could live through the fall I'd seen him take; the fellow was truly amazing.

Then came a dire warning. "Look out, mate! The little bleeders has got a *jingal!*"

A *jingal?* What the hell was a *jingal?* I peered apprehensively over my shoulder and saw two Chinese not a hundred feet away pointing a twelve-foot musket straight at me!

"Holy Moses, they're going to blow me right off this ladder!" I screamed piteously.

I scrambled up the last few rungs as the monster musket roared. Whizzing shrapnel blasted past my ears, and an awful blow caught me in the hindquarters, sending me screaming over the wall to land sprawling amongst a squad of Tommies crouching on the far side.

Dazed, I lay there fighting off a growing darkness. The last thing I heard was a thundering volley from the defenders, which sent the Boxers howling for cover, followed by the sound of Von Arnhem clambering over the parapet while calmly humming a Wagnerian tune.

Then everything went black.

43

I awoke in a darkened room. As my head cleared, I realized that I was lying facedown on a cot, and unless I was greatly mistaken, I was naked from the waist down. Someone, moreover, was ministering to my savaged posterior. I raised up and glanced over my shoulder. It was Fu Chou. And with him was Lou Hoover!

"Lieutenant, I'm glad to see you're stirring at last," she chirped, oblivious to my nakedness. "You had us all worried to death."

"What happened?" I croaked through a parched throat.

Lou refreshed my memory of my close call with the Boxers and told me that Fu Chou had insisted on ministering to me himself. "It seems he's taken a liking to you, Fenwick. He whipped up a paste made from local herbs that he vowed would combat any infection."

Fu Chou beamed at this. "Mak'ee you like new."

"What about Von Arnhem? Did he follow me over the wall into the settlement?"

"The Prussian?" asked Lou. "Oh, yes, he made it across the wall with a whole skin. Not a scratch on him, I understand."

That did nothing to lift my spirits. Misery loves company; if I had to be wounded, then it would have pleased me no end to learn that Von Arnhem had been mangled as well. Not only was he a bastard, but he was a lucky bastard to boot.

"We were worried about your wound. It looks quite a fright, but Fu Chou assures me that you will recover completely. I certainly hope he's right. In China, unfortunately, any wound is potentially lethal because of infection. Even scratches can be worrisome in this land."

I craned my neck around for a better look at myself. Lou was right; my hindquarters were a mess. One cheek was badly gashed; both had ugly bruises. I looked as though I'd sat on a meat grinder. "How bad is it?" I asked.

"Believe it or not, Fu Chou swears it's only a flesh wound."

"That right, Missy Hooer," insisted Fu Chou with a vigorous nod of his head. "Only small cut. No big cut. Honorable Fen'wi be fine, no time. Just need plenty rest."

I lay back on the cot, exhausted. "Do whatever you think best," I said.

"That's the good boy," beamed Lou with a look of maternal solicitude. "Just lie there and let Fu Chou make it all better."

And make it better he did, for in only a few days I was up and around once more. During this period Lou was constantly fluttering about to see to my needs. While Herbert was off seeing to his affairs around the settlement, Lou and I became quite close. Of course it would be too great a stretch of the imagination for me to expect that Lou derived any erotic thrill from our friendship. Yet I always wondered. After all, women have always had difficulty withstanding my rugged good looks, and perhaps Lou Hoover was simply another poor girl on the threshold of losing her heart, and a great deal more, to hot-blooded Fenny!

Since my return from Hsiku Arsenal, the foreign enclave in Tientsin had swollen with a steady stream of reinforcements rushed to China from all parts of the world. The massive Taku forts had been seized in a daring amphibious operation, thereby clearing the way to Tientsin, and the railroad from the coast was now hauling troops and supplies into the foreign settlement around the clock. By the time I regained my feet, in fact, there were sixteen thousand Western troops in the vicinity of Tientsin—so many, in fact, that the Boxers were holed up within the native city.

This show of martial strength greatly buoyed my flagging spirits, for you can rest assured that if I had thought Tientsin was about to turn into another Alamo, I would have pleaded incapacity in order to stay off the firing line. But despite Admiral Seymour's fiasco, I had a pretty good idea that the Chinese were going to lose this little tussle in short order. So, with the help of a wary Liu Chi, I donned my uniform, darned trousers seat and all, and hobbled about town to catch up on the latest events.

"Fenwick, old man!" hailed Hoover as soon as he saw me. "Good to see you fit once more."

"Thank you, Hoover. Those damned Chinamen were nearly the death of me," I laughed bluffly. "It's wonderful to be able to get a breath of fresh air."

"I can well sympathize with that," Hoover assured me. "I'd imagine that a professional soldier like yourself doesn't take kindly to confinement."

I gave a hearty yet appropriately modest smile at this; Lou had already informed me that the night ride Von Arnhem and I had made was the talk of the foreign settlement. "Why don't you accompany me down to the railroad station?" suggested Hoover. "I understand there's a trainload of American troops due to arrive shortly. You might see someone you know."

"You're on," I replied, happily enough. "It would be a tonic for me to see some familiar faces."

As we set off, Hoover remarked, "By the way, Sir Edward and his men were rescued at last. A battalion of American marines was sent out to fetch him in; the Boxers and the imperial troops just melted into the countryside and offered no resistance. They seem to fight for a week or so and then disappear. A strange way to make war, I must say."

No doubt the sudden influx of a host of foreigners into Tientsin, all armed to the teeth and wild-eyed for vengeance, explained the sudden shyness of the Chinese. However, I didn't bring this obvious fact to Hoover's attention; instead I gave a manly grunt and spat, "A damned ridiculous race of heathens, if you ask me."

"I heartily agree," concurred Hoover, "but nonetheless, the relief of Seymour was quite a feather in the caps of our gallant leathernecks."

As we neared the station we heard the shriek of an approaching train whistle. "Ah, right on time," said Hoover. We got to the station just as the train pulled in. The arriving cars were crammed with many young "goddamns," as American troops called themselves, and upon seeing my uniform they cheered lustily. I waved back with a broad grin until I saw a visage that froze the smile on my face: It was Col. Emerson Liscum, glaring at me with undisguised contempt! As soon as the train strained to a halt, Liscum leapt from his car and marched directly toward me.

"Welcome to Tientsin, sir!" I called with false cheer, snapping a quick salute, which Liscum ignored.

"What the hell are you doing here, Travers?" he demanded.

"I'm assigned to the American legation in Peking, sir. But at the moment, I don't seem able to get there."

"From now on you're assigned to the 9th United States Infantry," Liscum snapped. "Do you understand me, Mister?"

"I don't think the admiral will understand, sir," I said.

"Admiral? What admiral?" asked Liscum irritably.

"Why, Admiral Seymour, sir, of the Royal Navy. He attached me to his staff."

"You're on the staff of a limey admiral, Travers?" asked Liscum incredulously. "Well, I've got news for you, Mister; you're in the American army, not the damned British navy. There's no Shafter to hide behind here, Travers. When I take this regiment into battle, I'm taking you along with it. Do I make myself clear?"

The maniacal blue eyes glaring out from his wizened face told me that there was no point in arguing. "Yes, sir," I muttered resignedly; I was back in the 9th once more.

"Good," grunted Liscum. "Major Lee," he called, turning to his second in command, "this is Lieutenant Travers. He'll be joining us."

I was perplexed; who was Major Lee? "Where's Major Whittaker?" I asked.

"Whittaker left the service, you might say," retorted Colonel Liscum. "He died of yellow fever on the way home from Cuba."

"Damned bad luck" was all I could think to say.

"Yep," agreed Liscum, adding caustically, "but then Whittaker had more than his share of bad luck." Turning to Hoover, Liscum demanded, "And who are you?"

"I'm Herbert Hoover, Colonel. An American civil engineer here in Tientsin."

"Excellent," said Liscum. "Since you're familiar with this neck of the woods, I'll ask you to guide us to our cantonment."

"My pleasure, Colonel," replied Hoover affably, and the two of them headed off for the settlement, with the companies of the 9th following along as quickly as they dismounted from the train. I took a deep breath and traipsed along morosely in Liscum's wake.

With the arrival of the 9th Infantry, the concentration of Western power in Tientsin clearly outgunned the Boxer masses in the native city. Moreover, with the new troops came new commanders; Admiral Seymour was packed off to deep water and replaced by another Britisher, Maj. Gen. Sir Alfred Gasalee.

General Gasalee, however, was able to exert only nominal control over the allied contingents, and for the most part each went about its own merry way. For example, an overall American commander soon arrived on the scene: Maj. Gen. Adna Chaffee, a Cuba veteran recently engaged in the Philippines. Chaffee had no intention of being dictated to by either the Chinese or Gasalee. In fact, the only thing that unified the fractious Western contingents was a unanimous desire to thrash the uppity Chinese.

Soon a campaign plan to do exactly that was worked out. It was agreed that the allied force would first clear the Boxers from the native city in Tientsin and then drive up the Pei Ho all the way to Peking, hauling supplies in barges as it went. Of course, the only way to properly kick off a campaign was with a suitably impressive parade. General Gasalee, in the finest British tradition, decreed a general review of his forces on the eve of the assault on the native city. The allied army was to troop down the main thoroughfare of the foreign settlement, known appropriately enough as Victoria Way. I begged off from marching in the ranks of the 9th because of my wound, and instead joined Hoover on the reviewing stand.

As the spectacle began, led by a brass band composed of Italian sailors, Hoover gasped rapturously, "Isn't it a marvelous sight? There must be five thousand men in that column."

"About that," I agreed as a stream of soldiery from around the world marched by us smartly: rugged Welsh fusiliers in scarlet jackets, turbaned Bengal lancers mounted on splendid Arabians, blue-coated French Zouaves, and a small detachment of pith-helmeted German marines. Surprisingly, Von Arnhem was not among the German contingent. In fact, I hadn't seen Von Arnhem since our midnight ride. A strange one, that Prussian, I thought.

"Look, here come the Americans!" sang out Hoover.

"Ah, yes," I said, catching sight of Old Glory. Down the street they came, with a fine martial stride. A rugged-looking bunch of men all right, both the 9th Infantry and the regiment of United States Marines marching behind them. But the Americans' uniforms were a bit of a disappointment; they wore their functional field garb consisting of blue tunics over dusty tan trousers and khaki leggings, all set off with their characteristic slouch hats. The marines were indistinguishable from the soldiers, with the sole exception of the globe and anchor pinned to their slouch hats. Compared to their gaudily arrayed allies, the Americans looked more like a band of rowdy prospectors coming to town on a Saturday night than the cutting edge of a brand-new colonial power.

"Oh, my God!" moaned Hoover suddenly in a scandalized tone. "Would you look at that?" The 9th had already swung by, and now the marines were passing the reviewing stand. Their commander, Colonel Meade, ordered eyes right and brought his saber up in salute. This was all very proper, of course, except that Meade, who suffered from inflammatory rheumatism, had wrapped himself from head to toe in liniment-soaked flannel rags. The effect was as though he had dressed with his long johns over his uniform rather than the other way around. In short, he looked the perfect buffoon.

"Haw, haw!" I burst out. "It looks as though our friends in the marines are being led by a fugitive from a riverboat minstrel show!"

"It's not a laughing matter, Lieutenant!" Hoover reprimanded me sharply. "That man is making us look like fools in front of our allies!"

Of course Hoover was right. Already guffaws were rising from the reviewing stand and even the "rice Christians" lining the parade route— those Chinese who had embraced Christianity and were forced to seek shelter in the foreign settlement—were tittering at the spectacle.

"No harm done," I smiled broadly. "After all, Colonel Meade's only a marine. At worst this can only reflect badly on the navy."

"That's a fine attitude for an American officer!" fumed Hoover, and he stalked off, no doubt to see what pressure he could bring to bear to get Colonel Meade back into a regulation uniform. As for me, I was not a bit taken aback by Hoover's outburst; my attitude was doctrinally correct. It had been drilled into me at West Point that anything that reflected discredit on the navy was to be welcomed by the army. Meade's antics were merely a minor victory in the real war: the one between the United States Army and the United States Navy.

So I was in quite a good mood as I turned to watch Hoover go. I had had quite enough of the parade. After four years at West Point, you see, I had already endured enough parades to last me a lifetime. My wound was throbbing as well, so I decided to saunter back to Hoover's digs. Who knew, maybe Lou was around and we could have one of our pleasant chats. This happy thought was still in my mind when I rounded the last corner before Hoover's place and I spied a sight that stopped me dead in my tracks.

Liu Chi was in the lane before the Hoovers' door, and a crowd of Chinese was gathered around her: domestics and menservants from neighboring residences to judge from their appearance. She was screaming in anger at the top of her lungs. I shoved through the crowd of Chinese to see what the matter was and froze once more. There at Liu Chi's feet sprawled Fu Chou, his head bloody and his eyes rolling helplessly in his head. Liu Chi wielded a rolling pin in her hand, and on the ground was a pannier of rice, the grains spilling into the dirt.

I sized up the situation at once: Fu Chou had either spilled the rice or bumped into Liu Chi, who had then spilled it. Whatever the sequence of events that had led to this moment, two things were blazingly clear. First, Liu Chi was furious, and, second, she wouldn't stop flailing Fu Chou until he was dead. The skinny fellow was simply no match for her.

The curious thing was, the crowd of Chinese was hanging back as though Liu Chi was entitled to pummel the old codger to death. Now, I'm no saint; I'm not above lying, abetting gunrunning, or seducing any handsome women I chance upon. But I have my limits, and beating an old man's brains out in a public lane was on the other side of the line as far as I was concerned.

"Hold on, Liu Chi!" I cried, raising my hand to stay her next blow.

She turned to glare at me, and spat out something in Chinese. Then she hissed in English, "This not your affair!"

"Well, I'm making it my affair, my dear," I assured her levelly, stepping over Fu Chou's prostrate form.

Liu Chi raged at me in Chinese and then raised the rolling pin again. She was clearly determined to destroy the object of her wrath despite my intervention. Only she wasn't quick enough; I grasped her wrist and held it tight.

The crowd of Chinese issued a collective "Ohhh!" at this but did nothing to either help me or hinder Liu Chi.

"Damn you, white foreign devil!" she cried in her fury.

"Oh, white devil is it?" I smiled. "Well, if you have such a bad opinion of me, I have nothing to lose then, do I?"

So saying, I carried her over to where a bench was propped against a wall. I sat down and hauled her kicking and screaming over my lap. Then I hitched up her gown to reveal two shapely, almond-colored buttocks. With one hand I held her down and with the other I slapped her pretty behind until it was as pink as her furious face. The onlooking Chinese shouted and hooted in glee at Liu Chi's comeuppance, which only drove Liu Chi to struggle all the more fiercely. She was no match for my strength, however, and only when I judged that she had been thoroughly humiliated did I release her.

Liu Chi instantly sprang to her feet, her fury at her public chastisement evident in her eyes. She unleashed a string of maledictions at me in Chinese. The assembled Chinese "Ahhhed!" as one at this verbal broadside and fled the scene.

When we were alone with Fu Chou, Liu Chi looked at me with pure venom and vowed, "I will remember." Then, as best as her blistered bottom would let her, she stalked off down the street.

I got poor Fu Chou into the house and toweled the blood off him with cool water until he showed signs of reviving. Then I propped him up on a sleeping mat in the corner of the Hoovers' kitchen. He showed his thanks with feeble hand gestures and, all in all, I thought he'd probably pull through all right.

If I had arrived on the scene five minutes later, I knew, the end for Fu Chou would have been much different. I made a note to discuss this incident with the Hoovers. Liu Chi was clearly a menace; the sooner she was let go the better.

44

I was up after dawn the next day. The Hoovers never did arrive home, both of them being engaged in the feverish preparations for the day's assault. I donned a fresh uniform, wolfed down a quick breakfast, and then set out to find the allied army. I found it under a heavy morning fog, massing on the plain facing the native city. I stole over to where Colonel Liscum stood before the ranks of the 9th and tried to melt unobtrusively into the bevy of officers clustered around him. It didn't work.

"Travers," demanded Liscum, "where the hell have you been? The regiment formed hours before dawn."

"Er, there were a few legation matters I had to attend to yesterday, sir," I lied. "But that's all been resolved now and you have my undivided attention."

"I said you were to stay with the regiment, goddamnit!" retorted Liscum. "If you slip off one more time, Lieutenant, I'll see that you're court-martialed."

"Very good, sir," I murmured contritely.

"You're damned right it's very good," growled Liscum. Satisfied that I was properly chastened, he fired home a final barb. "I'm returning you to A Company. I'm sure Captain Harris will be delighted to have you back."

"Harris?" I asked, dumbfounded. Never in my worst nightmares had I expected to lay eyes on that misfit again.

"That's right, Mister" came a voice from behind me. I turned to see the menacing visage of Captain Harris. "Welcome home," he added, laughing mirthlessly.

I smiled back with studied nonchalance, knowing how much my insouciance grated on him. "Captain, it's so good to see you survived the Cuban campaign."

"I can see you haven't changed, Travers," sneered Harris. "Still the same damned upstart you always were—just as snide as the day is long. Well, let's see how damned sassy you are when this day is over. If you're still around, that is." He laughed harshly at his own black humor; none of the assembled officers joined him.

Before I could frame a suitably stinging rejoinder, Liscum interjected, "Where in the blue blazes is that fellow Hoover?"

"Hoover?" I asked. "Don't tell me he's going with us."

"Yes, he's going to guide the marine regiment through this mist, then we'll follow on their heels."

Well, that explained Hoover's absence. He was such an unspontaneous plodder that no doubt he'd been up all night tracing and retracing the route of the attack so that nothing would go awry. Which was fine with me, for this attack was likely to be trouble and I rather liked the idea of having a knowledgeable guide. I knew enough about the general plan of attack to understand that the native city, like most Manchu strongpoints, was ringed by two concentric palisades separated by an open space of about a half mile. The outer wall was constructed of mud bricks and would be fairly easy to breach. The inner wall was constructed of hewn stone and would be a much tougher nut to crack. Once the outer wall was breached, the allies would have to negotiate the maze of dikes that crisscrossed the extensive rice paddies beyond in order to reach the inner wall. Behind the inner wall lay the native city itself, where our spies estimated that thirty thousand Boxers and imperial troops lurked, along with the civilian population of some one million souls.

The plan of attack called for the Japanese to move forward under the cover of British artillery to pierce the outer wall. This done, the French, Austrians, and Americans, along with the Japanese, would surge forward toward the inner wall, again under cover of the British guns, and break into the city. The key to success was ensuring that once the various columns had penetrated the outer wall, they advanced along the raised dikes and did not attempt to cross the boggy paddies, which would hopelessly impede the advance. Normally, this would not pose a problem, but on a day like this, with a heavy fog reducing visibility to a few yards, a guide was needed. Hence the need for Hoover's presence to commence the festivities.

From out of the fog Colonel Meade shuffled up to Colonel Liscum, the penetrating odor of liniment preceding him. Hoover was with him. Hoover looked like a wreck; his eyes had dark shadows under them and he appeared distracted. This was something more than mere lack of sleep, I realized instantly; something serious was on Hoover's mind.

"What's wrong, Herbert?" I asked with concern, hoping that nothing was wrong with Lou.

"It's Fu Chou," he answered. "He was found dead a short while ago. Disemboweled. It was horrible."

"Dead? Fu Chou?" I was incredulous.

"Yes," Hoover grimly confirmed. "Who could have done such a thing?"

I knew, of course, but I didn't have time to tell Hoover, for Colonel Meade interrupted just then.

"C'mon, Hoover, let's go. We'll move forward as soon as the Nips crack the outer wall."

"Very good, Colonel," Hoover replied.

"Good luck, Meade," said Liscum, crinkling his nose involuntarily. "We'll be right behind you."

The fumes from Meade's ointments caused Liscum's officers to give way several feet, and a few of them actually gagged. I couldn't help but think that all we really needed to do to capture the native city was to hurl Meade over the ramparts with a catapult. In half an hour the Boxers would be streaming out of the place by every available exit!

Just then the crack of musketry in the gloom reached our ears. "Brisk enough," opined Liscum, trying to gauge the source of the firing. "Repeating rifles. It must be the Japanese."

It looked as though the game was on, but as I had learned in Tampa Bay, nothing is so true in war as the old adage "hurry up and wait." Tensed for action, we waited in the mist for the order to advance, but nothing happened. Then the fog thinned a bit, and Major Lee sang out behind me, "Look, Colonel, there's a semaphore on the wall ahead. I think the Japs have breached the wall!"

I peered into the haze and couldn't make out a thing, but apparently Lee was right, for in minutes orders came down the line. The marines were finally moving out. Soon we too were on the move.

"Gentlemen, report to your companies," ordered Liscum gravely. "I expect every man to do his duty today."

"That means you, too," growled Captain Harris at my side. "I'm going to have my eyes on you constantly in case you decide to ride shank's mare from the action."

With my instincts screaming that combat was imminent, I numbly took my place beside Harris at the head of A Company. There I found Lieutenant Longbottom; I hadn't seen him since my Plattsburgh Barracks days. There too was First Sergeant Richmond, the white chevrons on the sleeves of his blue tunic standing out in the fog. Richmond eyed me without emotion and said nothing.

"Well, if it isn't Lieutenant Travers," Longbottom greeted me frostily, eyeing Harris for an explanation of my sudden reappearance in the company.

"Travers is back with us for the duration" was all that Harris offered.

Longbottom, used to Harris's ways, pried no further. "Good to have you, Travers," he said without meaning it. "We heard you did a fine job in Cuba. And, of course, all about your ride from Hsiku Arsenal. You've made quite a name for yourself, although I must confess," he added pointedly, "I once had profound misgivings about you."

At this Harris gave a "harrumph" and rolled his eyes; Richmond merely spat a great wad of tobacco juice into the putrid water of the paddy below us.

"Kind of you to say so, Longbottom," I replied, uneasy at this cool reception. Looking around, I realized that one familiar face was missing: Charlie Hobart. "Where's Lieutenant Hobart?" I asked.

"In the Philippines," growled Harris. "I booted him out of the regiment right after we left Cuba."

"Booted him out? But why?" To my knowledge, Charlie hadn't disgraced himself under fire, and it would take a misdemeanor of that magnitude to provoke banishment from one's regiment.

"I booted him because he took your part back in Plattsburgh," snarled Harris, livid at the memory. "I would have sent him to the North Pole if it were in my power, and you with him."

Just then our little reunion was mercifully interrupted. The word came down the column to move out, and we duly advanced. As we trod forward in silence, I quickly became aware that the odor of Meade's ointments had been replaced by a far more pungent fragrance. From the paddies on either side of us wafted up the nose-numbing scent of human fertilizer, or "night soil," as Lou Hoover had euphemistically referred to it. Indeed, though I'd been in China only a few weeks, the smell of night soil was so pervasive that it seemed to me the Chinese wallowed in shit, and that their vaunted empire rested on mountains of it.

We reached the outer wall without incident; it was heavily pockmarked from Japanese bullets, and the gate had been blown clear off its hinges. We hurried past dead and wounded Japanese interspersed with moaning Boxers.

Once inside the outer wall, however, things began to quickly go awry. The column inexplicably halted, and the troops stood along the top of a dike peering forward, trying to learn the cause of the halt. After twenty minutes of this, Harris snapped, "Lieutenant Longbottom, take over here! Travers, follow me. I'm going forward to see what the hell's holding us up."

He walked briskly forward to the head of the column, only to find Lee and Liscum in total confusion. "Where the blazes did those marines go, Major?" demanded Liscum. "They couldn't have disappeared into thin air!"

Lee, clearly embarrassed, answered, "I don't know, Colonel. One minute they were in plain sight in front of us and the next minute they vanished into this damned fog. If the haze wasn't so thick, we could see them right now. They can't be more than a few hundred yards from us."

"It's the fog in your thick skull that worries me, Major!" stormed Liscum.

"We can't just stay here, Colonel," chimed in Harris, a note of concern in his voice. "We don't dare risk getting too far separated from the rest of the army."

Liscum pondered this and then made up his mind. "We have to push forward, guide or no guide. Stay on top of the dikes and try to head for the sound of the guns."

How we were to do that was a mystery to me, for in the heavy fog it sounded as though gunfire were coming from all around us.

"This way!" announced Colonel Liscum, heading off down the dike. Cautiously we followed, with the regiment tagging along behind us like a large, blind python feeling its way along a limb. Gradually, to our consternation, the sound of firing began to fade.

"Colonel," I suggested as we tramped along, "perhaps we'd better call a halt until this fog lifts. It sounds like we're actually moving away from the firing, which means we're moving away from any possible support."

"He's right," agreed Major Lee nervously. "It's too damned quiet for this to be the route of the main attack. We're lost, sir."

"The two of you make a fine pair," spat Liscum, turning on his heels to face us. "If General Grant had had advisers like the two of you, he'd never have beaten Sherman!"

Eh, how's that? I thought. Evidently the wound that Liscum took in Cuba was more serious than anyone suspected. I eyed Major Lee quizzically, but all he could do was shrug his shoulders in resignation. With Liscum's non sequitur, we shelved all attempts to talk sense to him. For his part, Liscum took our pained silence as begrudging respect, spun about once again, and continued to march into the void. As we advanced, the sun gradually rose in the July sky and the fog at long last began to thin. Then, as though a curtain had been suddenly lifted, the battlefield was revealed to our anxious eyes.

We were heading for the inner wall all right, but we'd strayed more than a half mile to the right of the main attack! Far to our left we could see the Japanese, French, and our marines advancing along a wide causeway toward the main gate of the native city, and apparently meeting with stiff resistance. Behind them was the redoubtable British artillery, peppering the howling defenders with a hail of shot. Although the Boxers were putting up a good fight, it was clearly only a matter of time before they yielded to the allies.

"Wouldn't you know it!" spat Liscum as he took in the scene revealed by the lifting fog. "We're in the wrong damned place!" Nobody had the temerity, however, to point out that it was he who had led us into this predicament.

"All's not lost, sir," I insisted hopefully. "We can simply retrace our path and come up behind the main force. With the mist gone, it'll only take an hour or so to get over to that causeway." And let's hope that by then, I told myself, the fighting will be over.

"Only an hour or so!" exploded Liscum. "The battle of Chancellorsville was decided in a matter of minutes, you young pup! Minutes, do you understand?"

"Does that mean we aren't going back?" asked Major Lee fretfully.

By way of an answer, Colonel Liscum thundered: "War is always a matter of minutes and inches, gentlemen! This entire battle may well hinge on what this regiment does here and now."

He paused meaningfully, staring hard down the narrow causeway that led straight toward the inner wall ahead, no doubt hoping that his fiercely martial mouthings were being duly noted for posterity by his underlings. "Gentlemen, the enemy is before us. Major Lee, sound the advance!" Drawing his saber, Colonel Liscum marched determinedly forward.

Major Lee shrugged again and I rolled my eyes skyward. "Get moving, Travers," growled Harris, giving me a none-too-gentle shove to set me off. Obediently, the regiment moved forward carefully, rifles leveled and pistols cocked. To our right I spied a small collection of mud huts surrounded by an expanse of rice paddies, looking for all the world like a lonely atoll in a sea of green. Major Lee saw the huts, too. "Colonel Liscum!" he called out. "Should we send out a patrol to secure those huts on our flank?"

"Send the patrol, Major," allowed Liscum, "but keep the main body moving forward. I don't want to be strung out on this damned strip of dirt any longer than necessary."

"Yes, sir!" replied Lee and hurried back down the column to carry out the order.

A platoon was duly sent off toward the huts. With a cold sweat trickling from my brow, I watched the thin skirmish line approach its objective. I knew that if there were Chinese in those huts armed with modern rifles, the regiment would be a sitting duck as it presented its flank on top of the dike. What's more, with a large part of the regiment already past the huts, if there was a Chinese force in them, we'd be trapped between the inner wall ahead and the huts behind, with the only route of withdrawal being along the exposed dike. I looked nervously at the rice fields to our right and left. They were at full flood, no doubt a final touch by the Chinese to hamper our attack. They would also, I realized grimly, hamper any retreat.

Suddenly gunshots erupted from the huts. "Ambush!" came the cry from the column.

"Holy shit!" bellowed Captain Harris and bolted to the rear in panic. I whirled in my tracks, uncertain which way to run. I saw a screaming mob of Boxers erupt from the huts and tear into the approaching patrol with swords swinging. The startled troopers got off only a few shots, then they went down before the sudden onslaught. A volley from the horrified ranks on the dike ripped into the exulting Boxers and sent the survivors reeling back into the shelter of the huts whence a withering fire soon came. Quickly, more troopers went down.

"Deploy off the causeway!" ordered Major Lee.

As one man, the entire regiment scurried down the far side of the dike away from the Chinese fire. The troops leveled their Krags on the Boxers and soon a lively exchange was underway. I clambered down into the foul muck of the paddy along with the others, but the disgusting slime quickly coated my uniform and so I moved off to a slight hummock above water level, where I took stock of the situation. I found I could rest somewhat more comfortably here while I waited for the troopers to drive off the Boxers on the far side of the causeway, whereupon we could all resume our advance.

But my rest was quickly disturbed. "Z-zing!" By God, a shot had whistled through the crown of my hat! I looked behind me and damned near fainted. There were Boxers behind us on this side of the causeway, too! We were surrounded by the little savages!

"Boxers!" I yelped, diving headlong into the paddy waters. When I came up, dozens of troopers were bobbing in the mire with me.

"Form a perimeter!" I heard Major Lee call. The rest of the troopers, who had been on the causeway pouring a hot fire on the Boxers in the huts, now slid down into the stinking mire and formed tight defensive circles, trying as they did to keep their rifles and cartridges above water level.

"Rally, boys, rally!" I heard Liscum cry. I poked my head up out of the muck far enough to see the old fool actually standing in a paddy next to the regimental color sergeant, Old Glory fluttering fitfully above them in the heavy air. Suddenly the big sergeant spun as a bullet slammed into him and he fell with a splash. Liscum grabbed the banner and held it only a few seconds before a great patch of crimson appeared on his tunic and he sagged.

"Arrghh, I'm done for, boys!" he moaned. Spying me peering at him not fifty feet away, he called out weakly, "Travers, take the flag, man, take the flag! I'm done for!"

Take the flag? My God, was Liscum stark raving mad? Oh, I'm a great one for saluting the flag on parade, and there's nothing I like better than the looks I get from the ladies when I snap to as Old Glory passes by on the Fourth of July. But at that moment I'd rather have hand-fed a slavering wolverine than to have grabbed the wavering flag from Liscum's dying hands. Getting killed just to keep a few yards of material flying in the air wasn't my idea of smart fighting, you see. So without so much as a look back, I turned and paddled off strongly in the opposite direction—and bumped right into First Sergeant Richmond.

He shot me a look of pure contempt. "You cur, Travers!" he spat. "I've always had my suspicions about you after I saw you gun down that Injun out in Arizona. Some would've thought that was murder, but I gave you the benefit of the doubt. And I didn't pay no never mind when I heard those rumors in Plattsburgh Barracks about you and my Ida! I thought it was jes' a bunch of folks talkin'. But now everythin' about you is clear. Yer a yella dog, Travers, and when we git t' hell out of this mess, I'm goin' to tell the world the truth about you!"

I was frozen with fear, both from the Chinese bullets whipping through the air around me and from the fact that Richmond was a witness to what small minds might consider cowardice under fire. And as a first sergeant, he was a damned credible witness! I'd be drummed out of the service in disgrace and shipped home with no chance of ever cozying up to George Duncan! Why, I'd never hold Alice again! It was all over; my world was crashing down around my ears.

Behind me Liscum gave out a groan and fell, his last words being, "Keep up the fire, boys!" Then he slipped into the fetid water as a storm of shots fell around him. First Sergeant Richmond, seeing the flag slowly falling, jumped to his feet, splashed to Liscum's prostrate body, and began to plant the colors firmly in the mire. But before he could do so, he too suddenly lurched forward with a look of disbelief put his hand to his throat where a geyser of crimson was erupting. Richmond sagged against the flagstaff and then slumped beside Liscum.

Then, to my complete amazement, a third figure splashed toward the flag! It was Olson, the woebegone private whom Richmond had sheltered over the years. Olson, ignoring the bullets snapping around him, quickly dragged Richmond behind a nearby dike and then made the perilous return journey to retrieve Liscum's carcass. Incredibly, Olson then made the dangerous passage a third time to drive the staff of the flag deep into the muck beneath the dark paddy waters. Old Glory, firmly planted now, waved gaily as the surrounding Boxers did their best to shoot it to pieces. Returning to the dike, Olson tenderly cradled Richmond's head until the rugged first sergeant finally gave up the ghost.

Two disjointed thoughts wandered through my stunned mind as I watched this carnage unfold. The first was that I never would have imagined that Olson was capable of such purposeful action, and the second was that Ida Richmond was now free to sample whatever wares struck her fancy, and I wondered wistfully if she were still at Plattsburgh Barracks.

The remainder of that day was pure hell, I can assure you. We bobbed about in those rancid paddies under a broiling sun that baked our brains, and more than one poor fellow went howling mad from the strain of it all. Oh, the goddamns fought back as best they could, but if a soldier rose up from the mud high enough to get off a well-aimed shot, he immediately became a target for scores of unseen marksmen. So I, like most of the men, kept my head down and wondered dully how we would ever get out of this fiasco alive.

Fully aware of our predicament, the jeering Boxers, clanging cymbals and blowing horns to further unnerve us, pressed in from all sides, and slowly the regiment was forced away from the causeway and into the middle of the paddies, until by nightfall we were compressed into a single defensive mass with Boxers hemming us in from every direction. Gradually the firing died off as the light faded and we waited grimly in the growing dark with bayonets fixed.

45

As I floated miserably in the mire—thinking bitterly that none of this would have happened if only I'd jumped from that train that took me to Fort Grant years ago—I heard someone softly calling my name.

"Travers, where are you?" It was Major Lee.

"Over here!" I whispered softly in reply, fearful that any noise might allow the Chinese to zero in on the sound.

Lee paddled up to me in the dark. "Travers, we need to talk," he panted, exhausted.

Lee's hat was gone and he was covered with mud and blood; he looked more like a huge swamp lizard than a man. I knew I looked no better than he, and the thought made me feel even more despondent. "What do we need to talk about?" I asked listlessly. The last thing I needed to hear was a half-baked scheme to break out of this fix with a bayonet charge or some similar act of lunacy.

"We have to get—" Lee began.

"For God's sake, keep your voice down!" I hissed. The sound of Chinese sharpening their blades a short distance away was clearly audible.

Major Lee nodded his understanding and began more quietly. "We have to get help somehow. We can't hold on without more ammunition and reinforcements."

"Right," I agreed unenthusiastically. "What do you suggest?"

Lee paused meaningfully. I could see where this conversation was going; Lee wanted me, the hero of Hsiku Arsenal, to sally forth once more. Well, there wasn't any pony to mount here, and there was no cossack guide to find the way and to step between me and any Boxers who might take a notion to lifting my head from my shoulders. No siree, not Fenny this time, I thought adamantly.

"Listen, Major," I balked, "nobody's going to slip past those Boxers in this muck! It would be suicide to even try, I tell you."

"Well, I understand if you're reluctant to go, Travers," allowed Lee, "but we're desperate, man, and you know the lay of this land better than any of us. There's really no alternative."

Oh, yes there is, I thought grimly. I could shoot this fool right here and now and nobody would ever be the wiser. In fact, I was toying with the trigger on my Colt and eyeing Lee sideways when somebody else splashed over to us. It was Lieutenant Longbottom.

"Major Lee," whispered Longbottom, "the men are down to one bullet apiece on the far side of the perimeter! By dawn, we'll be completely out."

"Damn!" swore Lee. "Travers, we've got to get reinforcements. If we don't, this whole command could be lost."

"Sir, permit me to volunteer," offered Longbottom.

Eh, what's this? Why, I could scarcely believe my ears! I quickly eyed Longbottom to see if he wasn't perhaps suffering from battle shock, but he was clear-eyed enough, and I relaxed a bit at having escaped Lee's suicidal mission.

"Excellent, Longbottom," whispered Lee, gratification evident in his voice. But then he added, "I'll send you and Travers out together. The two of you should be able to get through." Lee's desperate mind was so obsessed with seeking relief that he couldn't quite grasp the idea that I didn't care to stir from the relative safety of the regiment.

"Now wait a minute—" I began.

But Longbottom brusquely cut me off. "That's a fine idea, sir. That way we can cover each other and hopefully avoid an ambush."

Then I saw Longbottom's scheme. He wanted to become a damned hero just like me, and he saw our present predicament as his chance to do so! He was willing to risk his neck—and mine to boot—to get a coveted citation for gallantry. Oh, how I raged at Longbottom's damned interference. I might have been able to pop Lee off in the dark and pin the deed on the Chinese, but two dead officers in close proximity to me with Colt slugs in them might be just too much of a coincidence for a military tribunal to accept. Glumly, I stopped toying with my revolver.

"I agree, Longbottom," concurred Lee. "Two men can get through where one couldn't. It's terrible to have to ask you both to take such a risk, but, well, there just isn't any choice in the matter."

"There's not much time left before dawn," declared Longbottom. "We must go now if we're to make the greatest use of the night."

"Right you are," agreed Major Lee. Before I could protest, he ended with, "Gentlemen, I'm proud of you both. Good luck and godspeed."

With that Longbottom turned to me and asked, "All set, Travers?"

I was stunned. I'd been blindsided by Longbottom's thirst for glory and Lee's willingness to throw us both to the dogs. But what could I do? It was either bleat and croak and be branded as a coward should we all survive this disaster, or hold my peace and try to figure a more subtle escape from the dilemma these two fools had thrust me into. Predictably, I chose the latter course. "I'm as ready as I'll ever be," I gulped at length.

"Then let's get going," said Longbottom grimly, and to Major Lee added, "So long, sir." With that he slithered off into the gloom and was soon swallowed up in the night.

I hesitated, hoping against hope this was all a bad dream and that I'd awaken at any instant. "Get going or you'll lose him," hissed Major Lee, giving me a shove that propelled me in the direction Longbottom had taken. Reluctantly, I began crawling forward, guiding myself on the soft splashes I heard ahead. My movements were strained, for my buttocks still ached, and I expected annihilation at any moment. I paddled along with a heavy heart for some minutes until I suddenly bumped into something. It was Longbottom.

"Why'd you stop?" I demanded almost hysterically. "I thought you were a Boxer, for God's sake!"

"We're making too much noise," explained Longbottom patiently. "This is not going to work. We've got to split up and go separate ways. That will double our chances of getting through."

"You're crazy!" I hissed, forcing back my rising panic. "If we split up, we're guaranteed to get lost!" My God, the thought of wandering alone in a rice paddy filled with cutthroat Boxers was beyond bearing. "What's more, you're the one who just told Major Lee we'd have a better chance to get through together! What the hell are you trying to pull here, Longbottom?"

"Trust me, Travers," whispered Longbottom calmly. "It's the only way. You'll see."

Trust him? I'd sooner wave the Union Jack at a Fenian rally on Saint Patrick's Day than trust Longbottom. Then it dawned on me: The bastard wanted more than just an opportunity to be a hero; he wanted to show me up in the process! He must have hatched this scheme in an instant back there with Lee. First he got Lee's blessing to get us out into this no-man's-land; now he wanted to leave me behind to show that he, not Travers, the hero of Hsiku Arsenal, was truly deserving of being mentioned in dispatches.

"No way, Longbottom!" I argued fearfully. "You're not leaving me out here to die alone!"

"Get hold of yourself, Travers. You're not going to die if we're quiet. If we stay here arguing, though, every Boxer in the neighborhood will soon be down on us."

"Why can't we stay together?" I whined in protest. "I don't see why we have to split up."

But Longbottom had already made up his mind. "I'm not going to argue with you. I'm going on alone. I suggest you try to get through by a different route. Or you can stay here for all I care. But I'm determined to succeed, and I can best do that alone."

He slithered off again without so much as a fare-thee-well, leaving me alone in the awful dark. Goddamn him! I raged. If I got sliced up by some fanatical Boxer because of his treachery, I vowed to haunt him the rest of his life. If it wasn't for Longbottom, Lee might not have insisted on this insane scheme in the first place. I fought for self-control, knowing full well that my very life depended on what I did next. Should I go back? No, it was too risky. I rejected the option of simply staying put for the same reason. If dawn found me isolated among the Boxers, I would be a goner. The only feasible solution was to make my way onward to the outer wall. Why, it was even possible that I'd already penetrated the ring of our besiegers, and the way was clear for my escape. Once out of the paddies, I'd be able to find some of our allies. Safety in numbers, and all that.

My decision made, I damned Longbottom once more, sighted on the stars, and began paddling. The tall rice stalks obscured my view, and I was not able to pick out a single useful landmark along the way. I prayed that my bearing on the stars above was accurate enough to get me back to safety.

Suddenly I bumped headfirst into something again! "Holy smokes!" I cried, my eyes blinded by flashing lights from the collision. I blinked them away only to find myself gaping into the eyes of an equally stunned Chinaman!

"Help!" I screamed, leaping to my feet. The Boxer did the same, thoroughly alarmed by my antics. I drew my revolver and he produced a curved dagger. I pulled the trigger and nothing happened—the piece was clogged with mud and completely useless. For an instant I hesitated; then, with resolve born of extreme desperation, I sprang into action.

"Get out of my way!" I roared, slamming a shoulder into my opponent and driving him off his feet and into the muck. Like a frightened mallard trying to lift off from a lake, I commenced to scamper across the paddy with scarcely a thought of the Boxer's companions lurking all around me.

Hoping that I was near our allies, I began to scream piteously, "Don't shoot! I'm an American! Don't shoot!"

I splashed across the paddy in a blind panic, half expecting to be cut down with a bullet in the back from some unseen marksman, when suddenly someone reached up and grabbed my foot, and I went headfirst into the foul-smelling mire.

Only the muck in my mouth kept me from screaming, Don't kill me! I surrender! What came out was, "Mmmmmmmph!"

"Shaddup!" hissed a deep voice. "Every goddamn Boxer for miles around can hear you!"

It was an American! Thank God, I was safe! I'd broken through! "Where am I?" I asked tremulously when I'd spat out enough mud to speak.

"Right back where you left from, Travers," came another voice. It was Major Lee. "Where's Longbottom?" he demanded.

"I don't know," I gasped. "We split up. He got a little rattled out there and thought we'd each have a better chance alone. I must have, er, gotten disoriented and circled back."

"So it seems," agreed Lee evenly. "Did you see many Boxers out there?"

"Dozens," I lied. "They're everywhere, I tell you," hoping against hope that Lee wouldn't order me out once more. "I blundered into a nest of them after I left Longbottom. It was close work with blades for a few minutes, and I nicked a few, but I had to run when more joined the fray. God, how I wanted to pay them back for what they did to the colonel."

Suddenly the trooper who had tripped me tensed. "What's that?" he whispered.

"I don't hear anything," I hissed back.

"Shhhhh!" commanded Lee. "Something's out there!"

I leveled my useless revolver at the night and held my breath. Suddenly a huge form loomed up from the shadows.

Major Lee gasped and I flinched. "Halt!" boomed out a trooper on my right. "Who goes there?"

"Don't shoot, chaps!" retorted a hale British voice.

"Hold your fire, men," ordered Major Lee, quickly regaining his composure. "Who's there?" he demanded of the apparition.

"Captain Ollivant, 1st Chinese Regiment" came the reply.

"First Chinese Regiment?" I repeated, not recognizing any such outfit. "Damnit, man, are you with us or against us?" I demanded in a no-nonsense tone, while around me the bolts on Krags slammed home for emphasis.

"Oh, I'm with you," answered Captain Ollivant quickly. "I've come to fetch you blokes out!"

"Praise the Lord!" I exulted as Captain Ollivant emerged from the gloom with a crowd of Chinese in khaki jackets and straw hats, all armed with quite serviceable Martini-Henry rifles, swarming forward on his heels. The 1st Chinese Regiment, I surmised, was a levy of the locals in the British service. Many of the Chinese were leading sturdy mules burdened with ammunition cases.

"Ammo!" exclaimed Major Lee. "You're a sight for sore eyes, Captain! How'd you ever manage to slip past the Boxers?"

"Quite simple," he explained. "We came through the rice paddies. The Chinese don't care to walk through them at night; they're full of vermin. The Chinese are a very civilized race, so most of our Boxer friends were clustered on the causeway above you, or at least they were until you unleashed that wonderful diversion of having one of your men run around the paddies hallooing at the top of his voice. That completely unnerved the enemy, it seems, and the lot of them slipped off into the night. I congratulate you on your ingenuity."

At this Major Lee eyed me approvingly. "Good job, Travers," he said.

"You mean we can just walk out?" I asked incredulously.

"Most assuredly," replied Captain Ollivant, "or at least you can until dawn breaks. General Gasalee realized by late afternoon yesterday that you were pinned down over here, and he elected to extricate you under cover of darkness. I think that plan will work splendidly under the circumstances."

I was instantly in a whirl of motion, hurrying through the rice paddies to spread the word. In ten minutes the ammunition had been distributed, Liscum's and Richmond's bodies had been strapped to two of Ollivant's mules, and the lot of us were heading out.

"Stay close behind me," warned Ollivant. "We wouldn't want anyone to wander off in the wrong direction, would we?"

The bedraggled 9th, shot up and demoralized, followed close on the heels of its savior. We'd gone only a hundred yards when I stepped on something that was not mud.

"Yiii!" I screeched.

"What the hell's wrong?" demanded Lee behind me.

"There's something down there!" I retorted.

"Let's have a look-see," suggested Captain Ollivant, peering down at the muddy water. "Ah, it's a body!" Reassured that it was not a submerged Boxer lying in ambush to slit my throat, I peered over Ollivant's shoulder. "It's an American," observed Ollivant.

"Is it Longbottom?" asked Lee, concerned.

"By God, it's Harris!" I blurted, failing to keep the glee from my voice. I hadn't seen the bastard since he'd fled at the sound of gunfire, and until that moment I hadn't given a thought to his whereabouts. It was clear from his mangled appearance that he'd died an awful death beneath those terrible Chinese fighting swords.

"The poor sod," muttered Major Lee. "Travers, have some men strap him to a mule. We'll take him out, too." In short order Harris's cadaver was secured to a laboring animal, and the column pushed on once more. As we trudged forward I could not help but think that a day that'd had all the earmarks of a complete disaster had turned into a banner day after all. First, I was unscathed, and second, both Liscum and Harris had been swept away in one fell swoop, with First Sergeant Richmond thrown in to boot!

My only regret was that I had been too badly frightened to fully enjoy the demises of Liscum and Harris. As for Richmond, well, he wasn't really a bad fellow, just too straitlaced and too damned brave for his own good. The truth of the matter was, if he had survived, I'd have been finished in the army, so there was no point in mourning the poor bastard, was there?

Dawn was breaking by the time we reached the breach in the outer wall secured by the Japanese a short twenty-four hours earlier. We filed silently through and went into bivouac in a dry field beyond. In minutes most of the exhausted men were fast asleep.

But my nerves had been too frayed by my brush with death to allow me any shut-eye. As onerous as I found life in the army from time to time, I wasn't about to depart from it without a fight, by God. So I fished out my silver flask and took a great swallow. Feeling somewhat calmed, I went through the breach once more and sat down with my back against the wall to eye the brooding, silent bulk of the native city a half mile away.

46

"Mind if I join you, old man?" I looked up to see Ollivant standing over me.

"Not at all, Captain," I said. "It would be my pleasure. I'll drink with any man who saves my hide."

Ollivant hunkered down next to me, and I offered him my flask. He drank deeply. "Superb stuff! Smooth, yet with a powerful kick. Some sort of rye, perhaps?" he ventured.

"Nope," I said. "Sour-mash bourbon, the pride of Tennessee. Guaranteed to make a lion out of the most abject coward."

"Is that so? In that case, I'll take a wagon load for my lads!" he chuckled.

"Tell me, Ollivant, how long have you been in China?" I queried him.

"Oh, years and years," he answered vaguely. "Sometimes I forget the precise number."

I eyed the man as he sat beside me and relaxed with a great sigh. He was a powerful fellow, a little shorter than I, with the ruddy good looks of an English rustic. He sported a vigorous-looking handlebar mustache and impressive muttonchop whiskers that made him look older than he probably was. I pegged him as being in his midthirties, forty at the outside.

He gave me the impression of a man who had been around the block, but there was in him none of the haughty disdain for Americans so evident in the officers on Admiral Seymour's staff. I suspected that Ollivant, being as he was an officer in a colonial regiment, came from a lower stratum of society than those blue bloods.

"Whatever prompted you to come to the Orient in the first place?" I inquired.

Ollivant smiled with good grace; this was clearly a question he was accustomed to answering. "It was either here or India, and I can't stand curry," he replied. "It's damned hard to get a commission in one of the Queen's regiments, Travers, unless you've got a family name and a bloody fortune to keep up the necessary life-style. The colonial service was my only opportunity."

So I had been right about him, I thought. "Well, here's to you for saving our bacon out there tonight," I said, raising my flask and taking another sip. "I'm afraid that, left to our own devices, we'd have been done for in a few hours."

"It was nothing, Travers," replied Ollivant, abashed. "I'm sure that if the tables had been turned, you'd have done the same for me."

Not damned likely, I knew, but I smiled nonetheless.

Just then our exchange of compliments was interrupted by a great explosion that split the dawn from the direction of the native city.

"Holy Moses!" I exclaimed, leaping to my feet. "What the hell was that?"

"Look!" shouted Ollivant, pointing down the broad causeway that led to the inner palisade, where a crowd of figures could be seen by an immense gate, now battered and hanging off its hinges. "It's the Jappoes! They're pouring into the city! They must have run a mine under the main gate!"

Ollivant was right. In the glaring light of the fire ignited by the blast, I could see hundreds of tiny figures swarming into the gap in the city wall, and above them fluttered the Rising Sun banner of Japan.

"They've done it, by Jove!" whooped Ollivant excitedly. "The little blighters have taken the city!"

All around in the dull gray dawn the cry was taken up. Soldiers rolled out of their blankets, seized their arms, and, in groups and individually headed for the fray. "I say, this is going to be a much shorter campaign than I'd envisioned," mused Ollivant. "Shall we stroll over there, Travers, and see what the sons of Nippon have wrought?"

"Absolutely!" I agreed heartily, especially since from where I stood it looked as though the serious fighting was already done. We headed off down the wide causeway past the strewn wreckage of yesterday's battle. The heaps of dead Chinese and Japanese made me realize there was no love lost between those boys.

"Bloody good show," declared Ollivant approvingly when we reached the inner wall. "The Jappoes did a first-class job in blowing this gate."

"I'll say," I concurred, eyeing the blown portal. The blast had been quite clean and left the Chinese no chance to regather their wits and rally; evidently the little pieces of yellow paper so prized by the Boxers as talismans were no protection against engineering skills and modern explosives. "Those Jappoes certainly know how to take care of business, all right."

"Come along, Travers," called Ollivant merrily, heading into the now strangely silent native city. "No doubt there's a good time being had by all within."

"You're probably right," I replied, "and it seems that nobody wants to miss the party." I nodded at the steady stream of soldiery flowing past us into the breach. We had gone only a few blocks into the labyrinth of streets within before the reason for all the excitement became apparent.

Loot! Everywhere I looked, Europeans and Japanese were scrambling to gather up coins and rare vases, demolishing houses and callously abusing noncombatants in their search for hidden treasures. We stood aside as several burly Sikhs staggered past under the weight of burlap sacks crammed with plunder.

"I'd say these lads are determined to make this campaign pay for itself," grinned Ollivant, not at all taken aback by the mayhem unfolding around him.

"I can't say as I really blame them," I replied matter-of-factly. Up until then, I had simply assumed that my China tour would not be remunerative; that misconception was fast dying as I eyed the riches being harvested all around me.

We rounded a corner and came upon a huge building several stories in height. Flames were leaping from the windows on the upper floors, and scores of people were dashing in and out of its smoke-filled main portal.

"Whatever can be in there that's worth risking life and limb to loot?" I wondered aloud.

"Only a fortune in silver," came the casual reply.

"What?" I cried.

"My dear Travers," explained Ollivant, evidently amused by my lack of knowledge of all things Chinese, "yonder lies the Imperial Mint of Tientsin! It holds a king's ransom within its mighty walls."

I had to make a conscious effort not to run into the smoking mint right then and there. Gibbering Japanese ran past us clutching shoe-shaped ingots of pure silver and satchels filled with taels, the silver coins of Imperial China. Although I had to fight the urge to display my cupidity, Ollivant appeared able to take in this scene of great fortunes being made with seeming tranquility. Either he was a saint or a complete dolt!

"Aren't you the least bit interested in joining the fun, Ollivant?" I asked, half hoping he'd take offense and huff off to leave me free to stuff my pockets with gold and silver.

"Not at all!" he laughed. "In fact, I find the spectacle of these poor fellows scurrying off with what they think are their fortunes really quite pathetic."

"Pathetic? Are you crazy?" I asked, fighting to subdue the hysterical whine that creeps into my voice whenever I'm in the presence of easy money. "Those little monkeys are becoming millionaires before our very eyes!" As if to make my point, a squad of Japanese scurried by us lugging enough silver among them to buy an estate in Newport and a harem of white women with which to stock it.

"Calm down, chap," soothed Ollivant. "Those creatures aren't going to keep any of this booty."

"What the hell are you talking about?" I asked, totally confused.

"It's rather simple, Travers," he explained patiently. "Once those chaps get back to camp, their officers will turn the men out, shake them and their gear down, and confiscate every last ounce of silver. They will be forcibly reminded that they exist only to fulfil the will of their lords, and their lords will unquestionably desire that these lackeys hand over the proceeds of their night's work. So, you see, Travers, the loot from this mint will flow mainly into the coffers of the great families of Japan. As for the Sikhs we saw, never forget that they have British officers."

I got his point. Then I noticed that his gaze was wandering and I followed it toward the mint's portal. A gaggle of Chinese in khaki uniforms emerged from the smoky interior clutching coffers embla-zoned with official-looking seals, their haversacks stuffed to overflowing with silver ingots. I recognized these fellows instantly as hailing from the 1st Chinese Regiment, Ollivant's own outfit!

By the light of the flames I saw a broad smile crease Ollivant's rugged features. "And what about you, Captain?" I demanded. "Will your coolies turn over their loot to you?"

"Of course, old boy," he smiled. "And if they don't, I'll flog their yellow hides blood red. After all, one doesn't serve in a native regiment for Queen and country only, you know. Certain, er, perquisites are expected."

"So I see," I retorted sullenly, quite put out that no troopers from the 9th Infantry were on the scene so that I could introduce them to the pecking order attendant on such occasions.

"Of course, Travers," offered Ollivant, "the real reward for our many travails won't be had until we reach Peking."

"You mean there's another mint there?" I asked eagerly.

"Another mint?" roared Ollivant, launching into a paroxysm of howling laughter. Recovering, he explained, "My dear fellow, Peking is more than merely the capital of a nation. It's the seat of an empire! The wealth of many lands has been carried there and laid at the feet of the decadent Manchu rulers! Inside Peking is a separate city called the Tatar City. That is where the mandarins who rule this land reside. Inside the Tatar City is the Forbidden City, the home of the Dowager Empress herself and the repository of one of the most fabulous treasures the world has ever seen. When we take the Forbidden City, my friend, fortunes will be made in minutes. Why, it'll be like having the keys to Buckingham Palace in the palm of your hand with all the Beefeaters away on holiday!

"A fortune, you say?" I breathed raptly, almost mesmerized by Ollivant's description of the treasure that awaited us in Peking.

"Yes, indeed, lad," Ollivant assured me. "Gold and silver by the wagon load. Furs from the wilds of Manchuria and pearls from the Japanese Sea. Why, the very etchings on the walls of those treasure chambers are worth more than either of us could hope to earn in a lifetime."

"Fascinating," I drooled, my spirits soaring at the prospect, but then they sank as reality hit me. This situation was all well and good for the likes of Ollivant, who had a regiment of little yellow beggars at his beck and call to do his plundering for him. I, in contrast, had nothing but my own two hands. Moreover, I was an American officer, and from what I knew of General Chaffee, I suspected that he would not take kindly to a member of his command systematically looting conquered Chinese cities.

Then I got a grip on myself; I decided that morose pining over life's inequities wouldn't do. It would take a bit of doing to find a way around these obstacles, but I was confident that a grasping mind like mine would do exactly that!

"Shall we call it a night, Travers?" suggested Ollivant.

"Yes, I believe so," I answered, truly exhausted. But as we turned and made our way back to our respective bivouacs, I could think of nothing but the fabulous treasures awaiting me in the Forbidden City!

47

"Ho! Longbottom," I called. "Aren't you a sight for sore eyes!"

"And you, Travers," replied Longbottom, studying me coolly for any signs of obvious damage. "After all, I haven't seen you since the night we spent together in the paddies outside of Tientsin."

Around us, the allied army, now eighteen thousand men strong, was finally on the road to Peking, hot on the heels of the defeated Boxers who had fled Tientsin in tatters only days before. The majesty of our array was beyond description; there were regiments of Sikhs from India's Punjab, squat little Gurkhas from the foothills of the mystical Himalayas, proud Bengal lancers, arrogant Italian Bersaglieri with raven-plumed pith helmets, British Royal Marines, and French fusiliers marins. But these boys weren't just for show; no, indeed, General Gasalee was driving his forces hard, trying to keep the enemy from rallying and turning on us before we reached the beleaguered legations in Peking.

I reined in my mount beside the dust-covered column of the 9th Infantry to chat a moment. "You mean the night you tried to strand me alone with the Boxers, Longbottom?" I prodded dryly.

Longbottom eyed me angrily at this but said nothing; he knew I was onto his game. What made it all the sweeter was the fact that after he'd left me on that terrible night, he'd wandered about in circles for hours and was finally rescued from the paddies at dawn by two Japanese privates, who'd had to carry him back to camp on a litter because he was so exhausted from his exertions. I, on the other hand, was applauded as the fellow who ran off the Boxers so that we could be reached by Ollivant's relief column.

Controlling his anger at my good fortune, Longbottom demanded stiffly, "Just where have you been keeping yourself, Travers? You're a member of the 9th, and last I heard, you were assigned to this company. I've a mind to talk to Major Lee about your unexplained absence over the last few days."

"Oh, that's all been changed, friend," I explained breezily. "I spoke to Major Lee and he agrees that it's time I got back to my legation duties. I'm working very closely with General Gasalee and his staff now. All very sensitive matters, of course."

Longbottom glowered anew at this, but from his silence I knew he suspected that what I said was the plain truth. And it was, for you see, after having been shanghaied by Liscum and bullied about by Harris, I simply couldn't bear the thought of laboring in A Company under Longbottom, who had been breveted to captain after Tientsin. So I had nagged Major Lee to release me, and after a day or two of indecision, he'd done so.

Ostensibly, I was released to allow me to return to weightier affairs of diplomacy, but in reality I had simply gotten the old heave-ho from Major Lee, who, despite his years of professional education and training, had the heart of a fishwife. You see, he viewed me as a jinx and the source of the bad medicine that had plagued the regiment ever since Liscum had pressed me into the ranks back in the foreign settlement. There was no arguing the fact that since I'd marched under the 9th's banner, one man in every ten had become a casualty, and Liscum, that hitherto indestructible war-horse, was dead and in his grave. With a record like that, it had not been overly difficult to convince Major Lee to set me free. On the other hand, he viewed me as a genuine hero, the man who'd pulled Seymour's chestnuts out of the fire at Hsiku Arsenal and the fellow who had come upon Captain Ollivant that pitch-black night when the 9th had been threatened with annihilation by the Boxers. To Lee, then, I was a bit like a Greek god: I was to be admired, but from afar if at all possible.

"Tell me, Longbottom," I asked, more amiably this time and changing the subject somewhat, "has the regiment seen any action since it's been on the road?"

"A spot or two," answered Longbottom. "The Boxers have been digging great ditches across the route of our advance, forcing us to deploy for an assault, only to see them scamper off again. It's been time-consuming, but the action hasn't been too terribly hot."

"Oh, I wouldn't imagine it would be," I laughed heartily. "After the what-for we gave them in the native city, it will be a long time before these heathens ever attempt to stand against white men in a test of cold steel, eh, Longbottom?"

Longbottom's eyes danced with rage; was this the same mewling Travers who had been so petrified of being hacked to death by Boxers on that terrible night only days before? It was almost more than one man could stand, and he had to visibly struggle for control before my cocksure facade. "I suppose so, Travers," was all he could rasp in reply.

"That's the spirit of the 9th, Longbottom!" I trumpeted inanely. "God, wouldn't poor Liscum be proud of us today? God rest his soul, eh?"

"Amen," hissed Longbottom, not trusting himself to a wordier reply.

By then it was clear even to me that Longbottom had had quite enough of my scintillating company. "Well, I must be getting along now, partner," I smiled, gathering my reins. I patted my saddlebags, which were stuffed with hardtack and bottles of potent Chinese wine. "Urgent dispatches, you know. The general can't wait long for these." I tugged the brim of my campaign hat down over my brow in farewell, and put spurs to my mount. As I thundered past the ranks I waved my hat and called, "Give the little bastards hell, boys!" A thunderous cheer from a hundred parched throats saw me off as I left Longbottom fuming in my dust.

And the dust was quite serious that summer, you see, for campaigning in August in North China is no picnic. If the rains are sparse, as they were in 1900, the soil turns to dust and the dry wind fills the air with gritty particles that scour the eyes and clog gun bolts. This, coupled with the searing heat that blew in from Mongolia, turned what should have been a rather ordinary march into an ordeal that seemed akin to walking through a sandstorm inside a steel foundry. Although we'd been marching only a few days, the heat and the brutal pace had many of the troops staggered. Nonetheless, they slogged doggedly northward, following the incessant beat of infantry drums and the staccato notes of cavalry bugles.

But the travails of the common troopers meant little to me, of course. As a staffer once more, I wasn't expected to fight in any of the nasty little brawls we encountered en route to Peking. Moreover, since I had access to a splendid mount, I thought nothing of galloping down to the Pei Ho for a refreshing dip whenever I became overheated. It was to the river I was headed at this very instant as I guided my mount off the main track and down a brush-covered bank toward the high bamboo stands that marked the course of the river. I was quite alone and eagerly anticipating the welcoming coolness of the water when who should I see canter into sight but Von Arnhem!

"Travers!" he called. "I see that you have mended well!"

I trotted over to him and reined in. "That I have, Von Arnhem," I answered. "Running about like a jackrabbit, I am. But what of you? I can't say that I've seen very much of you in the past several weeks. Not since Hsiku Arsenal, in fact."

"That is true. But, I have my own business to attend to."

"Of course, friend, of course," I smiled. But what business could that be? I wondered. The Prussian hadn't volunteered for General Gasalee's staff, nor had he been asked to do so. Most of the officers on the staff—especially the French—avoided Von Arnhem like the plague and spoke his name only in low whispers. What was more, although the German contingent in Gasalee's expedition was commanded by a colonel, that officer made no attempt to rope in this mere *Hauptman*, as Liscum had done to me. It was all mighty strange, I can assure you.

"I stopped by the Hoovers' to see you after the arsenal ride, Travers. I was concerned for your health," he said unconvincingly, and added with a strange titter, "Life is so tenuous in the Orient."

"That was very kind of you," I retorted guardedly, thinking all the while that life had indeed become tenuous for the poor cossack Von Arnhem had batted from his mount and left as bait for those wild Kansu Muslim riders.

But Von Arnhem suddenly wasn't listening to me. Instead, he cocked an ear toward the undergrowth by the river and hissed, "Shhhh! Do you hear that?"

I stilled my mount. "I didn't hear a thing," I replied nervously.

"There it is again," insisted Von Arnhem. I strained my ears, but all I heard was a flock of water birds calling softly from the Pei Ho.

"There they are!" announced Von Arnhem suddenly.

"There is who?" I demanded with exasperation, when suddenly a small squadron of lancers clad in sky blue robes burst out of a bamboo thicket.

"Don't move, Travers!" warned Von Arnhem.

Was he mad? thought I. Those were imperial cavalry, by God! It was the Glorified Tigers, Prince Tuan's personal guard! He had pointed them out to me himself a month ago when they'd confronted Admiral Seymour's column at the bridge at Yang T'sun. My hand stealthily slipped to the Colt at my side.

"Touch that revolver and we are both dead!" Von Arnhem warned under his breath, his eyes on the approaching riders. Just as stealthily, my trembling hand slid away again.

"For God's sake, man," I pleaded in a feverish whisper, "let's make a run for it! The column's only a hundred yards away. We can make it!"

"Relax, Travers. Leave this to me," soothed Von Arnhem. He looked alert but not unduly alarmed at our predicament. Had he been unhinged from the strain of our Hsiku Arsenal ride? I wondered frantically. But all hope of flight was gone; the lancers were upon us. To my astonishment, however, instead of running us through right then and there, they motioned us to go toward the thicket from which they had just emerged. Without the slightest hesitation, Von Arnhem spurred off as ordered. Not wanting to be left behind in the dubious company of the Glorified Tigers, I hurried after him. Once in the shadows of the bamboo thicket, Von Arnhem dismounted.

"Get down, Travers," he ordered. "You are about to meet royalty."

"What?" was all I could manage before a blow from a lance staff across my shoulders sent me tumbling to the ground. No sooner did I stagger to my feet dazed than another company of Glorified Tigers materialized from the shadows. At their head, clad in an iridescent gold robe and mounted on a magnificent ebony charger, was Prince Tuan himself!

"Prince!" breathed Von Arnhem with a deep bow.

The Glorified Tiger who had unhorsed me motioned for me to make obeisance, too, and I hurriedly bobbed my head like a coolie before the emperor. I would have gotten on my knees and eaten dirt if I thought it would convince the little heathens to set me free, I'll readily admit. But a simple bow was all they wanted; then Von Arnhem got down to business.

"This is an American, Excellency," announced Von Arnhem, motioning to me. "Travers, this is Prince Tuan, crown prince of the Chinese Empire!"

Under the circumstances, I felt obliged to acknowledge the immensity of the privilege being accorded me by being admitted to such august company, but all I could do was croak "Hello."

Prince Tuan gazed at me impassively, much like an entomologist studying some rare beetle that had just blundered unknowingly into his laboratory. And I studied him right back; a young fellow, he was, with the shiny obsidian eyes of a true killer. His face was rouged, I was startled to see, and he sported a wispy little mustache that I guessed to be the height of fashion in these parts. I noticed the nails of his bejeweled fingers were fully four inches long, giving him an unreal and sinister appearance. Then the apparition spoke. "Your general appears to be on his way to complete victory," he said to Von Arnhem in flawless English. I was amazed; the little bastard was civilized after all!

Von Arnhem bobbed his head in agreement. *"Ja,* the Boxers are finished."

Prince Tuan remained silent, his lizard eyes flicking from Von Arnhem to me and back. "Then we must treat with the conquerors," he announced flatly.

Von Arnhem promptly agreed. "That is so. These Boxers, they move much too quickly. They give no thought to their actions."

Again Prince Tuan was silent. He moved not a muscle, but instead sat his mount, eyeing us both coldly. The silence was deafening; I had to forcibly remind myself that this was real and that I was not dreaming. Then Prince Tuan stirred and a hard look passed across his face. "I go now, *Hauptman.* The next time we meet," he announced potently, "it will be in Peking."

With that he wheeled his mount, and the bamboo thicket closed about him like a curtain. In an instant his escort of lancers thundered off and Von Arnhem and I were alone once more.

"Let us go, Travers," called Von Arnhem nonchalantly. "We don't want to be found by the Boxers all alone so far from the column."

Spooked by what had transpired, I leapt into the saddle. Although the idea of safety in numbers was quite appealing, my still-reeling mind demanded answers. When it found none I turned to the Prussian sphinx galloping alongside me.

"I don't understand what happened back there, Von Arnhem. I thought the imperial government had thrown in with the Boxers, for God's sake, but there you were having a pow-wow with a Chinese crown prince as thought it were something one did every day of the week.

Damnit, this is all highly irregular, I tell you! And what's more, just whose side is this Prince Tuan fellow on?"

Von Arnhem smiled broadly as he rode. "Prince Tuan is on the side of Prince Tuan," he offered enigmatically. "To him, the Boxers are like the locusts; they are a force of nature. You never learn to like them, but you learn to live with them."

"Just what the hell does that mean?" I demanded peevishly. The last thing I needed at the moment was another goddamned riddle. There was something sinister going on, and for my money, Von Arnhem was in the middle of it right up to his stiff neck!

But Von Arnhem wasn't of a mind to enlighten me further. He merely spurred his mount to greater speed and galloped off like a Ulan at the charge. I spurred my horse on to keep pace, thirsting for some meaningful answers.

"Damn you, Von Arnhem!" I shouted after him. "Doesn't it even bother you to be collaborating with the damned enemy like that?"

But Von Arnhem was finished making conversation. He leaned forward over the neck of his mount and pulled away from me, try as I might to lash my horse to greater speed. "Good-bye, Travers!" he called merrily as he pounded away to the rear of the great column of troops that was once more visible before us.

Disgusted, I reined in and slowed my mount to a trot. I was furious with Von Arnhem; I'd been used somehow, but for the life of me I couldn't figure out how. What was the purpose of the meeting I'd just "happened" to witness? And where did Von Arnhem's true loyalties lie? I knew that my interest lay in keeping my miserable hide in one piece, but I suspected that the Prussian was playing a game on a much larger board and for much greater stakes. I had to put all this into some kind of order. If I were a good soldier, of course, I would report all these shenanigans to the proper authorities at once. But then again, I'm not a model soldier, and treating with the enemy doesn't particularly offend me as long as I'm not endangered in the process.

Still I was troubled: Why had the normally inscrutable Von Arnhem allowed me to view this spectacle in the first place? Surely he realized he was in peril if I were to report his liaison with the foe. Then I saw the villain's ploy: Von Arnhem, sly fox that he was, knew that a meeting with Prince Tuan in broad daylight was so improbable that even if he misjudged me and I reported it, nobody in a position of responsibility would believe me. And he was right, by God. Why, I'd seen it, and I could hardly believe my eyes! No, I had to keep my mouth shut now or be thought a complete loon. I turned the problem around in my mind and viewed it from every possible angle, and by the time I'd rejoined the column, my mind was made up. I'd keep silent for the time being— at least until I determined how to turn all of this to my advantage.

48

The allied army moved irresistibly northward like a shadow on the land. We reached Yang T'sun, the site of Admiral Seymour's embarrassment, and, after some desultory long-range skirmishing, brushed aside the few Boxers barring our way across the railroad bridge. It was by then common knowledge among the Boxers that their little pieces of yellow paper wouldn't stop the bullets of the foreign devils, and they tended to run off as soon as a few well-placed rounds fell anywhere near their vicinity. The ferocity they had displayed at Tientsin was gone, a development that went a long way toward bolstering my cautious spirit. I mustered the élan to boldly gallop forward to the enemy's entrenchments, secure in the knowledge that the mere appearance of a Westerner at that point was enough to cause any group of Boxers to bolt. Ah, war can be fine sport when you're facing an enemy who knows he's beaten!

It was not just I who had the bit in his teeth: The whole army sensed that the game was about up for the heathen Chinese, and every man redoubled his pace toward Peking. The Jappoes were in the van of the column, less from any formal march order directed by General Gasalee than from an ardent desire in their yellow breasts not to be outdone by their Caucasian allies. This direct challenge was answered by the Russians, who'd taken a visceral dislike to the Jappoes. As a result of this rivalry, reveille on the march resembled the start of a collegiate footrace; Ruskies and Jappoes would tumble out of their blankets to the beat of the morning drumroll and hit the trail more asleep than awake. Often in the course of a day's march, the two contingents would roughly jostle each other aside, straining to make the other eat its dust. At such moments broad Slavic curses would fill the air only to be met with jeers from the squinty-eyed sons of Nippon.

But for the fact that we'd need all the rifles we could muster to storm
Peking, I could have cared less if the lot of them ran each other through
and died in droves in the dust of the road. My sole concern was pressing
forward with all possible speed, hoping fervently that Ollivant was
right and that the treasures of the Forbidden City would make the spoils
of Tientsin look like a beggar's cache.

On August 14 we arrived before the very walls of Peking itself. To
my disappointment there was nothing about the appearance of the place
from the outside to suggest that within lay the treasures of the ages.
I was fairly bursting with eagerness to storm the ramparts before the
Dowager Empress and her lackeys slipped out the back door with the
family silver, so to speak. But to my consternation, nothing of consequence happened that first day, other than the killing of all the Chinese hapless enough to be caught outside the walls. That night I slept
barely a wink, for my mind swam with visions of treasure. I'd be rich
on the morrow, or at least comfortably well off, I told myself, and I
prayed for the sun to rise so that I could set about the first major heist
of my life.

I was up at dawn and stamping about impatiently. It seemed to take
forever to get the groggy soldiers on their feet and into their ranks
for the assault. General Gasalee had assigned each allied contingent
a different gate of the Tatar City to storm. The plan, you see, called
for each contingent to seize its assigned gate, then to drive for the Imperial
City. Once there, we were to relieve the Legation Quarter, which abutted
the Imperial City, and finally drive to the inner sanctuary, that holiest of holies—the Forbidden City itself. By Jesus, I told myself, it would
be a payday that none in this army would soon forget!

Not quite certain where to place myself for maximum advantage
during the big attack, I decided finally to attach myself to the American contingent commanded by Maj. Gen. Adna Chaffee. Chaffee, a
square-chinned veteran of the Indian wars and the Cuban and Philippine campaigns, thought little of the Chinese and even less of our allies.
Besides the 9th Infantry, Chaffee had at his disposal the 14th Infantry, the 5th Artillery, and several marine battalions. I cantered up to
where he was gathered with his staff and several regimental commanders.
General Chaffee had his field glasses trained on his objective—the Tung
Pien Men gate—and the Tatar City beyond.

Major Lee at his side saw me coming. "Ah, Travers," Lee greeted
me, "there'll be fighting aplenty soon. No doubt you're quite up to it!"

"Well, that's why we're here," I replied cheerily.

"Travers?" growled Chaffee, putting up his glasses. "*The* Lieutenant Travers?"

His tone was cutting and gruff. Instantly I was on my guard; was he on to me? Had there been more eyes about than I realized when Prince Tuan trotted out of the brush back on the Pei Ho?

"Yes, sir," I managed to squeak. "I'm Lieutenant Travers."

"The hero of Hsiku Arsenal, sir!" added Major Lee, beaming.

"I've been told you acquitted yourself with great gallantry before the walls of Tientsin as well, young man," said Chaffee.

I silently heaved a sigh of relief and said the first silly thing that popped into my head. "Sir, you honor me, but it's nothing more than any man here would have done under the same circumstances."

A muted chorus of approval went up from the assembled officers, but Chaffee merely squinted and fixed me with a penetrating gaze. I immediately sensed that here was a man who could tell horseshit from honey and that I'd better not try to play the role of the abashed Horatio too strongly.

Others were not quite so discerning. "He's a marvel, sir," burbled Major Lee. "To hear him talk, saving the lives of hundreds of men is as easy as falling off a log. I wish there were more like him."

"I think I get your drift, Major," retorted General Chaffee curtly. Taking the none-too-subtle hint, Major Lee fell silent and drew his horse apart. Eyeing me squarely, General Chaffee intoned, "Travers, I've mentioned you in dispatches to the War Department. If you don't get killed, you might have a future."

That was clearly about as effusive as Chaffee was going to get, so I stammered awkwardly in reply, "Yes, sir, thank you."

Chaffee turned from me to study the city wall once more, and the interview was clearly over. "Where's that signal that General Gasalee promised us?" he demanded of a nearby aide.

"It should be coming at any moment, General," this worthy assured Chaffee.

Just then a cannon shot split the dawn stillness from somewhere to the rear. "Is that the signal?" demanded Chaffee.

"Er, I don't think so, sir," replied the aide, visibly flustered. "The British said the signal would be communicated by semaphore flags, not with cannons. I don't know what that shot was all about."

The mystery was instantly clarified when before our astounded eyes a thick column of Russian infantry in white tunics thundered past us headed right for the Tung Pien Men!

"Where do those Ruskie bastards think they're going? That's our goddamned gate!" bellowed Chaffee furiously. "Captain Riley!" he sang out.

Captain Riley, a renowned artillerist of long service whose battery was laid to cover the gate to our front and the walls to either side of it, spoke right up. "Sir?"

"Riley, train your guns on those Russians!" ordered General Chaffee. "Blow them the hell out of our way."

Major Lee turned ashen. "You can't do that, sir!" he squeaked. "They're on our side!"

"They may be on our side," fumed Chaffee, "but I'm not on their side. Captain Riley, do as I say. Blow those vermin back to Siberia!"

"Yes, sir!" snapped Riley smartly and was about to ride off to execute Chaffee's order when I cried out in further amazement.

"By God, here come the Jappoes!"

"What?" sputtered Chaffee. As he turned, a full regiment of howling Japanese ran by under banners of white emblazoned with the red orb of the Rising Sun, heading pell-mell for the Russians straight ahead.

"What the hell's going on here?" demanded Chaffee.

The situation was quite evident to me, so I piped up. "The Nips refuse to let the Ruskies get the better of them, sir," I explained hastily. "They're determined to better the white man even if they all get killed in the process."

"Riley!" roared Chaffee. "Blow those damned Nips away with the Russians! Nobody steals my damned gate and gets away with it!"

But Riley was stayed once more as Col. Aaron Dagett, commander of the 14th Infantry, cantered up to General Chaffee.

"Aaron!" cried Chaffee. "Get back to your regiment. I'm having Riley's battery clear away that rabble and then I'm sending in your regiment!"

"Paatooee!" responded Dagett, sending a huge wad of tobacco arcing to the ground. Then he doffed his slouch hat and scratched his pate. "That'll never work now, Gen'l," he observed with a deep Southern drawl. "The Chinee are all over those Jap 'n' Ruskie fellers like ticks on a hound. If'n we go in, they'll slice us up, too."

Dagett was right. From where I sat, the sounds of fighting coming from the wall were fierce—and the Chinese were more than holding their own.

"Better jus' forget 'bout attackin' that gate, Gen'l. It'll be a full day's work fer those danged fools t' fight through that hornet's nest," Dagett suggested, pointing to the mass of soldiery struggling for their lives before our eyes.

A hellacious fight it was, mark my words, what with men laying about themselves with cold steel and the devil take the hindmost. All for the sake of nothing more tangible than national pride, whatever the hell that was. As best I was able to learn afterward, the Russians had vowed to themselves to be the first over the Tatar Wall. So before dawn they stealthily crept to within striking distance of what they thought was their proper objective—the Tung Chih Men—which was actually across the Imperial Canal from where the American assault was to go in. The Russians planned to launch their attack before Gasalee gave his signal for a general assault, but in the faint light of dawn they got totally misdirected; without any artillery support whatsoever, they charged headlong at the Tung Pien Men—the American objective. There they were promptly taken under fire by determined Chinese imperial troops. The Jappoes, getting wind of all this, were determined not to be bested by the despised Russians. So they quickly headed for the Tung Pien Men as well, although General Gasalee had assigned them a different gate, the Ch'i Hua Men, to storm. In minutes the Jappoes and Ruskies were fiercely engaged; before it was all over, several hundred of the hotheads were dead, and all for naught.

"Damn!" swore Chaffee, acknowledging Colonel Dagett's eminent good sense. After a moment's inner struggle, he growled, "What do you suggest, Aaron?"

"We ought'a sidle a little to the left o' the gate. Right about thar'," Dagett opined, pointing to a quiet spot on the wall of the Tatar City to our left front. "We might be able t' slip in without too much of a fight if'n we move out smartly."

Chaffee mulled the idea over and then nodded. "All right, do it."

Twenty minutes later I was dismounted and standing before the ranks of the 14th at Colonel Dagett's side. Before me loomed the towering wall of the Tatar City. I could see the now-familiar dragon-toothed flags of the imperial banner men hanging limply from the ramparts. The Chinese knew we were coming, you could bet on that, and the little heathens were probably sharpening their wicked fighting swords and praying to their ancestors. Ordinarily, such a thought would have paralyzed me with fear and sent me packing to the rear with a sudden attack of "battle dysentery." But this fight was different: It was business, plain and simple!

"Let's go, boys!" called out Colonel Dagett. "F'ward, ho!" he ordered,

his saber flashing above his head. The 14th gave a cheer and went
forward, the solid blue ranks rushing to the foot of the Tatar Wall,
sweeping me along with them. At any moment I expected the stinging
crash of musketry from above, but strangely none came. The sound
of furious volleys could be heard to our right as the Russians and
Jappoes fought for their lives, but from above us there was only silence.

In the shadow of the wall, I cried to Dagett, "I don't know why
the Chinese haven't already spotted us, but they're sure to any minute
now. We can't stay down here like this too long!"

"Yer right, Lieutenant," replied Colonel Dagett calmly. Turning to
the troopers huddled tensely behind him, he asked quietly: "I need a
volunteer t' climb this heah wall. Who'll go?"

I expected dead silence to meet this request for a suicide mission,
but to my surprise a voice piped right up. "I think I can do it, sir!"

I turned to see the regimental bugler, a mere stripling, standing tall
under his colonel's gaze. He's loco, I thought.

"What's your name, son?" asked Colonel Dagett quietly.

"Titus, sir! Calvin Titus!"

Dagett looked down at the ground a second, no doubt certain he
was sending the lad to his death. Then he looked up. "Okay, Titus.
Up you go."

The slender bugler nodded calmly, and without further ado went up
the thirty-foot wall with the innate climbing skill of a mountain goat.
The ancient rampart had buckled over the centuries since its construction, and numerous fissures and cracks offered purchase for a determined climber. Once atop the wall, Titus stood and calmly gazed about.
Miraculously, he was not instantly killed.

"Come on up!" he hollered jubilantly. "There's nobody here!"

"They must'a lit out!" exclaimed Colonel Dagett.

That was all I needed to hear. "Out of my way!" I bellowed, and
in a heartbeat I was clambering up after the nimble bugler, dozens of
troopers right on my heels. I quickly reached the top and sprawled
flat on the wide, smooth surface of the parapet, fearful of lurking
Chinese snipers. As I lay there getting my bearings, the top of the wall
became crowded with milling troopers as the 14th flowed up the wall
behind me.

From my vantage point, I studied the city beyond. Immediately
below me was the Tatar City, an incredibly dense collection of hovels
cut by meandering streets. Of more immediate concern, however, was

a knot of imperial troops who had suddenly appeared on the wall not a hundred yards away. Several of them had *jingals* and were laboriously bringing them to bear in our general direction.

"Let 'em have it, boys!" ordered Colonel Dagett, who had been manhandled up the wall by his loyal men. Their Krags began to spit lead, knocking over the Chinamen like pins on a bowling green.

Now was the time, I realized; the empress's wealth would wait no more. "Up and at 'em, boys!" I cried, drawing my Colt and my saber and sprinting after the fleeing foe. With a rumbling huzzah, the 14th pounded after me down the parapet to where the surviving Chinese had disappeared. There we discovered massive stone steps leading to the city below. In seconds we were in the deserted streets, rushing as quickly as we could for the Imperial City. Behind us I heard a rousing cheer erupt as the Russians finally forced the Tung Pien Men and stormed into the Tatar City to join us. It was over; the Chinese were on the run everywhere!

49

As we ran down the twisting streets I caught sight from time to time of panicked defenders, and I fired a shot or two to hurry them on their way. They scattered like chickens before marauding foxes. "Run, you beggars!" I laughed, feeling in fine fettle, drawing my saber to give the few laggards the flat of it across their backs. All around me was the sound of battle and tumult; clearly the entire wall was in our hands, which meant that not only the Russians but also the rest of General Gasalee's army was pouring into the city.

Giddy with exertion, and literally licking my lips in anticipation of the rewards yet to come, I pushed down smoke-blackened streets, for fires were by then burning as both Chinese and Westerners gave themselves over to arson and pillage. Suddenly I rounded a corner and found myself confronted by six yellow-turbaned cutthroats!

These buckos stood their ground, not the least bit frightened of me. I instantly recognized them; they weren't craven Chinese; they were *Ten nai*, Manchu Tiger Men, in their characteristic black-and-yellow–striped tunics. These were the same fanatical fellows who'd held the railroad bridge over the Pei Ho at Yang T'sun in the face of Admiral

Seymour's artillery. I knew immediately that I was facing some rough customers.

I turned to order a volley poured into the bastards—but to my horror discovered that there was no one behind me! In the excitement of the chase, I had become separated from the regiment. There was nothing to do but brazen it out, so I brandished my saber and growled fiercely, "Be off, you vermin!" I stamped my foot for emphasis as though I were confronting a pack of mongrels rather than a group of trained fighting men.

The *Ten nai* were unimpressed. "Yeee-ahhh!" screeched the leader, or *Shih chang,* swiping at my head with a gleaming scimitar. I was barely able to deflect the blow with my saber.

"Get back, you brutes!" I screamed in desperation, leveling my Colt in their faces. They froze but didn't run. "Be off, damn you!" I bellowed, squeezing the trigger. The Colt roared and the *Shih chang* toppled dead in the street. The remaining *Cheng ping* (common soldiers) looked at him, then at me, and then closed in, blood in their eyes. I pulled the trigger again. The hammer fell with a click. The Colt was empty— I'd fired all six chambers! Damning myself for a fool for not keeping track of my shots, I threw the useless Colt at the Tiger Men and scampered off the way I'd come just as a dagger sailed over my head and clunked uselessly against a wall.

Quick as wolves, the *Ten nai* were on my heels, screaming, "Kill! Kill!" In an instant it became clear that they were much fleeter of foot than I; in a straight race, they'd run me down in no time! I whirled in desperation and swiped at them with my saber.

"Get back, I'm warning you!" I cried, terrified, as though the beasts could understand me. The foremost of them, sensing my fear, bore straight in with his sword raised. Don't ask me where I got the fortitude, or why I didn't drop to the ground and roll about howling for mercy. Perhaps it was because I sensed there was no mercy to be found there. Whatever the reason, I lunged forward, burying my blade in his belly. He convulsed and fell, his dying body blocking the onrush of his fellows in the narrow alley, and a moment was all I needed.

Quick as a frightened stoat, I propelled myself through an open window, rolled to my feet, and ran through a tiny room and out into a garden in an open courtyard. Seeing no way out, and hearing the *Ten nai* crash through the window behind me, I hurled myself toward one of the courtyard's walls, leapt hard while kicking out, and barely managed to grasp the wall's top. Just as the first Tiger Man burst into the courtyard and began to whirl his deadly grappling hook over his head, I heaved for all I was worth, pulled myself over the wall, and dropped down the other side.

I hit the ground and fell flat on my back. Dazed, I looked up to see hundreds of French fusiliers marins and their Indochinese lackeys, the Tonkinese Tirailleurs, trotting by. The French and the Tonkinese had been conspicuous in the campaign thus far by their absence, content to let others give their blood for the cause. Lured by the scent of spoils, however, they were second to none in élan. With martial cries, they hurried forward toward the Forbidden City. In an instant I was on my feet and hurrying among them, not wanting to be left behind for the tender mercies of the *Ten nai*.

In minutes we were out of the Tatar City and into the Imperial City, whose gates had been only lightly defended by the demoralized Chinese. Before us loomed the smoking ruins of the Legation Quarter. The siege of Peking had been lifted, by God! Men, women, and children hailed us from the battered walls, many of them weeping and cheering at the same time. Other columns arrived at about the same time, for already I could see red-turbanned Sikhs and Welsh fusiliers. From behind the walls of the Legation Quarter we could hear praise being given to Jehovah for deliverance, although in my opinion those poor souls would have been better off offering praise to Messrs. Krag and Jorgensen— gentlemen who had a far more direct hand in their salvation.

In a very short time the Britons and the Americans were on the scene in strength and set about the task of giving aid and comfort to the survivors. The Frogs, however, looked to their leader for guidance. This officer, a slick little dandy of a *commandant* (major), with heavy lids and a great Gallic mustache, who looked more like a Tenderloin pimp than a military man, had eyes not for the ruined legations, but instead for the as-yet-untouched walls of the Forbidden City. He wrestled with his humanitarian principles for a second or two; being poorly developed, however, these quickly yielded to his well-honed instincts for larceny. He turned toward his expectant troops, drew himself erect, and pointed at the nearest gate to the Forbidden City with his saber. "Forward!" he shrilled.

Here's a bucko after my own heart, I knew instantly, leaping to join the French as they set to. There would be plenty of time later to dig widows and orphans out of the ruins; it was time to settle accounts with the heathen Chinese. The French surged toward the nearest gate to the Forbidden City and began to belabor it with a makeshift battering ram, but it quickly became apparent that strength alone would never budge that massive, iron-bound portal. Orders were barked out, and in moments a squad of tiny Tonkinese trotted forward pulling a wheeled pack howitzer. In the twinkling of an eye, they laid their piece, aimed it at the wall just to the side of the gate, slammed a shell into the breech, and yanked the lanyard.

The howitzer roared, and a great shower of dust erupted where the shell slammed into the wall. But when the dust settled, the results showed that the shell had gouged out only a tiny pockmark in the wall; there was no real damage. Undeterred, the Tonkinese reloaded and fired again. Quickly finding a rhythm, they soon commenced a lively tattoo that threatened to take the great wall apart brick by brick.

All the while, the French infantry were cheering and capering about with gold fever. I joined right in, giggling and dancing at the prospect of the orgy that was about to unfold. It seemed that the breach was only minutes away, and the Tonkinese still had plenty of ammunition. "Give 'em hell, you little bastards!" I cried to the gunners in encouragement. "One or two more shots should do the trick!"

So I thought; but at that very moment a phalanx of British staff officers galloped onto the scene and planted themselves between the howitzer and the wall. Hold on, I thought, what's all this? From where I stood, it looked as though the staffers were trying to dissuade the Frogs' leader from carrying out his assault! I shoved myself forward to better hear the exchange.

"I'm telling you, old boy," an elegant guards major was calmly explaining to the *commandant,* "General Gasalee has already decided the matter. No allied troops are to advance a step farther. You're to cease your attack this moment. Is that quite clear?"

I guess it was, for the Frenchman stamped his foot and swore, "*Merde!*" Then he ranted on about the sexual preferences of Englishmen in general and this major's mother in particular. Working himself into a paroxysm of fury, he turned toward the gunners and screamed, "Continue the attack!"

The howitzer roared in reply, narrowly missing the major, whose mount reared skittishly. This time, rather than merely raising a cloud of dust, the shell collapsed an entire section of the wall. As the dust and rubble settled, a silence fell over the scene as each man strained his eyes, hoping to catch a glimpse of the marvels that lay within. A puff of wind cleared the last of the dust from the air, and suddenly my eye caught a metallic glint. Could it be? Dare I hope? Yes, it was!

"Silver!" I cried hoarsely. "Why, there's a king's ransom in there!"

For a second, nobody seemed capable of movement. The English major, so commanding and self-possessed moments before, stared in gape-jawed amazement. Then the Frogs sprang into action.

"Soldiers!" cried the French *commandant,* "Quick! Carry the silver to our camp!"

At once the French and Tonkinese rushed into the breach. They quickly began stuffing silver ingots into their haversacks and scurrying off as ordered. Push as I might, however, the French made sure that I didn't get close enough to snatch as much as a single ingot. I did get close enough, however, to peer into the breach and realize that the Frogs had blasted their way into a royal mint! There had to be millions of dollars' worth of bullion in there!

The English major quickly recovered. "Get back, you damned papists!" he cried, laying about him with the flat of his sword as the French flowed past him with their silver. To the rear of all the excitement, the French *commandant* stood smirking, arms akimbo with a dreamy, faraway look in his eyes. Shades of Ollivant, I fumed. The little pipsqueak was seeing his pension being assured, while I couldn't scoop up so much as a plug nickel! I was so outraged at this injustice that I practically cheered when a battalion of Welsh fusiliers trotted up on the double to physically eject the French and Tonkinese from the Forbidden City.

"*Ce n'est pas possible!*" groaned the *commandant.* Then, bowing to the inevitable, he called off his minions.

I didn't see what the hell he was so put out about. After all, his troops had managed to haul off a small fortune before the Limeys had arrived to restore law and order. But what about poor Fenny? I lamented. I wasn't a penny richer than when this campaign had kicked off. What was so damned wrong with robbing the Chinese blind anyway? This was war, by God, and to the victor belonged the spoils! Didn't our oaf of a commanding general understand that basic principle? Or had he already made his fortune in other campaigns and no longer gave a tinker's damn for plunder?

Disgusted at our military hierarchy, I stormed off toward the United States legation to get an explanation for General Gasalee's sudden morality. I found my way to Legation Street, which ran down the center of Legation Quarter, passed over a much-disputed barricade that marked the entrance to the customs house, and was strolling past the French legation when I noticed a decidedly Western-looking building with a shot-torn sign dangling over the doorway that announced it as the Hotel de Pekin. From inside came the strains of laughter and a rollicking piano. Intrigued, I entered.

It took my eyes a moment to adjust to the shadows within, but soon I could make out a crowd of European officers gathered around the bar in the saloon. I saw Captain Ollivant, and *Hauptman* Von Arnhem, and a smattering of officers from what appeared to be every regiment in the allied army. A victory celebration was well under way.

"Travers!" cried Ollivant jovially upon spotting me. "Come join us, old chap!"

Putting my rage aside for the moment, I sauntered into the bar, forcing a smile to my scowling face. "My pleasure, Captain," I said with as much grace as I could manage. "I hope this establishment has some decent sour-mash whiskey."

"I'm afraid not, old boy," replied Ollivant. "You'll have to settle for something lighter." He thrust a glass of bubbly wine into my hand. "Drink up, lad, the war's over!"

I took a sip. "By God, that's champagne! And what's more, it's chilled! Where in heaven's name did you get this?" I cried.

"From the wine cellar, of course," replied Ollivant blithely. "The ice, however, is probably from Manchuria. The Boxers may be fanatics, but they do come from civilized stock. Seems they kept up ice deliveries right through the hostilities."

"Well then," I toasted, raising my glass, "here's to civilized stock!"

"Here, here!" seconded Ollivant, draining his glass, as did all those around him.

Even Von Arnhem raised his glass happily, and then continued a conversation he was having with a Japanese colonel at his side. I knocked back my glass with one gulp and wiped my mouth with the back of my sleeve. "Ollivant, what's all this about not entering the Forbidden City?" I asked. "Are we or are we not at war with these bastards?"

"Legally, no, Travers," he answered. "Moreover, it seems that things have gotten devilishly sticky of late. Now that we have the Boxers on the run, there's a new wrinkle in the game."

"How's that?" I demanded, pouring myself another glass of champagne.

Ollivant filled his own glass, swallowed a great draught, and continued. "It appears that the Dowager Empress has been in contact with General Gasalee. The old bitch wants to keep up the facade about her never throwing in with the Boxers. Wants Gasalee to play along with her story that the nasty Boxers held her and her entire court hostage while they rampaged across the countryside."

"Don't tell me that Gasalee is going to buy that line," I scoffed. "Even a British general can see that the hag was in on this donnybrook from the very start."

"I agree, Travers," replied Ollivant, unruffled, "but even an American general would see that it's better to go along with her charade than to offend her curious Chinese sense of etiquette, and perhaps thereby touch off partisan warfare that could last well into the next century. Why not simply pretend that she had nothing to do with this sordid affair and thereby wind up the campaign into a neat package?"

"I see," I said glumly, things becoming clearer to me by the moment. "And if she was not involved in all this unpleasantness, Gasalee has no right to plunder her imperial palaces since technically she was never a belligerent."

"Precisely, Travers," beamed Ollivant.

"Nonetheless," I grumbled, "it's a damned shame that those of us who've sweated and bled to relieve these blasted legations should go home with no more than a worthless medal or two for our troubles."

Ollivant chuckled genially at my penury. "But you've also got the thanks of your grateful nation."

"My grateful nation be damned!" I retorted.

"Buck up, lad," Ollivant consoled me, "there's plunder aplenty in the Outer City alone. Ming vases by the hundreds and silk screens fine enough to bring a pretty penny anywhere in Europe or America. They're fine works of art, those screens," he breathed rapturously, closing his eyes. "Why, I can almost see them. . . ."

I bet he could, I thought bitterly, for just then his entire regiment was out picking the streets bare for him. No wonder it was so easy for him to accept Gasalee's cordon around the Forbidden City with equanimity. I drained my second glass and poured a third. Damn, I thought, there had to be some way to turn a profit from this war!

"Travers," hailed Von Arnhem, leaving his Jappoe friends and wandering over to me. "You look so sad that the war is over."

"I am a bit down at the moment, now that you mention it," I admitted disconsolately. The irony didn't escape me; if someone had told me six months before that I would ever be sad to see a shooting war stop, I'd have wagered that would be the day that pigs grew wings and flew away.

"Never fear, my friend," chuckled Von Arnhem dryly, "there will be other wars. Mark my words." With that he finished his drink, belched, and staggered off into the street.

Cocky bastard, I thought, watching him go. Knowing him, he was probably well on his way to hatching those other wars. Piss on him, I decided, melancholy welling up in me. I grabbed another bottle of bubbly and started to do some serious drinking.

50

It was well after midnight when I awoke to find myself sprawled on the floor of the saloon, my tunic ripped and my head ringing. Around me lay a half-dozen equally besotted fools. Groggily I rose to my feet and looked about. Ollivant sat snoring on a barstool, his head lying on a platter of rice and vegetables. Von Arnhem was gone. I shook my head to clear the cobwebs enveloping my brain and stumbled out the door.

The street was completely silent, the allied troops being exhausted by the attack and their looting spree afterward. I straightened out my tunic, pulled on my hat, and set off to find something warm to eat and a safe place to sleep off my hangover. Then the thought hit me: Why not take advantage of the night's tranquillity to slip into the vaunted Forbidden City and have a little look-see? There might be a priceless necklace or two lying about that nobody would miss. Besides, there should be little risk of discovery by Gasalee's staff, since they too were probably exhausted from the day's rigors.

I deliberated a moment, weighing the odds of success against those of discovery. Moral principles had no role here, you can rest assured; they'd become an issue only in the event of discovery, in which case I would whine pathetically about remorse and my fervent wish to mend my larcenous ways and other such drivel. Sure, it was a two-faced attitude, but don't forget I had just spent the better part of two months dodging bullets fired by these wild-eyed Chinese and eating the dust of this incomprehensible land. For the life of me, I couldn't understand why, if it was permissible—nay, positively laudable—to send the little yellow vermin off to a reunion with the Great Buddha in the sky, we should then turn on a dime and quibble about the propriety of snatching a few trinkets from the imperial treasure rooms while we were about the task. I'd have no part in such hypocrisy, thank you! If I was fit to murder these damned heathens, I was fit to rob them as well!

I patted my holster, only to discover that it was empty; I'd thrown my Colt at those damnable *Ten nai*. I didn't care to go traipsing unarmed into the den of the head Manchu herself, so I slipped back into the Hotel de Pekin and relieved an unconscious Bersaglieri officer of his revolver. I checked the chambers to ensure that they were loaded and tucked the pistol into my holster. Then I was off.

I hugged the shadows like a professional thief, not daring to slip across a street until I peered up and down to ensure that the way was clear. Although I didn't care to be challenged by the provost marshal's guard, I was also not unmindful that recalcitrant Boxers and imperial troops might still be lurking in the city, hoping to slit the throat of any unwary foreign devil they might chance upon. I didn't see any Chinese, but I did see dozens of sleeping allied troops lying in the streets, many of them still clutching empty bottles of potent Chinese rice wine looted from the shops of the Tatar City.

In a short time I had made my way back to the breach blown in the wall of the Forbidden City by the French. I stood silently in the shadows searching the night for any hint of danger. At first it seemed that the breach was unguarded, but then in the shadows of a nearby alley I saw them: a corporal's guard of Britishers, no doubt posted to keep looters like me out of the breach. Their arms were stacked, and they were fast asleep to the last man! From my hiding spot, I could hear their snores in the night.

I waited several minutes to assure myself that they were truly asleep and not merely playing possum in hopes of catching an unwary looter. Then, with the stealth of a Mescalero, I padded across the street, careful to avoid the rubble strewn in my way. I lightly made my way over the pile of debris at the foot of the breach and entered the yawning chamber beyond.

My heart began pounding wildly, for all around me were stacks of silver ingots! The mere proximity to such wealth made me so giddy

that I had to stop and take several deep breaths to regain my equilibrium. I considered whether to simply snatch some ingots and be off.
It would be a modest gain at small risk. But true avarice was beginning to stir deep within me. Why content myself with a pittance when
a bit of nosing about might uncover plunder enough to put me on easy
street for the rest of my life?

The logic of my argument was unassailable, so I pushed on. I crossed
the darkened chamber of the imperial mint and found a door on the
far side of the room. Cautiously, I unlatched the door and pulled it
open a crack. I found myself peering into the inner courtyards and gardens
of the Forbidden City. All appeared quiet; in the moonlight I could
see broad avenues running in various directions, dividing the gardens
into separate parks.

I listened intently for some hint of ambush outside, but there was
none. I slipped out the door and scurried across a wide boulevard into
a dark grove of trees. Around me there were several imposing buildings. Clearly, I would not have time to search them all for plunder. I
thought a moment about how to proceed. The Dowager Empress, I
concluded, like any grandee I'd ever heard about, would probably want
to live in the most impressive house on the street, so to speak. So I
carefully eyed the monstrous edifices around me, wondering which
one was the nest of the queen bee.

My eyes settled on a palace a short distance away; it had pink walls
that glowed eerily in the moonlight and impressive crimson columns
that seemed to be carved of marble. Around it was a moat, and the
only means of entrance was a drawbridge, which luckily hadn't been
raised. If that's not the home of the Dowager Empress, I decided, then
I'll be a volunteer for a yellow-fever experiment. I hugged the shrub-
bery until I was near the moat, then paused to listen. Only the sounds
of crickets reached my ears, so I rose and quietly scampered across
the lowered drawbridge. Once inside the beckoning portal I paused
again, ready to hightail it for safety at the slightest hint of danger. By
that time my heart was pounding so wildly that I thought it would burst,
and my throat was so parched with fear that I couldn't have screamed
for help had the Manchus set upon me then and there. All told, I was
thoroughly shaken and on the verge of soiling my britches. My common sense screamed at me to flee, but my lust for easy riches impelled
me forward. Swallowing dryly and shaking like a leaf, I stepped into
the darkness within.

I tiptoed down a wide, marble-floored corridor. Set into the wall were ornate bronze holders for torches, which if lit would undoubtedly have brightened up the place like a horse show in New York's Madison Square Garden. The lack of glowing torches heartened me, however; it told me that the place was vacant and had probably been that way since before sunset. I slowly followed the corridor deeper into the recesses of the palace. At regular intervals I encountered smaller passageways intersecting the main corridor at right angles. I explored each of these lesser passageways in turn, finding empty chambers furnished with numerous sitting mats and low-slung tables. In this way I had soon explored the first floor and determined that it was quite empty. No riches were to be found here, for apparently this level was given over to meeting halls and council chambers. The living quarters, and the treasures that surely waited within those walls, must be on the upper levels.

I located a broad staircase with banisters of dark teak that spiraled upward to the next floor. I quietly ascended the stairs and recommenced my explorations. Things looked much more promising up there, for I immediately stumbled across some small anterooms that were so richly furnished they could only have been the chambers of retainers for some exalted personage. My instincts were fairly crying out that I was slowly closing in on the mother lode! With exquisite care I made my way down the central corridor until my way was blocked by massive double doors of solid bronze. The doors were fully ten feet high and were inscribed with Chinese characters and a hideous-looking dragon of inlaid jade and porcelain.

A dragon! I thought. Didn't Ollivant say that the Dowager Empress sat on the Dragon Throne? Of course, that was it, I'd found the old girl's chambers!

My hands shook uncontrollably as I pushed on the massive doors. To my surprise they swung open easily, no doubt crafted by master artisans to open at the touch of a female hand. Slipping past the doorway, I entered an even darker passageway. Apparently even the dim light of the moon, which filtered freely into the rest of the palace, did not reach into these dark recesses. Groping forward in the pitch blackness, I suddenly felt a heavy silk curtain across my path. I drew it aside and found myself on the threshold of a chamber dimly lit by a stand of incense-impregnated candles. It was the biggest room I had yet encountered!

In the middle of the chamber was a massive canopied bed, and strewn all about were exquisite furnishings and delicately painted silk screens.

On a mahogany table near the bed was a black lacquered chest about the size of a bread box. I went to it and raised its lid—and found myself staring at a collection of the largest rubies I had ever seen!

"Holy cow!" I gasped involuntarily, and then bit my tongue to silence it. I grasped handfuls of the glowing scarlet stones and thrust them deep into my pockets. Clearly, this was the place I had sought; this surely was the bedchamber of Tzu Hsi, the Dowager Empress!

On the far side of the chamber I saw sliding doors to what appeared to be closets lining an entire wall. I hurried over and slid open the doors. Inside were row after row of priceless furs—ermines, minks, sables. Why, the pelts in that closet alone were enough to make me wealthy for life, I thought ecstatically. I wanted to whoop at the top of my lungs, but contented myself instead with a little jig of glee.

It was time to get to work in earnest, I told myself. I studied the entire chamber anew; there wasn't much time, and I had to work as efficiently as possible. I would have to forgo the furs since they were too bulky and concentrate instead on items that were easily transportable. Accordingly, I set about opening every drawer in the place, and quickly turned up boxes of pearls from the Japanese Sea, fine emeralds, and incredible diamond brooches to go along with my newfound ruby collection. The exquisite vases and silk screens would have to stay, I decided sadly. Satisfied at last that I'd ransacked every square inch of the chamber, and with my pockets bulging with riches, I determined that it was time to leave.

It was then I heard the voice: "So, we meet again, Fenwi!"

Whirling about, I came face to face with Liu Chi, the Hoovers' serving wench! Only she was dressed in a fine silk robe, not the dreary black peasant's garb in which I had always seen her. Behind her stood two of the largest Chinamen I had yet seen. The giants stood with arms akimbo, silently eyeing me; clearly they were at Liu Chi's beck and call. In the flickering candlelight I could see that each wore a wicked-looking two-handed killing sword in his sash.

"Liu Chi," I stammered, forcing a smile to my face, "how good to see you again. I, er, that is, I meant to say good-bye back in Tientsin. I never had the chance to tell you how, er, much I enjoyed your cooking—"

"Silence!" Liu Chi commanded with a ring of authority in her voice that brought me up short. I noted with disquiet that she had dropped her affectation of Pidgin English; she apparently could speak English as well as that devil Prince Tuan! Things were looking more and more worrisome by the second.

Then Liu Chi barked out a command in her heathen tongue; before I could move, her two retainers sprang forward and seized me roughly by my arms. "Please, Liu Chi," I begged, fear rising high in my voice, "let me explain! I only laid hands on you to stop you from killing Fu Chou. It was nothing personal! Can't you see that?"

I was silenced by a stinging blow to the side of my head delivered by one of the giants. "If you are not silent, Fenwi," promised Liu Chi menacingly, "I will have your tongue removed like those of my eunuchs who are holding you. If you persist in being disrespectful you will only force me to make you more like my eunuchs than I had originally planned."

"Whaa . . . ?" I sputtered, only to be walloped across the head once more. What the hell did the bitch have in mind? I wondered fearfully.

Liu Chi began gibbering to her retainers rapidly now as a third eunuch appeared in the chamber. He was carrying a brazier filled with glowing coals, which he set down at his mistress's feet, and then bowed low. Liu Chi went to the brazier and withdrew a heated iron rod, grasping it by its wooden handle. The metal glowed a dull red in the dim light of the chamber. It was a branding iron, by God!

"It was most fortunate that you came to me, Fenwi. If you did not, of course, I would have arranged for your kidnapping. You see, ever since"—she paused here, her voice breaking a bit, but then she caught herself and continued as steely as before—"that day in Tientsin, I have kept you under observation."

I smiled wanly. "And I've thought of you often, too, my dear. It's clear that we've got a special magic between us—" Another thundering blow from a eunuch stilled my wildly wagging tongue.

"You must pay for your foul deed against me, Fenwi," she announced icily. "For not only did you shame Liu Chi on that day, but you also shamed the house of my esteemed husband, Prince Tuan."

My ears perked up at this. "Prince Tuan?" I cried. "You mean he and you are . . . ? I had no idea, you must believe me!" The little hellcat was a Manchu, by God, and a royal one at that! No wonder her feet were unbound; that was a torture inflicted on Chinese women, not Manchu gals! I damned myself for not immediately realizing that the first time I laid eyes on Liu Chi back in the Hoovers' kitchen.

Another robed figure suddenly glided into the chamber. The light fell upon his face, and I saw myself gazing into the obsidian eyes of Prince Tuan himself. At his side stood a wrinkled old crone in crimson robes emblazoned with the same dragon I'd seen on the doors to the chamber. It was Tzu Hsi, the Dowager Empress! Her ancient eyes held mine, and in them I saw a deep loathing for me and for all things Western. I sensed that next to her tender mercies, the cruel Prince Tuan would seem like a Vienna choirboy. There was no mistaking the fact that I was in deep, deep trouble, and the whole family was gathering around to see me off to the next world in proper style.

The Dowager Empress was not pleased to see me in her boudoir, for she turned and rounded on Prince Tuan something hellacious. He endured her tongue-lashing silently for a while and then barked something back at her that calmed the old girl right down. Her wizened visage broke into what I guessed was a smile and she rubbed her benailed claws together. I figured right then that Tuan had told her his plan for my imminent demise.

Then Prince Tuan spoke, and I knew I had guessed right. "Yes, Lieutenant, you had the great misfortune to select my number-one wife as an object of humiliation. I could have easily executed you back on the banks of the Pei Ho, but I spared your miserable life so that I could relish this moment."

"You don't understand!" I bleated hysterically. "This is all a mistake—" was all I could manage before the pommel of a sword cracked across the back of my head and drove me to my knees, sobbing.

"You will not speak again!" ordered Liu Chi. "You have disgraced my husband's royal house and caused his ancestors pain. I was in Tientsin to serve as the eyes and ears of my honored husband. I expected danger, but I did not expect to be treated with animal cruelty. Before you depart to your ancestors, Fenwi, you will experience some of the pain and humiliation you have inflicted on me."

At this she plunged the metal branding iron once more into the coals and rolled it about noisily. "You have branded me," she continued in an ominously detached voice, but with piercing eyes that caught mine and shriveled my worthless soul with terror. "Now I will brand you— in a manner involving the most excruciating pain! You will suffer as though the demons of the netherworld themselves possessed you!"

At this she again shrilled out an order to her eunuchs. They roughly hauled me over to the bed and tied me securely between the posts of the great canopy. It wasn't until one of them ripped my tunic down to my waist that the finality of what was about to befall me struck home! She planned to brand me as a vaquero would a steer and then kill me when she'd had her fun. After the way she'd finished poor Fu Chou, I had no doubt she'd relish personally pushing a blade into me.

"No, Liu Chi, for sweet Christ's sake!" I wailed. "You can't do this to me. Please, don't, I beg of you! It's, it's . . . unchristian!"

51

"Yes, it is very unchristian!" she laughed demonically. "But this revenge is very Chinese, I think you'll find."

My bonds were tightened, making escape impossible. From behind me came the awful sound of the heated branding iron being drawn through the coals once more before its final plunge home.

"After this torment," said Liu Chi, chuckling with diabolical glee, "you will hardly feel the cut of the blade when I personally send you into the next world!"

"No! Stop!" I howled, like a dog caught in a steel trap. "You can't do this! This is all a horrible mistake, I swear to God!"

Liu Chi stepped behind me and fiercely grasped one of my buttocks. "You are now mine, Fenwi! I will do with you as I please!"

You can believe me when I tell you I was praying then. Oh, Lordy, how I prayed. I called on Christ, his mother, his father, his brothers and sisters. I prayed to my guardian angel and any saint I'd heard of during my wasted youth. I promised God that if he would only transport me away from my fiendish captors immediately, I would forthwith commit myself to a monastery, take vows of chastity and poverty, and devote the rest of my miserable existence to silent contemplation. Oh, please Christ, save me, I prayed. I'll mend my wastrel ways, I swear it! As the heated rod neared me, I went out of my mind with fear and bawled like a frightened calf!

"Don't do this, please! I'll do anything you ask, just leave me alone!"

"I knew you were not a man," sneered Liu Chi contemptuously. "You are only a dog in human form. Like the dog you are, you will be destroyed, piece by piece!"

Just as the rod was about to ram home, I heard a silk curtain being pulled aside and the heavy sound of Western boots echoing on the marble floor. "Ach, Prince Tuan. You wanted to see me?" Liu Chi hesitated.

I looked up in shock; it was Von Arnhem! "Help!" I screamed. "Save me from this crazy bitch!"

"Travers, my friend," Von Arnhem greeted me cheerily, not the slightest bit of surprise registering on his face over the fact that I was in the chamber or that I was about to be hideously tortured by Liu Chi. "I see that Liu Chi has finally gotten her hands on you!" Then the bastard actually laughed uproariously at my situation.

"What?" I croaked incredulously. "You . . . you mean that you knew all along that this she-devil was on my trail?"

"Of course, Travers," Von Arnhem laughed merrily. "I would have told you, of course, but it would only have caused you to worry unnecessarily. After all, escape was impossible for you."

Worry me unnecessarily? Was he mad? I could have fled the country if only I'd realized the extent of the peril facing me! Then it hit me; Von Arnhem didn't alert me to the danger because he wanted me to be taken by the yellow bastards! But why? It just didn't make any sense!

Although Von Arnhem clearly wasn't there to rescue me, his presence had given me a respite, for Liu Chi backed off a bit, not wanting to enjoy her pleasures under another barbarian's eyes.

"Your Highness," said Von Arnhem, addressing himself to the old woman, "it is so good to see you. But Prince Tuan and I have business to discuss."

There was no indication of comprehension in the expression on either Prince Tuan's face or that of the old crone. In fact, they gazed at Von Arnhem as though he were an insect crawling up the wall. Despite Von Arnhem's bluff manner, there was something in his eyes that told me that he was unsettled to find Tzu Hsi at Prince Tuan's side. But since Prince Tuan remained silent, Von Arnhem continued, "Tell the empress that the alliance between China and the Kaiser of the German Empire can still be achieved."

"It seems," countered Prince Tuan quietly, "that events dictate otherwise."

"Well, the situation is not completely favorable, I agree," admitted Von Arnhem. "But all is not lost. I have received a cable instructing me to inform her majesty that thirty thousand German troops are being loaded onto transports today in Hamburg. They will be here within two months."

Incredible, I marveled. Von Arnhem was plotting with these monkeys to form a Chinese-German alliance! What's more, if there really were thirty thousand German troops on the way, they'd outgun the eighteen thousand troops that General Gasalee could muster. If Von Arnhem's little plan worked, he would succeed in linking the world's biggest arms producer with the world's most populous country. The resulting union would be a powerhouse that could rule the earth! Such an alliance would be anathema to Tzu Hsi, who clearly detested foreigners, but it would appeal to a young turk like Prince Tuan, who saw the need for change within China, especially in relation to military matters. I suspected that Von Arnhem had broached his scheme with Prince Tuan and expected the prince to depose the Old Buddha to pave the way for the German-Chinese pact.

But it appeared that Prince Tuan was no longer dancing to Von Arnhem's tune. "The war is over," said Prince Tuan flatly. "China will be a British and Japanese colony for the next several decades, not a German ally."

"I don't understand, then," protested Von Arnhem angrily. "If that is your position, why did you bother to summon me?"

"The reason is simple, *Hauptman*," replied Prince Tuan. "The allies extended the hand of reconciliation today. They did not plunder the Forbidden City even though it was within their power to do so. My honored mother, the Dowager Empress," here he bowed to the old witch, "wishes to make a gesture of reconciliation to the allies in return."

"What sort of gesture?" demanded Von Arnhem warily, acutely aware that his collaborator, Prince Tuan, had deserted what he perceived to be a sinking ship.

"Your head, respected *Hauptman,* will be delivered to General Gasalee tomorrow" came the reply.

Craning my neck to look over my shoulder, I saw Von Arnhem stiffen, and then laugh harshly. Blackguard though he was, you had to admire that boy's audacity! "And what makes you think, my dear prince, that the British will not see your gesture as merely one more of your barbaric murders? There have been so many recently, you know."

"Perhaps General Gasalee will think precisely that," conceded Prince Tuan. "But there are other eyes in the allied expedition, eyes that know precisely why you came to this land, *Hauptman*. Those eyes have regarded your activities with trepidation."

I suddenly realized why other Europeans had universally shunned Von Arnhem, especially the French, who always hopped about like mongooses near a cobra whenever Von Arnhem came around.

"The discovery of your head at General Gasalee's door," continued Prince Tuan, "will be understood and much welcomed."

Von Arnhem fell silent, the muscles of his jaws working furiously, which caused the scar on the side of his rugged face to glow white. Clearly this conversation was at an end. If Prince Tuan had spoken the truth and Von Arnhem had come to China to forge an alliance of global proportions, it appeared the jig was up. Who knows what might have happened had the Boxers held out longer or the Germans gotten their army to China quicker?

The world would never find out, for suddenly Von Arnhem made his move. "Travers, look out!" he yelled, at the same time whipping out an automatic pistol from the holster on his hip. He fired twice, dropping the eunuchs behind me. Then, before anyone could move, he had his saber out and slashed me free of my bonds.

I whirled away as Liu Chi rushed for me with the hot poker. "I will see you dead, Fenwi!" she vowed as she closed for the kill.

I ducked as she swung for my head, driving a fist into her midsection as I did. I caught her with a solid punch just below her breasts. "Ugh!" she grunted, staggering backward and tripping over the brazier. Before my horrified eyes she tumbled upon the glowing coals and her silk garments burst into flame!

"Yeeee!" she shrieked, jumping to her feet and running off in a solid ball of flames. Prince Tuan pulled an ancient flintlock pistol from his robes and leveled it at me, but Liu Chi running by caused him to flinch as he squeezed the trigger. The pistol roared. I felt the ball graze my cheek and ricochet harmlessly off the far wall. Before Prince Tuan could reload, I dropped to all fours and scuttled off like a crab caught at low tide. Behind me more eunuchs stormed into the chamber, and Von Arnhem bowled over a few more with pistol shots until I hopped to my feet, shucked my tunic back in place over my shoulders, drew my Italian automatic, and began firing as Von Arnhem reloaded. The Chinese, including Prince Tuan and the Old Buddha, scattered.

"Travers," ordered Von Arnhem, "run for it!"

In a flash I was running for my life, pausing only to scoop up a discarded scimitar as I went. I bolted through the great double doors like a frightened deer and down the corridor I'd followed earlier, Von Arnhem right on my heels. I reached the spiral staircase and bounded down the stairs two and three at a time. Reaching the ground floor, I dashed headlong down the main corridor for the portal that led to the drawbridge. Up ahead I saw the growing glow of moonlight. Only a few more steps and we'd be safe!

Suddenly a figure loomed up in the darkness ahead, drawing back an arm as if to hurl something. Instinctively I ducked, and whatever it was sailed over my head.

"Arrghh!" grunted Von Arnhem heavily. "Throwing star!"

I had no time to wonder what a throwing star was as I crashed into the assailant, my sword slashing madly. "Eee-igh!" yelped the fellow as my blade bit deep into his neck, dropping him like a rag doll. His weight wrenched the scimitar from my grasp as he fell, but I was not about to take the time to retrieve the damned thing. I leapt over his body even before it hit the floor and pounded for the drawbridge like a fox with the pack on its trail. Wounded or not, Von Arnhem managed to stay right with me, determined not to be taken and used as a human olive branch by Prince Tuan.

We flashed across the drawbridge at a dead run, heedless of the possibility of bushwhackers lurking in the shadows, and sprinted down the boulevard leading to the breach through which I had entered the Forbidden City. Behind us I could hear the footfalls of pursuing eunuchs. Casting a fearful eye over my shoulder, I was horrified by the sight of curved blades gleaming in the moonlight as the eunuchs came on.

"They're gaining!" I gasped to Von Arnhem, whose labored breath told me that his wound was sapping his strength. Ahead was the mint through which I knew we must flee to reach the breach. Without slowing to see if Von Arnhem needed assistance, I sped up the steps to the mint, through the open door, across the silver-strewn inner chamber, and out the breach into the streets of the Imperial City.

"Halt!" cried a gruff voice, reinforced by the sound of a bolt being thrown home. Eunuchs or no eunuchs, I froze, only to be knocked to the ground by Von Arnhem as he hurtled through the breach behind me. We were hauled roughly to our feet and held at bayonet point.

"O'right, you blokes," said a suspicious English sergeant, his face pushed near mine. "What are ye goin' on about 'ere? Out for a bit of lootin', are ye? There's a general order out against that, y' know. Looters is bein' shot."

I took a deep breath. Having escaped the insane machinations of Liu Chi and her equally deranged husband, I realized I was within a hairbreadth of being dragooned by a cockney sergeant and then shot by my own side. "Now hold on there, Sergeant," I countered crisply. "I am Lieutenant Travers, United States Army. And this," I nodded at Von Arnhem, "is *Hauptman* Von Arnhem of the Imperial German Army. We are certainly not looters. We are carrying important intelligence for General Gasalee, and I will brook no delay in getting it to him!" I reasoned that any equivocation or vacillation would seal our fates, you see. I had to seize the high ground right off and hold onto it doggedly.

"Bring a bloody torch over 'ere," ordered the sergeant, wanting to do his duty for queen and country, of course, but at the same time not wanting to make a career-ending faux pas. A torch was quickly produced as I prayed silently that he would not order me searched: I had enough contraband on me to warrant execution twice over! I waited tensely, fearing both the English before me and the eunuchs behind me. But no sound came from the breach, and I concluded that the eunuchs had given up the pursuit once we'd fled the confines of the Forbidden City.

The torch was lit, its flame illuminating our inquisitor's chevrons. "Well, ye both have the look o' officers, at that," the sergeant allowed cautiously. I cast a sideways glance at Von Arnhem, standing ramrod straight in the torchlight with what appeared to be half of a sheriff's badge protruding from his shoulder. So that's a throwing star, I thought grimly.

"Wait a minute, Ser'gint," interjected one of the other sentries who were crowding around us now. "I recognize these'uns. They's the blokes what galloped out o' that Chinee arsenal when all o' us was surrounded with Adm'ral Seymour!"

"Is 'at right now?" demanded the sergeant, still suspicious but more conciliatory.

"He's exactly right, Sergeant," I assured him, sensing that the danger had passed. "At the moment, we're on another dangerous mission. I urge you not to delay us further, since General Gasalee will not look kindly upon any interference with his most trusted agents."

That made up the sergeant's mind. "Of course, sir, I understand completely. Pass on, an' a very good evenin' t' ye, sir."

Von Arnhem and I exchanged salutes with the Britishers and walked off into the night, exhausted but relieved to still be in one piece. No sooner had we rounded the first corner and slipped once more into the shadows than Von Arnhem gripped his shoulder, groaned quietly, and collapsed to the street in a dead faint.

52

"Arrghh! *Mein Gott!*" murmured Von Arnhem groggily.

"Ah, coming to at last, are we?" I inquired brightly. "Well, hop to, amigo, and share a glass with me."

It was about an hour past dawn, and we were back in the saloon of the Hotel de Pekin. All the revelers had roused themselves and slunk back to their units, so I'd dumped Von Arnhem unceremoniously on the floor among the glass shards and spilled champagne and began pouring myself congratulatory toasts: I was wealthy beyond my wildest imaginings! Despite the fact that I'd dropped some of my plunder during my near execution at the hands of Liu Chi, the stones I'd managed to retain had to be easily worth millions. The only problem was to figure a way to smuggle my loot out of the country, but I was confident that I'd hit upon a feasible scheme. Then all that remained to be done was to see to it that the army discharged me, and I'd be free to embark upon a life of luxury and ease.

"My arm!" gasped Von Arnhem, tenderly holding his shoulder where the throwing star still protruded.

"I'd be more than happy to yank that thing out for you," I offered with a smile.

Von Arnhem glowered at me. "Don't touch it. If it's not carefully worked out, the nerves could be severed and my arm will be paralyzed."

"Suit yourself," I replied airily, quaffing another glass of the bubbly. "But for my money, it looks like a nice clean wound. As long as that star hasn't been dipped in poison, I'd say you have a good chance of pulling through, at least, if you can avoid gangrene."

"So, Travers, I'll live unless I die?" growled Von Arnhem grimly.

"Bull's-eye," I affirmed cheerily. "Your mind is really so sharp."

"Travers, you are a cold bastard," spat Von Arnhem bitterly.

"Oh, perhaps," I conceded, "although coming from you it's a little like the pot calling the kettle black, don't you think?"

Von Arnhem ignored the small talk and went straight for the jugular. "Travers, I know why you were in the palace. From this moment on, you will follow my orders or I will see to it that your General Chaffee learns of your crimes against the Chinese throne."

It was vintage Von Arnhem I was seeing. Take a setback and turn it to his advantage. He'd lost China for his master the Kaiser, but he suddenly saw a chance to turn me into a German agent. But I wasn't alarmed; in fact, I laughed in his impudent face. "So what?" I countered. "I happen to know why you were in there as well, my friend." I'd be damned if I'd let this would-be world conqueror intimidate me!

"You bluff, Travers," declared Von Arnhem. "There is nobody who would believe you if you told your tale of what went on between me and Prince Tuan."

"Oh, I wouldn't be too sure of that, Von Arnhem," I countered. "Think of the French, for instance."

Von Arnhem pondered that in silence. Then he raised the ante in our game of liar's poker. "I know that your President McKinley has cabled General Chaffee to prevent looting, on pain of death."

I smiled bravely, but I had no doubt that Von Arnhem could intercept American cables. "You seem to know more about what goes on in the American army than I do."

Von Arnhem gave a sinister smile, his blue eyes as cold as ice. "Travers, you have violated the orders of your president. I can have you ruined if I make that information known to the right people."

It was my turn to ponder. I was sure that he was right; he could ruin me if he put his mind to it. On the other hand, I wouldn't make much of a spy for him. After all, I'd spent the last few years resisting any meaningful cooperation with my own army, so I'd be damned if I'd cooperate with the Prussian army. Was his real goal to intimidate me into silence? I wondered. If that were the case, he could save himself a lot of effort, for I had no intention of reporting his shenanigans to the authorities. That would only open the door for an inquiry into my own nocturnal wanderings.

Then another thought crossed my mind: Maybe Von Arnhem wasn't motivated by lofty goals of service to country after all. Maybe the bastard wanted a share of my loot for himself! Now that was a threat I would not tolerate; I went over to the offensive with a vengeance!

"Listen here, *Hauptman*," I sneered, "can you imagine the furor in England and France if their daily newspapers got wind of a plot to steal China for the German Empire? You know how touchy the French are about you Prussians, especially since 1870. If such a circumstance were to come to pass, I wouldn't be at all surprised if the French decided to vent their spleen against the nearest German possession, like, oh, say, Alsace-Lorraine, for instance."

Von Arnhem bridled visibly at my mention of the disputed provinces lying between France and Germany, which Bismarck had seized in his conquest of France in the Franco-Prussian War.

"No self-respecting newspaper would print such rubbish!" exploded Von Arnhem venomously.

"No *German* paper," I conceded. "And perhaps no British or French paper, at least at first. But American papers will print anything—the more scurrilous the story, the better. You were in Tampa, Von Arnhem. You read the drivel published by Hearst and Pulitzer. Now tell me," I demanded, leaning over the wounded Prussian, "do you *really* think that American newspapers wouldn't print whatever tidbits I might happen to send them about your China escapades? Don't forget, I count a few correspondents among my acquaintances," I added menacingly, thinking of Crane and Davis.

Von Arnhem pondered my words in silence, no doubt recalling my dalliance with the fourth estate in Tampa, and in his silence I sensed my victory. We sat together awhile longer without speaking as he nursed his shoulder and I nursed my drink. Then, Von Arnhem grunted painfully and rose to his feet.

"Travers, I must go now. We shall meet in the future, of that you may be certain." So saying, he turned and walked out the door.

With Von Arnhem gone, I finished another bottle of champagne. I was lost in reverie and feeling on top of the world. With exquisite pleasure I planned my new life as a world-class bon vivant. I'd take a town house in Manhattan, of course, and maybe a farm up near Saratoga close by the gambling tables. And I'd need a summer home, thirty rooms at least, in Newport to entertain all the nubile lovelies my newfound wealth would undoubtedly attract. Yes, I thought with languid weariness, there was much to do as soon as I left the army.

But it was time to put dreams of paradise behind me, I thought, reminding myself that I'd better be off to the American legation, since technically I was assigned there and had been since I'd been run out of Havana by Marguerite and Colonel Quinlon. No doubt the chargé d'affaires would be curious as to the whereabouts of his military attaché.

So I performed a quick toilette in a basin of water I found behind the bar, dusted the grime from my uniform as best I could, put a sheen on my boots with a bar towel, and set out toward the Legation Quarter.

I sauntered down Legation Street and crossed over the wooden bridge spanning the Imperial Canal. Although things were slowly returning to normal within the Legation Quarter, great piles of sandbags and spent cartridges still littered the ground, attesting to the ferocity of the siege. I stood in the center of all this destruction, trying to decide which of the battered buildings around me might be the United States legation, when in a nearby doorway I spied an elderly gent in a black morning coat and top hat.

Could it be? I thought. Yes, by God, it was! "Harlock!" I roared. "What the hell are you doing here?"

Harlock turned at the sound of his name. "Ah, young Travers. What a pleasant surprise. I rather thought our paths might cross again."

Of course he did, I instantly realized. He knew I'd been posted to Peking and probably had kept an eye out for me. "A pleasant surprise, my sweet behind, Harlock!" I bellowed, storming over to him with half a mind to throttle him right there in the street. "If you hadn't abandoned me when I sought your help, I never would have been sent to this hellhole in the first place!"

"Now, now, Lieutenant Travers," he admonished me primly. "Temper tantrums are useless and so unseemly. Besides, all this campaigning seems to have agreed with you. You look fit as a fiddle."

"It's only by pure luck that I haven't had my carcass ventilated with hot lead or sliced open a dozen times over since I've been here!" I retorted angrily. "As for campaigning, I've had enough of it to last me a lifetime, thank you."

Harlock was not the least bit alarmed by my rantings. "I've received reports about your exploits, Lieutenant Travers. Most impressive, I must say," he said, and sounded so sincere that I almost believed he meant it, until he added pointedly, "It's so hard to keep real soldiers away from the sound of the guns, isn't it?"

Guns! Of course, I thought; so that was why the old troll was there. He intended to buy and sell guns before the dust settled and his competition began to arrive. It was Harlock's style, I realized, to set up shop on a pile of smoking ruins and bleeding bodies.

"Tell me, Harlock," I demanded. "How the blazes did you get here so fast? Why, Peking fell only yesterday."

Harlock gave me that enigmatic smile he used when he wished to remind me just what a dunce I was. "I have my own means of learning things, Lieutenant. After all, in my line of work, one must be very nimble. Yes, very nimble indeed."

That he was, I had to admit. Why, the old fellow hopped about more than a jackrabbit in a grass fire. "What's your game now?" I pressed him. "Are you buying or selling?"

"Selling at the moment, son," he replied with his Yankee twang. "The Boxers are gathering off to the north, and the price of good arms is still intriguingly high. But as soon as the last flicker of resistance is stamped out, the price of arms will plummet, and then I shall buy."

"No doubt you will, Harlock," I agreed. "Only this time, you'll have to find a new boy to help you sneak your booty out of the country. You and I are finished, bucko." With my pockets bulging with loot, I could afford to give Harlock a piece of my mind.

"It causes me great pain to know you feel that way, Lieutenant Travers," said Harlock, his face looking anything but pained. "But in truth, I knew we could not, er, collaborate further even before I laid eyes on you today."

"Eh? Just what's that supposed to mean?" I demanded suspiciously.

"Your orders have arrived from Washington, Lieutenant," he explained. "You've been cited for gallantry by General Chaffee for being the first American officer over the wall at Peking and the hero of Hsiku. You're bound for the United States to be decorated and feted. I understand you're to leave within a month."

"What? A hero?" I considered this a moment. Sure, I was a looter and a general ne'er-do-well, but then I had been under fire a time or two. Well, I decided, if my grateful nation wanted to roll out the red carpet and wine and dine me, I was game!

Seeing that I was distracted by his news, Harlock began to take his leave. With a tip of his hat he said, "Perhaps we can do business on some other shore."

I drew myself up at this. "I hardly think so, you double-dealing snake!"

Harlock merely chuckled again and murmured disapprovingly, "Temper, temper, Lieutenant Travers." With a tip of his hat he set off on his way.

I watched him go and damned him at each step he took. But just then a thought occurred to me. "Harlock!" I called.

Harlock stopped in his tracks and turned, his lizard eyes revealing nothing. "Yes, Lieutenant?" he inquired mildly.

"Perhaps, er, well, that is, maybe I've been just a bit *too* hasty," I apologized. "If I have, then please blame it on the strain of the campaign. It's been hell out here, you know."

Harlock said nothing as he stood watching me.

"Well, the point is this, Harlock. Perhaps we can do business together," I proposed.

Harlock didn't blink an eye at my volte-face. "How?" was all he said.

"Not here," I insisted, glancing meaningfully at the passersby.

Harlock understood, of course, since no business scheme I was likely to raise with him would withstand the light of day. "Come this way," he directed. He led me right back through the doorway where I had first spied him. Inside was a shredded American flag hanging limply from a bamboo pole. This was obviously the United States legation, and we were strolling through the place with nary a sideways glance from the harried clerks laboring at the stacks of documents piled on their desks, paperwork that no doubt had accumulated during the recent unpleasantness. Why, I thought with astonishment, Harlock acts as though he owns the place!

We passed an impressive-looking door with a brass plate that announced Mr. Clairborne, United States of America. Directly adjacent to this was an equally impressive-looking door bearing a brass plate proclaiming Yankee Clipper Limited. By God, Harlock was doing business right out of the American legation, I realized with shock.

With me right behind him, Harlock opened the door, and we entered a comfortably appointed office. He crossed the room to where a sturdy wooden desk stood and seated himself on the leather chair behind it. No wonder Harlock was so well informed about international affairs, I realized; he probably had members of the diplomatic corps on his payroll!

"Now, Travers, what's on your mind?" asked Harlock bluntly.

I decided to be equally direct, or at least as direct as I was capable of being. "Well, it seems I've come into possession of a certain number of, er, objects."

Harlock's eyes glinted like those of a hog that's just had slop dropped in front of it. "What sort of objects?" he demanded.

"Jewels," I answered quietly.

"I see," said Harlock. "And how does this concern me?" He was toying with me and I knew it.

"I need to get these stones out of the country, Harlock," I explained levelly, "and you're just the man to do it."

"Oh, dear me, Lieutenant Travers, are you proposing that I smuggle jewels of dubious ownership out of China? That would violate a half-dozen imperial edicts and customs regulations," he said with mock horror.

"Let's not be coy, Harlock," I countered squarely. "I'm proposing the sort of business deal that you engage in every day of the week. Are you with me, or do I get another partner?"

A thin smile crossed Harlock's face, then he sat back in his chair and eyed the ceiling. "Tell me your proposal, Lieutenant."

"I'll give you the jewels, and in return you'll give a properly drawn bearer note for their worth, minus, of course, a generous commission for your services."

That had been a flash of genius on my part; I'd transfer the incriminating stones to Harlock and take home with me an innocent bearer note that could never be tied to my larceny. Harlock would have the jewels, which he would be able to smuggle out of the country with little risk through the network of operatives he'd undoubtedly cultivated, and I would have a negotiable instrument that could be easily secreted on my person when I left the country. It was a foolproof plan.

Harlock mulled over my proposition for a few minutes. At length he asked, "Where are the jewels now?"

By way of an answer, I dug into my pockets and piled the rubies, pearls, and diamonds on the desk. Harlock sat there dumbstruck at the opulence before him. His shifty blue eyes flared with a light I'd never seen in them before and a thin trickle of drool escaped his lips.

When at last he was able to look away from the jewels and back at me, he croaked: "What's your price?"

"I want an even million for them. You'll have no difficulty selling them for twice that in New York or London."

I expected haggling, but there was none. "Wait here," was all Harlock said as he left the room. He returned in a few moments with a diminutive clerk in tow. "Mister Peer, here, read the law before coming out to China. He'll prepare your note."

Peer sat himself down at the desk, put pen to paper, and drew up the document as directed. Upon finishing, he blew on the ink to dry it, gave the paper a shake or two, and handed it to Harlock. Harlock eyed it sharply, nodded with approval, and handed it to me.

I studied it carefully. It looked regular enough to my unpracticed eye. Of particular importance to me was the part about an unqualified promise to pay to the bearer a million dollars in gold certificate dollar bills upon presentation to Harlock's bank, the Nassau Bank, in New York. I prayed that Harlock hadn't guessed at the extent of my ignorance of financial matters; I didn't want to be cheated out of what was rightfully mine by some legal sleight of hand.

"That note is fully negotiable," volunteered Mr. Peer, as though fathoming my concerns.

Harlock cleared his throat pointedly. "I trust you find everything satisfactory?"

"Perfectly," I said.

I slid the note to Harlock, who signed it with a flourish, blew on the ink to dry it, and handed the note back to me. In return, I slid the pile of jewels across the desk to him, and he eagerly scooped them into his pockets. Folding the note carefully and placing it in my tunic pocket, I rose to take my leave.

"Good day, Lieutenant," said Harlock in farewell. "I believe you can find your own way out."

"Of course, Mister Harlock," I said, even giving a bit of a bow as I took my leave, so elated was I by the day's bit of work. Once outside I took a deep breath of air and held it. I had to gain control of my reeling mind. Why, I was as giddy as a schoolboy in a brewery. In twenty-four hours my life had changed completely and the world was literally at my feet! I set off with a jaunty tune on my lips, determined to enjoy a day of mild debauchery, all thoughts of my official duties banished from my mind. After I'd had a proper congratulatory fling, all that remained to be done was to escape the army's grasp. I knew I would succeed in that regard, for as the day's events had proven, no obstacle was too big for me to overcome. Then I'd finally be able to slip into a premature retirement and savor a life of dissolute bliss!

53

November 25, 1900
New York City
Three months later I steamed into New York harbor. Fireboats greeted my steamer as it entered the harbor, sending great geysers of water up into the air. A flotilla of private yachts escorted me to dockside where thousands of well wishers waited and a brass band struck up a rousing chorus of "The Battle Hymn of the Republic." As we slid against

the dock and the hawsers were made fast, I stood at the rail waving to the crowd below and striking what I thought was a suitably heroic pose. My admirers shouted and applauded and pushed each other about so much that it was sheer chaos below on the dock.

The gangplank was dropped and the captain came down from the bridge and marched straight up to me. "Lieutenant Travers," he intoned gravely, "would you do me the very great honor of allowing me to escort you to the dock?"

"Sir, the honor would be all mine," I replied with as much humility as I'm capable of mustering, and together we descended into the roaring assembly below.

"Fenny, we love you, boy!" they screamed and others called, "Three cheers for the Hero of Peking!" Only a straining thin line of New York's Finest kept the exuberant mob from surging forward to crush the object of its ardor.

"Fenwick! Fenwick, boy!" called a familiar voice. I turned to see the incredible sight of Uncle Enoch Sheffield rushing toward me, his eyes streaming tears of joy! Evidently he had gotten word that I was a rising star in the world and had decided to mend fences with me. He must have learned of my expected landfall and traveled all the way from Illinois to be at dockside when I arrived. The old hypocrite ran straight at me, arms outstretched, his coat flapping absurdly behind him in the breeze. I had to fight a sudden instinct to duck, but then he had me, crushing me to his burly chest.

"Oh!" he burbled emotionally, "it does this old fool's heart good to see you again!"

I was at a loss as to how to react to Enoch; after all, never before had he actually been glad to see me. So I tentatively hugged him back. "It's good to see you too, Judge."

That seemed to hit the mark, for Uncle Enoch reared back and cried in a choked voice, "Do you mean it, Fenwick? Truly?"

I nodded. "Of course I mean it," I lied.

"Oh, Fenwick, we've missed you so," he bawled as tears streamed anew down his craggy cheeks. "I've badly misjudged you, boy. I never thought you'd be the man you are! I was wrong, Fenwick, dead wrong! Do you forgive me?"

He was hugging me so hard that for an instant I feared that the wrong answer could have dire consequences for me. "What's to forgive?" I smiled smoothly. "All's well that ends well, right?"

"Ah, Fenwick, thank you, thank you," Uncle Enoch sobbed. "I'll make it up to you, son, I promise I will. When we get back to Elm Grove, things'll be different, you'll see."

Of course I had no intention of ever returning to Elm Grove in this lifetime, but I had no time to tell that to Uncle Enoch, for just then we were interrupted by a dessicated old hag who shoved herself roughly between the Judge and me. "Fenwick, dear child, welcome home!"

I blinked a time or two before I even recognized her; it was Aunt Hannah Sheffield. Apparently she too had undergone a change of heart about me.

"Why, Aunt Hannah," I stammered awkwardly, not at all pleased to see her but not wanting that to show at the moment. "it was good of you to come." I gave her a perfunctory peck on the cheek and moved back for a bit of breathing space. The past eight years had not been good to her; she looked like a shriveled-up apple, and it seemed that she'd lost several inches of height. But then I looked at the Judge blowing his bulbous red nose into a handkerchief and I thought that it was a wonder Aunt Hannah looked as well as she did considering the company she kept.

Just then we were joined by a military delegation. "Lieutenant Travers, welcome home." I looked up to see Brig. Gen. Leonard Wood, the former commander of the Rough Riders and the ex–military governor of Cuba. Then I saw the two gleaming stars on each epaulet: it was Major General Wood!

"Thank you, sir. It's a pleasure to be here," I replied, taking advantage of this development to thrust Aunt Hannah into Uncle Enoch's arms.

"Let me be the first to congratulate you on your promotion, *Captain* Travers," beamed General Wood.

"Promotion?" I said, flustered. "I hadn't heard anything about a promotion."

"Of course you didn't, Captain," explained the general genially, "because it was intended to be a surprise. And I'm happy to see that's the case."

He handed me a small velvet-covered box. I opened it to see the silver bars of a captain twinkling back at me.

"Congratulations, Travers," he said again, shaking my free hand. "It's well deserved."

An aide expertly slipped forward and handed General Wood a sheet of paper. "This is the order promoting you to captain," he explained, handing it to me. "It's dated the day after we heard about the glorious capture of Peking. As you can see, it was signed by President McKinley himself."

And so it was, I confirmed with a glance. "You really must thank him for me, sir. It was very kind of him," I smiled, truly taken aback by this token of esteem. It was nice to be appreciated, even if I intended to submit my resignation at the earliest possible time. Had I not intended to leave the army, that promotion would have been the fulfillment of a lieutenant's fondest dream, but as things were, it was no more than a fond gesture on my way out the door. I could tell, however, that General Wood completely misunderstood the reason for my composed reaction to the honors being showered upon me; he took my insouciance for well-bred humility, and I could tell from the approving glint in his steely eyes that he had marked me as very much his type of fellow.

"You can thank the president personally," he announced to my amazement. "President McKinley will be attending the ball that's being thrown in your honor this evening in the 7th Regiment Armory."

"A ball? In my honor?" I gaped incredulously. "Certainly you're joshing, sir." I'd always known what a splendid fellow I was, of course, but it was a bit of a shock to have the rest of the world come around to the same point of view in such a hurry.

"No, I'm not, Travers," General Wood assured me. "The City of New York, indeed the entire nation, wishes to extend to you its gratitude for the services you've rendered to the Republic."

"I don't know what to say" was all I could muster.

"I understand, son," said General Wood with a nod. Then he leaned over and whispered in my ear, "I think you'll be pleased to know that there's also a citation for gallantry that's slowly working its way through channels from General Chaffee in Peking. It will receive favorable consideration at the very highest levels of the War Department, if you know what I mean." Stepping back, he gave me a sly wink.

I fought the impulse to wink back. Instead, I growled bluffly, "Thank you, sir." Only the knowledge that Harlock's bearer note was tucked securely in my pocket allowed me to tolerate this overblown ceremony with such good grace.

"Come along, Captain," instructed General Wood, pushing past Uncle Enoch and taking me by the arm. "There are still a great many people who've come to see you." He led me to a waiting brougham when suddenly I saw a sight that froze me to the spot. There at the open door of the carriage stood a familiar figure clad in a loud plaid suit and with a derby perched precariously on his bull-like head.

It was Detective Becker! By God, although I thought I'd done him in what seemed like years ago, the bastard had somehow survived! I searched his eyes to see if he remembered me from the night I'd slashed his face and later tried to murder him. His scowl and the tough set of his jaw gave me my answer: He remembered me, all right!

My first impulse was to flee, and only the protective aura of General Wood at my side checked me. As we neared the brougham, Becker's hand drifted upward, and for an instant I thought he was reaching for the blackjack he always carried inside his coat. But instead, he tipped his hat politely!

"And a very good day to you, sir," he growled, the livid scar that ran down his cheek glowing an angry white.

"Good day to you, detective," I said coolly in return.

"It's *Lieutenant* Becker now," he corrected me. "I got promoted when I singlehandedly brought in Willy Delaney. Willy was wanted for the attempted murder of a policeman."

"Willy Delaney? Can't say as I recognize that name," I said with a shake of my head.

Becker merely grunted and rumbled on, "Willy's doing twenty years in the Tombs."

"Well, then, my congratulations on a job well done," I said, smiling nervously. Conscious of General Wood behind me, and eager to be away from Becker, I put up a foot to climb into the brougham when Becker spoke again.

"Some people say I got the wrong man, you know."

That, of course, bothered me not a whit, for a sidewinder like Delaney had certainly committed enough crimes to merit a lifetime behind bars long before I set him up. Nonetheless, I halted and eyed Becker levelly. "And what's *your* opinion on the matter, Lieutenant?" I asked carefully.

Becker fixed me with a cold stare and smiled mirthlessly. "Oh, I'm certain I nabbed the right fellow. The department would never make a mistake as big as that."

"I'm sure you're right," I breathed with a sigh of relief and heaved myself into the carriage. Becker had just voiced the great unwritten rule of the New York City police department. Bring the full weight of the law crashing down on the backs of suspected malefactors if they were poor and helpless, but treat the rich and powerful deferentially—yea, approvingly—no matter how stupefying their transgressions.

I realized as I settled back into the soft leather seat that I was permanently off the hook with Becker. You've done it again, Fenny! I congratulated myself smugly. Then General Wood climbed in next to me, and we were off at a trot. I watched the cheering spectators through my window and reveled in the knowledge that at last the world was my oyster; the moment had been a long time in coming, but it had been well worth the wait.

The carriage swung onto Fifth Avenue and headed uptown and into Grand Army Plaza, where it halted before a dais. "There's a little delegation here to greet you, Captain," explained the general. "You know, Travers, this is the same spot where New York raised a victory arch in honor of Admiral Dewey when he returned from the Pacific in '99. It's no small honor they're paying you, son."

I could see that Wood expected a suitably fawning reply, so I gave him one: "I'm overwhelmed, sir. I feel as though I don't deserve any of this." At least the last part of my statement was true.

We stepped out of the carriage and confronted a pack of the most unsavory-looking rogues I had ever laid eyes on. "Captain Travers," announced General Wood, "may I present the assembled leadership of Tammany Hall and other dignitaries representing the premier business interests of New York."

Oh, they were properly decked out in morning coats and top hats, all right, but their shifty eyes and debauched faces called to mind the more ruthless flesh peddlers I'd encountered in the bordellos of Cuba. And there right in the front row was George Duncan. He smiled most benignly at me, exposing all his small perfect teeth. That smile told me instantly that as far as Duncan was concerned the bad blood between us was history; my stock was rising and he clearly wanted to buy in.

Together General Wood and I mounted the wooden steps to the platform where a portly gentleman with the seedy air of a chief whoremaster advanced unsteadily toward us. "Mayor Van Wyck," said General Wood, "may I present Captain Travers."

Hizzoner smiled broadly at me and then belched loudly, the stench of whiskey quickly enveloping us all. From the look of his florid jowls and the distended veins in his nose, I guessed that the mayor was already three sheets to the wind, although it was barely past noon. Van Wyck turned to a disheveled aide, who handed him an ornate brass key to the city. Without a word, and with an inane smile plastered on his wide face, Van Wyck attempted to hand the key to me, missed, and instead thrust it at General Wood.

Wood harrumphed gruffly and folded his hands across his chest disdainfully, giving the inebriated mayor a look that could have curdled cow's milk at ten paces. Van Wyck squinted blearily, got my range in his mind, and thrust the key once more, this time right into my outstretched hand. "S'onor, my boy, s'onor," he mumbled incoherently. Then he belched again and would have fallen from the dais had not his aide quickly grasped his arm to steady him.

I took the old sot's hand and pumped it vigorously. "Thank you, Mister Mayor, I shall never forget this moment," I promised. General Wood shot me a glance to see if I was being sarcastic, but my face was wreathed in an angelic smile.

Van Wyck then commenced to speak, rambling on about manifest destiny and similar rot. It was clear that the mayor was just getting warmed up, but General Wood was finished here. Brusquely interrupting, he said, "Thank you, thank you, Your Honor." Then he seized my arm and steered me back to the carriage. The crowd, taking their cue from us and thinking that the ceremony was over, broke into hearty hurrahs while behind us Van Wyck carried on with his soliloquy, oblivious to the fact that we had left.

General Wood escorted me back to his carriage, where we were joined by George Duncan, who slapped my back and told me how fine I looked and how damned proud of me he was. I, of course, was beyond amazement by that point and took it all in as though it were my natural due. General Wood looked at his timepiece and muttered, "Where does the day go? I'm afraid I need to be off to confer with the president, gentlemen."

"Leave this young paladin in my charge," insisted Duncan. "I'll see to it that he's at the ball, General." And so we took our leave with handshakes all around, and Duncan promptly took charge of me for the rest of the day. He insisted that I was to abide with him for the duration of my stay in the city, and he bundled the Sheffields off in their hansom to a complimentary suite in the Waldorf-Astoria. Then we were off in his sky blue landau trimmed in gold, and in a short while we arrived at his manor by Central Park.

I was shown to a magnificent guest bedroom to rest before the evening's festivities. A nap sounded like just the thing and I had just stripped to my drawers when the door unexpectedly swung open and in walked Alice!

"Fenny!" she cried with a sob, rushing to me, "I heard you were back and I couldn't wait to say hello!"

"Alice, dearest!" I gasped, making no effort to cover myself as she rushed into my arms. "It's grand to see you again. I haven't heard from you since that night I left New York en route for Cuba."

"I know, dearest, I know," she said, laughing through her tears. "Uncle George forbade me to contact you. He was adamant that I put you out of my mind, and he encouraged a parade of suitors to pay court to me."

Suitors? I thought. That was a damned ominous development. "And?" I asked anxiously. "Were any of those suitors . . . successful?"

"Well . . . ," she demurred, casting her eyes down. A tremor of fear shot through my body.

"Alice, tell me true," I stammered. "Have . . . have you married while I was off to the wars?"

When she looked up again she was smiling. "No, I haven't, Fenny, but if I had, you would have deserved it for all the heartache you've put me through."

I laughed heartily with relief. "You poor girl. I know this has been hard on you."

"You'll get no argument from me there," replied Alice tartly, but I could see from the light in her eyes that she was ready to let bygones be bygones and to take up where we had left off so long ago.

"But I've changed, Alice," I insisted, moving closer and putting my hands on her shoulders. "I was an irresponsible boy back then. But now I'm a—"

"Now you're an irresponsible man!" she interrupted impishly, slipping from my grasp and going to the bed, where she began to turn down the covers for me.

I slipped up behind her and held her by the waist. "Now Alice, you can't truly be holding any grudges about what happened in the past, can you?"

She straightened up and turned to me, smiling. "No, I can't say that I do. I was every bit as thrilled as the rest of the country when I heard of your great deeds. I always knew you were brave, but I could scarcely believe that it was the same Fenny I had known as a young private who was performing such great feats of arms." Then she stopped, as if fearing she had overstepped her bounds and insulted me.

"It's okay, Alice," I soothed. "Why, I wasn't too certain how the army would turn out for me, either. But now that it's over, I can look back and see just how lucky I was."

That bit of modesty did the trick! As I gazed at her with my large, soulful blue eyes, I could see tears of gladness and desire welling up in her green orbs. "You've changed, Fenny," she sighed. "A young boy went off to war, but it's a man who has returned. A very strong, handsome man."

"Then give me a kiss, dear Alice," I coaxed, "and welcome me home."

Alice obediently tilted her head up to give me a polite peck, but I landed a great wet smack on her lips with such force that she teetered against the edge of the bed and then, off balance, fell. Over she went onto the bed with me right on top of her. As her lovely bottom hit the covers her feet came off the floor and I took advantage of her awkward position to flip her skirts and petticoats up above her waist.

"Oh, you conniving thing!" giggled Alice, struggling unsuccessfully to pull down her skirt.

"Now let's not be prudish, love," I laughed in return. "After all, there shouldn't be any false modesty between us, don't you agree?"

"Let me loose, you . . . you octopus!" she demanded by way of an answer, but without any great conviction. Instead of releasing her, however, I drove home my ardor even more resolutely, kissing her hard on her mouth and letting my hands roam freely up her skirts. In minutes all resistance ceased and Alice began to respond passionately to my caresses.

"How long did you say you would be in New York?" she asked huskily.

54

Several hours later I was awakened by pounding at my door. It was Duncan himself. "Fenwick, it's time, boy!" he called. "We don't want to be late on this night!"

I arose groggily. Alice was gone, my bags were carefully stored in the huge walk-in closet adjacent to my bed, and my dress blue uniform had been pressed, brushed, and was hanging in my wardrobe. My new rank, indicated by two gold trefoil braids, was expertly sewn on the sleeves, I noted with pleasure. I quickly bathed, and with the help of a valet I dressed and in short order was standing tall in the main salon.

"Oh, Fenwick!" cried Alice when she beheld me in all my glory. "You're beautiful!"

Duncan snorted and muttered something about damned foolish females, but I saw that he grudgingly agreed with Alice's appraisal that I was quite a sight to behold. Duncan, Alice, and I took our leave and were soon heading across town in Duncan's carriage to the 7th Regiment Armory, located at Park Avenue and 66th Street. When we neared the place I saw that it was a massive building, a full city-block square.

"By God, it looks as forbidding as a Manchu fort," I breathed in awe.

Duncan grunted in agreement. "In a way it is, I suppose, Fenwick. It's the stronghold of the richest families in New York. You don't become a member of the 7th Regiment unless your name is Vanderbilt, Whitney, or Clinton, or you're one of their allies." As if to drive home the enormity of the honor being rendered to me by the city, he added in an aside, "Although your Uncle Enoch might be a man of some substance back in Illinois, a judge even, if it hadn't been for your deeds in China, he would not be setting foot within this armory on this or any other night."

A uniformed footman met Duncan's coach at the portcullis and assisted us to the cobblestones. Alice took my arm, and we entered the massive gates of the armory. Although the ball was already in progress, no sooner had we entered the hall than the music suddenly stopped, and a bank of trumpets sounded a staccato tattoo. Then all heads turned our way.

"Ladies and gentlemen!" bellowed the regimental sergeant major, "I give you Captain Travers, the Hero of Peking!"

A chorus of cheers went up around the hall, which prompted a self-conscious bow on my part. Then the band struck up a lovely waltz and the floor cleared. The intent was obvious: The floor had been yielded to the young hero and his lovely lady. I gave Alice my arm and led her away as Duncan stood gawking. I guided her to the center of the hall and took her in my arms. Together we swept gloriously across the floor, the very picture of rapturous young love.

Alice's face was radiant; she was in the arms of her true love and all of New York's high society was looking on with approval.

"Fenny, I love you," she sighed breathlessly as I whirled her about.

"And I love you," I assured her warmly, and it was true. Alice was one of a kind. I knew that if I could just stay in one place long enough to love her properly, I was sure she could make a passable husband out of me. Not that I was certain I could stay away from other women totally, mind you, but any philandering I might do would be strictly discreet out of respect for Alice's sensibilities.

Then the music was over and the hall exploded with congratulatory applause. We were surrounded by men and women who shook my hand and patted my back. As we stood there accepting the adulation of the crowd, General Wood stepped forward and paid his compliments to Alice. "Ma'am, I need to steal this young fellow from you for a moment if you don't mind."

"Of course not, General," smiled Alice. "But I want him back when you're done." She gave me a smile that promised a night of sweet delights and then turned to rejoin Duncan, who stood where we'd left him upon our entrance.

As Alice withdrew, the band struck up a jaunty tune and couples filled the dance floor once more. Wood laid a hand on my arm and drew me aside. "Travers," he said, "I'll get you in to see the president as soon as possible. He's closeted in the Veterans' Room with Vice-President–elect Roosevelt at the moment."

"Roosevelt?" I echoed, astounded. "Not the same—?"

"*The* very same," General Wood assured me with a chuckle. "Don't tell me you didn't know?"

"I had no idea," I said. "After all, in the places I've been in the past year they didn't have regular newspaper deliveries. I'd heard that McKinley had been reelected, of course, but I hadn't heard any news about Colonel Roosevelt being his choice for a running mate."

"Well, he wasn't exactly *chosen* by McKinley, son. There has been bad blood between those two ever since Teddy denounced McKinley to the press for ineptly handling the war with Spain. No, McKinley didn't choose Teddy, Captain; the delegates at the Republican convention did it for him. They stampeded from McKinley's choice and nominated Roosevelt by acclaim. Believe me, Teddy's a political force to be reckoned with."

I suddenly understood how Wood had risen from lieutenant colonel to two-star general in two short years. He had hitched his wagon to Roosevelt; the two of them were apparently unstoppable. But the thought of a horse-toothed buffoon like Roosevelt in the White House was so absurd that I had difficulty accepting the notion. Of course, I shared none of those thoughts with Wood. "If the president's in conference, sir, I think I'll just wander about and make the acquaintance of some of these wonderful people."

"Fine, son, fine," said General Wood, giving me a clap on the shoulder and hurrying off to the Veterans' Room.

Alice and Duncan rejoined me, as did Uncle Enoch and Aunt Hannah, both of whom had been in the hall when I arrived. Uncle Enoch had overheard the tail end of General Wood's comments and was astounded beyond his ability to contain himself. He sidled up to me, his normally dour features illuminated with excitement.

"An interview with President McKinley!" he fairly wheezed. "Why, I can scarcely believe my ears! Who would have thought that you—" but then he caught himself.

Right, I thought. Who would have thought that Emma's little bastard would have come so far? But I was in a magnanimous mood, not a vindictive one, so I simply smiled. "It's only a gesture, Judge. He'll just give me a pat on the back and send me along my merry way."

Uncle Enoch shook his head in amazement. "I can't believe you're taking all this adoration so calmly, Fenwick. Why, if I were in your boots, I'd be trembling with fear."

Fear? What was fear to me after campaigning my way around the world for a couple of years? I had changed during that time and I knew that it would take more than a chat with McKinley to rattle me after what I'd been through. And because I'd changed, I decided to teach Uncle Enoch that he wasn't dealing with the same boy he once knew: "After a man's been through the hell of China," I said gruffly, giving my mustache a fierce tug, "it takes quite a lot to ever shake him again. Do you understand me?" I demanded, eyeing him searchingly.

Uncle Enoch nodded dutifully, and a bit uncomfortably, under my glare. "I guess, er, I guess I do, boy . . . er, that is, Fenny."

As Duncan watched me take Uncle Enoch down a peg or two, I could see that his own estimate of me rose accordingly. I swelled with pride and satisfaction at the knowledge that I was at last a power in my own right, and more than able to hold my own with anyone. I took a glass of champagne from a passing waiter, gulped it down in one swallow, and handed the glass to Uncle Enoch. "I think I'll mosey around the room," I announced. I gave Alice's hand to Duncan and sauntered off, leaving all of them staring wonderingly at each other in my wake.

In truth, I had much better things to do than to chatter with Uncle Enoch, Duncan, or even President McKinley for that matter. With a note worth a fortune in my pocket, I could care less about gaining the respect and admiration of others; by God, if I wanted such things in the future, I could damned well buy them! What I wanted now was women and song. Lovely, sweet Alice was an excellent start in that regard but, the truth was, she merely whetted my appetite. In the crowd I saw many likely wasp-waisted conquests draped in silks and jewels, quite a few of whom where signaling invitations my way with their eyes.

I selected a raven-haired beauty as a likely target—I wasn't married to Alice yet, right?—and marched her way. Unfortunately I never got there, for my path was suddenly blocked by a slender gent in evening clothes. His skull was completely shaved. It was Harlock!

"Ah, Captain Travers, so good to see you again," he oozed insincerely.

"Harlock! What the hell are you doing here? This ball is for the elite of New York society."

"And so it is, Captain Travers. I happen to be well known to the Knickerbockers, you see. And many of them, er, do business with me." He smiled maliciously before continuing. "You're evidently unaware of the fact that I'm an honorary member of the 7th Regiment. Have been for years."

"No, I didn't know that," I admitted. There was no way I could have, of course, but nonetheless it didn't surprise me; after having seen Harlock's tracks all around the globe, I wouldn't have blinked an eye to learn that he was a member of the pope's College of Cardinals. But small talk with Harlock made me uneasy, so I demanded brusquely, "What's on your mind, Harlock?"

"I merely wish to add my congratulations to those of the citizens of this great metropolis, Captain," he smiled, showing thin, straight teeth. "I salute you, sir."

I snorted contemptuously. "I rather doubt your sincerity on that point, but since you're here, Harlock, let's talk business. There's a little matter of the bearer note you signed and which I happen to hold. Remember?" I tapped the pocket of my tunic meaningfully.

"Oh, I do remember, Captain Travers," replied Harlock easily. "If you inquire at the Nassau Bank on 13 Nassau Street in the morning, you'll find that an account has been opened in your name."

"Excellent!" I smiled, much relieved, for I had been expecting some last-minute chicanery from Harlock. "I trust you deposited the full one million?"

"One million?" asked Harlock, a look of innocent bewilderment on his face.

Suddenly I sensed trouble. "Yes, one million!" I repeated firmly, my voice rising an octave in anger.

"I'm afraid you're mistaken, Captain Travers," insisted Harlock. "Our agreement was that I pay you five thousand dollars. That's the amount you'll find on deposit."

"Five thousand?" I cried, aghast at Harlock's duplicity. "Why, you swindler, you owe me a million, and you damned well know it!" My outburst drew stares, so I fought to regain my composure. "Harlock," I rasped, "I swear to God that if you think you're going to get away with this cheap trick, you're sadly mistaken! I'll sue you in court, you cur! That note's a legal obligation and I'll force you to honor it!"

Far from being alarmed, Harlock merely chuckled. "Come, come, my dear captain," he clucked, as if reasoning with an overgrown schoolboy. "There are legalities, and then there are legalities. I quite agree with you that if you were to sue on the note you possess, you would likely prevail on the merits. A judgment would be entered in your favor, and you would be entitled to levy execution against any of my considerable assets in this city to satisfy that judgment."

"That's right," I assured him forcefully. "And don't think I won't!"

"But that's just the point," Harlock explained, unperturbed. "You won't sue me, Captain Travers, because there are other aspects of this transaction to be taken into account."

"Like what?" I snarled.

Harlock crinkled his brow pensively, looking for all the world like a professor trying to get a point across to a dunce. "Well, here are a few for your consideration. First, when I executed that note, I was in Peking and the city was in a state of war. That's verifiable from the date on the note. Now, what do you suppose a young and—excuse me, Captain—poorly paid officer might possess that was of so much value that I would give him a note worth a million dollars to secure?" He paused theatrically, and then his face lit up as though the answer had only just then occurred to him. "Ah, of course! Loot! That must be it."

"You could never prove that in court, Harlock," I sneered. "It would be your word against mine and, if you haven't noticed, I'm rather well regarded in these parts. I suspect that my testimony might carry a great deal more weight than yours. Besides, all of that is irrelevant, and you know it. I have the note and that would be the end of the matter."

"Well, yes and no, Captain," conceded Harlock in his maddeningly pedantic tone. "It would be the end of the civil suit, of course, but since I would insist on making my allegations in open court, I'm sure that the local papers would pick up on them. Why, I can see the headlines now: 'War Hero Accused of Looting: Violates Presidential Order.'"

I blanched. "What presidential order?" I demanded.

"The one President McKinley sent to General Chaffee before the assault on Peking. It prohibited looting by Americans."

Damn, I thought, he was right! Von Arnhem had told me about that order when he tried to blackmail me in the Hotel de Pekin. Harlock had me shaken now, damn him, but I couldn't let him see me sweat, so I plunged on.

"So what?" I said, scowling. "Do you think I care if I'm smeared? I'll have your money to tide me over for the rest of my life. I won't need the groveling goodwill of anyone. So you see, Harlock, your scare tactics won't work!"

"Oh, you'll have my money," admitted Harlock almost gaily, "at least for a little while."

"What do you mean 'for a little while'?" I demanded suspiciously.

"Exactly that, Captain," he explained calmly. "After the fuss I kick up about your activities in China, a military court will probably look into my allegations. Looting, Captain Travers, is a capital offense. And there are witnesses to your transgressions. Myself for one, and the clerk who prepared the note for another. You remember Mister Peer, don't you? If there should be a need for additional witnesses, rest assured they will be, er, produced."

I was dumbstruck! I felt my knees buckling as the import of what he was saying penetrated my skull. Desperately, I fought for equilibrium and tried to counterattack. "What about you, Harlock? You're just as guilty as I am. If I'm convicted, you won't be too far behind!"

Harlock laughed dryly at this. "I'm afraid you're mistaken there, Captain. The military code hardly applies to me, since I'm a civilian. What's more, the American penal code has no applicability beyond our own borders. So you see, there's no statute that in any way proscribes the conduct of a private United States citizen residing in China. When I'm abroad, Captain Travers, I'm free to loot to my heart's content."

My brain went numb. I had walked into this hall with the world in the palm of my hand. Suddenly, my dreams had been shattered to bits. I was humbugged, by God, and the game was up. A few thousand dollars would keep me in wine, women, and horses for a while, make no mistake, but I could hardly afford to turn my back on a captain's salary. It looked as though I would never escape from the army! My face drained of all color, and for a few minutes I was speechless. When I regained my voice I asked shakily, "What's that address again?"

"It's 13 Nassau Street," he answered, contempt for me dripping from each syllable; he had me beaten and he knew it. Seeing the fight leave my eyes, Harlock bowed mockingly and took his leave. "Please excuse me, Captain. I trust the rest of your evening will be equally pleasant."

His departure barely registered with me. Like a ship with its rudder shot away, I wandered erratically across the floor, oblivious to people trying to catch my eye or engage me in conversation. Only a sharp tug at my sleeve brought me up short.

"Fenwick, what's the matter with you?" It was Duncan. He had seen me closeted with Harlock and hastened over to discover the nature of our caballing, but had been too late to overhear anything. "Surely the champagne could not have affected you in this short a time?"

"No, it's not that, Mister Duncan," I murmured, my guts churning in despair.

"Call me George," he insisted with a tight smile.

"Well—George—it's just, er, I received some bad news. A very close friend of mine has suffered a personal tragedy."

"A pity," clucked Duncan perfunctorily. It was clear that seeing Harlock and me together had put a notion in his brain and he was anxious to share it with me. He got right to the point. "Fenwick, there's a subject I've been meaning to raise with you, and now's the time to do it."

"Oh, what's that?" I asked, looking past Duncan for a waiter. I needed another drink badly.

"I don't know quite how to say this, so I'll just come out with it. I know you and Alice have had warm feelings for each other over the years, ever since you both met back in Arizona. What's more I admit that I haven't treated you as fairly as perhaps I should have. That is, well, I haven't exactly encouraged your affections for Alice. The fact is, I never thought you had much of a future, to be blunt about it. That was the reason I helped pack you off to West Point the way I did. I thought you'd fail miserably and be sent off to oblivion and out of Alice's and my lives forever."

A drink arrived and I gulped it down thankfully. "Yes, yes, I know all that," I said impatiently. The last thing I needed was an emotional confession from Duncan telling me what a bastard he was. I already knew that; besides, I was more in need of comforting at the moment than he was.

"The point is, son, you've achieved more than I ever dreamed possible. You're a war hero and a veteran of campaigns around the world. Why, you're even on speaking terms with the president of the United States. What I'm saying, Fenwick, is that I think you're the type of man I need at Duncan Enterprises."

I did a double take; Duncan suddenly had my full attention! "You want *me?* At Duncan Enterprises? But I thought you'd rather die than let me have a piece of the pie—er, that is, let me into the business."

"That's all changed, Fenwick," Duncan replied. "I want to find a place for you in the firm."

"What? You want to take me in?" I fairly stammered. Why, maybe my fortune was made after all! "Mister Dun—er, George, you honor me greatly," I bubbled. "This is all so sudden. I mean, I hope I have some talents that may be of use to you."

"That you do," Duncan quickly assured me. "Talents that I need very much at the moment."

Perhaps it was his tone of voice or perhaps it was my deep knowledge of Duncan and his miserly ways, but whatever it was, something told me to proceed with caution.

"And just what might those talents *be?*" I asked gingerly.

Here Duncan shifted uncomfortably before answering. "As you may know, I've, er, been in a bit of a financial squeeze over the past few years."

"Financial squeeze?" I echoed. "I had no idea. . . ."

"Yes, a squeeze," continued Duncan. "Ever since the Panic of '93 I've had trouble securing capital to expand and improve my Arizona copper mines. The equipment is aging at a time I have to dig ever deeper to bring up profitable ore. To make matters worse, the damned miners are organizing into unions and demanding higher wages. Even if I were inclined to boost their pay, I don't have the money to do it."

"That's all very sad," I tut-tutted for his benefit, "but how can a setback in your mine operations threaten the mighty Duncan Enterprises? After all, you have other business interests. Some of them must be making a profit, right?"

Duncan gave me a peeved looked as if to say that perhaps he had overestimated me after all, but then took a breath and tried to impart some of the facts of life to me. "Yes, I have other interests, and yes, many of them are profitable. That's why they were accepted by the bankers as collateral for the loans they made to me years ago when I first developed my mine operations. What I'm saying is that I'm mortgaged to the hilt, and now the cash to pay those mortgages is starting to dry up. I've got to do something about it and do it fast; if this keeps up much longer, I'm on my way to the poorhouse. *Now* do you understand?"

"I think so," I said, nodding slowly. "But surely you've got reserves for just such eventualities?"

"I used to, yes, but I liquidated them in 1893 just to stay solvent, and I haven't been able to build them back up again. There's nothing left, Fenwick, nothing. I either get those mines back to profitability or I go under. If it weren't for the managers I have out there working for half pay, I might have gone under long ago."

For a second I wondered if I'd heard him right. "Your managers are on half pay?" I asked with trepidation.

"Yes, I haven't the cash to give them a full salary, and I won't until we get this situation straightened out." Looking me square in the eye with all the earnestness he was capable of mustering, he asked directly: "Will you help me out, Fenwick?"

"Er, exactly what kind of help are we talking about here, George?" I asked carefully.

"I want you to go to Arizona, Fenwick, and salvage whatever you can. Get the miners settled down again and run off those damned union organizers. I know that you're handy with a gun; you're a natural for the type of work I have in mind. Once the labor situation settles down, I can cut the miners' wages back to a point where I can amass the capital I need to modernize the mines enough to get at the deeper ores. It can be done, I tell you. Those mines have years of useful life remaining, but first I have to get over my present difficulties. Will you do it, Fenwick? Can I count you in?"

My eyes opened wide with disbelief; Duncan didn't want a junior executive; he wanted a slave overseer! No wonder he was glad to see me return from China! "But if cash reserves are your problem," I stalled, "why not get together with your, er, friend, Mister Harlock? He's helped you in the past and perhaps he'll help you now."

Duncan's face darkened at the mention of Harlock's name. "Never!" he vowed. "Yes, we were close once. We were business partners."

I suspected as much. "In the gunrunning business," I said accusingly. "Yankee Clipper Limited."

Duncan eyed me narrowly, then nodded. "Yes, back in the Civil War. We ran guns into Savannah and Charleston."

I started visibly at that revelation; Duncan was a New Yorker, by God. What he was describing was outright treason.

Duncan caught my look. "Don't presume to judge me, Fenwick. Sure I had a good name, but my side of the Duncan family was poor as church mice. If I was to make it in this world, I knew I'd have to rely on my own wits. Harlock in those years had a few ships and some big plans, so we combined our efforts. I was the one who thought up the clipper ship as the symbol of our business; it seemed a fitting symbol for what we did. And a good business it was, but as soon as I could after the war I went into legitimate pursuits. Oh, I lent Harlock ships and men from time to time, and in return he was there when I needed loans to make it through the hard times. But I'm done with that whole dirty business now—only Harlock isn't. There's a side of him that delights in mayhem, you know. What I'm saying is that to take a loan from him would mean returning to that sordid life I left behind. No, I'm done with Harlock and I like it that way. Now, what do you say, Fenwick?"

So that was their relationship, I thought. It was much as I had suspected. But the important point was that, for the time being at least, Duncan had scratched Harlock off his list of potential contributors. And, Duncan's protestations notwithstanding, I was sure it had nothing to do with any late-found ethics; Harlock probably wanted too high an interest rate or, even more ominously, a piece of Duncan Enterprises in exchange for credit. Whatever it was, it was obviously a price that Duncan was unwilling to pay—yet.

My immediate problem was that Duncan was eagerly awaiting my reply, and I cast about for some way to escape his clutches gracefully. Clearly, performing honest labor at half pay was beyond bearing, but

I couldn't bring myself to say so straight out, so I stonewalled the old goat. "I, er, that is, this is all so sudden, George."

"I know, I know, but things have worked up to a crisis and I had to lay this before you. There's one more thing, Fenwick. With a partnership, of course, comes Alice. I'll make sure that there are no more obstacles for you in that department, if you follow me."

I followed him, all right. I looked across the ballroom to where Alice stood uncomfortably with Uncle Enoch and Aunt Hannah. She caught my glance and, even at that distance, I could see her eyes glow with love at the sight of me. No, I decided, Alice wasn't Duncan's to give away any longer; she was mine for the taking. Duncan was playing with chips he'd already lost.

"Think on it then, Fenwick," urged Duncan, clasping my shoulder. "I need you, and," he added significantly, "Alice needs you." He gave me a thump for emphasis and released me.

Mercifully, General Wood picked that moment to reappear. "Captain Travers, the president will see you now."

I excused myself and hurried after Wood, who led me down a corridor and through an oaken doorway. As I followed, I surveyed my options. My coveted fortune was gone, and I retained only a modest windfall. I rejected out of hand Duncan's ludicrous proposal that I hie myself to the wilderness and labor as a strikebreaker. What then was left? No sooner had I framed the question than I knew the answer: the army.

And then I was ushered into the presence of the president of the United States. "Sir," said General Wood, "may I present Captain Travers."

"Ah, Captain Travers," gushed McKinley, coming at me from across the room with his arm outstretched. His girth was so massive and his wattled chins swung so alarmingly as he advanced that I had to fight an impulse to sidestep his charge like a toreador facing an onrushing bull.

Instead I stood bravely to and took his proffered hand. "Mister President," I heard myself say, "you honor me." Behind McKinley stood Roosevelt, beaming at me as maniacally as ever; shades of San Juan Hill, I thought.

"Now, Captain," began McKinley, "General Wood here tells me you are one of our foremost experts on irregular warfare. I understand you've seen action in both Cuba and China."

"That's correct, sir," I replied dutifully, alarmed that our meeting wasn't shaping up quite like the quick pat on the back and out the door affair that I had imagined. What in damnation is going on? I thought.

"Good, my boy, good," grinned McKinley, leading me to where a large globe stood in a far corner of the room. "Captain Travers, I need a special man for a special mission. General Wood has recommended you, and the vice-president agrees."

"Special mission, sir?" I fairly squeaked. "What mission?"

"Ah, what an eager devil he is!" laughed McKinley heartily. "He can't wait to get down to the details! I like that in a man." He pointed to the globe and rested a pudgy finger on the Philippines before continuing. "It's this Aguinaldo fellow in the Philippines, Travers. He's made a pretty mess of things, I'm afraid. Now, here's what I want you to do. . . ."

I stopped listening. The Philippines? My God, could this be happening? Surely I was in a nightmare and would awaken at any minute! Only I didn't, and McKinley droned on. "Once you get to Manila, Travers, you're to contact General MacArthur. . . ."

I stopped listening again. It was no dream; I was on my way to the Philippines. I looked helplessly at Wood and then at Roosevelt as they shook their heads in emphatic agreement with every word McKinley said.

Was it too late, I wondered wistfully, to volunteer for bordello duty in Old Havana?